THE

BAD

DAUGHTER

By Joy Fielding

All the Wrong Places
The Bad Daughter
She's Not There
Someone Is Watching
Shadow Creek
Now You See Her
The Wild Zone
Still Life
Charley's Web
Heartstopper
Mad River Road
Puppet
Lost
Whispers and Lies
Grand Avenue
The First Time
Missing Pieces
Don't Cry Now
Tell Me No Secrets
See Jane Run
Good Intentions
The Deep End
Life Penalty
The Other Woman
Kiss Mommy Goodbye
Trance
The Transformation
The Best of Friends
Home Invasion—a special project designed
to encourage adult literacy

The Bad Daughter

A NOVEL

JOY FIELDING

SEAL BOOKS

SEAL BOOKS, 2019

THE BAD DAUGHTER
Seal Books/published by arrangement with Penguin Random House Canada
Doubleday Canada edition published 2018

Library and Archives Canada Cataloguing in Publication

Fielding, Joy, author
The bad daughter / Joy Fielding.

ISBN 978-1-4000-2681-4 (softcover).

I. Title.

PS8561.I52B33 2019 C813'.54 C2017-904904-6

Cover design: Scott Biel
Cover image: Nagib El Desouky/Arcangel Images

Printed and bound in the USA

www.penguinrandomhouse.ca

2 4 6 8 9 7 5 3 1

For my two wonderful daughters,
Shannon and Annie

THE BAD DAUGHTER

—ONE—

The tingling started in the pit of her stomach, a vague gnawing that quickly traveled to her chest, then spread upward and outward until it reached her neck. Invisible fingers wrapped around her throat and pressed down hard on her windpipe, cutting off her supply of oxygen, rendering her dizzy and light-headed. *I'm having a heart attack,* Robin thought. *I can't breathe. I'm going to die.*

The middle-aged woman sitting across from her didn't seem to notice. She was too engrossed in her own troubles. Something about an overbearing mother-in-law, a difficult daughter, and a less-than-supportive husband.

Okay, get a grip. Concentrate. The woman—*what the hell was her name?*—wasn't paying her a hundred and seventy-five dollars an hour to receive a blank stare back in response. At the very least, she expected Robin to be paying attention. You didn't go to a therapist to watch *her* have a nervous breakdown.

You are not having a nervous breakdown, Robin admonished herself, recognizing the familiar symptoms.

This isn't a heart attack. It is a panic attack, plain and simple. You've had them before. God knows you should be used to them by now.

But it's been more than five years, she thought with her next breath. The panic attacks she used to experience on an almost daily basis were part of her past. *Except the past is always with you. Isn't that what they say?*

Robin didn't have to wonder what had brought on the sudden attack. She knew exactly what—*who*—was responsible. *Melanie,* she thought, picturing her sister, older by three years, and thinking, not for the first time, that if you removed the L from her sister's name, it spelled "Meanie."

A message from Melanie had been waiting on her voice mail when she'd returned to her office after lunch. Robin had listened to the message, debating whether to return the call or simply pretend she'd never received it. In the midst of her deliberations, her client had arrived. *You'll just have to wait,* she'd informed her sister silently, grabbing her notepad and entering the room she reserved for counseling clients.

"Are you all right?" the woman asked her now, leaning forward in her upholstered blue chair and eyeing Robin suspiciously. "You look kind of funny."

"Could you excuse me for just a minute?" Robin was out of her seat before the woman could answer. She returned to the smaller room off her main office and shut the door. "Okay," she whispered, leaning against her desk with the palms of both hands, careful not to look at the phone. "Breathe. Just breathe."

Okay, you've identified what's happening. You know

what caused it. All you have to do now is relax and concentrate on your breathing. You have a client in the next room waiting for you. You don't have time for this crap. Pull yourself together. What was it her mother used to say? *This too shall pass.*

Except not everything passed. And if it did, it often circled back to bite you in the ass. "Okay, take deep breaths," she counseled herself again. "Now another one." Three more and her breathing had almost returned to normal. "Okay," she said. "Okay."

Except it wasn't okay, and she knew it. Melanie was calling for a reason, and whatever that reason was, it wasn't good. The sisters had barely exchanged two words since their mother died, and none at all since Robin had left Red Bluff for good after their father's hasty remarriage. Nothing in almost six years. Not a congratulatory note after Robin graduated from Berkeley with a master's degree in psychology, no best wishes when she'd opened her own practice the following year, not even a casual "good luck" when she and Blake had announced their engagement.

And so, two years ago, with Blake's encouragement and support, Robin had ceased all attempts at communication with her sister. Wasn't she always advising clients to stop banging their heads against the wall when faced with an immovable object and insurmountable odds? Wasn't it time she followed her own sage counsel?

Of course, it was always easier to give advice than it was to take it.

And now, out of the blue, her sister was calling and leaving cryptic messages on her voice mail. Like a cancer you thought had been excised, only to have it come roaring back, more virulent than ever.

"Call me" was the enigmatic message Melanie had left, not bothering to state her name, taking for granted that Robin would recognize her voice even after all this time.

Which, of course, she had. Melanie's voice was a hard one to get out of your head, no matter how many years had passed.

What fresh hell is this? Robin wondered, taking several more deep breaths and refusing to speculate. Experience had taught her that her imagination couldn't compete with her reality. Not by a long shot.

She debated calling Blake, then decided against it. He was busy and wouldn't appreciate being interrupted. "You're the therapist," he would tell her, his eyes wandering to a space behind her head, as if someone more interesting had just walked into view.

Pushing thoughts of Blake and Melanie out of her mind, Robin tucked her chin-length curly blond hair behind her ears and returned to the other room, forcing her lips into a reassuring smile. "Sorry about that," she told the woman waiting, who was a first-time client and whose name Robin was still unable to recall. Emma or Emily. Something like that.

"Everything okay?" the woman asked.

"Everything's fine. I just felt a bit queasy for a second there."

The woman's eyes narrowed. "You're not pregnant, are you? I'd hate to start this process only to see you quit to have a baby."

"No. I'm not pregnant." *You have to have sex to get pregnant,* Robin thought. And she and Blake hadn't made love in over a month. "I'm fine," she said, trying desperately to recall the woman's name. "Please, go on. You were saying . . ."

What the hell had the woman been saying?

"Yes, well, I was saying that my husband is absolutely useless as far as his mother is concerned. It's like he's ten years old again and he's afraid to open his mouth. She says the most hurtful things to me, and he acts like he doesn't hear any of it. Then when I point it out, he says I'm exaggerating, and I shouldn't let her get to me. But my daughter has picked up on it, of course. And now she's being just as rude. You should hear the way she talks to me."

You think you have problems? Robin thought. *You think your family is difficult?*

"I don't know why my mother-in-law hates me so much."

She doesn't need a reason. If she's anything like my sister, she despises you on principle. Because you exist.

It was true. Melanie had hated her baby sister from the first moment she'd laid eyes on her. She'd been instantly jealous of their mother's suddenly divided attention. She would pinch Robin while she lay sleeping in her crib, not stopping until the infant was covered in tiny bruises; she'd hacked off Robin's beautiful curls with scissors when she was two; when Robin was seven, Melanie had pushed her into a wall during a supposedly friendly game of tag, breaking her nose. She was constantly criticizing Robin's choice of clothes, her choice of interests, her choice of friends. “The girl’s a stupid slut,” Melanie had sneered about Robin’s best friend, Tara.

Oh, wait—she was right about that.

“I’ve done everything to make peace with that woman. I’ve taken her shopping. I’ve taken her for lunch. I invite her to have dinner at our house at least three times a week.”

“Why?” Robin asked.

“Why?” the woman repeated.

“If she’s so unpleasant, why bother?”

“Because my husband thinks it’s the right thing to do.”

“Then let *him* take her shopping and out to lunch. She’s *his* mother.”

“It’s not that simple,” the woman demurred.

“It’s exactly that simple,” Robin countered. “She’s rude and disrespectful. You’re under no obligation to put up with that. Stop taking her shopping and to lunch. Stop inviting her over for dinner. If she asks you why, tell her.”

“What will I say to my husband?”

“That you’re tired of being disrespected and you’re not going to put up with it anymore.”

“I don’t think I can do that.”

“What’s stopping you?”

“Well, it’s complicated.”

“Not really.”

You want complicated? I’ll give you complicated: My parents were married for thirty-four years, during which time my father cheated on my mother with every skank who caught his roving eye, including my best friend, Tara, whom he married five short months after my mother died. And just to make matters truly interesting, at the time, Tara was engaged to my brother, Alec. How's that for complicated?

Oh, wait—there's more.

Tara has a daughter, the product of a failed first marriage when she was barely out of her teens. Cassidy would be twelve now, I guess. Cute kid. My father adores her, has shown her more love than he ever gave any of his own kids. Speaking of which, did I mention that I haven't talked to my sister in almost six years?

"Some people are toxic," Robin said out loud. "It's best to have as little to do with them as possible."

"Even when they're family?"

"*Especially* when they're family."

"Wow," the woman said. "I thought therapists were supposed to ask questions and let you figure things out for yourself."

Were they? God, that could take years. "Just thought I'd save us both some time."

"You're tough," the woman said.

Robin almost laughed. "Tough" was probably the last word she would have used to describe herself. Melanie was the tough one. Or maybe "angry" was the right word. For as long as Robin could remember, Melanie had been angry. At the world in general. At Robin in particular. Although to be fair, it hadn't always been easy for Melanie. Hell, it had *never* been easy for her.

Double hell, Robin thought. *Who wants to be fair?*

"Are you sure you're all right?" the woman asked. "Your face . . ."

"What's the matter with my face?" *Am I having a stroke? Is it Bell's palsy? What's the matter with my face?*

"Nothing. It just got all scrunched up for a second there."

"Scrunched up?" Robin realized she was shouting.

"I'm sorry. I didn't mean to upset you—"

"Would you excuse me for another minute?" Robin propelled herself from her chair with such force that it almost tipped over. "I'll be right back." She opened the outer door to her office and bolted into the gray-carpeted hallway, running down the narrow corridor until she reached the washroom. Pushing the door open, she darted toward the sink to check her image in the mirror. An attractive thirty-three-year-old woman with deep blue eyes, pleasantly full lips, and a vaguely heart-shaped face stared back at her. There were no unsavory warts or blemishes, no noticeable scars or abnormalities. Everything was where it was supposed to be, if a little off-kilter because of her slightly crooked nose. But there was nothing that could be described as "scrunched up." Her hair could use a touch-up and a trim, she realized, but other than that, she looked decent enough, even professional, in her rose-colored blouse and straight gray skirt. She could stand to put on a few pounds, she thought, hearing Melanie's voice in her ear reminding her that despite her achievements and *"fancy degree,"* she was still *"flat as a pancake"* and *"skinny like a stick."*

She felt the stirrings of another panic attack and took

a series of preventive deep breaths. When that didn't work, she splashed a handful of cold water on her face. "Okay, calm down," she told herself. "Calm down. Everything is fine. Except your face *is* all scrunched up." She examined her reflection once more, noting her pursed lips and pinched cheeks and making a concerted effort to relax her features. "You can't let Melanie get to you." She took another series of deep breaths—in through the nose, out through the mouth, inhale the good energy, exhale the bad. "There's a woman patiently awaiting your wise counsel," she reminded herself. "Now, get back there and give it to her." *Whatever the hell her name is.*

But when Robin returned to her office, the woman was gone. "Hello?" Robin called, opening the door to her inner office and discovering that room empty as well. "Adeline?" She returned to the exterior hallway and found it likewise deserted. *Great. Fine time to remember her name.*

Obviously, Adeline had fled. Scared off by Robin's "tough" facade and "scrunched-up" face. Not that Robin blamed her. The session had been a disaster. What gave her the right to think she could counsel others when she herself was such a complete and utter fuckup?

Robin plopped down into the blue chair that Adeline had abandoned and looked around the thoughtfully arranged space. The walls were a pale but sunny yellow, meant to encourage optimism. A poster of colorful flowers hung on the wall opposite the door, meant to suggest growth and personal development. A photograph of autumn leaves was situated beside the door to her inner sanctum, a subtle reminder that change was both good and inevitable. Her personal favorite—a collage depicting a curly-haired woman with glasses and a worried smile amidst a flurry of happy faces and abstract raindrops, the capitalized words WHY DO I GET SO EMOTIONAL? floating above her head—occupied the place of honor behind the chair she usually sat in. It was intended to be humorous and put clients at ease. She'd found it at a neighborhood garage sale soon after she and Blake had moved in together. Now he was increasingly "working late." How long before he brought up the idea of moving out?

"Why do I get so emotional indeed?" she asked the woman in the collage.

The woman smiled her worried smile and said nothing.

The phone in Robin's inner office rang.

"Shit," she said, listening as it rang two more times before voice mail picked up. Was it Melanie, phoning to berate her for not returning her previous call promptly enough? Robin pushed herself slowly to her feet. *What the hell, might as well get this over with.*

The first thing she saw when she entered the adjoining room was the telephone's blinking red light. She sank into the comfortable burgundy leather chair behind her small oak desk, a desk that had been Blake's when he first began practicing law; he'd passed it on to her when he graduated to a bigger firm with a bigger office, one that required a more imposing desk.

Was that why they'd never followed through on their plans to marry? Was she not sufficiently imposing for a man of his growing stature?

Or maybe it was the pretty new assistant he'd hired, or the attractive young lawyer in the next office. Perhaps the woman he'd smiled at while waiting in line at Starbucks had been the source of second thoughts on his part.

How long could she continue to ignore the all-too-familiar signs?

She picked up the receiver, listened as a recorded voice informed her that she had one new message and one saved message. "To listen to your message, press one-one."

Robin did as directed.

"Hi, this is Adeline Sullivan," the voice said. "I'm calling to apologize for running out on you like that. I just didn't think we were a good fit, and to quote a therapist I know, 'I thought I'd save us both some time' and just leave. I hope you aren't angry. You can bill me for the session. You *did* give me some things to think about." She left the address where Robin could send the invoice. Robin promptly erased the message. *Would that everything else was so easy to erase.* She closed her eyes, her fingers hovering over the phone's keypad.

"Go on," she urged herself. "You can do this." She pressed the button to listen to her sister's message again.

"First saved message," the recorded voice announced, followed by her sister's abrupt command.

"Call me."

Robin didn't have to look up Melanie's phone number. She knew it by heart. It was chiseled into her brain. She punched in the digits before she could change her mind.

The phone was answered almost immediately. “Took you long enough,” her sister said without preamble.

“What’s wrong?” Robin asked.

“You better sit down,” Melanie said.

—TWO—

The next morning, Robin woke up in a strange bed in an unfamiliar room, the conversation with her sister playing on an endless loop in her head.

"It's Dad," Melanie had said, her voice flat and unemotional.

"Is he dead?"

"He's in the hospital."

"Did he have a heart attack?"

"No."

"A car accident?"

"No."

"Someone shot him?"

"Bingo."

Robin pressed the Pause button in her brain, temporarily freezing the conversation that had been haunting her all night. The exaggerated frown she imagined on her sister's face froze as well, a frown that had always kept her from being the beauty their mother had predicted she would become.

Robin climbed out of the too-hard queen-size bed and shuffled toward the bathroom. *Why do all motel rooms look alike?* she wondered. *Is there some union rule that dictates they all be uninteresting rectangles in shades of beige and brown?* Not that she was an expert in motel decor, having stayed in only a few over the years. She'd gone from her parents' crowded house in Red Bluff to a dorm room at Berkeley, back to her parents' house to work and earn money to continue her education, on to a small shared apartment off campus, then back and forth between Berkeley and Red Bluff to help care for her mother, then on to a cramped studio apartment in Los Angeles, and finally to the spacious two-bedroom unit she shared with Blake.

Blake, she thought, silently turning the name over on her tongue as she stepped into the tub. *What must he be thinking?* She turned on the faucet for the shower, then had to brace herself against the wall as a torrent of ice-cold water shot from the showerhead.

Blake would be furious with her.

She hadn't called him since yesterday afternoon. Even then, she hadn't spoken to him directly, but just left a message with his pretty new assistant to the effect that she had to go to Red Bluff to deal with a family emergency and she'd call him later. Then she'd canceled the week's remaining appointments, gone home to pack a small suitcase, and taken a cab to the airport, where she'd boarded the first available flight to Sacramento, arriving at almost six o'clock in the evening. The bus to Red Bluff didn't leave till the next morning, but the thought of renting a car and making the drive herself had proved too daunting, and in truth, she was in no hurry to get there. Instead she'd found a motel close to the bus terminal and checked in. She'd eschewed dinner, instead wolfing down a Three Musketeers bar she got from the vending machine down the hall.

She also resisted turning on the TV, hoping to avoid reports of the shooting. She could handle only so much information, process only so much. She really didn't want to know every awful detail yet.

She thought about calling Blake again, but then remembered he'd said something about a dinner meeting with clients, so why bother? He was busy. He was always busy. Too busy to phone, obviously. Too busy to spare a few seconds to inquire as to what sort of family emergency would necessitate her taking off like that, to return to a place she'd sworn never to go back to. Would it have been so hard for him to interrupt one of his seemingly endless meetings to call her, to feign at least a modicum of interest?

So maybe he wouldn't be furious that she hadn't tried contacting him again. Maybe he'd be relieved. Maybe she'd finally handed him the ammunition he'd been waiting for to end their relationship once and for all.

Not that he could do anything to help the situation, she reminded herself. His specialty was corporate law, not criminal law. And it wasn't as if he even knew her father. Or her sister. Or any member of her screwed-up family, except her brother, Alec, who lived in San Francisco, so they'd actually met only twice. She'd left a message for Alec, but he hadn't called her back either. So screw both of them, she'd decided, turning off her cell phone and climbing into bed at barely eight o'clock.

She shouldn't have turned off her cell phone, she thought now. What if Blake or Alec *had* called? What if Melanie had been trying to reach her?

"It's Dad," she heard her sister say. She fast-forwarded her memory of the conversation as the shower gradually lost its icy sting and settled into a tepid spray. Someone had shot their father.

"Who?"

"We don't know."

"When?"

"Last night."

"Is he all right?"

"Of course he's not all right. He was shot. In the head. He's in a coma."

"Oh, God."

"They operated, but it's not looking good."

Robin fumbled with the wrapping on the tiny bar of soap lying in the soap dish, tossing the paper to the bottom of the tub and watching it stick to the top of the drain like a plug, causing the water to begin rising, puddling around her ankles. The soap produced almost no lather, no matter how hard she scrubbed. "Great," she muttered as it slipped from her hands and disappeared beneath the rising water. "Just great." She positioned herself directly under the shower's spray, feeling her wet hair flatten against her scalp, then wind around her head like a layer of Saran Wrap.

"He was shot. In the head. He's in a coma."

She turned off the shower and stepped onto the too-small ivory-colored bath mat, wrapping herself in one of the two thin terry-cloth towels provided, then returned to the bedroom. She glanced at the clock on the nightstand. Just after seven A.M., which meant she had three hours to kill before her bus left. Add to that the two-plus hours it would take to travel the hundred and twenty-five miles of boring highway to the middle of nowhere known as Red Bluff. Which meant at least five hours for the conversation with her sister to ricochet around in her head like a pinball.

"I don't understand. How did this happen? Where's Tara?"

"Still in surgery."

"In surgery? What are you saying? She was shot, too?"

"And Cassidy."

"What?"

"You heard me."

"Someone shot Cassidy?"

"Yes."

"I don't believe it. What kind of monster shoots a twelve-year-old girl?"

Robin opened her suitcase and removed some fresh underwear, a blue-and-white-striped jersey, and a pair of jeans. She dressed quickly, debating again whether to turn on the television in case the local station was carrying news of the shooting. *"Prominent Red Bluff developer Greg Davis, his wife, and stepdaughter are clinging to life in the hospital after being shot,"* she imagined a perky yet paradoxically somber-faced reporter announcing.

Once again, Melanie's voice interrupted her musings. *"It's looking like some sort of home invasion,"* she was saying, her voice growing faster and less steady with each word. *"Apparently sometime after midnight last night, someone entered their house and . . . and . . ."*

"Okay. Okay. Slow down. Take deep breaths."

"Please don't tell me what to do. You aren't here. You haven't been *here."*

Well, that didn't take long, Robin had thought, every muscle in her body constricting. It was the same refrain she'd been hearing ever since their mother's death. *"Just tell me what happened."*

"I told you. It looks like a home invasion."

"What does that mean exactly? Do the police know who did it? Do they have any leads, any suspects?"

"Not that they've told me."

"Have you spoken to Alec?"

"I called him. He hasn't returned any of my messages."

"I'll try to reach him."

"Are you coming home or not?"

"I don't know. I'll have to make arrangements, find out what flights, what buses . . . It could take time."

"Fine. Whatever. Your choice."

Robin sank back onto the bed, lowering her head into her hands and staring at the worn beige-and-brown carpet at her feet. No matter how many times she went over the conversation with her sister, she couldn't wrap her head around it. It was like a disturbing dream that bolted from your memory the second you tried to make sense of it.

She sat motionless until she felt her stomach start to rumble. She hadn't had a proper meal since yesterday's soup-and-sandwich lunch. Probably she should grab a bite of breakfast before the bus left. Who knew when she'd have the opportunity to eat once she got to Red Bluff? She pushed her bare feet into her sneakers, grabbed her purse, activated her cell phone, and headed for the door, vaguely recalling there was a diner across the street.

The phone rang as her fingers were reaching for the doorknob.

"Blake?" she asked, lifting it to her ear without checking the caller ID.

"Alec," her brother answered. "What's going on?"

"Have you spoken to Melanie?"

"Thought I'd call you first. What's up?"

"Brace yourself."

"Fully braced."

Robin took a deep breath. "Dad's been shot."

There was a brief pause, followed by a nervous laugh. "Is this a joke?"

"It's no joke. He's alive, but probably not for long."

"Did Tara do it?"

"No." She suppressed a smile. That had been her first thought as well. "She was shot, too."

"Tara was shot?"

"And Cassidy."

"Tara's been shot?" Alec repeated. "How is she?"

"I don't know. She was in surgery when I spoke to Melanie."

"I don't understand. What happened?"

"Melanie says it appears to be some sort of home invasion."

"Wow." A second of silence. Robin pictured her brother, younger than her by three years, lifting his hand to his face to massage his jaw, something he always did when he was upset. "Guess it serves them right for building the biggest fucking house in town."

"I'm on my way there now. You should probably come, too."

"No, not a good idea."

Robin was trying to come up with something she could use to lure her brother back to Red Bluff when she realized he was no longer on the line. She returned the phone to her purse, deciding to call him back when she had more information and he'd had more time to think.

She opened the door to her motel room and stepped into the adjacent parking lot. A blanket of heat immediately wrapped itself around her shoulders. Mid-April, not even eight A.M. and already the thermometer was edging past eighty. It would be even hotter in Red Bluff, where the temperature averaged more than ninety degrees a hundred days a year. Just the thought of it made her heart rate quicken.

"Okay, stay calm," she whispered to herself as she crossed the street to the fifties-style diner. "A diner is not a suitable place for a panic attack." But waves of anxiety were already sweeping over her as she stumbled through the restaurant's heavy glass door. She sidled into a booth by the window, her hand knocking against the small jukebox at the side of the Formica tabletop, and she cried out.

"You okay?" the waitress asked, approaching with a pot of hot coffee.

"I will be," Robin managed to say, trying to find a spot on the lumpy red vinyl seat that she wouldn't stick to. "Once I get some of that."

The waitress poured her a cup. "You need a menu?"

"No. Just the coffee." Robin reached for the cup, returning her hands to her lap when she realized they were shaking. She glanced toward the counter running along one wall, three of the five stools in front of it occupied by men with heavy-looking tool belts around their waists. A list of the diner's specialties was written in black paint on the long mirror behind the counter. *Sundaes. Blueberry Pancakes. Waffles. Western Omelets.* "Do you have any bagels?"

"Sesame seed, poppy seed, cinnamon-raisin," the waitress rattled off.

Oh, God. "Sesame seed."

"Toasted?"

Shit. "Yes, please."

"Buttered?"

Help. "Okay."

"You sure you're all right?"

Robin looked up at the woman, who was around fifty and at least that many pounds overweight. She had a sweet bow-shaped mouth and a twinkle in her kind brown eyes. *Just smile and tell her you're fine.* "My father's been shot," Robin said instead, the words tumbling out of her mouth before she could stop them.

"That's horrible. I'm so sorry."

"And his wife, Tara. She was shot, too," she continued, hearing her voice rise with each sentence. "She used to be my best friend, and my brother's fiancée. Until she married my father." A strangled chuckle escaped her mouth. *You're hysterical,* she told herself. *Stop talking. Stop talking now.* "And her daughter, Cassidy. She was shot, too. She's only twelve."

The waitress looked stunned. She slid into the seat on the opposite side of the booth, depositing the pot of coffee on the table and reaching across to take one of Robin's shaking hands in her own. "That's so awful, honey. Did it happen here? I haven't heard anything . . ."

"No. It happened in Red Bluff. I'm on my way there now. As soon as the bus comes." She glanced toward the terminal. "I live in L.A. There are no flights to Red Bluff anymore because nobody in their right mind wants to go there. There's a municipal airport, but it hasn't been used in years. That's why I have to take the bus."

"Are you alone?"

"My sister's meeting me at the bus stop."

"Well, that's good," the waitress said.

"Not really," Robin said with a smile. "She hates me." *Why am I smiling? Stop smiling!*

"I'm sure she doesn't . . ."

"Oh, yes, she absolutely does. She thinks I've had it so easy all my life. That I've had all the breaks. That I got to go away to college while she had to stay in Red Bluff and look after our mother when she was dying. Which isn't exactly the truth, because even though I had a partial scholarship, I paid for the rest all by myself. My father said a master's degree in psychology was a waste of time and money and he wasn't going to contribute to it, which is why it took me so long to finish my degree." *Okay, that's enough. She's not interested. You can stop now.*

Except she couldn't stop the words that were already pouring out of her.

"That plus the fact that I was traveling back and forth all the time to see my mother," Robin continued without pause, her words picking up speed, like a runaway train. "My sister conveniently leaves that out, along with the fact that she had to stay in Red Bluff anyway because of her son. She has a son, Landon. He's eighteen now. He was named for this actor. He's dead now. The actor, not Landon. Landon's autistic. I'm sure she blames me for that, too." Robin's smile stretched toward her ears. She began laughing, then crying, then laughing and crying at the same time until she was gasping for air. "Oh, God. I can't breathe. I can't breathe."

The waitress was instantly on her feet. "I'll call an ambulance."

Robin reached out and grabbed the woman's apron. "No, it's okay. It's just a panic attack. I'll be fine. Honestly. I don't need an ambulance."

"I have some Valium in my purse. Would you like a couple?"

"Dear God, yes."

A minute later, the waitress was back, two small pills in the palm of her hand.

"I think I love you," Robin said.

At ten o'clock Robin boarded the Greyhound bus for Red Bluff. Any residual feelings of embarrassment she'd had about her mini breakdown at breakfast—*I'm a therapist, for God's sake. I just spilled my guts to a waitress in a diner*—had long since disappeared into the pleasant buzz from the Valium, and she slept for most of the more than two-hour journey north along Highway 5. "Everything's going to be okay," she whispered into the palm of her hand as the bus drew closer to Red Bluff, located at the base of the snow-covered Cascades, about halfway between Sacramento and the Oregon border, on the banks of the Sacramento River, the largest river in California.

"Everything's going to be okay," she repeated as the bus made its way down tree-lined Main Street in what was generously referred to as Historic Downtown Red Bluff. If memory served, there were about one hundred and fifty businesses located in the downtown core, all just blocks from the river. Most of the residents lived in the surrounding suburbs—fully a fifth of them below the poverty line—and her father had played a major part in developing its 7.7 square miles.

Your father is invincible, Robin told herself. *He isn't about to let a little bullet to the brain slow him down. And Tara's no shrinking violet. At the very least, she's a survivor. Hell, the word was coined for her. And little Cassidy will be fine. She's twelve. She'll bounce back in no time. You'll see—all three of them will pull through. You'll visit them in the hospital, they'll laugh in your face, and you'll get the hell out of Dodge.*

Robin was feeling almost peaceful as the bus passed the State Theatre and the gold-hatted clock tower—both regularly referred to in local guidebooks as "historic"—before pulling to a stop at the far end of the street.

Then she saw Melanie waiting by the side of the road.

Robin stepped off the bus, the colorful Victorian architecture of Main Street blurring behind her as she took her small suitcase from the bus driver's outstretched hand, then walked toward her sister.

Melanie wasted no time on pleasantries. "Tara's dead," she said.

—THREE—

Approximately 14,000 people live in Red Bluff, most of them white and straining toward middle class. The town's motto is A Great Place to Live, although Robin had always thought A Great Place to Leave would probably be a more suitable slogan. *Unless you loved rodeos,* she thought. The annual Red Bluff Round-Up had become one of the West's largest rodeos and most anticipated events, ranchers coming from all over the country every April to have their bulls compete. She said a silent *Thank you, God,* that she had just missed it.

Aside from its rodeo, Red Bluff was perhaps best known for being the place where a seventeen-year-old girl was kidnapped by a deranged couple and held captive in a box under their bed for seven years. The kidnapping had occurred back in May 1977, and as far as Robin knew, nothing much of note had happened in the town since.

"You look like crap," Melanie said as they climbed into the front seat of her candy wrapper–strewn, decade-old Impala.

Robin had been thinking the same thing about Melanie, but was too polite to say it. There were deep bags under her sister's hazel eyes, and her preternaturally dark hair hung in lifeless waves past her rounded shoulders, her hair the victim of years of bad dye jobs, her shoulders the victim of years of bad posture. "I didn't get much sleep. How's Dad?"

"Still breathing."

"When did Tara die?"

"About an hour ago."

"That's so awful."

Melanie lowered her chin, looking sideways at Robin with undisguised skepticism as she threw the car into drive and pulled away from the curb. "You were hardly her biggest fan."

"I never wished her dead."

"No? Guess that was Alec. Were you able to reach him?"

Robin nodded, taking note of the few trees scattered across the vast expanse of mostly empty space between downtown Red Bluff and the hospital on its outskirts. Nothing much had changed since she'd left. "I don't think he'll be joining us."

"Not exactly a big surprise." Melanie glanced toward Robin without taking her eyes off the road. "You don't think . . ."

"I don't think . . . *what*? That Alec had something to do with this?" Robin heard the defensiveness in her voice, a leftover from her childhood. It had always been Robin and her brother against the world, "the world" at the time being Melanie.

"You said it," Melanie replied. "I didn't."

"You *thought* it."

"Don't tell me it never crossed your mind."

"Alec loved Tara," Robin said, refusing to admit there was even the possibility that Melanie could be right.

"And hated our father."

"Not enough to do something like this!"

"You're really so sure of that?"

"Yes." *Was she? Wasn't there a tiny part of her that had wondered the same thing?*

St. Elizabeth Community Hospital was located on Sister Mary Columba Drive, about five minutes from downtown. Robin repeatedly stole glances at her sister, waiting for her to ask questions about Robin's life, about Blake, about her health, about *anything*. "Have there been any other developments?" she asked when Melanie failed to do so.

"Like what?"

"I don't know. Did Tara say anything to the police before she died?"

"No. She never regained consciousness."

"What about Cassidy?"

"It's touch and go. The bullet hit just below her heart and exited out her back, what the sheriff calls a through-and-through. Miraculously, it missed her lungs, but she's lost a tremendous amount of blood, and her condition is still critical. The doctor said it could go either way."

"Is she awake?"

"She drifts in and out. They've tried talking to her, but so far she hasn't said a word."

"So they still have no idea who's responsible."

"They are absolutely clueless," Melanie said, emphasizing each word.

"Does she know about her mother?"

"Not to my knowledge." Melanie turned off the road into the small hospital's surprisingly large parking lot. "Guess we'll find out soon enough." She located a parking space across from two police cars and shut off the car's engine, then opened her door. An explosion of hot air shot toward Robin, as if someone had tossed a grenade at her head. "Coming?"

"Wait," Robin urged, feeling an unwelcome tingle of anxiety in her chest. Clearly the Valium was starting to wear off.

"What for?"

"I just thought . . . Could we sit here for a few minutes?"

"And do what?"

"I don't know. Maybe we could talk."

"About anything in particular?"

"Not really. I was just kind of hoping to get acclimated."

"Acclimated," Melanie repeated, drawing out each syllable. "Fine. I guess Dad can wait. It's not like he's going anywhere." She sank back against her seat, although she left her car door open. "Okay. So . . . talk."

Robin felt beads of perspiration line up across her forehead and didn't know whether she was reacting to the heat or to her sister's directive. The years hadn't softened Melanie one bit. "How've you been?"

"Good."

"Are you still working?"

"Yep."

"At Tillie's?" Tillie's was a combination antiques-and-gifts shop located in the middle of Main Street. Melanie had worked there on and off for the last twenty years.

"Yes. At Tillie's." She paused. "Of course, I'll have to take some time off now."

"What about Dad's office?"

"What about it?"

"Is there anyone in charge . . . ?"

"His CFO is managing things temporarily."

Robin waited several seconds for Melanie to volunteer more information. She didn't. "How's Landon?"

An impatient release of breath. "Fine," Melanie said, managing to make the one-syllable word sound even shorter.

Robin debated asking more questions about her nephew, aware that Landon had always been a sensitive subject where Melanie was concerned. The product of a one-night stand with the captain of the high school football team when Melanie was just seventeen, Landon had been diagnosed with autism at the age of three. As far as Robin knew, his father had never contributed a dime toward supporting his son. In fact, he had moved to Colorado soon after graduation and worked as a personal trainer, then eventually bought into a moderately successful fast-food franchise. Meanwhile Melanie had been forced to abandon any hope of the modeling career she'd always dreamt of to stay in Red Bluff and look after the boy.

Even though Landon was relatively high functioning, he was also subject to wild mood swings and was for the most part silent and uncommunicative, a prisoner of his own mind. Despite living under the same roof for years, Robin couldn't remember the last time he'd said more than two words to her or the last time he'd looked her in the eye.

Of course, having a son with autism had only increased Melanie's anger. At the world in general. At Robin in particular.

"He must be pretty tall now."

"Six feet, two inches."

"How's he doing?"

"He's doing great. Why all the questions about Landon? He had nothing to do with what happened."

"Of course not. I wasn't suggesting . . ."

"I'll tell you the same thing I told the police: Landon was home with me that night. All night. Just because he's autistic doesn't mean he's violent. He hasn't had any major outbursts in years. He's certainly not capable of anything like this. He would never hurt anyone, let alone his grandfather. Or Cassidy. For God's sake, he loves that girl."

"Melanie, please. I was just curious about how he's doing. He's my nephew."

"Yeah, well, I guess you'll have to remind him of that."

Robin unfastened her seat belt. "Okay. Let's go inside." *Safe to say I'm sufficiently acclimated.* She climbed out of the car, her shoulders slumping in the oppressive heat that was rising in almost visible waves from the pavement. Or maybe her defeated posture was the result of the load of shit her sister had just dumped on her.

"Dad's in the east wing," Melanie said, marching past Robin through the parking lot to the front entrance of the sprawling single-story white building.

The powerful combined odors of sickness, disinfectant, and flowers hit Robin as soon as she stepped inside the hospital. *The smell of suffering,* she thought. Instantly she was seven years old again, holding her mother's hand and clutching her own broken nose as they followed the doctor down the winding corridor. In the next second it was twenty years later, and she was standing beside Melanie at their mother's bedside, watching her waste away, the color of her skin grayer than the sheets she was wrapped in. She remembered reaching for Melanie's hand and her sister pushing her away. *"Nice of you to make it back for the grand finale,"* she heard Melanie say. Would she say the same thing again if their father succumbed to his wounds?

"Place looks the same," Robin said, glancing only fleetingly at the warren of familiar corridors as they walked by the reception desk. Her cell phone rang as they were passing a sign reminding visitors that the use of cell phones was forbidden. Robin quickly removed the phone from her purse and raised it to her ear.

"What the hell's going on?" Blake demanded, his voice filling her head. "I must have called you at least ten times last night. I called again this morning," he continued before she could speak. "I left half a dozen messages. Why'd you turn off your phone? Why didn't you call me back?"

Robin stared at her cell phone, trying to make sense of what he was saying. "I'm sorry. I haven't checked my messages. I took some Valium and I'm still a little loopy."

"You took Valium? Who gave you Valium?"

"It's a long story. Can we talk about it later?"

"I don't know. Can we?"

"Of course."

"What's going on, Robin?"

The phone started making crackling noises.

"My father . . . He's been shot."

More crackling noises, louder this time.

"What? I didn't hear you. You're breaking up. Did you say something about your father?"

"I said he's . . ."

"Hello? Hello, Robin? Are you there?"

Robin followed her sister as she turned down a hall leading to the east wing. "Blake? Can you hear me now?"

"Yes, that's better."

"We're not supposed to use our cell phones."

"What? Why not?"

"This way," Melanie directed, leading Robin past another nurses' station, where two policemen were conferring with a bald, heavyset man wearing a beige uniform. "That's Sheriff Prescott," she said, acknowledging him with a nod.

"What's that about a sheriff?" Blake asked.

Robin gave Blake a quick recap of everything she knew. "We're at the hospital now."

"This is it," Melanie said, stopping outside the closed door to room 124.

"Holy shit. Are you all right?" Blake asked.

"I don't know," Robin replied honestly.

"You need to turn that off now," her sister said.

"Look. This really isn't a good time. Can I call you back later?"

"I'm in meetings all day. I'll have to call you."

"Okay."

"You'll answer your phone?"

"I'll answer."

"You won't take any more Valium?"

"I don't have any more," Robin said, her voice a whine.

Blake chuckled. "Good. You're strong. You don't need it."

I'm not strong, Robin thought. *I need* you.

"Robin," Melanie said again. "Are you coming?"

"I have to go." Robin disconnected the call before Blake could say goodbye and returned the phone to her pocket.

"Ready?" Melanie opened the door to their father's room and stepped inside.

Robin took a deep breath, feeling it waver as she released it.

"Robin?" her sister said again.

Robin forced one reluctant foot in front of the other, crossing the threshold and closing the door behind her.

Her father was lying in a narrow bed in the middle of the small private room, his heavily bandaged head elevated by two pillows. Myriad wires and tubes connected him to life, a monitor registering his every breath and heartbeat. Amazingly, he still managed to look imposing. Or maybe that wasn't so surprising. At sixty-two, he was still relatively young and in excellent shape. He exercised regularly and often boasted of never having been sick a day in his life. His skin was tanned, his arms muscular beneath the short sleeves of his hospital gown. "I can't believe how good he looks," Robin stammered.

"He's a handsome devil, all right."

Hooray! Something we agree on.

Robin approached the bed, staring down at the man under the stiff white sheets. *Who did this to you?* she asked silently, running her fingers along the bed's railing and fighting the urge to cover her father's fingers with her own.

"Are you crying?" Melanie asked.

Robin wiped the tears from her eyes. Truthfully, she was as astounded as her sister by their sudden appearance. Their father was a bastard. There was no other word for it. *Oh, wait . . . there were actually a bunch of other words: prick, cad, asshole. How about jerk, scoundrel, son of a bitch?* In fact, there was no shortage of words she could use to describe her father, almost none of them complimentary.

She heard the sound of a door opening behind her and turned to see Sheriff Prescott step into the room. He was a big man, at least six and a half feet tall, with a barrel chest that strained against the buttons of his khaki shirt, his sheriff's badge—a seven-pointed star framing a picture of a bull, the words "County of Tehama" scrawled above the bull's head, the single word "Sheriff" below—proudly on display. His hard stomach protruded over his belt, and his khaki pants were too short, revealing scuffed brown leather cowboy boots. His eyes were small and close together, his hands large, his head bald and shiny, as if he'd just waxed it. A large-brimmed cowboy hat dangled between his thick fingers.

A casting director's dream sheriff, Robin couldn't help thinking.

"Sheriff Prescott," Melanie acknowledged.

"Melanie," he said in return.

There was no warmth in either of their voices.

"This is my sister, Robin."

"Sheriff," Robin said.

Sheriff Prescott nodded. "I was wondering if we could have a few words. When you have a minute . . ."

"Certainly." *I have nothing but minutes.*

"I'll be in the hall. Take your time. Whenever you're ready."

Robin glanced back at her father. *Serves you damn right,* she thought, fighting back another onslaught of unwanted tears. "I'm ready now," she said.

—FOUR—

"How are you holding up?" the sheriff asked, leading Robin toward a small waiting room at the end of the hall and motioning for her to sit down.

"I'm okay." Robin sank into one of the green vinyl chairs in front of a window that showcased the mountains in the distance. Sheriff Prescott lowered himself into another chair and pulled it toward her, their knees almost touching. He leaned forward in a gesture that was curiously both intimate and intimidating.

"I understand you just got in from Los Angeles."

Robin nodded. "That's right. What can you—"

"You drive?" he interrupted.

"No. I flew to Sacramento yesterday, then took the bus here this morning. What—"

"I guess Red Bluff's not the easiest place to get to anymore," he said, interrupting again, clearly determined to be the one conducting the interview. "They tell me you're a therapist."

"That's right. What can you tell me about what

happened?" she asked in one breath, refusing to give him the opportunity to interrupt a third time.

"Unfortunately, not much more than what I assume your sister has already told you," Sheriff Prescott answered. "I was actually hoping you could tell *me* a few things."

"Such as?"

"Such as if there's anyone you can think of who might have had a motive to shoot your father or Tara."

It would be harder to think of someone who didn't, Robin thought. "I haven't seen or talked to either of them in over five years," she told the sheriff. "I have no idea who might have done this." She stopped abruptly. "Wait. I thought it was a home invasion."

"That's one of the scenarios we're considering," he said. "But until little Cassidy is able to tell us something, we have to consider all possibilities."

"How is she?"

"Hard to say. The doctors are cautiously optimistic, but they said it might be some time before she's out of the woods."

"So you haven't told her . . ."

"About her mother passing? No. There doesn't seem to be much point at the moment. We don't know how much, if anything, is registering. In the meantime, we're trying to get as good a grip on this thing as possible, so anything you can tell us about your father and his wife would be helpful. I understand you and Tara used to be friends."

You understand a lot more than you're letting on, Robin thought. "Yes, that's true."

"Best friends, I hear."

"Since we were ten years old."

"But not anymore."

Robin sighed with frustration. "It's kind of hard to stay friends with someone who ditches your brother to marry your father, especially so soon after your mother's funeral."

A small smile tugged at the corners of the sheriff's lips. "I imagine it is."

"Is this relevant?"

"Indulge me," Sheriff Prescott said. "What was Tara like?"

Robin paused to consider her answer. "I'm probably the wrong person to ask, since she obviously wasn't who I thought she was."

"And who was that?"

"My friend, for starters."

Another tug at the corners of his lips. "What else?"

Again, Robin paused to consider her former friend, but no thoughts came. Her mind was like a blank canvas, and no matter how much paint she threw at it, nothing stuck. She felt the familiar tingle stirring in her chest. "I'm sorry, Sheriff. I'm tired and more than a bit overwhelmed. I don't think I'm ready to have this conversation after all."

He nodded. "I understand. We can talk later." A statement, not a request.

"If you could just tell me what happened . . ."

Sheriff Prescott stared down at his boots, the top of his head reflecting the glare of the overhead fluorescent lighting. "The nine-one-one call came in about half past midnight the night before last," he began, raising his head as he spoke, until once again his eyes were level with Robin's. "It was Cassidy, screaming that her parents had been shot. And then the dispatcher heard what sounded like a gunshot, and the line went dead. The police got to the house as fast as they could. They found the front door open and your father and Tara lying on the living room floor, their bodies riddled with bullets, Tara's face pretty much blown off."

Oh, God. Tara's beautiful face. Gone. Robin fought the almost overwhelming urge to throw up and zeroed in on the sheriff's eyebrows in an effort to still her growing panic attack. His eyebrows were darker and bushier than she'd first realized. They lay like two caterpillars across the bottom of his forehead. "And Cassidy?"

"She was upstairs in her bedroom, sprawled across her bed. Unconscious. Barely breathing. The front of her pajama top soaked through with blood. Phone still in her hand."

What kind of monster shoots a twelve-year-old girl? Robin asked herself again. Then, out loud, "What else?"

"The safe in the den was open and empty, so it looks as if whoever did this was after something. 'Course, we don't know what was in the safe. Hoping you might be able to help us with that." He ran a hand across the top of his smooth head. "And dresser drawers and items of clothing were all over the floor in the walk-in closet of the master bedroom."

That doesn't mean anything, Robin thought. *Tara wasn't exactly a neat freak.*

"It's also looking as if Tara's rings had been forcibly

removed. She wasn't wearing any, and there was bruising on both her ring fingers."

Robin pictured the brilliant round three-carat diamond solitaire and accompanying diamond eternity band that her father had bought Tara and that she'd never been shy about showing off. Nor had she been reticent about wearing the few good pieces of jewelry that had once belonged to Robin's mother, pieces that her father had showered on his new wife, leaving the less-valuable items for Robin and Melanie to fight over. Except that Robin had had no stamina for further conflict, and so she gave in to all of Melanie's demands, settling for the simple amethyst ring her mother had owned since girlhood, which Robin wore on a thin gold chain around her neck. Her fingers went to it now.

"We'd like you and your sister to go through the house with us tomorrow morning, if you're up to it," Sheriff Prescott said. Again, he made it more of a statement than a request. "See if you can figure out what might be missing."

Robin nodded, although she didn't see how she could help. She'd never even seen her father's new house—let alone set foot inside it. It was right next door to his old house—the one she'd grown up in, the one where Melanie and her son still lived. "Do you know how many people were involved, if there were more than one . . ."

"We don't know," the sheriff answered before she could finish her question. "There's been no rain. Never is at this time of year, so it's not like there are any telltale footprints in the mud or anything like that. Not like on TV. We're still dusting for fingerprints, but it's unlikely we'll find anything useful. The house is brand spanking new. Apparently, workers were still going in and out of it all the time. Plus your father and Tara had just thrown a big house-warming party a few days before." He shook his head, his small eyes narrowing into tiny slits as his bushy eyebrows converged into a single straight line. "Not to mention we just had the annual rodeo, so there've been lots of strangers in town."

"So what you're essentially saying is that it could have been anyone."

"Except there was no sign of forced entry."

"Meaning?"

"Meaning that either the front door was unlocked or your father or Tara opened it."

"I can't imagine that they would leave the front door unlocked."

"Can you imagine them opening it to strangers after midnight?"

Robin felt her windpipe closing, as if being squeezed by invisible fingers, and a dry cough escaped her throat.

The sheriff continued, oblivious to her discomfort, "If you can think of anyone who might have had a motive . . ."

"My father didn't exactly make a secret of his wealth, Sheriff. It seems pretty obvious from everything you've just told me that robbery was the motive, regardless of whether or not my father knew his attacker. And with workers coming in and out of the house all the time, it would seem logical that one of them—"

"Would that life was always logical," the sheriff interrupted again, this time with a rueful shake of his head. "Guess we'll just have to wait till little Cassidy is able to tell us something."

"Can I see her?"

"Absolutely." Sheriff Prescott pushed himself to his feet.

Robin did likewise, then stumbled, her mounting panic all but propelling her into the sheriff's arms.

"Whoa, there. You all right?"

"Just clumsy. Sorry."

"No need to apologize. This way." He took her elbow, as if he was afraid she might stumble again, and led her down the corridor to a room at the far end where an armed officer was standing guard.

"Is that necessary?" Robin asked.

"Just a precaution," Sheriff Prescott explained. "Till we find out what happened." He pushed the door open, then stood back to let her enter.

Robin took a deep breath, feeling it bounce against the air like a rubber ball as she released it and stepped inside the room. "Oh, God," she whispered, inching forward, her mind trying to grasp what her eyes were seeing.

What she was seeing was the past—a little girl who so resembled her mother at that age that it took away what little breath Robin had left, and she fell back against the sheriff's burly chest, the gun in his holster burrowing into the small of her back.

"You all right?" he asked her again. "Do you want me to get your sister?"

Robin shook her head. *God, no.* "She just looks so helpless, so young."

In fact Cassidy looked even younger than her twelve years. Eyes closed, skin the color of skim milk, stringy light brown hair hanging limply past bony shoulders, only a hint of breasts beneath the bandages encasing her torso. *More larva than butterfly,* Robin couldn't help thinking, staring down at the child's sweet, unlined face. *Tara's face,* she thought.

"Pretty much blown off," the sheriff had said.

She stifled yet another cry.

"You can talk to her if you'd like," the sheriff urged.

Robin recognized the command inside the gentle request. "What do I say?"

"Anything."

Robin reached for Cassidy's hand, finding the child's fingers cold and unresponsive inside her own. "Hi, sweetheart," she began. "My name is Robin. I don't know if you remember me. I haven't seen you in a long time. But I used to be good friends with your mother." She received no response and glanced back at Sheriff Prescott.

Keep going, he said with his eyes.

"We met in the fifth grade. I was in Miss DeWitt's class, and she was in Miss Browning's, and for some reason I got transferred into Miss Browning's class about halfway through the year—I don't remember why. We were ten years old and I was very shy. I didn't have a lot of friends. Your mother was the exact opposite. Everybody wanted to be friends with her. 'A real little firecracker,' my father used to say." *Oh, God.* A deepening pressure on Robin's larynx put a temporary stop to her words. "Anyway, for some reason," she continued, scraping the words from the back of her throat, "your mother decided she liked me and she took me under her wing, made sure that everybody was nice to me."

Everybody but Melanie, who'd always been impervious to Tara's charms.

Strange that it had been Melanie who'd been the one to accept Tara's marriage to their father, Robin thought with her next breath. *That it had been Melanie who'd made nice and continued to live under the same roof with her until construction had been completed on the house next door.*

"We were best friends all through high school," Robin continued, putting the brakes on her interior monologue. "We were pretty much inseparable, your mother and I, even after she married your father. In fact, I was maid of honor at their wedding."

Robin pictured Tara, stunning in the secondhand wedding gown she'd paid for herself, standing in front of the justice of the peace beside dark-haired, charismatic Dylan Campbell, the archetypal bad boy she'd fallen for and married right after their high school graduation, despite her parents' disapproval. Or maybe because of it.

It soon became clear that Tara's parents had good reason to be concerned about Dylan, who turned out to be even worse than anyone had imagined.

The abuse started when Tara was pregnant with Cassidy, and it had continued until Dylan was jailed for breaking and entering in the third year of their marriage. Tara had seized the opportunity to file for divorce. She was all of twenty-one.

Where was Dylan now? Did Sheriff Prescott know about him? Was he in prison somewhere? Was he a suspect? Had he shot his former wife? Had he tried to murder his own child?

Robin spun toward the sheriff, about to voice these thoughts out loud when she noticed Melanie standing just inside the doorway, a bemused look on her face. *When had she come in? How long had she been standing there?*

"Please don't let me interrupt this little jaunt down memory lane," she said.

More not-so-gentle pressure on Robin's windpipe. "Your mother was so beautiful," Robin said, turning her attention back to Cassidy and squeezing her hand. "She was the most beautiful girl in Red Bluff."

"*Was* being the operative word," Melanie said, only half under her breath.

Cassidy's eyes opened wide.

"Melanie, for God's sake."

The child's enormous brown eyes moved from Robin to Melanie, widening even further in alarm.

"Hey, kiddo," Melanie said. "You know who I am, don't you? It's Melanie. And this is Robin. You probably don't remember her. You were still pretty little when she moved away."

"How are you feeling today?" Sheriff Prescott asked, approaching on the other side of the bed.

Cassidy's eyes traveled from one face to another, although she showed no signs of recognition, or even that she understood what they were saying.

"Cassidy," the sheriff said, "can you hear me? Do you know where you are?"

The girl stared at him, said nothing.

"You're in the hospital," he continued. "You were shot. Do you remember that?"

No response.

"Can you tell us anything about what happened?"

Cassidy shifted her gaze from the sheriff to Robin to Melanie.

"Cassidy," Sheriff Prescott repeated, "can you tell us who did this to you?"

Cassidy's eyes drifted up toward the ceiling, then closed.

"Maybe we should go," Robin suggested after several seconds had elapsed. The air had become very thick inside the small room. She was having trouble breathing.

"Guess we'll try again tomorrow," the sheriff said.

Robin nodded, although returning to the hospital was the last thing she wanted to do. She'd hoped to be on a bus back to Sacramento by then, followed immediately by a plane to Los Angeles.

That was unlikely to happen until some of the sheriff's questions had been answered. She'd already agreed to accompany him to her father's house the next morning, so she'd likely have to hang around at least a few more days. Maybe by then Cassidy would be able to tell them something.

Assuming the child survived.

Who could have done such an awful thing?

Robin had watched enough television to know that if a crime wasn't solved within the first forty-eight hours, it likely never would be. How could she leave without knowing who was responsible? How could she leave Red Bluff before she knew whether her father would survive his injuries?

How could she stay?

In the next instant, the room was spinning, and the floor was falling away. Robin tried to cling to Cassidy's hand but felt her fingers slipping. She heard Sheriff Prescott's voice in the distance—"Can we get a nurse in here?"

The last voice she heard before she lost consciousness belonged to her sister. "She always was a drama queen," Melanie said.

—FIVE—

"Well, what do you know? She awakens," Melanie said from behind the wheel of her car as Robin opened her eyes and bolted upright in the passenger seat, her eyes darting in all directions at once. "Relax. You were only out a few minutes."

Robin stared out the window at the few middle-class houses scattered among the profusion of vacant lots. A street sign revealed that they were at the corner of South Jackson Street and Luther Road. They turned left, heading west toward Paskenta Road.

"How many of those pills did you take, anyway?" Melanie asked.

Obviously not enough, Robin thought, picturing the young doctor with short, frizzy red hair whose huge green eyes had been the first thing she'd seen when she came to on the floor of Cassidy's hospital room. The doctor had checked her blood pressure and listened to her heartbeat before pronouncing a diagnosis of stress and writing out a prescription for Ativan. Robin had filled the prescription as soon as they left the hospital, running into the pharmacy next to the clock tower on Main Street while Melanie waited in the car, then swallowing two of the tiny white pills without the benefit of water before even walking out the door. The last thing she remembered was climbing back into the front seat and trying to block out the excruciating sound of Enya on the radio by closing her eyes and pretending to be floating on her back in the ocean.

"What's the matter—you didn't do enough drugs at Berkeley to develop a tolerance?" Melanie was asking now. "I thought that was the whole point of going there."

Actually, Robin had *stopped* doing drugs at Berkeley, her panic attacks having abated once she was a safe distance from Red Bluff. Until then, drugs had been part of her regular routine. A few tokes to get her through the day, a mild sedative at night to help her sleep.

Tara had been her chief supplier.

Should she tell Sheriff Prescott that*?*

"You didn't recognize Dr. Simpson, did you?" Melanie was saying.

"Should I have?"

"Think. Red hair, green eyes, a nose full of freckles. Of course she tries to hide them with all that makeup."

"Oh, my God," Robin said, vaguely recalling the Annie look-alike who'd been a year behind her in high school. "That was Jimmy Kessler's little sister, Arlene?"

"She married Freddy Simpson a few years ago. He was president of the student council the year I graduated. Captain of the debate team. A real know-it-all. Surely you remember *him*."

Robin shook her head. She'd done her best to forget everything about Red Bluff.

"She's calling herself Arla now."

"Oh, my." The sisters shared a welcome laugh. "She should have said something."

"She probably didn't think it was the best time to play catch-up. Or maybe she was just embarrassed."

"Why would she be embarrassed?"

"I guess some people find murder embarrassing." The car crossed Paskenta Road, continuing west.

Murder, Robin repeated silently, flipping the word over on her tongue, the pleasant buzz from the Ativan softening its impact. *Tara didn't just die. She was murdered.* "Has anyone notified Tara's parents?"

"I doubt it."

"Should we?"

"I wouldn't have a clue where to find them. Would you?"

Robin shook her head, concentrating on the increasingly barren vista beyond her side window. She tried picturing Tara's parents, but all she managed to conjure up was a vague outline. Tara had never been close to either her mother or her father, and they'd all but disowned her after she'd married Dylan. They'd separated the same year that Cassidy was born, and Tara's father had run off to Florida soon after with the woman who cut his hair. Her mother had joined some religious cult and disappeared into the wilderness of Oregon at least a decade ago. Who knew if either of them was even still alive?

“Almost home,” Melanie announced unnecessarily, turning onto Walnut Street.

So intense was her revulsion that Robin had to fight the impulse to open the car door and hurl herself out, despite the Ativan. *Maybe I should have stayed in a hotel,* she was thinking. Except she’d already decided that this trip, however unplanned and unpleasant it might be, presented a good opportunity to mend fences with her sister, however high those fences might be. And Melanie had been adamant that it would give the locals more to gossip about if Robin stayed anywhere but the family home and that the press would likely hound her. She wouldn’t be here long in any event, and this way they’d be able to maintain at least some control over the situation.

Robin watched the space between houses grow as they continued north. Less than a minute later, they turned onto Larie Lane. An enormous wood-and-glass house appeared, surrounded by the yellow tape that identified it as a crime scene and warned the curious to keep their distance. Two police cruisers and a white van were parked in the long driveway leading up to the three-car garage.

“And there it is,” Melanie said, slowing her car to a crawl. “What is it they say? ‘A man’s home is his castle’?”

“It certainly stands out.”

“I think that was the intention.”

“It’s huge.”

“Over eight thousand square feet.”

Which makes it probably the largest home in Red Bluff, Robin thought. The majority of houses in the area were a quarter that size and worth a fraction of what she estimated it had cost to build this place. It sat in the middle of an acre of land, almost daring the general population to come and get it.

"Serves them right for building the biggest fucking house in town," Robin remembered her brother saying. She wondered idly when he'd seen it, the thought slipping out of her mind as quickly and quietly as it had slipped in.

"They used some hotshot decorator from San Francisco, and it's all very grand inside," Melanie said. "Grand and bland, if you ask me." She picked up speed. "Of course, no one did." A short distance farther along, Melanie turned in to the long driveway of the much smaller house next door. "Home sweet home." She shut off the car's engine and was about to open her door when she stopped and swiveled toward Robin. "Are you ready, or do you need time to *acclimate*?"

Robin stared at the two-story house she'd grown up in, trying to recall at least one happy memory contained inside those walls. She was surprised to realize that there were several, almost all of them involving her mother. However, even those memories were tainted by the fact that her mother's brain had been so riddled with cancer in those final weeks after Robin came home from Berkeley to be with her that she had no idea who Robin was.

All her other happy memories included Tara: bringing her new friend home after school one afternoon and introducing her to her parents, who were as impressed by Tara's bubbly nature as Robin was; she and Tara sharing adolescent hopes and dreams in her upstairs bedroom, and later, trying to mask the smell of the joint they'd just smoked with copious sprays of her mother's

Angel perfume; her pride whenever one of Tara's clever put-downs left Melanie speechless; her thrill at holding Tara's newborn baby in her arms when Tara came to visit; her relief when Tara confided that she was leaving Dylan; her joy when, seated around the dining room table five years later, Tara and Alec announced their engagement, and her naïve conviction that she would have a real sister now. *"Think that might be a little too much woman for you,"* she remembered her father telling his son. *"She's a real little firecracker."*

Neither Robin nor Alec had suspected that one day that little firecracker would explode in their faces.

So much for happy memories, she thought. She opened the car door and stepped onto the gravel of the driveway, watching a cloud of dust rise in the thick air like smoke. She stood staring at the old house, its white clapboard exterior in dire need of a fresh coat of paint, its dull veneer an obvious consequence of the prolonged construction next door.

Still, the house managed to send shivers up and down her spine. Four bedrooms—five, if you counted the tiny mudroom off the kitchen. Her brother had claimed that space as his own after Melanie's son grew too big to sleep in the same room with her, and the boy had moved into Alec's bedroom. Robin could still hear the rhythmic banging of Landon's chair as he rocked it back and forth compulsively against the hardwood floor for hours every night.

Now she looked toward that bedroom window and was startled to see a hulking figure staring back at her. "My God. Who's that?"

Melanie was getting Robin's suitcase from the trunk and replied without bothering to look up. "Who do you think?"

"Is that Landon?"

"No, it's George Clooney. Of course it's Landon."

Robin waved. The hulking figure promptly disappeared.

Robin followed Melanie up the front walk. "Does he understand what's going on?" She tried to take her suitcase from Melanie's hand, but Melanie shooed her away, holding firm in her grip.

"He understands. Being autistic doesn't make him an idiot."

"Has he said anything to you about it?"

"What's he supposed to say?" Melanie dropped Robin's suitcase to the patch of concrete by the front door and fumbled in her purse for her house key.

Robin looked toward the police cruisers next door. "Does the sheriff really consider him a suspect?"

"Who would be more convenient than the crazy boy next door?" Melanie found the key and jammed it angrily into the lock. "Think of the accolades if they can wrap this up quickly. Think of the great publicity: small-town sheriff solves big-time crime. I can picture the cover of *People* now, with *Dateline* and *48 Hours* fighting over an exclusive. Wouldn't that asshole Prescott love to be at the center of that."

Sheriff Prescott hadn't struck Robin as an asshole, but she decided to keep that opinion to herself as she followed Melanie into the front hall of the old house.

It was as if she'd never left.

Thank God for the Ativan, she thought. It was the only thing that was keeping her upright.

Melanie dropped her keys onto the side table to the left of the front door and walked toward the staircase in the middle of the center hall. "Landon," she called out. "Come say hello to your long-lost auntie. Landon," she called again when he failed to materialize after several seconds. She turned back to Robin. "So, what do you think?"

"Looks the same," Robin said without looking.

"Well, I made a few changes after Dad moved out. Couldn't afford to do much, of course. Not that I have any right to complain. He *did* leave behind all the old furniture."

Not to mention letting you continue to live rent-free in the home he's provided for you and your son these past eighteen years.

"Dad and Tara bought all new stuff when they moved. Well, they had to, really. Nothing here was suitable, and Tara wanted to 'put her own stamp on things,' as she put it. Guess she'd lived with Mom's 'stamp' long enough. Can't say I blame her. I'm getting a little tired of it myself. You want something to drink?"

"Maybe a glass of water."

"I don't have any of that fancy bottled water you probably like."

"Tap water's fine."

"Well, you know where the kitchen is. Help yourself." Melanie turned back toward the stairs. "Landon, get down here right now!"

Robin moved slowly past the stained-oak staircase and

the downstairs powder room to the eat-in kitchen at the back of the house. She glanced only briefly into the living room to her left and the dining room to her right, refusing to allow enough time for familiar objects to register. She proceeded directly to the sink, ignoring the view of the backyard from the window above it and turning on the cold-water tap while reaching into the cupboard on her right for a glass. She filled one with water and drank it down, then rinsed it and put it in the dishwasher.

"You know that it's not good to rinse things first," Melanie said from somewhere behind her. "Leaves a film."

"I didn't know that."

"I thought therapists were supposed to know everything."

"Guess I'm not a very good therapist."

Melanie shrugged, as if accepting Robin's appraisal.

"Where's Landon?" Robin asked. "I thought he was coming down."

"Apparently not. You hungry?"

"Not really."

"We usually have dinner around six. That too early for you?"

"Six o'clock sounds good."

"It won't be anything fancy. Chili, most likely. You're not a vegetarian, are you?"

"No. Chili sounds great."

"Well, it's not great. But Landon likes chili, so it'll have to do. You want to go upstairs, unpack, get settled?"

Get settled? Are you kidding me? I've never felt less settled in my life. "Sure."

"It's your old room. Actually, it was Cassidy's before they moved into the new house. Now it's yours again. Seems we've come full circle." She looked at Robin, apparently surprised to find her still there. "You don't need me to show you the way, do you?"

"I think I can manage."

"Feel free to have a nap before dinner," Melanie said as Robin was leaving the kitchen.

"Thanks. I just might do that."

"Good," said Melanie. "You need it. You look like crap."

–SIX–

Robin was asleep the minute her head hit the pillow.

The dreams started almost immediately.

In the first dream, she was walking down Main Street searching for Tillie's. She was supposed to be meeting her mother and she was already late. But Tillie's wasn't in its usual location. Robin ran up and down the street, crossing to the other side and back again, then running into the drugstore and asking the pharmacist behind the counter where the popular shop had moved.

"Take these," he said. "You'll find it."

Suddenly Robin was standing in front of a large window full of silver picture frames and quasi antiques, the name Tillie's painted across the glass in letters of swirling gold. She entered the store. "If you're looking for Mommy," Melanie called from behind an old-fashioned cash register, "you're out of luck. She just left."

"Where did she go?"

"She's in a coma," Melanie said. "Now go away. Can't you see I'm busy with a customer?"

The customer turned around.

It was Tara.

She didn't have a face.

Robin groaned in her sleep and flipped over onto her side as that dream faded and another one took its place.

She was in her office, and the phone was ringing. It was Adeline Sullivan, calling to say she wouldn't be able to make their next session. She'd shot her husband. "He was cheating on me," she told Robin.

"All men cheat," Robin said.

"What do I tell the police? They're expecting a confession."

"Tell them you're autistic," Robin advised. "Just because you're autistic doesn't mean you're a killer."

That dream melted seamlessly into dream number three.

She was trying on bridesmaid dresses in the middle of a huge warehouse. "I like this one," Tara said, pulling a bright yellow gown off a nearby rack and handing it to Robin.

"What do you think?" Robin asked a couple of minutes later, emerging from behind the curtain of a makeshift dressing room.

Tara doubled over with laughter. When she stood up, she'd morphed into Melanie. "You look like a giant banana."

"I have another dress to show you," said a salesgirl with bright red hair and huge green eyes.

"Dr. Simpson?" Robin asked.

"Call me Arla."

"I didn't know you worked here."

"I thought therapists knew everything."

"I'm not a very good therapist."

"So I hear. Anyway, I have to go. Your father is waiting."

"What's he waiting for?"

"He's waiting to die," Arla said before fading into nothingness.

The warehouse disappeared and a hospital corridor rose to take its place. Robin raced down the sterile hall, peeking into room after room, finding each one empty. And then, in the last room, she saw Cassidy.

The child sat up as Robin entered the room, the front of her pajamas dripping fresh blood. "They broke in and shot me," she said, pointing to a second bed only a few feet away.

Robin approached the bed and pulled down the sheet, revealing Blake and his pretty new assistant naked and tangled up in each other's arms. "What are you doing here?" Robin demanded of her fiancé.

"Same thing I've been doing for years," Blake said. "No surprises here."

Robin heard a strangled cry escape her lips.

"Robin," Melanie said from somewhere above her head.

She felt a hand on her shoulder.

"Robin," Melanie said again, shaking her, her voice piercing Robin's dream. "Wake up."

"What?"

"You're having a nightmare," Melanie told her.

Robin opened her eyes, saw Melanie looming above her, a gun in her hand. "What are you doing?"

"Sorry about this," Melanie said, pressing the gun against Robin's forehead. "It has to be done."

She pulled the trigger.

Robin screamed and bolted up in bed. "Holy crap," she whispered, wiping a swath of perspiration from her forehead and coming fully awake. "What the hell was that?"

It was then that she saw him. She caught no more than a fleeting glimpse—a tall young man, wide-shouldered and slim-hipped, long hair falling across his forehead into his eyes. "Landon?" *How long had he been standing there?*

In the next second, he was gone.

"Landon?" Robin called again, getting to her feet and crossing to the bedroom door. She peered down the hall but saw no one. The door to Landon's bedroom was closed. *Had he been there at all? Had she dreamt him, too?*

Robin returned to her room and sank down on the bed. She checked her watch and saw that it was almost five o'clock, which meant she'd been asleep for more than an hour. *Had he been watching her the whole time? Had he been watching her at all?*

She reached for her purse on the floor beside the double bed, her fingers searching blindly for the small notepad and pencil she kept inside it. She wanted to jot down her dreams before she forgot them, something she often advised her clients to do. Not that she was any good at deciphering their meaning, despite the various books she'd read on the subject and the extra courses she'd taken. Sure, she could recognize the difference between a dream of wish fulfillment and one of anxiety, but the individual symbols contained in these dreams always eluded her. "No surprises here," she muttered, borrowing Blake's phrase and scribbling it down, although the rest of her dreams were already evaporating, bursting like bubbles in the air. By the time she'd finished recording that simple sentence, the only image that remained from any of the dreams was that of Blake and his pretty assistant lying naked in each other's arms.

"Tara is dead," she said out loud. "Your father's in a coma. Cassidy is still in critical condition. And you're worried that your fiancé is cheating on you. Way to put things in perspective!" She fell back against the pillow, dropping the notepad and pencil to the floor and staring at the ceiling fan whirling gently above her head.

Gradually she gave in to curiosity and looked around the room, noting the changes that had been made. Her bed, once covered with plain white sheets and a blue blanket, now sported flowered sheets and a frilly pink bedspread; rose-colored broadloom lay atop the hardwood floor she'd grown up with; the formerly beige walls were now a soft shade of ivory. Large posters of the Eagles and the Grateful Dead had been replaced by even larger posters of Beyoncé and Taylor Swift. The only thing that was the same was her old desk. It stood in front of the window, a small TV occupying its center, the space around it littered with a motley collection of snow globes that Cassidy had clearly outgrown and abandoned in the move to the larger, grander house next door.

"Some house," Robin said, walking to the window and leaning against the desk, staring across the expanse of mottled grass at the imposing structure. "More like a hotel." She picked up one of the snow globes and turned it upside down, watching as hundreds of tiny white flakes swirled around the assortment of miniature animals trapped inside its underwater zoo. "I should have stayed in a hotel," she whispered to the tiny giraffe standing next to a blue plastic whale. She wondered idly if the Hotel Tremont was still considered Red Bluff's finest.

Instantly she found herself standing in the middle of its elegant lobby. She and Tara, both sixteen, had ducked into the hotel to use the washroom on their way home from a school dance. They were giggling about Lenny Fisher making out with Marie Reynolds in full view of the school principal, and wondering where Sheila Bernard had bought her dress, since it was obvious it hadn't come from any of the shops in Red Bluff, when they saw him. The laughter immediately stopped, sticking in their throats like stale popcorn.

What they saw was a tall, handsome man, his arm around a curvaceous brunette roughly half his age, as he strutted across the lobby toward the reception desk.

"Oh, my God," Tara said, grabbing Robin's arm and pulling her behind the nearest pillar.

Not that it mattered.

Her father clearly didn't care who saw him.

"Who's that with him?" Tara asked.

"Her name's Kleo. She works in his office," Robin replied, tears forming in the corners of her eyes.

"Maybe it's not what it looks like," Tara said. *"Maybe they're here for a meeting or something."*

They watched the man's hand slide down the woman's back to cup her right buttock. *"He's supposed to be out of town on business. He told my mother he wouldn't be back till tomorrow."*

Tara wrapped her arm around Robin's waist, hugging her tight. "*I'm so sorry.*"

"*Why? It's not your fault.*"

"*I'm the one who dragged you in here. I'm the one who couldn't wait to pee until we got home.*"

"*I probably would have found out sooner or later,*" Robin said. "*I mean, look at him. He's not even trying to be careful.*"

They watched her father sign the hotel register and walk toward the elevators at the rear of the lobby, his arm now draped proprietarily across the young woman's shoulders, his fingers stretching toward the cleavage that was on ample display.

"*Duck,*" cautioned Tara. "*Wait. What are you doing?*"

What Robin was doing was standing up, confronting her father, blocking his path.

Had she been trying to shame him into a tearful recognition of what he was about to do, followed by his even more tearful apology? Had she been expecting him to get down on his knees and beg her forgiveness? Had she been hoping that, at the very least, he would push the young woman aside and promise never to stray again?

"*Don't tell your mother,*" he said instead. "*It would break her heart. Now go home. You didn't see me.*"

And so her father's betrayal became her responsibility.

By not telling her mother, by rationalizing that it would indeed break her heart, Robin had become complicit, a passive participant in the betrayals that inevitably followed. Although she never caught him outright again, she heard the whispers and knew that the rumors always swirling around him, like specks of dust in the sunlight, were true. He continued to "work late" at the office; his business trips became more frequent, lasted longer.

How could her mother not know? How could she not see what was happening right under her nose?

"Go home. You didn't see me."

So nobody saw.

And everybody knew.

"My father cheats, too," Tara had confided some time later.

"How do you know?"

"My mother told me."

"She told you? What did she say?"

"That they all do it."

"And she's okay with it?"

"I guess. She has her Bible."

"Doesn't the Bible say you're supposed to stone adulterers?" Robin asked.

"Don't think there'd be too many people left if we did that," Tara said.

And they'd laughed, although the laughter was joyless.

"What would you do if you found out Dylan was cheating on you?" Robin had asked her friend after she'd announced she was getting married.

"Probably cut his balls off."

"Seriously."

"I am *serious."*

"More seriously."

"I guess I'd give him a taste of his own medicine. You know the expression—what's good for the goose . . ."

"You could do that?"

Tara took a deep drag of the joint they were sharing, then passed it back to Robin. *"I can do anything I want."*

And she had, Robin thought.

And now she was dead.

"I would never stay with a man who cheated on me," Robin remembered telling Tara.

"Then you probably shouldn't bother getting married," had been Tara's instant response.

Was that why she and Blake had never followed through on their plans to wed? Despite all Robin's efforts to steer clear of men who even remotely resembled her father, did she secretly suspect she'd chosen a man just like him?

Robin stared at the house her father had built next door. *His castle,* she thought.

His tomb.

"Robin!" her sister called from downstairs. "Landon! Dinner's ready."

Robin looked at her watch, stunned to see it was already six o'clock. *How long have I been standing here?* She turned away from the window. "Be right down."

She crossed the hall and entered the bathroom. "I *do* look like crap," she said to her reflection in the mirror over the sink. She tugged at her hair, trying to force its curls into some semblance of order, then gave up, washing her hands and splashing warm water on her face, before tugging on her hair again. "Much better," she muttered without conviction as she left the room.

The door to Landon's bedroom was closed, and she approached it cautiously. Inside she could hear his rhythmic rocking. "Landon," she said, knocking gently on the door. The rocking stopped. "Supper's ready."

She waited for some form of acknowledgment, but there was nothing.

"Robin! Landon!" Melanie called up the stairs. "Dinner's on the table."

Robin waited outside Landon's door for several more seconds. Only after the rocking resumed did she give up and go downstairs.

—SEVEN—

Melanie was already eating when Robin entered the kitchen.

"Sorry I'm late," Robin said, pulling up the chair across from her sister at the square wooden table and sitting down.

"That's Landon's seat," Melanie said.

Robin promptly moved to another chair, so that she and her sister were sitting at right angles to each other. *Within striking distance,* she thought, recalling the time Melanie had reached over to spear the back of her hand with a fork when they were children. Instinctively she brought her hands into her lap.

"Something wrong?" Melanie asked.

"No." She looked at the large bowl of chili in the middle of the table. "Smells delicious."

"Help yourself. We don't stand on ceremony around here."

Robin spooned a small helping of chili onto her plate.

"That's all you eat? No wonder you're nothing but skin and bones."

"I'll probably take seconds."

Melanie shrugged. "There's bread in the breadbox, if you want any. I didn't bother with a salad. Landon never eats salads, so I've pretty much stopped making them."

"No worries."

"Who said I was worried? God, I hate that expression."

Robin felt her stomach twist into a large knot. She raised a forkful of chili to her mouth, praying she wouldn't gag. "It's really good," she said after she'd successfully swallowed one forkful and was about to attempt another.

"You sound surprised."

"I'm not. I wasn't . . ." *Let it go.* "Melanie, do you think we could . . . ?" She stopped. *What's the use?*

"Do I think we could . . . what?" Melanie asked. "You don't want to talk again, do you?"

Robin put down her fork. "I was just hoping we could . . ."

"What? For God's sake, Robin, just spit it out."

". . . be a little nicer to each other," Robin said. "I mean, we haven't seen each other in a long time. Maybe we could stop with all the barbs and snide remarks."

"I wasn't aware you'd made any."

"I haven't."

Melanie nodded knowingly. "So this isn't about *us* at all. It's about *me,* what *I* do wrong."

"You haven't done anything wrong. I'm just asking you to lighten up a bit."

"Tara's dead; our father probably won't make it through the night; it'll be a miracle if Cassidy survives; whoever did it is still out there; the sheriff thinks Landon is guilty and that I'm lying to protect him. And you want me to 'lighten up'?"

"That's not what I meant."

"It's what you said. What is it you want exactly, Robin? You want me to tell a few jokes?"

Might be nice. "I just want us to be civil."

"How am I not being civil?" Melanie responded. "I picked you up at the bus station. I acted as chauffeur all afternoon, driving you to the hospital and waiting at the drugstore while you got your supply of happy pills. I made you dinner. What's the matter—is chili not *civilized* enough for a fancy L.A. therapist?"

Robin put down her fork with more force than she'd intended. *Don't bite,* she told herself, but it was already too late. "That's exactly what I'm talking about. I never said anything about the chili except it was delicious. I like chili. That's not the issue."

"And what, pray tell, is 'the issue'?"

"That I'm not some fancy L.A. therapist."

"You're not a therapist? You don't live in L.A.?"

"Yes, I live in L.A. Yes, I'm a therapist. It's the word 'fancy' . . . "

"You don't like the word 'fancy'?"

"Not in that context, no."

"So, the *issue* is about *context*?"

Robin's head was spinning. A corkscrew of anxiety twisted through her chest. "I'm just saying . . ."

"Yes, please. What *are* you saying?"

"That I'm not the enemy here."

"And I am?"

"No. I'm just asking you to . . ."

"Lighten up?"

"Be kind."

"Uh-huh," Melanie acknowledged. "So now I'm not only uncivil. I'm also unkind."

Robin bowed her head. "Forget it. I'm sorry I said anything."

"Apology accepted," Melanie said with a smile. "That was me lightening up," she added, the smile spreading to her eyes.

Robin couldn't help smiling in return. "Have you heard anything more from the hospital?" she asked, scooping another spoonful of chili onto her plate.

"Not a word."

"I guess that's good." She got up from the table, went to the sink, and poured herself a glass of water, her heart racing despite the "happy pills" still in her system. "Would you like some?" she asked her sister.

"No, thanks. But you can pour Landon a glass."

"Is he coming down?"

"If he wants to eat. I don't do room service."

Robin returned to the table, depositing Landon's full glass of water next to his empty plate. "Have you spoken to him since we got home?"

"No. Why?"

"I was just wondering how he feels about my being here."

"Don't know. You'd have to ask him."

"I knocked on his door before. But he didn't answer."

"Well, I'm sure you'll run into each other eventually."

"Is he seeing anyone?" Robin asked.

"You mean, like a girlfriend?"

"No."

"I see. You mean someone like you?"

"Well, preferably someone who specializes in autism."

"We don't have a lot of specialists in Red Bluff, remember?" Melanie said. "We were seeing this one doctor for a while," she continued, surprising Robin by elaborating. "But Landon didn't like him very much, so we stopped."

"Is he on medication?"

"The doctor or Landon?" Melanie asked. "Sorry," she went on, immediately qualifying her statement. "Another attempt at levity." She dragged Landon's glass of water across the table and took a sip, then pushed it back with her index finger. "The doctor prescribed something. Can't remember the name. Sometimes Landon takes it; sometimes he doesn't. Says it makes him dopey. Anyway, there's not much I can do about it. He's a little big for me to force-feed."

Robin knew that the teen years could be a time of major stress and confusion for those who suffered from autism. They became painfully aware that they were different from other kids. Subsequent hurt feelings and the problems of connecting with others often led to depression and increased anxiety. And if there was one thing Robin understood, it was anxiety. "Is he still in school?"

"No. He quit a few years back."

"Does he have friends?"

"Not really. There's this one kid, but—"

The doorbell rang.

"Are you expecting someone?" Robin asked.

Melanie pushed herself away from the table. "Nope."

Robin followed her sister out of the kitchen to the front door. She watched Melanie peer through the peephole, then take a step back. "Speak of the devil . . . ," she said, opening the door to a slender young man whose black hair and pale skin emphasized the intense blue of his eyes. He was wearing black jeans and a plain black T-shirt, and Robin estimated his age as late teens.

"Mrs. Davis," the boy said to Melanie.

"*Miss,*" she corrected him, sounding as if this wasn't the first time she'd made such a clarification. "How are you, Kenny?"

"Not so good," he said. "I heard about Cassidy. Can I come in?"

Melanie stepped back to allow him entry.

"Is she all right?" He stopped abruptly when he saw Robin.

Melanie followed the young man's gaze. "This is my sister, Robin."

The boy managed a weak smile. "How you doin'?"

"This is Kenny Stapleton," Melanie said. "We were just talking about you, as a matter of fact."

"You were?"

"My sister was asking if Landon had any friends. You're pretty much it, I guess. Although you haven't been around much recently, have you?"

"I'm really sorry about that. Been kind of busy," Kenny said. "How's Cassidy? Is she gonna be all right?"

"We don't know. She's still critical. You heard about her mother?"

Kenny lowered his gaze to his black boots. "I can't believe it. Who'd do this?"

"I don't know."

"They're saying it was, like, a home invasion or something."

"That's what they're saying," Melanie agreed.

"What about Mr. Davis?"

"It's not looking good."

"But he's still alive," Kenny said. "That's something, isn't it?"

"Maybe."

"He's pretty tough. He'll pull through. Cassidy, too. You'll see."

"Guess we will."

"How's Landon?"

"Well, you know," Melanie said. "It's hard to tell for sure."

"Can I see him?"

"Sure." Melanie moved toward the staircase. "Landon! Kenny's here."

There was no response.

"You might as well go on up."

"Great." Kenny was halfway up the stairs when he stopped and turned back toward Robin. "Nice meeting you."

"You, too." Robin watched him disappear at the top of the stairs, heard the door to Landon's bedroom open and close. "He seems like a nice boy."

Melanie shrugged.

"It was thoughtful of him to come by."

"I guess." She started back toward the kitchen. "You feel like some ice cream? I think there's some in the freezer."

"Ice cream sounds great," Robin said.

"It's nothing fancy. Just plain old vanilla."

"Vanilla's my favorite."

"Really? Mine, too. Guess we're related, after all." She scooped the ice cream into two small bowls, then tossed the now-empty container into the garbage bin under the sink.

The sisters resumed their seats at the table, the only sound the scrape of their spoons against the sides of the ice cream bowls. "Do you think Kenny's right that Dad and Cassidy will somehow pull through?" Robin asked after a silence of several minutes.

"Well, Cassidy's young and she might stand a chance," her sister said. "But Dad was shot multiple times from close range, once in the head. To be honest, I don't know how he's managed to hang on this long."

"Can I ask you something else?" Robin asked.

"Can I stop you?"

Robin smiled in spite of herself. "Was he different?"

"What do you mean?"

"After he married Tara. Did he change?"

"You mean, did he cheat?"

"No. I meant change, in general. Wait. Why? Did he?"

"Who knows? Maybe. There were rumors . . ."

"What kind of rumors?"

"You know the kind."

"That he was cheating?"

"Well, there are no videos, if that's what you're after."

"Had Tara heard the rumors?"

"Beats me. We weren't exactly confidantes."

"But you lived in the same house, you managed to get along . . ."

"Maybe because we minded our own business," Melanie said pointedly.

Robin felt fresh stabs of anxiety poking at her chest. "I can't imagine Tara putting up with Dad cheating on her."

"Yeah, well, she wasn't exactly Miss Innocent in that department, from what I understand." Melanie got up from the table, gathering the empty dishes and depositing them in the dishwasher.

"What are you saying? That Tara was cheating, too?"

What's good for the goose . . .

Melanie shrugged.

"Does Sheriff Prescott know about this?"

"I can't imagine he doesn't."

"Holy shit," Robin said.

Melanie slammed the dishwasher shut. "That pretty much sums it up."

—EIGHT—

Robin had just slipped into her nightgown when her cell phone rang.

"Blake?"

"Alec," her brother said.

"Where are you?"

"In my apartment. You?"

"I think this might actually qualify as hell."

"Which means you're home. Congratulations. You're a better man than I am, Gunga Din."

"Are you coming?"

"Are you crazy?"

"Tara's dead."

Silence.

"Alec? Are you still there?"

"Tara's dead," he repeated, his voice flat, without inflection.

"She died this morning without regaining consciousness."

Another silence, longer this time. "So she never talked to the police. They don't know who . . ."

Robin heard the despair in his voice. *"Despair or relief?"* she heard Melanie whisper in her ear. "I'm so sorry, Alec," she said, pushing Melanie's imagined voice out of her mind. She knew her brother still harbored feelings for his former fiancée, even after all this time and despite everything. He would never . . . He *could* never . . .

Robin filled him in on what had happened since her bus arrived in Red Bluff. She refrained from telling him about the recent rumors regarding both their father and Tara, not sure how he'd react.

"Dad's still hanging in there, I take it?"

"He's a tough old dog," Robin said.

"So Tara dies and he survives. Figures."

"Come home, Alec," Robin urged. "I could really use the support."

"Where's Blake? Isn't that his job?"

Robin had been wondering the same thing. "He's pretty busy these days. He just can't pick up and leave whenever—"

"Whenever his fiancée's family gets slaughtered?"

"Nice talk," Robin said.

"I should go."

"You should come home."

"Talk soon," Alec said, then disconnected the call.

Robin tossed her phone on the bed, picturing her brother's handsome face—their mother's soft gray eyes, their father's sturdy jaw, the light brown hair that was a mixture of both, the sardonic sense of humor that was entirely his own. How many times had he reduced Robin and Tara to a puddle of helpless tears with one of his wry observations? *"Oh, God,"* she remembered Tara squealing at the conclusion of one of Alec's spontaneous comic riffs. *"I think I just peed my pants!"*

"How could she do this?" Alec had asked Robin after Tara had eloped with their father. *"I mean, it's bad enough leaving me for a man almost twice her age. My father, no less. My father no more,"* he'd proclaimed with a sad shake of his head. *"But how could a woman who loves to laugh marry a man without a single funny bone in his entire body? Shit, the man wouldn't know irony if it bit him in the ass. You know what he is, don't you?"* he'd asked, pausing before adding the killer punch line. *"He's irony deficient!"*

Robin still chuckled over that one.

It was true. Greg Davis had absolutely no sense of humor. His relentless pursuit of success and the almighty dollar had left little time or room for anything else. Oh, he could be charming. He knew the right things to say. He could even tell a pretty good joke. But there was something hollow behind his easy laugh and seductive manner. Not that it mattered. He'd learned that money went a long way toward filling pesky hollows.

And it seemed that Tara had loved money even more than she loved to laugh.

"She'll be sorry," she heard Alec say, trying to block out the words that had followed. *"Karma, baby. What goes around comes around. Sooner or later, she'll pay for this. They both will."*

Of course her younger brother was just being overly dramatic. He'd been justifiably hurt and angry. *"It would be way easier if she were dead,"* he'd said.

But that was almost six years ago, Robin told herself

now. *He didn't mean . . . There was no way . . . Besides, he'd been hundreds of miles away at the time of the shootings.*

She took a deep breath, determined not to let unwarranted suspicions hijack the rest of the night. She wouldn't allow such inane conjecture to keep her from getting a good night's sleep. She needed her rest for what was promising to be an exceedingly trying day tomorrow. So where was Blake? she wondered, transferring her anxiety about Alec to her fiancé. Why hadn't he called? "Goddamn it. Where are you?" *Are you alone? Who are you with?* She grabbed her purse from the floor and removed the small bottle of Ativan. *Only eight left,* she thought, counting them out and shaking two into the palm of her hand.

Her cell phone rang as she was lifting them to her mouth. Caller ID identified Blake as the caller.

Finally. "Hey," she said, folding her fingers over the pills, as if trying to hide them from Blake's sight, knowing he would disapprove.

"How are you?"

"Okay. Getting ready for bed."

"It's seven-thirty," he said.

Robin pictured his eyebrows inching together at the bridge of his patrician nose. His worried face, she called it. Oddly enough, it made him even better-looking than he already was.

"You haven't taken any more Valium, have you?"

"No," she said, which technically was not a lie. "I'm just tired, that's all. Apparently murder takes a lot out of you."

"I'm so sorry. How's your dad?"

"The same."

"Do they have any idea who did it?"

Robin shook her head.

"Robin? Are you there?"

"Sorry. No, they don't know who did it. They're thinking home invasion, but . . ."

"But?"

"They don't know." She didn't have the energy to recount her earlier discussion with Melanie. *Were the rumors true? Had her father been cheating on Tara? Had Tara been cheating on her father? And ultimately, did it make any difference? Would they still be alive if the rumors proved to be unfounded?*

"Have you been cheating on me?" she wanted to ask. "How are *you*?" she asked instead.

"Me? I'm fine. What about your sister?"

"Hard to say. One minute we seem to be doing all right; the next, not so much."

"And her son? Sorry, I forget his name."

"Landon."

"Oh, yeah. He was named after that actor . . ."

"Michael Landon." Robin pictured the long-dead star of *Bonanza,* a popular western that Melanie used to watch in reruns on TV. *Who names their son after an actor she's only seen in reruns?* "He keeps pretty much to himself. I haven't actually talked to him." *I can hear him, though,* she thought, glancing at the wall separating their two rooms. He'd resumed his incessant rocking as soon as his friend, Kenny, left.

"Must feel weird to be back there," Blake said.

"It does."

"How's the weather?"

Really? "Hot." *We're actually talking about the weather?*

"Do you have any idea when you'll be home?"

"Probably not for a few days at least. The sheriff wants us to go through my father's new house with him tomorrow, see if we can figure out what's missing." *Why? Are you concerned about being caught off guard? Is someone there with you?*

"How do you feel about that?"

Robin chuckled. "That's supposed to be *my* question. I'm the therapist, remember?"

Not a very good one.

"It won't be easy," Blake said.

"True. But when has anything about my family ever been easy?"

"Do you want me to come up there?" he asked.

Please say no, Robin heard him add silently.

"Not necessary," she obliged him by saying. "You're busy."

"I can manage a few days off."

"I'm fine. Really."

"You *do* sound pretty good."

"Do I?" *I guess we hear what we want to hear.*

"Yeah. Tired, but okay."

"I *am* tired."

"Guess I should let you go and get some sleep."

"Yeah. Probably a good idea." *Although a better idea would be for you to drop everything and get your ass up here. An even better idea would be for you to stop asking what I want and figure out what I need.*

"Okay," he said.

"Okay."

"You'll call me as soon as you know anything?"

"I'll call you."

"I love you," he said, so softly that Robin wasn't sure he'd said anything at all. *Another case of hearing what we want to hear?*

"Love you, too," she whispered. She tossed the phone back to the bed and deposited the two pills she was holding on the tip of her tongue, then swallowed both at once. One of them stuck in her throat, and she tried clearing it, but that seemed only to make things worse. She opened her door and stepped into the hall, crossing to the washroom and leaning over the sink to drink the cold water directly from the tap. It dribbled down her chin and neck and disappeared inside the front of her nightgown.

She washed her face and brushed her teeth, then spent a few minutes pulling on her hair before recognizing it as a lost cause and leaving the bathroom. She could hear the TV on in Melanie's bedroom at the end of the hall. Her sister hadn't wasted any time in taking over the master bedroom, with its convenient en suite bathroom, after their father and Tara had moved out. Robin wasn't sure exactly when that had been, and she hadn't thought to ask, but Sheriff Prescott had mentioned something about a recent house-warming party and that workers were still going in and out of the house on a regular basis. So, probably sometime in the last month, Robin surmised, returning to her room.

He was standing beside her bed, his back to her. He was tall and barefooted, with impressive biceps straining against the sleeves of his checkered shirt, which hung loosely over a pair of baggy blue jeans. Thick brown hair fell toward his slumped shoulders, and his body rocked back and forth as if he were praying.

"Landon?"

The boy spun around, dark eyes darting from Robin's face to her breasts.

Robin raised her hand to her chest, aware that her nipples were clearly visible beneath the thin white cotton of her nightgown. "It's so nice to finally see you," she said, wondering what he was doing in her room. "We missed you at dinner."

Landon said nothing, his gaze shifting to the floor.

"Did you eat anything? There's lots left, if you haven't. It's really good. Your mother makes excellent chili."

Again, no response.

"She said it's one of your favorites. Although she told me you don't like salads. I don't like broccoli." *Really? Since when didn't she like broccoli? Why had she said that?* "I can't believe how tall you are. The last time I saw you, you were still a little kid. Well, you weren't even a teenager. And now look at you. You're a man." *A great big silent man with bulging muscles who was in my room doing God only knows what.* "Did you come to say hello?"

Landon shifted his weight from one foot to the other, refusing to make eye contact.

"Would you like to sit down?" She inched forward. "We could talk, get reacquainted."

He took a step back, stopping only when his leg came in contact with the bed.

Robin heard footsteps behind her.

"What's going on here?" Melanie said. "Landon, what are you doing in Robin's room?"

Landon shot past both Robin and his mother with neither a word nor a glance in their direction.

"It's all right," Robin called after him. "You can stay."

Seconds later, his bedroom door slammed shut.

"He wasn't doing any . . ."

"Can you please refrain from entertaining my teenage son in your nightgown?" Melanie interrupted. "You can see right through that thing, you know."

"I wasn't entertain— I went to the bathroom. He was here when I came back."

"Whatever. I'd just like you to be a little more discreet instead of parading around the halls half-naked."

"I'm hardly half-naked."

"I can see your pubes," came Melanie's stinging retort.

Robin glanced toward her groin, her cheeks growing warm, as if Melanie had slapped her. She heard her sister's footsteps receding down the hall, and didn't look up again until she heard Melanie's bedroom door close. Then she crawled into bed, pulling the pink-flowered bedspread up over her head in an effort to keep unwanted ghosts at bay.

—NINE—

"You ready?" Melanie asked from the doorway. It was just past nine A.M.

Robin took a final sip of her coffee, followed by a deep inhalation, then used her exhale to push away from the kitchen table. She wiped her sweaty palms on the front of her jeans and walked to the sink.

"Uh-uh," Melanie cautioned as Robin was about to rinse out her mug. "Dishwasher."

"Sorry. I forgot."

"Let's go," Melanie instructed. "Mustn't keep the sheriff waiting."

Robin put the mug in the dishwasher, anxiety driving invisible nails through the soles of her sandaled feet, rooting her to the spot.

"Are you all right?" Melanie asked.

"Do you really need me? I mean, I've never even been inside the house. I wouldn't have a clue what's missing."

"You want me to go alone?"

Yes. "No." *Yes*. "I'm just not sure I can do this."

"Look, I know it won't be easy," Melanie said. "But the faster we get over there, the faster we can get back."

Maybe that's what I'm afraid of.

"Maybe you should take another pill. Don't want you passing out on us again."

"I already took one." *Two, actually. Unfortunately, they have yet to take effect.*

"Then let's go," Melanie said, hanging on to the word "go" until Robin was forced to comply.

One foot in front of the other. One step at a time.

"I'm trying to understand why you're so upset," Melanie was saying. "These were people you hadn't spoken to in more than five years. People you'd all but disowned. You don't see me falling apart, do you? And I'm the one who was here every fucking day—"

"I'm coming, for God's sake."

"Good. Maybe you could walk a little faster. Landon!" Melanie called up the stairs as they moved through the hall toward the front door. "We're leaving now. Be back in about an hour. In the meantime, don't answer the phone. Don't let anyone in. Do you hear me?"

"Did he hear you?" Robin asked as her sister opened the door without waiting for a reply.

"He hears everything." They stepped into the bright sunshine, Melanie walking briskly despite the already intense heat, Robin struggling to catch up.

She glanced over her shoulder at the house, saw Landon watching them from his bedroom window.

"What now?" Melanie asked as Robin came to an abrupt halt.

"You just said he hears everything," Robin said, seeing

Landon disappear behind the curtains. “Did he hear anything that night?”

“Like what?”

“Like gunfire. Dad and Tara were shot multiple times. Did Landon hear gunshots?” Robin released a long, deep breath, feeling it slam against the heavy outside air, as if into a brick wall. “Did *you*?”

“It was after midnight. I was sound asleep.” Melanie dug her hands into the pockets of her denim skirt and resumed her former pace.

“But maybe Landon wasn’t.” Once again, Robin struggled to catch up. “The house is right next door. Maybe he heard shots and went to the window. He’s always standing there. Maybe he saw something. Maybe he saw the person who—”

“He didn’t.”

“How do you know? Did you ask him?”

“Sheriff Prescott asked him. Landon didn’t hear anything. He didn’t see anything. Are you done with the questions? I have no wish to get into this in front of everyone.”

“I didn’t mean—”

“Let’s just get this over with, okay?”

Robin felt a trickle of perspiration make its way between her breasts and cling to the underside of her white shirt. She followed Melanie in silence as they cut across the wide expanse of dry grass toward the mini-mansion next door. Two police cruisers were already parked in the long driveway, one so close behind the other that they were almost touching, leaving plenty of room for more cars, more prying eyes. The sheriff was standing at the front door, his wide-brimmed cowboy hat protecting his bald pate from the sun.

"Hello, ladies," he said, tipping his hat in greeting.

"Sheriff," Melanie said.

"Good morning," Robin whispered, her voice barely audible.

"All settled in?" he asked her.

Robin managed a weak smile as she felt the Ativan kick in. *Thank you, God.* "All settled in," she repeated, her shoulders inching slowly away from her ears. "Is that a camera?" She pointed with her chin toward a security camera positioned above the front door. Surely if there were cameras, there would be footage . . .

"Unfortunately none of the cameras have been connected yet," the sheriff said. "Apparently the electricians were scheduled to come this week to finish installing the security system, which I understand is state of the art. If they had . . ." The sentence hung unfinished in the space between them.

"Can we just do this?" Melanie said.

"Certainly. You gonna be all right?" he asked Robin.

"She'll be fine," Melanie answered for her.

"I just want you to be prepared. There's a lot of blood."

Oh, God. "I'll be okay," Robin said.

"Good." He opened the front door. "After you." He stepped back to allow them entry. "This is Deputy Wilson," he said, introducing them to the young uniformed officer waiting inside the circular foyer, the floor of which was a sprawling mosaic of tiny white and black tiles. The air-conditioning was on high.

Robin nodded hello, her attention captured by the giant crystal chandelier hanging from the twenty-five-foot ceiling, and behind it two sweeping staircases, one on either side of the center hall, each one leading to a different wing on the second floor. "Holy shit."

"That's one way of putting it," Sheriff Prescott said, motioning to his right. "The living room is this way. I have to caution you not to touch anything."

Robin saw the blood as soon as she crossed the threshold into the large rectangular room. It was everywhere—pools of it soaked into the white-and-silver rug, splatters of it streaked across the floral chintz sofa and the huge expanse of window behind it, more splatters across the white keys of the black grand piano that stood next to a chintz-covered wing chair that had somehow managed to escape the carnage.

"Who plays the piano?" Robin asked.

"Cassidy was going to start taking lessons," Melanie said.

Robin watched Deputy Wilson jot down this information.

"Do you notice anything missing?" Sheriff Prescott asked after a pause of several seconds.

"Not offhand," Melanie answered. "But then, they bought almost everything brand-new, so it's hard to say for sure. You should probably ask their decorator."

"Who would that be?"

"I don't remember her name. Sheila or Shelley. Maybe Susan. She was with some hoity-toity design firm in San Francisco. Cassidy might know. She'd drive down with Tara when my dad was too busy to go with her."

Too busy doing what? Robin wondered.

The living room led into a formal dining room filled with heavy oak furniture, including a long table with more than enough room for the twelve rust-colored leather chairs clustered around it. Next came a huge kitchen full of the latest in stainless-steel appliances. Shiny white cabinets and black granite countertops surrounded an enormous center island with an array of copper pots and pans hanging artfully above it. As with the rest of the house, windows took the place of walls. What walls there were were bare.

Melanie was right. Despite its size and impressive exterior, despite the crystal chandelier and sweeping staircases, despite the grand piano and expensive furniture, despite the stainless-steel appliances and granite countertops—or maybe *because* of all these things—there was something curiously generic about the house. How had Melanie described it? *Grand and bland.* It looked more like a hotel than a home.

Of course her father had always been partial to hotels.

But Tara?

Tara had always turned up her nose at gaudy chandeliers. She'd hated chintz. She'd been indifferent to copper pots.

Robin tried picturing Tara tagging along with the decorator—Sheila or Shelley or maybe Susan—to the various designer showrooms, trying to choose among the myriad fabrics and marbles on display. Had she been too overwhelmed to have an opinion? Had she shrugged her lovely broad shoulders and gone along with her husband's choices? Had she been intimidated by the decorator's pedigree and expertise?

Except that Tara had never been one to shrug and go along. She wasn't easily overwhelmed. She was rarely intimidated.

Maybe she'd been distracted. Or she just didn't care. Maybe decorating bored her. Maybe her heart wasn't in it.

Maybe her heart was elsewhere.

Were the rumors true?

"This way," the sheriff said, leading them out of the kitchen through a side door that brought them back to the center hall.

Robin followed Sheriff Prescott into the large empty room on their left. More windows. More blank walls.

"They were having a pool table custom-built. It's supposed to be ready next month," Melanie said.

They returned to the hall, proceeding into their father's home office.

"His computer's missing," Melanie said immediately.

"We have it," the sheriff said. "Our tech guys are going through his files."

"Can you do that?" Melanie asked. "Without a warrant?"

Sheriff Prescott looked surprised by the question. "Your father's a victim, Melanie. Not a suspect. We're trying to find out who's responsible for what happened. What's in his computer might be of help."

"Not if it was a home invasion."

The sheriff nodded. "We'll try to have it back to you soon."

Robin glanced around the wood-paneled den, a pleasant buzz settling comfortably into the nape of her neck. Unlike the other rooms, which appeared to be largely untouched, this one had been ransacked. The drawers of the large walnut desk in the center of the room were open, their contents strewn across the floor. Books that must normally have filled the built-in bookshelves now littered the masculine green-and-brown-checkered carpet that covered the hardwood floor. A large black-and-white photograph of their father, his arms around Tara and Cassidy, stood upended in front of an open and empty wall safe.

"The safe was located behind the picture," Sheriff Prescott explained unnecessarily.

Not exactly the most original place in the world to hide a safe, Robin thought. *Especially when the only thing on any of the walls was this stupid photograph.* She glanced at the upside-down smiles of her father and his young family. *They look so happy,* she thought. *Had they been?*

"Any idea what was in that safe?" the sheriff asked.

Robin shook her head.

"Cash, probably," Melanie said. "He liked to have lots on hand."

"Any clue how much?"

"Five, maybe ten thousand dollars. That's what he always had lying around at home."

"Anything else?"

"Jewelry?" Melanie suggested. "Your guess is as good as mine."

"What about his will?" the sheriff asked.

"What about it?"

"Any idea who the beneficiaries might be?"

"You should probably talk to his lawyer." Melanie gave Sheriff Prescott the attorney's name. "But my father's not dead yet, remember?"

"What about guns?"

"What about them?"

"Did your father have any?"

"A couple. Are they missing?"

Prescott nodded. "Do you know what kind they were?"

"A Smith & Wesson, I think. And . . . what's that big one?"

"A .357?"

"Sounds about right. Was it the murder weapon?"

"It's a possibility. Shall we go upstairs?"

"Why not? Any particular staircase you'd prefer?" Melanie asked, returning to the hall.

"Why don't we start with the one on the right?"

"Good choice."

"Wow," Robin said when they reached the master suite. She stepped inside the first of three huge rooms, her feet sinking into the plush ivory-colored broadloom covering the floor and feeling it tickle her bare toes inside her sandals. Three small blue velvet sofas were grouped around a large blue leather ottoman. An enormous flat-screen TV was mounted on the wall. Heavy blue drapes framed the picture window overlooking the backyard.

"I believe they referred to this as their 'bed-sitting room,'" Melanie said, moving into the bedroom itself.

"Double wow," Robin whispered when she saw the giant four-poster, complete with canopy and white chiffon curtains, that stood in the center of the cavernous room. A blue velvet divan was positioned in front of the bed, complementing the chairs of yet another sitting area in front of another long window. "Holy shit," she said, her startled eyes coming to rest on a large nude portrait of Tara.

She was sitting on a swing, her right hand gripping one of the flower-festooned ropes that held it in place, her left strategically folded in her lap, her full breasts prominently and proudly on display.

As was the pronounced gash that ripped through the canvas on a diagonal from top to bottom.

"Looks as if at least one person has good taste in art," Melanie remarked.

"Why would someone do this?" Robin asked, approaching the picture.

"We've been wondering the same thing," Sheriff Prescott said, coming up behind her. "It looks personal, doesn't it?"

"Not necessarily," Melanie said. "I mean, you read about vandals doing stuff like this all the time. Wrecking things, defecating on carpets, slashing paintings . . ."

The sheriff nodded. "Yup. Could be." He opened the door to the enormous walk-in closet, which was more like a room full of closets, all of them open, clothes pulled from their hangers, dozens of shoes flung across the floor. An island dresser, full of open drawers that had clearly been rummaged through, occupied the middle of the room. A jewelry box sat empty on the dresser's hand-painted surface. "You know what jewelry might be missing?"

"Looks like all of it," Melanie said with a shrug.

"Could you be more specific?"

"Tara had a necklace with a diamond heart, and a pair of diamond studs that my father gave her for her birthday. A few gold chains and earrings that used to belong to my mother, an emerald-and-ruby butterfly pin that was also my mother's."

Robin's hand played absently with the amethyst ring on the chain around her neck, as she pictured the butterfly brooch her father had bought her mother for their twentieth anniversary. Her mother wore it only rarely, not wanting to appear ostentatious. Tara had had no such qualms.

"Maybe also some costume stuff," Melanie said. "Tara didn't have the best taste."

"You said at the hospital that it looked as if someone took her wedding and engagement rings," Robin said to the sheriff, not wanting to contradict her sister. She'd always admired Tara's sense of style, although it was admittedly unique.

Which was exactly what was missing from this house, Robin realized.

Tara.

In spite of her nude likeness, Tara was missing.

"It appears that way from the bruising on her fingers, yes," the sheriff said, answering the question she'd already forgotten she'd asked. "This way," he said, leading them out of the closet into the marble-and-glass master bathroom. "Not much to see in here."

There was an elaborate Jacuzzi in front of a large window overlooking the side of the house, a glassed-in shower for two, a beige marble floor with matching countertops, double sinks on either side of the room, a separate stall for the toilet, a bidet, gold-plated faucets. *"A bidet? Gold-plated faucets? Are you kidding me?"* Robin could almost hear Tara squeal with disdain.

She followed her sister across the upstairs hall to the other wing.

"How are you holding up?" Sheriff Prescott asked as they approached Cassidy's room.

"I've been better," Robin told him, although in truth, she wasn't feeling as bad as she'd feared. The Ativan was doing its job.

That is, it was doing its job until she saw the blood covering Cassidy's bed and pictured the little girl sprawled across it, her phone in her hand. A burst of anxiety exploded like gunfire inside her chest. "Oh, God."

It was only later, after they'd finished the tour of the upstairs rooms—a guest bedroom, a home gym, a media room—and they were saying their goodbyes at the front door, that Robin realized how different Cassidy's new room was from her old one. The soft pinks and snow globes were gone, replaced by bold primary colors and shelves lined with video games. Posters of snarling hip-hop artists and half-naked models had usurped Beyoncé and Taylor Swift. Cassidy was growing up, she realized, becoming a teenager, moving inexorably from girl to woman.

Someone had tried to stop that from happening.

What kind of monster shoots a twelve-year-old girl?

"Goodbye, Sheriff," Melanie was saying when his cell phone rang.

He motioned for them to hold on a moment, then turned away, listening. "That was the hospital," he said when he turned back.

Oh, God, Robin thought. *Their father was dead.*

"Cassidy is awake," the sheriff told them instead. "She's talking."

"She's talking?" Melanie repeated. "What did she say?"

"Apparently she asked for Robin."

—TEN—

Fifteen minutes later, they were at the hospital.

"I don't get it," Melanie muttered as the sisters exited the backseat of Sheriff Prescott's patrol car. "Why would she ask to speak to you? I'm the one she lived with for the past six years, the one who listened to her bitch about her mother whenever they had a fight, the one who took her to buy tampons when she got her period last year. She hasn't seen *you* since she was a little girl. She barely knows you, for God's sake."

Robin shook her head, as confused as her sister. "You never really liked Cassidy," she offered, remembering Melanie's initial antipathy toward Tara's child. "Maybe she sensed that."

"I just don't trust kids with better vocabularies than mine."

It was true that Cassidy had always sounded more mature than her years. Tara had believed in treating Cassidy as an equal, disdaining baby talk and encouraging the toddler to speak in complete sentences. Robin smiled, recalling the look of astonishment on their father's face after spending several minutes with Cassidy when she was barely two years old. *"It's like talking to an adult,"* he'd marveled. To which Melanie had responded, *"It's spooky, if you ask me."* To which their father had replied, *"Nobody did."*

"You haven't been in touch at all over the years?" the sheriff asked, interrupting her thoughts as they entered the hospital's main lobby. "You haven't emailed or spoken on the phone?"

"There's been no contact whatsoever," Robin assured both the sheriff and her sister.

"It just doesn't make any sense," Melanie said as they headed toward the east wing.

Nothing about this makes any sense, Robin thought as they neared Cassidy's room.

"Hey," a voice called from down the hall.

They turned in unison to see a young man shuffling toward them, hands in the pockets of his tight black jeans.

"Kenny," Melanie said, her voice registering her surprise as he came to a stop in front of them. "What are you doing here?"

"I was hoping to see Cassidy." His eyes shifted between Robin and her sister while carefully avoiding the sheriff. "But they won't let me in." He nodded toward the uniformed guard at the door.

"And you are?" Sheriff Prescott asked.

"Kenny Stapleton?" the boy said, as if he weren't sure. He pushed some dark hairs away from his forehead, still refusing to meet the sheriff's eyes.

"And your connection to Cassidy?"

The boy shifted his weight from one foot to the other. "She's a friend."

The sheriff's eyes narrowed, his eyebrows forming their now-familiar straight line across the bridge of his nose. "A little young to be your friend, isn't she?"

"Well, she's not a friend exactly."

"What is she *exactly*?"

"I know her through Landon."

"Landon," the sheriff repeated, his eyes darting toward Melanie.

Kenny's hands sank deeper into his pockets, pulling his jeans down even lower on his slim hips. "Landon's just real concerned about her. Asked me to check on her."

"When was this?"

"Last night." Kenny looked to Robin and Melanie for confirmation. "When I was at your house."

"Neither of you thought to mention his visit to me?" the sheriff asked the women.

"It's been a rather busy morning," Melanie said, speaking for both of them. "Guess it slipped our minds."

"Hmm." Sheriff Prescott turned his attention back to the boy. "Why don't you have a seat down the hall," he told him. "There's a waiting area—"

"Yeah, I know. That's where I've *been* waiting, but . . ."

"But?"

"Maybe I should go. Come back another time."

"Maybe you should stay," the sheriff said, leaving no doubt that this wasn't a request. "I have a few questions I'd like to ask you."

"Sure thing." Kenny managed a weak smile. "Will you tell Cassidy I stopped by?"

"Sure thing," the sheriff repeated.

Robin watched the young man retreat down the hall.

"Anything else I should know about that might have 'slipped your minds'?" the sheriff asked the women pointedly.

"Not a thing," Melanie said, again speaking for the two of them.

"And from now on, let me decide what's relevant or not." He jotted Kenny's name in the notepad he pulled out of his shirt pocket as they continued toward Cassidy's room.

"Of course," Robin said.

"Bastard," Melanie muttered under her breath, her eyes shooting daggers at the sheriff's back.

They stopped in front of the closed door to Cassidy's room. Robin took a deep breath.

"Ladies," the sheriff said as he pushed the door open.

Cassidy was lying in bed, her eyes closed to the midday sun sliding through the slats of the blinds covering the side window. Her hair had been pulled away from her thin, pale face and secured with a bobby pin, making her appear even more vulnerable than she had the day before. Robin felt the air constrict in her chest like a closed fist.

"Cassidy?" the sheriff said gently, approaching her bed.

"She's asleep," Robin whispered, standing back, fighting the urge to flee. "Maybe we shouldn't disturb her."

"Cassidy," the sheriff repeated, touching her exposed arm above the IV protruding from the vein on the underside of her elbow.

The girl's gold-flecked brown eyes opened wide. A startled cry escaped her lips.

"I'm Sheriff Prescott," the sheriff said quickly. "You don't have to be afraid, Cassidy. You're safe now."

"Robin?" the girl asked, her gaze shooting around the room.

"She's right here," the sheriff said. He glanced over his shoulder at Robin, silently beckoning her forward.

"I'm here." Robin set one recalcitrant foot in front of the other until she was standing beside him.

"I'm here, too," Melanie said, approaching on the other side of the bed.

"Robin?" Cassidy said again, ignoring both Melanie and the sheriff.

"Right here, sweetheart," Robin said, finding her therapist's voice and taking the girl's hand as the sheriff stepped back a bit.

"Robin," the girl repeated, squeezing Robin's fingers. "I knew you'd come."

"You did?"

"My mother said she could always count on you."

"She said that?" Tears filled Robin's eyes.

"She was always talking about you, said she missed you so much."

"I missed her, too." Robin realized it was true. Her natural shyness had always made it difficult for her to make friends, and her trust issues had made it all but impossible to keep them. The truth was that she hadn't had a real friend since leaving Red Bluff. "What else did she tell you?"

"That I should call you if anything ever happened to her."

"Why would she say that?" the sheriff interjected, reasserting his presence. "Was she worried about anything in particular?"

The girl stared up at the ceiling for several long seconds, then closed her eyes. For a minute, Robin thought she might have drifted back into unconsciousness.

"Can you tell us what happened the night you were shot?" the sheriff prodded.

Cassidy's eyes remained shut, but she squeezed Robin's fingers so tightly that Robin had to fight to keep from crying out.

"It's okay, sweetheart. I'm right here. Can you tell us what happened that night?" Robin asked, repeating the sheriff's question. "Do you know who shot you?"

Cassidy opened her eyes, stared directly at Robin. "Someone shot me," she repeated, as if trying to force the words to make sense. "Oh, God. It hurts. It hurts so much."

"We'll get a doctor in here in a few minutes," the sheriff said. "But it's real important that we find out what happened the night you were shot, Cassidy, so we can catch whoever did this. Can you help us?"

"I don't know. I don't know. I don't know." Her voice rose with each repetition.

"Okay. It's okay. Calm down, sweetheart," Robin said. "There's no rush. We'll take this very slowly. Okay, Sheriff? Okay, Cassidy?"

Cassidy nodded, tears falling down her cheeks. The sheriff took another step back.

"Do you know who shot you, sweetheart?" Robin repeated after a pause of several seconds.

"No. They were wearing masks. I couldn't see their faces."

"They?" Sheriff Prescott interjected. "How many were there?"

"Two. Maybe three. I'm not sure."

"That's okay," Robin said. "Now we know that more than one person was involved. That's good, Cassidy. You're doing great."

"Could you tell if they were men or women?" the sheriff asked.

"Men, I think. They were tall. Big. They were dressed all in black."

"What kind of masks were they wearing?"

"Like for skiing."

"Okay," the sheriff said. "That's good, Cassidy."

"You're doing great," Robin said again, patting the child's thin arm.

"Do you know how these people got in the house?"

Cassidy shook her head. "No. It was late. I was asleep. I remember . . ."

"What do you remember?" Robin asked as Cassidy's eyes once again threatened to close.

"I remember hearing voices," Cassidy responded. "Really loud. They woke me up."

"Did you recognize the voices?"

"Just Daddy's."

Robin noticed Melanie's shoulders stiffen on the word "daddy."

"Could you hear what was being said?" the sheriff asked.

"No. There was just suddenly all this yelling. At first I thought it was my dad yelling at my mom about something . . ."

"Did they fight often?" Sheriff Prescott asked.

"No. Never. That's what was so confusing. They were so happy . . . Oh, God, oh, God." Her eyes widened, as if she'd just caught a glimpse of something horrific.

"Go on, Cassidy," the sheriff urged. "You were asleep. Loud voices woke you up . . ."

"I looked at the clock beside my bed. It was after midnight. I wondered who it was so late at night, and why they were so mad. I climbed out of bed, went into the hall, crept down the stairs. The voices got louder," she continued, speaking as if she were in a trance. "I got closer, and I saw two men," she said. "One of them was waving a gun and saying, *'Stop fucking with me, you piece of shit, or I swear I'll shoot the bitch,'*" Cassidy repeated in a voice not her own, the words jarring as they came from the child's mouth. "*'I'll shoot the bitch right now.'*"

"And you're sure you didn't recognize the man's voice?"

"I'm sure."

"What about the second man?"

"He never said anything. He just stood there."

"Think, Cassidy. Was there a third man, maybe standing guard in the hall?"

"I don't know. Maybe. I don't know."

"Then what happened?" the sheriff asked.

"All of a sudden Daddy lunged . . ."

Robin watched Melanie wince at the word "daddy."

"You saw him lunge?"

Cassidy nodded, relating the events as if she were narrating a scene from a movie. "And the man whacked him with the gun on the side of his head, and Daddy fell to his knees. And Mommy started screaming," she said, one sentence tumbling into the next, "and the other guy shot her . . . Oh, God! He just kept shooting her. I screamed and the men spun around. And I ran. I heard more shots. I turned back and saw a man coming after me. But he tripped running up the stairs and I got to my room and grabbed the phone to call nine-one-one. And then the man burst through the door. He pointed his gun at my chest . . ." She stopped, looking around helplessly, as if trying to connect a series of invisible dots. "I don't remember being shot."

"You're very lucky to be alive," the sheriff said.

There was silence, the word "lucky" ricocheting through the still air like a stray bullet.

"The man who shot you," the sheriff continued, "was he one of the men in the living room? Or was he someone else?"

"I don't know. Oh, God. They're dead, aren't they?" Cassidy wailed. "Mommy . . . Daddy . . . they're both dead."

More silence, then, "I'm afraid that your mother succumbed to her wounds yesterday morning."

Cassidy's strangled cry shook the room. "And Daddy?"

"It doesn't look good."

"What do you mean?"

"He's still breathing," Robin said, "but . . ."

"But he's alive?"

"Barely," Melanie said. "You can't get your hopes up."

"He's alive," Cassidy repeated.

"Yes," Robin said. "He's alive."

"He'll make it. You'll see," Cassidy insisted before bursting into tears. "Oh, God. My poor mommy. Why couldn't they just take what they wanted and leave us alone? Why did they have to shoot us?"

"Were your parents expecting anyone that night?" the sheriff asked.

"No, I don't think so."

"Can you think of any problems that either of them might have been having with anyone?"

Cassidy shook her head. "Everyone loved them."

Robin caught Melanie's smirk. Now was hardly the time to argue with Cassidy's perceptions, however misguided they might be.

"No arguments with any business associates or employees?"

"They never talked about that sort of thing around me."

"What about the workers? I understand men were in and out of the house pretty much on a daily basis."

"They all seemed really nice. Daddy said they were doing a great job." She looked from the sheriff to Robin. "I'm not much help, am I? I'm sorry . . ."

"Don't be," Robin said. "This isn't your responsibility."

"I want to help. I feel so stupid."

"You *are* helping and you're *not* stupid," Robin assured her. "You just might be the bravest person I know."

Cassidy's fingers tightened their grip on Robin's hand. "My mommy's dead."

"I know, sweetheart. I'm so sorry."

"What am I gonna do?"

"Let's not worry about that right now. For the moment, you have to concentrate on getting well."

"Where am I gonna go?"

"You'll come home with us," Melanie said.

This time it was Cassidy who winced.

"Are you in pain?" Robin asked her. "I'll get the doctor."

"It's okay," Cassidy said, refusing to let go of Robin's hand. "Don't leave me."

"I'll go," Melanie said. She paused, as if waiting for Cassidy to beg her to stay, then marched from the room when she didn't.

"Promise you won't leave me," Cassidy said, her eyes pleading with Robin.

"I'll stay as long as you need me," Robin heard herself say, anxiety stabbing her chest like a knife. *Had she really just promised to hang around Red Bluff indefinitely?* She leaned in to kiss Cassidy's forehead.

Cassidy quickly lifted her chin to whisper in Robin's ear. "My mother said you're the only one I can trust."

—ELEVEN—

"Can I ask you something?" Robin said to her sister at dinner that night.

Melanie glanced up from her leftover chili. "Knock yourself out."

"Why did you stay here? Why didn't you move out after Dad married Tara?"

"Where would I have gone?" Melanie asked. "With no prospects, no fancy degrees, and an autistic son?" She looked at Landon, who was sitting across from her, spooning chili into his mouth without pause, his eyes resolutely on his plate. "To San Francisco to find Alec? To L.A. to be with you? Bet you would have loved that." She leaned back in her chair, setting her fork down on the table. "I couldn't afford my own place on what I make at Tillie's, and Dad made it abundantly clear he wasn't about to pay rent on an apartment when there was more than enough room for me and Landon here. Tara wasn't thrilled, of course. It wasn't exactly the arrangement she'd been picturing, which I have to admit made it somewhat more palatable as far as I was concerned. I *did* love watching her squirm. She tried to change Dad's mind, but she learned pretty quickly who was in charge around here. Anyway, it's water under the bridge, as they say. She finally managed to talk Dad into building that monstrosity next door."

Robin's cell phone rang. She reached into her pocket, checked the phone's caller ID. "It's Blake," she said. "My fiancé," she explained to Landon, who hadn't said a word since joining them at the table ten minutes earlier.

"No phone calls at dinner," he said before Robin could answer the call.

Robin stared at her nephew, so shocked to hear him speak that she didn't immediately register the anger in his voice. "It'll just take half a second. I'll tell him I'll call him back."

"No phone calls at dinner," Landon repeated, louder this time.

Robin quickly tucked her phone back into her pocket, listening as it rang another four times before voice mail picked up. "I'm sorry. I didn't mean to upset you."

"He'll be fine," Melanie said.

Robin swallowed another forkful of chili. "So, Landon," she began, deciding to take advantage of Landon's sudden interest in communicating, "did your mother tell you that we saw your friend, Kenny, at the hospital today?"

Landon said nothing. The only indication he gave of having heard her question was the increasingly frantic shaking of his leg underneath the table.

"He told us that you asked him to look in on Cassidy."

Landon began making clicking noises with his tongue.

"The sheriff wouldn't let him see her," Robin continued, "but he did tell Cassidy, and I'm sure she appreciated your concern." Robin was lying; in fact, Cassidy had said nothing when they told her of Kenny's visit. "It was very thoughtful of you."

The phone in her pocket began ringing again.

Shit, Robin thought. "Honestly, this will just take two seconds—"

"No phone calls at dinner!" Landon banged on the table with both hands, his body beginning to rock back and forth.

"It's just that it could be important," Robin said, removing the phone from her pocket and rising from her chair. "I'll take it in the other room."

"No phone calls at dinner!" Landon jumped from his seat, lunging for the phone in Robin's hand.

"Wait!" Robin cried as he tore it from her grasp. "What are you doing? Stop!"

"No phone calls at dinner!" Landon hurled her phone against the far wall.

Robin watched in horror as the phone shattered, shards of plastic falling to the kitchen floor.

"No phone calls at dinner!" The words bounced off the walls as Landon ran from the kitchen.

Seconds later, Robin heard the front door open, then slam shut.

"Guess that settles that," Melanie said.

—

The first thing Robin did the next morning was to borrow Melanie's car and drive downtown to purchase a new cell phone.

Melanie declined to come with her. Landon was still in his room, having stayed out until well past midnight. He'd spent the balance of the night rocking in his chair while Robin lay awake in her bed, a prisoner of his rhythmic compulsion, wondering where he'd been. "He'll be back," was all Melanie had said, shrugging off Robin's concern and retreating to her bedroom to watch TV.

Robin had used the landline in the kitchen to call Blake, but he hadn't picked up. Nor had he returned either of the messages she'd left on his voice mail before she went to bed. She'd dozed off briefly, only to wake up when Landon returned, and when she finally *did* manage to fall asleep at almost five o'clock in the morning—courtesy of the two Ativan tablets she'd taken out of desperation the hour before—a small snake had slithered out of an unpleasant dream to bite her in the neck, its imagined sting keeping her awake until she finally pushed herself out of bed at seven A.M., exhausted and vaguely hungover from the drugs still in her system.

Main Street was surprisingly busy for ten o'clock on a weekday morning. Robin had forgone breakfast at home, not wanting to risk another unpleasant encounter with Landon. Instead, she chose to stop by the local Starbucks. In front of her in line were two women in matching pink beautician uniforms and a man in a business suit nuzzling the neck of his female companion. Behind her two young women were whispering.

"I was at their house-warming party last week," one of them was saying. "You should see that place . . ."

Robin turned slightly, trying to identify the women while pretending to be checking the clock on the wall. Both women were in their late twenties, ponytailed, and dressed in stylish workout clothes. Neither looked familiar. As Robin was turning back, she caught sight of a man standing outside the front window, his face pressed against the glass, one hand cupped over his eyes. There was something familiar about him, although she couldn't make out his features. *Are you looking at me? Do I know you?*

Don't be silly, she admonished herself. *Just because a man is looking through the window doesn't mean he's looking at you. He's probably checking how long the line inside is. You're being paranoid.*

"I heard there was trouble in Paradise," the woman in front of her was saying to the man nibbling on her neck.

"A friend of mine said he saw her cozying up to Donny Warren a few days before the murder," the man replied. "Rumor has it they were more than just friends."

"You think he had something to do with what happened?"

The man shrugged. "Wouldn't surprise me. He's kind of an oddball."

Who are *these people?* Robin wondered. *And who the hell is Donny Warren?*

"Excuse me," someone said.

Robin felt a tap on her shoulder and spun around.

"You're up," said one of the ponytailed women behind her, pointing at the counter.

A uniformed young man was gazing at her expectantly. "What'll it be?"

"A mochaccino and a cranberry muffin," Robin said, her voice so soft he couldn't hear her and she had to repeat her order.

"Afraid we just ran out of cranberry muffins."

"Whatever, then. You choose."

"The buttermilk blueberry muffins are my favorite," he offered with a toothy smile.

"Sure. Why not?"

She paid for her order and stepped aside, munching on the stale muffin while waiting for her mochaccino.

The outside door opened and a woman walked in, about to join the line. Suddenly she came to an abrupt stop. "Robin?" It was part question, part exclamation. "My God! You poor thing. I knew you'd come back. How *are* you?"

Robin recognized Sandi Grant's grating voice before she recognized her face, which was considerably fuller than the last time Robin had seen her. Though they'd gone through Red Bluff High together, sharing many of the same classes, they'd never really been friends, so Robin was somewhat skeptical of the other woman's concern. She swallowed the chunk of muffin she'd been chewing, feeling a blueberry stick to the roof of her mouth. "I'm okay. You?"

Sandi was clearly surprised by the question. "Me? I'm fine. Well, pregnant again. Obviously. My fourth. Jason's killer sperm strikes again!" She smiled, then frowned, as if realizing a smile might be inappropriate. "What's happening with your dad? Is he going to make it?"

"I don't know." Robin looked around the room uneasily, trying to extricate the errant blueberry from the roof of her mouth with her tongue. Sandi's voice had attracted the attention of everyone in the place. All eyes were now focused squarely on her.

"The whole thing is so crazy," Sandi was saying. "I can't believe Tara's dead. Do the police have any idea who did it?"

Whispers began swirling around her like a sudden summer breeze.

"Who is she?"

"That must be the other daughter."

"She's so thin."

"I heard little Cassidy's still critical. Poor sweet thing," Sandi said as Robin finally succeeded in freeing the stubborn berry. "Do you know when Tara's funeral will be?"

"No. I . . ." Out of the corner of her eye, Robin saw cell phones being lifted. She raised her hand to hide her face from the telltale click of prying cameras.

"Are you staying at Melanie's? She must be reeling. I mean, how much can one person take, what with that boy of hers . . . Is it true he's a suspect?"

"One mochaccino," a voice behind the counter called out.

"Mine!" Robin reached eagerly toward it.

"Are you Robin Davis?" someone asked. "You probably don't remember me, but . . ."

"No, sorry." Robin grabbed her mochaccino and fled the premises without looking back.

"Well, that was rather rude," she heard Sandi say as the door shut behind her.

—

There were two people waiting to be served when Robin entered the T-Mobile store at the end of the block. Luckily, she didn't know either of them. Nor did she know the young male employees assisting them, although she couldn't help wondering if they knew Landon. She made a concerted effort while she waited to avoid thinking about last night's incident with her nephew, which of course ensured that it was all she thought about.

"Wow," the employee, whose name tag identified him as Tony, exclaimed when she presented him with her shattered cell phone. "What happened here?"

"I dropped it."

"Down a well?"

Robin quickly selected a new phone, bursting into a flood of grateful tears when Tony told her that she'd be able to keep her old number.

"Wow," he said, "you must really like that number."

Robin was wiping away her tears when she caught sight of a man's shadow at the store window. *Was it the same man who'd been peering at her through the window at Starbucks?*

"Who's that?" she asked Tony.

Tony looked past her toward the street. "Who's who?"

"That man," Robin began, then stopped when she realized no one was there. *So, not only are you paranoid, but you're seeing things as well.*

No more Ativan for you, dear, she decided as she left the shop. *You're strong. You're in control. You don't need it.* With exaggerated resolve, she reached into her purse and impulsively chucked the tiny plastic bottle containing the remaining pills into a trash can at the corner, along with her empty coffee cup. Immediately she regretted her decision. As she was trying to figure out how she could retrieve the bottle, her gaze fell on the bright yellow newspaper box nearby.

MILLIONAIRE DEVELOPER GREG DAVIS FIGHTS FOR HIS LIFE, screamed the headline of the *Red Bluff Daily News*. Below it was the same photograph of her father, Tara, and Cassidy that had hung on the wall in her father's office, hiding the safe. *Tara Davis succumbs to her wounds; daughter Cassidy remains in critical condition,* read the caption accompanying the picture.

Berating herself for jettisoning the pills, Robin hurried down the street to where she'd parked Melanie's car, anxiety nipping at her heels like an overeager puppy.

"Excuse me, Miss Davis," a voice called as Robin was unlocking the car door.

Instinctively, Robin turned her head. A man with a camera stood less than ten feet away, furiously snapping one photo after another of her.

The same man who'd been watching her earlier? she wondered as he continued clicking away. "Get away from me!" she yelled. Head down, she quickly climbed into the driver's seat and pulled away from the curb, eyes barely clearing the top of the steering wheel as she sped down the street. She didn't stop until she reached the hospital parking lot.

She noted the two police cruisers still occupying their positions and wondered if they'd ever left. She left the engine running as she retrieved her new phone from her purse, quickly punching in the number of Blake's office.

"Okay," she said to herself, "get a grip." It was important that she sound in control.

Or, at the very least, sane.

The call was picked up in the middle of the second ring. "Blake Upton's office. Kelly speaking."

Robin recognized the plummy tones of Blake's assistant even before the young woman identified herself. She pictured the California beauty with her sun-kissed hair and bottomless blue eyes, imagined her balancing a legal brief in her hands while balancing her round little bottom on Blake's lap. "Is Blake there?"

"I'm sorry, no. He's tied up in meetings all day. Is this Robin?"

Robin was so surprised to hear her name on the younger woman's lips that for a second she was speechless.

"Robin?" Kelly asked again.

"Yes, this is Robin."

"Blake told me what happened. I just wanted to say how sorry I am."

"Thank you."

"Is anything new? Have they caught who did it?"

"Nothing's new," Robin said, answering both questions. "Would you please tell Blake that I called?"

"Of course. And Robin . . ."

"Yes?"

"Our prayers are with you."

Our prayers? "Thank you." Robin disconnected the call and tossed her phone back into her purse. "*Our* prayers?"

There was a knock on her side window.

Robin's head snapped toward the sound.

A man's face appeared against the glass, his sly smile filling the frame.

She knew him immediately, even though it had been more than a decade since their last meeting. He was even more attractive than she remembered. "You've been following me," she said, lowering the window and staring into his sea-green eyes with their impossibly long, girlish lashes. She shut off the ignition and stepped out of the car into the sauna-like heat.

"That I have," Tara's ex-husband, Dylan, acknowledged, his bad-boy grin widening. "Do I get a hug?" He stretched his arms toward her, well-defined muscles evident beneath his navy T-shirt.

Guess you had lots of time to exercise in prison, Robin thought, recoiling from his proffered embrace. "Do you want to tell me *why* you've been following me?"

"It seemed like a good idea at the time?" He lowered his arms, clearly enjoying her discomfort.

"Goodbye, Dylan."

"Okay, okay," he said. "Truth is, I didn't set out to follow you. But when I spotted you in Starbucks, I figured I might as well see what you were up to."

"Okay, well, now you've seen me."

"Now I've seen you."

"Now you can go."

"And not see my daughter?"

Robin froze. "Are you kidding me?"

"Not really the best time for joking around."

"You haven't seen Cassidy in . . . how many years?"

"Yeah, well, I've been kind of busy."

"You've been in jail," Robin corrected.

"Picky, picky." His grin spread, causing deep dimples to form on either side of his mouth. "Anyway, what difference does it make where I've been? The important thing is that Dylan Campbell is here now."

Robin looked toward her feet, trying not to picture Tara's beautiful face battered by Dylan's fists. "What were you in for this time?"

"This time," he repeated. "Ouch. Oh, well. Guess I deserved that. Assault. No big deal. Served two years."

"And you've been out how long?"

"Three months. Perfect timing, wouldn't you say?"

"Perfect timing for what?"

"My little girl needs me."

"You're the last thing she needs."

"She just lost her mother."

"You wouldn't have had anything to do with that, would you?" Robin surprised them both by asking. She heard the quiver in her voice and looked toward the hospital entrance. *Now would be a really good time for Sheriff Prescott to make an appearance.*

"Me? Of course not. How could you think such a horrible thing?"

Robin shook her head. "I'm sure the sheriff will be eager to talk to you about your whereabouts that night."

"More than happy to speak to the man." Dylan laughed. "Do you really think I'd be foolish enough to show my handsome face around here if I'd had anything at all to do with what happened?"

"I would never underestimate how foolish you might be."

He smiled. "Okay, maybe I deserved that, too. But why the hell would I shoot my own kid? I mean, shooting Tara and your dad, that's one thing. But my own flesh and blood? I'd have to be some kind of monster."

"You *are* some kind of monster."

"Not anymore. I've changed, Robin. I'm ready to be a real father to that little girl."

"How noble. The fact that Cassidy could come into a lot of money if my father dies has absolutely nothing to do with this sudden urge to be a parent?"

"Absolutely nothing," he repeated. "The thought never entered my mind."

"Thoughts rarely do."

The smile toying with the corners of his lips froze. "Shall we go inside?"

"*I'm* going inside," Robin said. "*You* can go to hell." With that, she pushed him aside and marched toward the hospital doors.

"See you around," he called after her.

—TWELVE—

Robin alerted the deputy outside Cassidy's room to Dylan's presence and asked him not to allow the man anywhere near his daughter. Then she spoke to Cassidy's doctor, who informed her that the child had shown a marked improvement during the night and that her condition had been downgraded from critical to serious, although she was by no means out of the woods.

"That's such good news, sweetheart," she said to the pale young girl sitting up in bed. "How are you feeling?"

"A little better." Cassidy dropped an issue of *Star* magazine to the bed, watching helplessly as it slid off the stiff white sheets to the floor. "Oh," she said, looking as if she was about to burst into tears.

Robin quickly scooped up the magazine. "My goodness," she said, perusing its headlines. "It seems that Jennifer Aniston is pregnant with triplets. Again. That must make at least fifty children she's had in the last five years."

Cassidy smiled, the effort causing her to wince in

pain. “She’s a real little firecracker, all right. That’s what Daddy would say.”

Yes, he would, Robin thought, smoothing some hair away from the girl’s delicate face, then gently kissing her forehead. “Did the nurses bring you these?” She noted that in addition to *Star,* there were also current issues of *People, Us,* and *Vogue* on the nightstand beside her bed.

“No. Kenny did.”

“Kenny Stapleton?”

Cassidy nodded. “It’s too hard to read them. I’m just looking at the pictures.”

“When was Kenny here?”

“This morning. I said it was okay. Was that all right? Did I do something wrong?”

“No, sweetheart. Not if you felt safe with him.”

“With Kenny? Why wouldn’t I?”

Robin hesitated.

“He’s not the man who shot me,” Cassidy said. The force with which she said it elicited another grimace of pain.

“How can you be sure?” Robin asked.

“Because he doesn’t look anything like the men who were in the house that night.”

“You didn’t see their faces,” Robin reminded her.

“I didn’t have to see their faces to know it wasn’t Kenny,” Cassidy replied. “Kenny’s tall and skinny. The men who shot us were way bigger, way more muscular. Like they worked out a lot.”

Like Dylan Campbell, Robin thought, pulling up a chair and sitting down. Another unwelcome thought intruded. *Like Landon.* She quickly brushed that thought aside. "Sorry. I didn't mean to upset you."

Cassidy attempted another smile, her lips quivering with the effort. "I like that you worry about me. Mommy was right about you."

Robin felt a pang of guilt pierce her heart. She'd cut Tara off without so much as a word of goodbye, and while Tara had tried reestablishing contact from time to time—seeking her out on Facebook and regularly sending her cards on her birthday—Robin had ignored or rebuffed every attempt. "You know that your mother and I had a falling-out."

"I know," Cassidy acknowledged. "She said you were mad at her for marrying Daddy."

"I was."

"Why?"

"It's complicated."

"Because of Alec?"

"Partly that."

"How come Melanie wasn't angry?" Cassidy asked.

Beats the shit out of me, Robin thought. Melanie was always angry about something.

"She was always nice to us."

"I'm glad."

"She said that the important thing was for Daddy to be happy, and if Mommy made him happy, then she was happy, too," she recited, as if from memory.

Robin paused, carefully considering her next remark. "So why do you think your mommy didn't trust her?"

Cassidy shrugged.

They sat in silence for several seconds.

"Tell me about my mother," Cassidy urged.

"What do you want to know?"

"Like, what she was like when she was my age. If she had any boyfriends. If she was, you know, popular."

"Your mother had more friends than anyone I've ever met. Girls *and* boys. The boys wanted to be around her; the girls wanted to *be* her."

"So she was, like, *really* popular."

"She was, like, *really* popular," Robin agreed.

"I've never been popular," Cassidy said softly.

"No? Me neither."

"Really? You're not just saying that?"

"It's the truth. I was always shy and a little on the quiet side."

"It's kind of funny," Cassidy said.

"What is?"

"That Mommy had so many friends in school."

"How so?"

"'Cause she really didn't have any now."

"She didn't?"

"Maybe Melanie, but they weren't exactly . . . Oh, there was Tom."

"Tom?"

"This guy she went to school with."

Robin searched her memory for someone in any of their classes named Tom. She couldn't think of anyone. "Tom who?"

"I don't remember. He lives in San Francisco now. We visited him a few times when we went to see the decorator."

A frisson of anxiety wriggled through Robin's chest. *Alec lives in San Francisco,* she thought, then banished the unwelcome thought from her mind.

"Can I ask you something?" Robin said.

"Sure."

"Was your mother happy?"

"You mean with Daddy?"

"Yes."

"They were *so* happy," Cassidy said. "They loved each other *so* much."

So what about the rumors of infidelity? What about this mysterious "friend," Tom? Robin wanted to ask, knowing she couldn't. "And my . . . *our* father?" she asked instead. "Was he a good father to you?"

"The best. I mean, Melanie always complained that he was spoiling me rotten, but then Daddy would tell her that you can't spoil a child with too much love."

Wow. "I'm sure that went over big," Robin said without thinking.

"What do you mean?"

"Nothing." Robin found herself wishing that she'd known the "Daddy" Greg Davis had been to Cassidy. *Would that he'd been so loving and magnanimous toward his own children.* "Do you ever wonder about your biological father?" she asked.

Cassidy studied Robin for several long seconds, as if trying to peek inside her brain. "He's here, isn't he?" she stunned Robin by asking. "Have you talked to him?"

"Yes, he's here. How did you know?"

"Because Mommy always said he'd turn up one day. She said that he was like a rash you couldn't get rid of."

Cassidy's already pale complexion turned ashen. She looked as if she was about to faint. "Do you think he's the one who shot us?"

"I don't know. He says no."

"Do you believe him?"

"I'm sure the sheriff will have his alibi thoroughly checked out."

"I don't want to see him."

"You don't have to."

"I don't want to see him," Cassidy repeated. "Ever. I already have a father. A *real* father. And he's going to be okay. He's going to be okay, right? He's not going to die."

Robin tried to form the words, but they wouldn't come. "I wish I knew," she whispered.

"What will happen to me if he dies?"

"Let's not worry about that now."

"Will they make me go live with *him*?" Cassidy asked, panic returning to her voice.

"With Dylan Campbell? No! Of course not." *Would they?*

"Because I'd run away if they did. I'd kill myself."

"Sweetheart, no. Don't talk that way."

"And I don't want to live with Melanie. I know she doesn't really want me. And Landon, well, he's nice and all, but he can be kind of scary sometimes. The way he rocks all the time and everything. I know it's not his fault, that he can't help it . . ." Cassidy reached over and grabbed Robin's hand. "I want to live with you," she said, her voice pleading. "If anything happens to Daddy, please, can I live with you?" Her eyes suddenly rolled back in her head and she collapsed against her pillows, unconscious.

Robin jumped out of her seat and ran to the door. "Get a nurse," she shouted at the officer stationed in the hall.

"Tell me again exactly what he said to you," Sheriff Prescott instructed Robin. They were in the waiting area down the hall from Cassidy's room, sitting in the same two chairs they'd occupied the first time they'd met. Cassidy's vital signs had returned to normal, although the doctors cautioned that everything could change in an instant.

For the third time, Robin relayed her conversation with Dylan to the sheriff, watching as he checked her story against the notes he'd already made. "You have any idea where he's staying?" he asked.

"None."

"Well, I guess it shouldn't be too difficult to find him." The sheriff ran his palm across the top of his smooth head. "From everything he said to you, it doesn't look as if he's going anywhere anytime soon."

"Are you going to check his alibi?"

"Soon as I know what it is," the sheriff said with a smile.

"Do you think he did it?"

"I won't know what to think till I talk to the man. Is there anything else you want to tell me?"

Robin debated informing the sheriff what had happened at the dinner table the previous night—Landon's violent reaction to the ringing of her cell phone, his fleeing the house and not returning until after midnight.

"He can be kind of scary," she heard Cassidy say.

"What is it?" Prescott asked.

Robin shook her head. The sheriff was already suspicious of Landon. Anything she said would only reinforce that suspicion, make him less likely to examine other possibilities. She couldn't betray her nephew. Not without tangible evidence that he'd done something wrong. "Nothing."

"You're sure? You look like you've got something on your mind."

"Who's Donny Warren?" Robin asked.

"Donny Warren," the sheriff repeated. "Why do you ask?"

Robin relayed the conversation she'd overheard at Starbucks, watching him copy it into his notepad. "Who is he?" she asked again.

"He's a war vet, did a couple of tours in Afghanistan, moved here about three years ago from Tacoma, Washington, and bought a small ranch on the outskirts of town. Kind of a loner. Owns a couple of horses. Drives a Harley. Never been arrested, as far as I know. You think he and Tara had something going on?"

"I don't know what to think. According to Cassidy, Tara and my father were madly in love."

"Which is what any child would choose to believe about her parents, but that doesn't rule out the possibility that Tara was seeing someone on the side. She had quite a history, as I'm sure you're aware. It certainly wouldn't be the first time that a young wife has stepped out on her much older husband."

The name Tom was on the tip of Robin's tongue. *What was stopping her from saying it out loud?*

Prescott stood, grabbing his hat before it could fall to the floor. "Guess I should try to locate Dylan Campbell, maybe have a little talk with Donny Warren. Can I drop you somewhere?"

Robin was in no hurry to return home. "I have my sister's car, thank you. And I think I'll stick around the hospital for a little while, be here when Cassidy wakes up."

"I'm sure she'll appreciate that." Sheriff Prescott placed his hat on his head, then tipped it toward her. "Oh," he said. "You wouldn't happen to know what kind of car your brother drives, would you?"

"My brother?" *Why was he asking about Alec?*

"Do you know what kind of car he drives?" the sheriff asked again.

Robin hesitated. "He used to have a Chevy Malibu. But that was a few years ago. He's probably traded it in by now. Why?"

"You happen to remember what color it was?"

"It was red. Why are you asking about Alec's car?"

"Just curious." He tipped his hat a second time. "Talk later."

Robin watched the sheriff amble down the hall. Only after he was no longer visible did she take her new phone out of her purse and call her brother in San Francisco.

He answered on the first ring. "What's up?" he said instead of hello.

"Why would the sheriff be asking about your car?" Robin said.

A second of silence.

"The sheriff is asking about my car?"

"The question was 'why?' "

"I have no idea."

"When was the last time you saw Tara?"

"What?!"

"Who's Tom?"

A pause that was just a fraction too long.

"Tom . . . ? What the hell are you talking about?"

"What's going on, Alec?"

"By the sound of it, my sister is having some kind of breakdown."

"Talk to me, Alec. I can't protect you if you don't tell me what's going on."

"There's nothing going on. I don't need your protection."

"Alec . . ."

"I have to go."

"Don't you dare hang up on me," Robin warned.

But it was too late. He was already gone.

—THIRTEEN—

Robin could recall the exact moment when she'd first suspected that something was happening between Tara and her father.

It was Thanksgiving, and Robin had come home from Berkeley to spend the holiday with her ailing mother. The family was seated around the dining room table, her father at one end, Alec at the other. Tara, who'd been engaged to Alec for the better part of a year, was on their father's left, with little Cassidy beside her. Landon sat on the other side of the narrow oak table, wedged between Melanie and Robin, rarely lifting his eyes from his plate. Sarah Davis, her body riddled with cancer, had been too weak to leave her bed. In two weeks she would be transferred to St. Elizabeth Community Hospital. She would die four months after that.

It was a subdued celebration, nobody feeling particularly thankful. The turkey Melanie had prepared was dry, the mashed potatoes tasteless, the green beans overcooked, and the mold of red Jell-O uninspiring. There was little conversation, the dinner's dominant sounds coming from the periodic clanking of cutlery against the plain white dishes and the occasional grunt from Landon.

"So, tell us about your classes," Tara had ventured at one point.

"They're fascinating," Robin said, grateful that someone at the table had expressed an interest. "I mean, they're really hard. I'm being run off my feet with work, but I'm learning so much."

"I think it's so exciting," Tara said proudly. "We're going to have a psychologist in the family."

"What's a psychologist?" Cassidy asked.

"Somebody who asks a lot of useless questions, then waits for you to answer them," Melanie answered. She held out her glass. "Could someone who *isn't* being run off their feet with work please pour me another glass of wine?"

"Allow me," their father said, removing the bottle of white wine from its ice bucket and refilling Melanie's glass. "Tara, how about you? A little more wine?"

"I don't know. I'm not sure if I should."

"You definitely should," Greg Davis said with a wink. "How about I just top you up a bit?"

Tara's smile was surprisingly shy as she held out her glass.

A wave of anxiety washed through Robin as she watched her father fill Tara's glass to the halfway mark. The wave turned into a surge, like an electrical charge, when Robin saw his hand brush her best friend's fingers as he returned the bottle to the ice bucket.

Robin shook off the unpleasant sensation, ignoring her instincts and telling herself that her sudden anxiety was the result of Melanie's attempts to belittle her. A classic case of transference, as one of her professors at Berkeley would no doubt explain.

"So, how are things going with you and Tara?" she'd asked Alec several days later. She was heading back to Berkeley, and Alec had volunteered to drive her to the bus station. "Everything good? You two getting along okay?" She threw the questions casually over her shoulder, like a lightweight sweater, as Alec was dropping her overnight bag into the trunk of his car. He'd bought the immaculately maintained red Chevy with the money he'd saved from working summers for their father, and it was his pride and joy.

" 'Course we're getting along. Why do you ask?"

"Just checking."

She had checked again at Christmas, when she and Tara were leaving the hospital after a brief visit with Robin's dying mother.

"I feel so helpless," Robin confided. "I just wish there was something I could do."

"You're doing everything you can."

"Not according to my sister."

"Your sister's a cunt."

"Tara!" Robin looked around to make sure no one had overheard. "You shouldn't say things like that."

"Why not? It's the truth."

"The truth won't protect you from Melanie."

"Yeah? Well, let her do her worst. I'm not afraid of her."

"Maybe you should be." Robin squeezed her friend's arm. She felt so lucky to have a friend like Tara, so grateful that the two would soon be family. She was sure that the unease she'd been experiencing was all in her head, a by-product of the guilt she was feeling about leaving her mother. "So what's happening with you and Alec? Any closer to setting a date for the wedding?" She felt an almost imperceptible stiffening of Tara's arm beneath her fingers.

"How can we?" Tara asked. "I mean, with things the way they are . . ."

The sentence trailed off into silence.

"But everything's good between the two of you?" Robin persisted. "You're still madly in love and everything?"

"Everything's good," Tara said, turning away.

Four months later, Sarah Davis was dead, and two months after that Tara ended her engagement to Robin's brother.

"She said she can't marry me," Alec had confided over the phone, sounding as numb as he undoubtedly felt.

"Did she say why?"

"Just that her feelings had changed and she couldn't go through with it."

"Does Dad know?"

"I told him this morning on the way to work." Alec had been working for their father full-time since graduating from high school, and they usually drove to the office together. According to Alec, Greg generally used that time to berate him for what Alec jokingly referred to as his "shortcoming of the day."

That arrangement came to an abrupt halt three months later when their father returned from a supposed business trip to Las Vegas with his new and astonishingly familiar bride in tow. Alec immediately quit work and left

Red Bluff. He spent the next year driving his prized red Chevy from one end of the country to the other and then back, eventually settling in San Francisco and working a succession of minimum-wage jobs.

Robin had returned to Red Bluff only to pack up what few possessions of hers remained in the house, vowing never to speak to her father or Tara again.

"If you'd just let me explain," Tara had pleaded.

"Seems pretty self-explanatory to me."

"I never expected this to happen. It wasn't something we planned."

"And yet, here we are," Robin countered. "I just don't understand how you're able to stomach sleeping with a man old enough to be our father. Oh, wait—he *is* my father. You can't seriously be trying to tell me that you're in love with him."

"He's been so good to me. And to Cassidy. She adores him."

"She's a child. You're a grown-up. And you haven't answered my question."

"You didn't ask one."

"Do you love him?"

"He'll take good care of us."

"Not an answer."

"I respect him. I admire him."

"How can you respect and admire him when you *know* what a bastard he is?"

"He's changed."

"He hasn't."

"He's not the same man he was when you were growing up."

"Really? I remind you that he just eloped with his son's fiancée!" Robin shook her head at Tara's willful naïveté.

"It would never have worked with Alec. He's sweet and everything, but he's never going to amount to much. He's a boy, Robin. Cassidy and I . . . we need a man."

"Amazing," Robin said. "How'd you do that?"

"How'd I do what?"

"I just saw your lips moving, but I heard my father's voice."

Tara blushed bright crimson.

"Do you honestly believe that marrying my father isn't going to end in absolute disaster?" Robin asked.

Oh, God, she thought to herself now, recalling those words, the last words she'd spoken to the person who had once been her dearest friend. She pulled Melanie's car into the driveway of her house, watching as Landon's shadow disappeared from the upstairs window. She turned off the car's engine and lowered her forehead to the steering wheel, her fingers grasping the amethyst ring dangling from the chain around her neck. She remained in that position for several minutes, feeling the hot air wrap itself around her and trying to slow the rapid beating of her heart.

"What's the matter? Are you sick?" came Melanie's voice from outside the car window.

Robin bit down on her lower lip as her hand dropped to her side. She hadn't heard her sister approach. She removed the key from the ignition and stepped out of the car. "No, I'm not sick."

"You weren't praying, were you?" Melanie sounded horrified by the thought.

"No. I wasn't praying."

"Well, thank God for that." Melanie chuckled at her own joke. "So—what's with the glum face? I haven't heard anything from the hospital, so I'm assuming our father is still with us."

"Nothing's changed."

"And Cassidy?"

"Seems to be okay."

"So what's the problem? You look like you could use a drink."

"Why don't we just take a little walk?"

"You want to *walk*? In this heat?" Melanie sounded even more horrified than she had before. *"Where?"*

"I don't know. Around the block, maybe?"

"Around the block," Melanie repeated. *"Really?"*

"It was just a suggestion. You don't have to come."

"No, I'll go for a walk. I like to walk." She motioned for Robin to lead the way. "After you."

Robin headed down the driveway, stealing a glance at their father's house next door. The police cars were no longer parked in the driveway, although the yellow tape remained. "I guess they finished going through everything."

"Do we have to *talk*, too?" Melanie deadpanned.

There was no sidewalk, so the sisters walked along the shoulder of the road. The nearest house was almost half a mile away.

"I'll probably regret this," Melanie said after several long minutes, "but something is clearly bothering you. Are you going to tell me what it is?"

"Did Tara ever mention running into someone we

went to high school with when she was in San Francisco?"

Melanie shook her head. "Not that I remember."

"Do you know anyone from Red Bluff who moved there?"

"Just our brother. Why? What are you getting at?"

It was Robin's turn to shake her head. She had no desire to further arouse Melanie's suspicions. To change the subject, she told her sister about her run-in with Dylan Campbell in the hospital parking lot.

"That piece of shit," Melanie muttered. "Although I guess it's not all that surprising for him to show up." She kicked at a small pebble. "Bet all sorts of lowlifes come crawling out of the woodwork now, anticipating a big payday."

"Speaking of lowlifes," Robin said, "what do you know about Donny Warren?"

Melanie came to an abrupt halt. "Who?"

"Donny Warren. According to some gossip I overheard in town, he and Tara might have been having an affair."

"That's a load of crap," Melanie said. "And I'd hardly call him a lowlife." She resumed walking, quickly picking up her pace, so that Robin had to run to catch up.

"So, you know him?"

"I've met him a couple of times. Seemed like a pretty stand-up guy to me."

"Do you think he and Tara . . . ?"

"Absolutely not." Melanie shook her head. "He wasn't Tara's type."

"What was her type?"

Melanie kicked at another stone, the scuffing sound mimicking the one coming from her throat. "Not poor."

A car drove by in the opposite direction, its occupants craning their necks in their direction. Both women instinctively turned aside.

"I'm going back," Melanie announced as they drew within a few yards of her neighbor's house. "It's too hot. You can keep walking if you want."

"No." Robin wiped the perspiration from her neck and forehead as they crossed the street. "That's enough torture for one day."

—FOURTEEN—

Robin went to bed that night at nine, though she lay awake listening to Landon's rhythmic rocking until almost midnight, when the rocking suddenly stopped. It was replaced seconds later by the sounds of his heavy footsteps as he paced back and forth, back and forth, from one end of the room to the other. After ten minutes, the pacing ceased, and Robin waited anxiously for the rocking to resume, cursing herself for having thrown away the last of her Ativan. She needed to sleep. Unconsciousness was her only respite from a reality that was becoming ever more bizarre. While her dreams might be troubling and incoherent, her waking hours were even worse. Dreams generally vanished within minutes. Reality wasn't so easy to dismiss. And her reality was that nothing about her life made sense anymore.

Had it ever?

Yes, she decided, thinking of Blake. When she was with Blake, her life had made sense. At least in the beginning.

She'd been working as an assistant to a social worker at a vocational school in the Silver Lake district of L.A., her first job since graduating from Berkeley, when her boss had invited her to a party a neighbor of hers was throwing that night. She'd spotted Blake the minute she'd walked through the door. Tall and movie-star handsome, he was surrounded by a coterie of adoring females. *Stay away from that one,* Robin told herself, making a beeline for the other side of the room and engaging in small talk with whoever was nearby, trying not to look in his direction.

Until suddenly he was standing right beside her. "Hello," he said, depositing a glass of white wine in her hand. "I'm Blake Upton."

Run, she thought.

"And you are . . . ?"

Her answer came from out of nowhere. "I'm the one who got away," she said, handing the glass back.

And *then* she ran.

Out the door and into the night.

She kept running until she found a cab, until she was safely in her own apartment, in her own bed, far away from Blake Upton's warm brown eyes and sensuous mouth, out of reach of the mischievous dimple in his chin, his thick brown hair, the soft command of his voice, all of which spelled trouble.

More than trouble.

Danger.

She spent the balance of the night alternating between congratulating herself for her resolve and berating herself for her stupidity. "The last thing you need is a man like that," she lectured herself out loud. *A man who can have any woman he wants. A man who will never be faithful.*

A man like your father.

"So what? At least you could have gotten laid," she told herself with her next breath. Then, as the sun was coming up on what had been a frustrating and sleepless night, "Oh, well. Too late. What's done is done."

Except it wasn't done.

Blake found out who she was, and he called her the next night.

And the one who got away quickly morphed into the one who wasn't going anywhere.

Which was precisely the problem, Robin realized now. The woman Blake Upton thought he was getting, the girl with the quick retort and the confidence to walk away, was nothing like the needy bundle of anxieties he ultimately found himself saddled with.

Which probably explained why he hadn't returned any of the messages she'd left on his voice mail earlier tonight. Perhaps he assumed that was message enough.

Robin felt a tug on her bladder and climbed out of bed to use the washroom. She was opening her door when she heard the door to Landon's room also open, and she quickly ducked back inside. Seconds later, she heard Landon's door close and his footsteps recede down the hall. Only then did she crack open her door and see him disappearing down the stairs.

She stepped into the hall, tiptoeing toward the top of the stairs, the hardwood floor creaking beneath her bare feet. She heard the front door open and close.

She thought of waking up her sister, but didn't want to risk Melanie's wrath. Instead, Robin headed down the stairs after her nephew. "This is not a good idea," she whispered as she opened the front door.

At first she saw nothing but the blackness of the night. Gradually, a curving sliver of moon appeared overhead, followed by a sprinkling of stars. A smattering of roadside trees swayed in the tepid midnight breeze.

And then she saw him.

He was standing at the end of the walkway at the side of the road, his body mimicking the swaying of the trees. "What are you up to?" she asked softly, watching her nephew take several steps toward her father's house, then stop, turn back, resume his swaying.

Stop, go, sway, repeat.

Then Robin heard a sound come from the distance—a low rumble that grew louder as it drew nearer. A motorcycle, Robin realized, watching as the large bike materialized, its unmistakable form piercing the darkness as it slowed, then stopped to allow Landon to climb on.

A second later, the motorcycle sped down the road and was swallowed up by the warm night.

Robin stood in the doorway, trying to process the scene she had witnessed. "What just happened?"

Again she thought of waking up her sister. Again she thought better of it. If Melanie knew of Landon's nocturnal wanderings, she was unlikely to explain them to her sister.

Robin closed the front door and hurried back up the steps, glancing repeatedly over her shoulder as she tiptoed past Landon's room, then stopped and turned around. *What the hell are you doing now?*

Throwing caution to the wind, she opened Landon's door and stepped inside his room, closing the door after her.

It was even darker inside the room than it had been outside, the tiny sliver of moon not strong enough to penetrate the sheer curtains. Robin debated turning on a light, then decided it was too risky.

"So what now?" she whispered, waiting for her eyes to adjust to the darkness. "What are you doing here? What do you think you're going to find?"

After several seconds, objects began to take shape in the darkness: the double bed in the center of the room, the night tables on either side of it, a dresser next to a small closet on the opposite wall; the rocking chair in front of the window.

Robin moved to the bed, falling to her knees in front of it and quickly running her hands underneath it. *Nothing but dust.* She ran around to the other side and repeated the process. *More dust.* Wiping her hands on the front of her nightgown, she opened the top drawer of the closest night table, her fingers brushing over an assortment of pencils and paper clips before closing around a large ball of something soft and wriggly. *Worms,* she thought, dropping the ball to the floor and feeling it bounce against her toes. "Not worms, you idiot," she said as she bent to retrieve it. *Elastic bands.* "Way to go, Nancy Drew." She returned the ball of elastic bands to the drawer, then opened the drawer beneath it. It was filled with comic books: *Archie, The Green Hornet, Superman.*

The second night table contained more of the same: comic books, paper clips, rubber bands, pens and pencils, scrap pieces of paper full of doodles and illegible scribbles. And something else. Something hard and dome-shaped. A snow globe, she realized, pulling it out from the back of the drawer and turning it upside down, watching hundreds of make-believe flakes dance around the tiny plastic ballerina at its center.

An odd thing for a teenage boy to have, she thought, wondering if Cassidy had given it to him. Or maybe he'd just helped himself from her collection after she'd moved out. *Odd, maybe, but hardly incriminating.* Robin returned the snow globe to its previous position and pushed the drawer closed.

Except it didn't close.

Robin tried it repeatedly, but the drawer would shut only halfway before getting stuck. "Close, damn you." She jiggled it, but it refused to budge. "Shit! Okay. Don't panic." A few measured breaths later, she reached back and found two crumpled pieces of paper wedged between the two drawers. She extricated them gently, ironing them across her thighs with the palms of her hands.

A girl's face stared back at her from both pages. The sketches were rendered in pencil. While they were somewhat slapdash and lacking in detail, the girl in both pictures was instantly recognizable, even in the dim light: Cassidy.

"You're just full of surprises, aren't you?" Robin muttered, wondering if Melanie was aware that Landon was such a talented artist and realizing that she couldn't ask her about it without giving away her snooping. *Would there be any more surprises?*

She folded the papers neatly in half and returned them to the drawer, releasing a deep sigh of relief as the drawer now slid easily back into place.

She crossed to the closet, examining the shirts and pants draped across the wire hangers, and rummaging through the shoes on the floor. There was nothing unusual. No jewelry secreted in the toe of a sneaker, no gun hidden in the back pocket of a pair of jeans.

Robin was moving toward the dresser when she heard the sound of car doors slamming. She hurried to the window and peered through the sheer curtains, careful to keep out of sight.

A car was parked at the top of her father's driveway. Two people were running toward the house.

Robin reached under the curtains to pry open the window several inches.

"It's so dark," she heard a girl say, her high-pitched voice magnified by the breeze. "You're sure this is the right place?"

"Of course it's the right place," her male companion answered. "Can't you see the police tape?"

Dear God. Teenagers.

"I can hardly see anything, it's so dark." The girl stopped. "It's really spooky. I think we should leave."

Yes, that's exactly what you should do.

"Come on. It's an adventure. Everybody's gonna be so jealous when we tell 'em we were here."

Robin watched in horror as the boy ran toward the house.

"Wait," the girl called after him, although she didn't move.

"Are you coming or not?"

And then another voice. "What the hell is going on out here?"

Melanie?

"Shit," the boy swore as Robin watched Melanie march toward them, a housecoat over her pajamas, something long and menacing in her hand.

Dear God, was that a rifle?

"She's got a gun," the girl cried. "No! Please don't shoot us."

"What the hell are you doing here?"

"We just wanted to have a look . . ."

"This isn't a goddamn tourist attraction. Get out of here before I call the sheriff."

Robin watched the two kids race back to their car and take off, the car's tires screaming in protest.

"Stupid kids," Melanie growled, lowering the rifle as she glanced up at Landon's window.

Immediately Robin dropped to the floor. Had Melanie seen her?

Shit.

She heard the front door close, followed by Melanie's footsteps on the stairs. The next moment, Melanie was standing outside Landon's door, knocking gently. "Landon," she called softly. "Landon, are you awake?"

Please go away. Please go away. Please go away.

Several long seconds passed before Robin realized that Melanie was no longer standing outside the door, and still more time went by before she was able to breathe without pain and get to her feet. Her knees wobbling, she closed the bedroom window, debating whether to continue her search. She decided not to press her luck. One close call was enough for one night. She might not be the world's best therapist, but she was an even worse detective.

What the hell was I thinking?

Better not to think at all, she decided, returning to her room and collapsing on the bed. A series of silent images replayed in her head as she closed her eyes: Landon swaying by the side of the road; a motorcycle pulling up in the dark; a wriggling ball of elastic bands; two pencil drawings of Cassidy's smiling face; curious teenagers creeping toward her father's house; Melanie walking toward them, a rifle in her hands.

The last thing Robin saw before she fell asleep was a tiny ballerina imprisoned in a plastic dome, snowflakes swirling around her head.

—FIFTEEN—

She woke the next morning to a house that was eerily quiet: no voices, no footsteps, no persistent rocking.

It was after ten o'clock, and both Melanie's and Landon's bedroom doors were open. Robin stole a quick glance inside Landon's room as she passed by, noting that his bed was neatly made, its covers all in place, as if it hadn't been slept in. Had he come home last night?

"Melanie?" she called out, hurrying down the stairs and walking toward the kitchen, her sister's absence palpable. "Melanie?" She half expected her sister to jump out at her from a corner of the room.

Some leftover coffee remained in the coffeemaker, and Robin poured herself a mug, then heated it up in the microwave. She glanced out the window over the sink to see if Melanie was in the backyard, but it was empty.

Where is everyone?

Mug in hand, Robin proceeded into the mudroom, which Alec had once claimed as his personal space. "What are you hiding, Alec?" she asked, noting that the cot he'd slept on stood folded up and abandoned in a corner. The small room was now a makeshift storage area for boots and forgotten household items, the sort of things that people never used but were loath to throw away "just in case." An empty glass-front cabinet stood against the wall beside the back door, across from a wobbly wooden bench. A rusty yellow toolbox lay open on the bench's scratched surface, a large claw hammer half in, half out of the slot intended for a screwdriver, the screwdriver tossed carelessly atop a pair of pliers. Robin was tempted to return each item to its proper place, but decided against it.

Several large cardboard boxes sat on the floor in the far corner of the room. Robin knelt to reach into the first one and removed a handful of pencil drawings. Many of them were little more than scribbles, but a number of them were surprisingly good. She sank back on her heels, marveling at a simple sketch of two horses and another of a helmeted man on a motorcycle. But the best ones were of a young girl as she morphed from child to adolescent: Cassidy.

Her nephew was quite the artist, Robin thought, returning the pictures to the box, grateful that Melanie had saved them. *Perhaps she could suggest sending Landon to art school, maybe even offer to help out . . .*

"*We don't need your help,*" came Melanie's imagined retort, even before Robin could finish the thought.

The second box was filled with old paperback books: *Rosemary's Baby; Kiss the Girls; The Shining.* Someone obviously loved suspense thrillers. *Nothing wrong with that.* Another title suddenly caught her eye, and she squatted down to retrieve the softcover book from the top of the pile. *Hunting Humans: The Rise of the Modern Multiple Murderer.*

Shit, she thought, shuddering as she dropped the book back into the box. *What the hell does that mean?*

"It doesn't mean anything," she said out loud, noticing some larger books protruding from the bottom of the pile, her heartbeat quickening when she realized that they were old high school yearbooks. Eagerly tossing the paperback books aside, she extricated the half dozen leather-bound books.

She started with the most recent—the year she and Tara had graduated. Surely if there'd been anyone named Tom in any of their classes, she would find him in these pages.

Surely if there'd been anyone named Tom, she would have remembered him, a nagging voice in her head whispered.

She flipped through the pages, her eyes scanning the series of black-and-white homeroom photos. *There was Sandi Grant, with her perpetually open, gossipy little mouth, and little Arlene Kessler, with her huge green eyes, freckle-covered nose, and Little Orphan Annie mop of curly red hair. Who'd have suspected she would grow into the sophisticated Dr. Arla Simpson?*

Who'd have suspected a lot of things? Robin thought, locating her homeroom photograph and searching the faces of the normally sullen teenagers smiling awkwardly for the camera: Vicki Peters, with her too-short skirt and too-tight sweater, perched on a bench in the front row; Taylor Pritchard standing behind her, her long bangs almost completely hiding her half-closed eyes;

Ron McLean, as tall as he was stupid; Chris Lawrence, a smug smile plastered across his round face; and Tara, front and center, as beautiful as always, her arm draped across Robin's shoulders.

And then there he was in the back row—tall, heavy-set, blond hair combed away from his not-quite-handsome face: Tom Richards, curiously insubstantial despite his girth. *My God, she'd forgotten all about him.*

Even now, staring into his blank eyes, Robin was hard-pressed to recall a single thing about him. He faded into the background. *Like wallpaper,* she thought, recalling Tara's caustic assessment.

Was it possible that he and Tara had reconnected sometime in the last five years? That, improbably enough, they'd become friends? Possibly even lovers?

Robin dropped the yearbooks back into the box, burying them beneath the old paperbacks and pushing herself to her feet. She marched out of the mudroom, not sure what to make of—or what to do with—this discovery.

She found herself in the living room, the first time she'd been inside this room since her arrival in Red Bluff. Sinking into the moss-green velvet sofa against the wall opposite the large front window, she pictured her mother lying back against its pillows, a smile on her face, watching the large-screen TV with a magazine in her hands, her feet resting on the rectangular oak-and-glass coffee table in front of her. It was her mother who'd suggested the decorative brick fireplace in the middle of the far wall, her mother who'd selected the pair of matching rust-colored armchairs placed in front of it. She'd found the two watercolors of bucolic landscapes that hung on the wall at either side of the fireplace at a garage sale. "*Can you imagine?*" she'd said with a squeal of genuine delight. "*Someone was actually going to throw these treasures out.*"

Robin rested her head against the pillow, studying the paintings and imagining her cheek pressed tightly against her mother's skin. "*You've always been my favorite,*" she heard her mother whisper, and she felt her heart swell with pride.

In the end, her mother had barely known who she was.

Robin stood up and crossed the hall into the dining room, with its gold-flecked, ivory-colored wallpaper that dated back to her childhood. She stood for several minutes at the head of the long oak table, which was surrounded by high-backed, orange leather chairs. Everything was exactly as it had been when her mother was alive.

Had Tara tried to change things?

Robin could imagine her friend wanting to be respectful of her mother's memory, at least in the beginning. But surely after a year or two, she would have wanted to "put her own stamp on things," as Melanie had suggested.

Yet there was nothing of Tara's anywhere.

Just as there'd been nothing of her in that oversize mausoleum next door. It was almost as if the free spirit Robin had known and loved all those years had disappeared completely once she'd married Greg Davis.

Had the search for the self she'd lost propelled her into an affair? And was that what had ultimately gotten her killed?

Robin pulled her cell phone from the side pocket of her robe and pressed 4-1-1.

"Information. For what city?" the recording asked.

"San Francisco."

"Do you want a residential number?"

"Yes."

"For what name?"

"Tom Richards."

A phone rang.

It took Robin a moment to realize that it was the phone in the kitchen and not the one in her hand. *The hospital,* she thought, calling to say that her father had passed away during the night. She quickly disconnected her cell and raced into the kitchen, grabbing the phone from the counter. "Hello?"

"Hello?" a woman said, her voice soft and quizzical. "Who's this?"

"Who's *this*?" Robin countered.

"Of course. Sorry. It's Sherry Loftus."

"Who?"

"Sherry Loftus?" the woman repeated, turning her name into a question. "From McMillan and Loftus Designs in San Francisco."

"McMillan and Loftus Designs," Robin repeated. The decorators of her father's new house.

In San Francisco.

Of course. That explained everything. Cassidy had said they'd run into Tom Richards when they were in San Francisco seeing the decorator. He obviously worked for McMillan and Loftus. "By any chance," Robin began hopefully, "does a Tom Richards work there?"

"Tom Richards? No. There's no one here by that name."

"You're sure?"

"Quite. We're not a large company."

"Shit."

"Excuse me?"

"I'm sorry. I have to go . . ."

"Please don't hang up," the woman said as Robin was about to disconnect. "It's important."

"What's important?"

"This is horribly awkward," Sherry Loftus said. "It's just that . . . are you related to Mr. Davis?"

"I'm his daughter. Robin. What can I do for you, Ms. Loftus?"

"Yes, well, as I said, this is very awkward under the circumstances."

"Then perhaps it could wait for a less awkward time," Robin suggested.

"Unfortunately, it can't," Sherry Loftus said. "It's about the pool table Mr. Davis ordered."

Oh, God.

"First, allow me to offer my sincere condolences. We heard about what happened . . . We're all so shocked. Is Mr. Davis going to be all right?"

"We don't know."

"Such a tragedy. Who could have done such a thing?"

"We don't know that either."

"And the little girl?"

"It looks like she'll be okay."

"Well, thank God for that. Such a sweet little thing, absolutely adored her father."

"You said something about a pool table . . ."

"Yes. Yes. It's here."

"It's here . . . where?"

"In San Francisco. It arrived this morning, three weeks ahead of schedule, which almost never happens. But your father had asked them to put a rush on things, and as I'm sure you know, he was . . . *is* . . . I'm so sorry . . . a very persuasive man. And, well, we were just wondering when we could have it delivered."

"Excuse me?"

"Believe me, I understand that this is hardly the best time to be having this conversation . . ."

"Then you understand correctly."

". . . but I'm afraid we don't have a lot of options."

"Just send the damn thing back."

"I'm afraid I can't do that. It was custom-ordered, and all sales are final. Your father was aware of that when he placed the order."

"My father is in the hospital with a bullet in his brain."

"Yes, and I'm so sorry. Such a lovely man. We spent many hours together, going over every aspect of the design on the new house, picking out the furniture. They were so excited. He and the little girl . . ."

"Well, you'll just have to figure something out . . . Wait. What about *Mrs.* Davis?"

"What about her?"

"You said you spent hours with my father and Cassidy, that they were so excited. What about Mrs. Davis? Wasn't she excited?"

"I didn't really see a lot of Mrs. Davis. She came only a few times, in the beginning. After that, she pretty much left things to her husband." Sherry Loftus cleared her throat, then cleared it again. "About the pool table . . . I guess we could put it in storage for the time being. There'll be a charge, of course."

"Fine. Do that."

"And there's the matter of payment. The table was ten thousand dollars."

"Ten thousand dollars!"

"And there's money owing on—"

"Look," Robin interrupted, "I really can't deal with this now. My sister will have to get back to you." She hung up before Sherry Loftus could say anything else. Then she poured herself another cup of coffee and gulped it down cold as fists of anxiety began pummeling her insides. "Okay. Breathe. Just breathe, goddamn it."

"What's going on?" her sister asked from somewhere behind her.

At the sound of Melanie's voice, Robin dropped the mug, which crashed to the floor, splintering into dozens of pieces. "Shit." She fell to her knees and began scooping up the ceramic shards, her hands shaking. "Oh, God. I'm so sorry."

"Relax. It's not exactly a family heirloom."

"I'll buy you another one."

Melanie lowered the bags of groceries in her hands to the kitchen table as the sound of Landon's feet thundering up the stairs reverberated throughout the house. "You're rather tightly wound this morning," she said, starting to unload the groceries and put them away. "Landon and I were only gone an hour. What happened?"

Robin gathered the remaining pieces of the shattered mug from the floor and dropped them into the garbage bin under the sink before relaying her conversation with Sherry Loftus.

"Sherry!" Melanie exclaimed. "That's it. I knew her name started with an S."

"I think you're missing the point here."

"The point being?"

"What are we going to do?" Robin asked.

"About the pool table?" Melanie shrugged. "Not my problem. What else?"

"What do you mean, what else?"

"It doesn't take a degree in psychology to see that something else is bothering you."

Robin took a long, deep breath. Was there any point in telling Melanie that she'd been on the verge of contacting Tom Richards when Sherry Loftus called? "It's something Sherry Loftus said," she said instead, then waited for Melanie to ask what that something was. She didn't. "She said that Tara only went to San Francisco with Dad a few times and then she lost interest."

"And this bothers you because . . . ?"

"You said that Tara made frequent trips . . ."

The phone rang.

"Busy morning," Melanie said, reaching over to answer it. "Hello?" An exaggerated roll of her eyes. "Why, hello, Sheriff. How are you this fine morning?" She balanced the phone between her ear and shoulder as she put a carton of milk and a pound of butter in the fridge. "No, I haven't spoken to my brother recently. No, he hasn't called." She looked to Robin for confirmation. "No, I have no idea where he might have gone. What makes you think he's gone anywhere?"

"What's he saying?" Robin asked.

Melanie ignored her. "You what? Why would you do that?"

"What did he do?"

Melanie swatted Robin's question aside with a brusque wave of her hand.

Robin pulled her cell phone out of the pocket of her robe and pressed her brother's number. It rang four times before voice mail picked up.

"Leave a message," came the terse directive.

"Call me," Robin said, equally abruptly. She disconnected the line at the same time Melanie was disconnecting hers. The two women stared at each other across the kitchen table. "What's going on?" Robin asked.

Melanie lowered herself into the nearest chair. "It appears our baby brother has disappeared."

–SIXTEEN–

"Information," the recording said. "For what city?"

"San Francisco."

"Do you want a residential number?"

"Yes."

"For what name?"

Robin lowered her voice, glancing toward the closed door of her bedroom. Melanie wouldn't be happy if she knew what she was doing.

"What—are you a detective now? You're being ridiculous." She could hear her sister scoff.

"Tom Richards," Robin said clearly into her cell phone.

Maybe she *was* being ridiculous. But it was obvious that the sheriff considered Alec a suspect in the shootings, and her brother wasn't helping his cause by taking off without a word to anyone. If she could confirm that Tara had been in touch with a man from her past, it might divert some of the suspicion away from Alec, and since she was stuck in this hellhole for at least a few more days, she might as well make herself useful.

"For what address?" the recording asked.

Shit. "I have no idea."

"Please hold for an operator."

Seconds later, a human voice replaced the recording, informing Robin that there were three Tom Richardses in the Bay Area. Robin jotted down their phone numbers, then called all three.

The first Tom Richards was at least eighty years old and partially deaf, so their conversation consisted mostly of the words "Sorry" (hers) and "What?" (his). The second Tom Richards was a lifelong resident of San Francisco and had never been to Red Bluff. She was about to phone the third Tom Richards when she heard her sister's voice.

"Robin," Melanie called from the hallway, "what are you doing in there? I thought you wanted to go to the hospital."

"I'll be ready in two minutes."

Robin waited until she heard Melanie retreat down the hall before completing the last call. It was answered after six rings, just as she was about to hang up.

"Hello," a woman said, the word a shout, as if she'd just run in from outside.

"Hello," Robin said. "I'm sorry to bother you. My name is Robin Davis and I was wondering if . . ."

"Just a minute," the woman said. "Tom, wait a second. I need to talk to you before you leave."

"Actually, it's Tom I was hoping to speak to," Robin said quickly.

"You want to speak to Tom?" The woman sounded surprised. "May I ask what about?"

"It's a long story. Please, if I could just speak to him. It's very important."

"Some woman wants to talk to you," the woman said. "What have you been up to?"

Robin heard shuffling noises as the phone was transferred from one hand to another.

"Hello?" came a child's voice seconds later.

"Oh, I'm sorry," Robin apologized quickly. "It must be your father I'm looking for—is he there?"

"She wants to talk to Daddy," the boy explained to his mother.

"It's okay, sweetie," the woman said, returning to the line. "You can go. Tell Jason's mother I'll call her later. Watch crossing the road. Hello," she said into the receiver. "Who did you say you were?"

"Robin Davis. From Red Bluff. I'm trying to reach an old classmate named Tom Richards. By any chance, is that your husband?"

There was a long pause. Robin could feel her heart pounding. She wondered if the woman was still on the line.

"My husband is dead," the woman said. "He died two years ago. Leukemia."

"Oh, my God. I'm so sorry."

"We haven't been back to Red Bluff in years. Was there something in particular that you wanted to talk to him about?"

"No. No," Robin stammered. "I was just looking through some old high school yearbooks and thought I'd . . ." Clearly, she had no idea what she'd been thinking. "I'm sorry to have bothered you."

The woman hung up without saying goodbye.

"Shit." She'd managed to locate her old classmate, only to discover that he'd been dead for two years. Which meant what? That someone had borrowed his name? That that someone was Alec? That he and Tara . . . ? She couldn't bring herself to finish the thought. "Shit."

"What are you swearing about in there?" Melanie asked from outside the door. "What's the problem now?"

Robin tucked her phone into the side pocket of her jeans and opened the door. "No problem. Let's go."

The sheriff was waiting for them when they arrived at the hospital.

"Well, well," Melanie said, her voice as stiff as her posture. "What a surprise."

"Ladies," he said, with a tip of his hat. "I was hoping we'd run into each other."

"Has something happened?" Robin asked.

"There are a few things I need to discuss with you," he answered. "Is Landon here?"

"Do you see him?" Melanie's voice was colder than the morning's leftover coffee.

"He's at home," Robin said. Was he? Or was he off somewhere, balancing on the back of a motorcycle, long hair blowing in the wind? She'd wanted to question Melanie about what she'd seen the previous night, but didn't want to undermine their uneasy peace. "Did you locate Alec?" she asked the sheriff instead.

"Not yet. Perhaps we could sit down." He motioned toward a nearby seating area where a cluster of beige leather chairs sat across from a long brown sofa.

"If you don't mind," Melanie said, "we're here to see our father."

"By all means," came Prescott's easy reply. "Whenever you're ready. I'll wait right here."

Melanie's eyes narrowed into a hard glare. She spun on her heel and headed toward the east wing, Robin trailing after her. Minutes later, the sisters stood beside their father's bed. "He's looking a little gray around the edges," Melanie remarked dispassionately, as if she were commenting on the color of the walls. "Doesn't look like it'll be much longer."

"Hi, Daddy," Robin whispered, her eyes once again welling up with unexpected tears.

"Don't tell me you're going to start crying again."

Robin shook her head, as confused by her tears as her sister was.

"Good news, Dad," Melanie announced, tapping on the bed's handrails. "Your pool table has arrived. Any suggestions what to do with it?" She waited several seconds. "No? I didn't think so. You were always better at creating problems than you were at solving them."

Robin stared down at the comatose man who was her father. His tan was fading, and his complexion had taken on an ashen tinge, all the more noticeable because of the white bandages wrapped around his head and the sheets tucked underneath his chin. He seemed to have shrunk since she'd last seen him, although perhaps that was her imagination. *Someone's finally cut you down to size,* she thought, turning away. *Dear God, please don't let that someone be Alec.*

"Where are you going?" Melanie asked.

"Doesn't seem to be much point in staying here. Might as well talk to the sheriff, get it over with. You coming?"

"No. I think I'll stay and keep Dad company." Melanie pulled up a chair and plopped down, stretching her legs out in front of her and folding her arms across her chest, as if emphasizing her resolve.

"What'll I tell Prescott?"

"Whatever you want."

Robin knew that it was pointless to argue. "Goodbye, Dad," she whispered on her way out.

Sheriff Prescott stood up as soon as he saw her walking toward him. "I take it your sister has decided not to join us." He motioned for Robin to have a seat, then reached for a large manila envelope lying beside him. He removed two photographs and handed them to Robin.

"What's this?" She studied the large prints, understanding that the red Chevy Malibu at the center of both photographs—one beside a pump at a Shell station, one passing through a highway tollbooth—belonged to Alec.

"Recognize the car?"

"I'm sure that my brother isn't the only person in the world who owns a red Chevy."

"They're his license plates," the sheriff said.

"Okay. So it's his car."

"You recognize the gas station?"

"Should I?"

"It's located about a mile from here. And this tollbooth," he said, pointing to the second picture, "is located about halfway between here and San Francisco. You want to know when these pictures were taken?"

Not really. Robin held her breath as Prescott returned the photos to their manila envelope.

"First one was taken the evening of the shooting, the second one around two the next morning. Two-eighteen, to be precise. Which would indicate that your brother was here in Red Bluff when the shootings took place."

"Are you implying that Alec was the shooter?" Robin said, jumping to her feet. "That's crazy." *Was it?* "There's no way Alec shot anyone. He loved Tara." *How many times could she have this conversation?*

"She betrayed him pretty badly."

"That was more than five years ago."

"Some men can nurse a grudge a very long time."

"He still loved her," Robin insisted. *Even after what she did. Even after all this time.*

"Maybe he did. But he hated your father."

"Lots of people hated my father. Including me."

"Yes. But you weren't in Red Bluff that night, and it appears your brother was."

"My brother isn't capable of hurting anyone, especially not a twelve-year-old girl. Why would he possibly want to shoot Cassidy?"

"Maybe he didn't. There was at least one other shooter. Remember?"

"Who you think could be Landon," Robin said, surprised by the anger in her voice. Didn't she harbor her own suspicions regarding her nephew? "You think they were in this together," she stated more than asked.

"I can't ignore the possibility."

"My brother had nothing to do with what happened," Robin reiterated, the slight tremor in her voice belying the certainty of her words.

"Then what was he doing here, and why did he run?"

"Who says he ran?"

"Why don't you sit back down?" Prescott suggested gently, waiting until Robin had resumed her former position before continuing. "After we got hold of these pictures, I contacted the San Francisco police," he explained. "I asked them to talk to your brother. They went to his apartment. He wasn't there. He hasn't shown up for work. His car's gone. Nobody's seen him." Prescott lowered his chin while lifting his eyes. "You didn't happen to mention to him that I'd been asking about his car, did you?"

Shit.

"Look," Prescott said, "I'm not saying your brother is guilty . . ."

"Then what *are* you saying?"

"That I'd like to talk to him, that's all. So if you *do* hear from him . . ."

"I'll tell him that you'd like to talk to him," Robin said, her head spinning from a sudden lack of oxygen. "My turn to ask *you* a few questions."

"Go ahead."

"Have you talked to Dylan Campbell?"

"He walked into the station first thing this morning and introduced himself."

"That cocky bastard. And?"

"He claims he was in Las Vegas on the night of the shootings, showed us a receipt from the hotel where he stayed, claims he did pretty well at the tables. We're waiting on video confirmation. Should have it by the end of the day."

Shit. "And Donny Warren?"

"I talked to him."

"And?"

"Says he knew Tara casually, but that they definitely weren't having an affair."

"Do you believe him?"

"Not sure."

"Does he have an alibi for that night?"

"He says he was home in bed. Asleep. Alone."

"So he *doesn't* have an alibi," Robin clarified.

"Or a motive," Prescott said.

"That we know of."

"That we know of," the sheriff agreed.

Robin debated telling Sheriff Prescott about the events of the previous night—how she'd seen Landon sneak out of the house after midnight, how she'd watched him climb onto the back of a motorcycle and drive off into the darkness. Anything to deflect suspicion from Alec.

"Are you all right?" the sheriff asked. "Your face is kind of . . ."

Scrunched up? Robin pushed at her cheeks with her fingers, as if trying to smooth away any errant signs of emotion. *Damn it.* "I'm fine."

"Is there something you want to tell me?" he asked after several seconds of silence.

Again Robin considered telling the sheriff about the events of the previous night. Again, loyalty toward her family won out. "No," she said finally. "There's nothing."

—

"Cassidy seems to be making great progress," Robin said to her sister as they were driving home. "The doctor said that if she continues to improve at this rate, she could conceivably be released by the end of the week."

"Which begs the question . . . where exactly is she going to go?" Melanie asked. "I know I said she'd come home with me, but I didn't mean forever. I have enough on my plate."

Robin gave the question a moment's thought. Melanie wasn't being unreasonable. And Cassidy had admitted to being scared of Landon. Her cavernous new home was a crime scene, her mother dead, her stepfather in a coma. She wanted nothing to do with her newly resurfaced biological father. Her grandparents were God knows where. Which left only foster care.

Or me, Robin thought. Was she really prepared to take Tara's child back to Los Angeles to live with her? What would Blake think of *that*? "Look. There's something I need to talk to you about. It concerns Landon."

"What about him?"

"I saw him. Last night."

Melanie's shoulders tensed. She turned the corner abruptly and pulled the car to a stop at the side of the road, shutting off the engine, then swiveling around to face her sister. "What exactly did you see?"

"I saw him go downstairs and out the front door. I followed him. Do you think we could leave the air-conditioning on? It's so hot . . ."

"You followed him," Melanie repeated, ignoring her request.

"It was after midnight. I was worried . . ."

"You were *curious*," Melanie corrected. "There's a difference."

Robin told her sister about Landon waiting by the side of the road and the motorcycle that picked him up, watching as Melanie's hands formed fists in her lap. "Help me out here, Melanie. I'm trying to understand."

"Your trying to understand is going to land my son behind bars. I'm sure the sheriff was salivating when you told him this."

"I didn't tell him."

"No?" Melanie looked momentarily relieved. "Well, that's something, I guess. Thank you for that." She restarted the car, pulling away from the curb with such a jolt that Robin's head almost hit the front window, despite her seat belt. Neither sister said another word for the duration of the ride home. "Who the hell is that?" Melanie asked as they turned onto Larie Lane.

Robin looked toward the late-model white Lexus sitting in her sister's driveway, her gaze shifting to the man beside it, who stood looking anxiously toward them. "Oh, my God."

"You know this person?" Melanie asked.

"I don't believe it," Robin said, barely recognizing the sound of her own voice. "It's Blake."

–SEVENTEEN–

She couldn't stop looking at him.

They were walking down the road, the same route she'd taken with her sister the day before, and every few seconds Robin snuck a peek at him, just to make sure he was really there, that he wasn't a figment of her overripe imagination.

They'd spoken only a handful of sentences since she stepped out of the car. She'd wanted to race into his arms, smother his beautiful face with kisses, but something about the rigidity of his stance, the set of his jaw, the flatness of his gaze, had stopped her, warning her to keep her distance. "Thank God you're here," she'd wanted to shout. "What are you doing here?" was what she'd said, stepping into an awkward embrace, Blake's lips missing hers to graze the side of her hair.

"Do you really have to ask?"

"I take it this is the fiancé," Melanie said, not waiting to be introduced as she walked past them to the front door.

"Nice meeting you," Blake called after her.

"When did you get here?" Robin asked.

He checked his watch. "About half an hour ago. I knocked, but no one answered. I debated going to the hospital, then decided I might as well just wait out here."

Robin glanced toward Landon's room, saw him staring down at them from the upstairs window. "You must be broiling."

"I'm okay. How's your father?"

"Not good."

"I'm sorry."

"But Cassidy seems to be getting stronger, so that's something." Robin looked toward her father's house, surrounded by its yellow fence of police tape. "That's the house . . ."

"I figured."

"Sorry. I guess it's pretty obvious." *As obvious as the distance between us,* Robin thought.

"No need to apologize."

When had they become so stiff, so formal, with each other? Robin felt a line of perspiration dribble down her neck, although Blake seemed comfortable enough. He looked as cool as ever in his crisp blue shirt and khaki pants.

"How are you holding up?" he asked.

"Me? I'm fine."

"You look exhausted."

Robin's hand flew to her hair, as if her unruly curls were the source of her fatigue. "Are you thirsty? Do you want to come inside, have a drink of something cold?"

"No. I'm okay. I think I'd rather take a walk, stretch my legs a bit, if you don't mind."

"A walk sounds good."

Robin strode down the long driveway, Blake falling into place beside her. She longed to take his hand, to hug him close, but settled for the occasional graze of the back of his hand against hers as they walked. *We might as well be strangers,* she thought.

Maybe that was what they were.

"You seem shocked that I'm here," he said after a few minutes of strained silence.

"I guess I am."

"Why does it surprise you?"

The question caught her off guard. *Maybe because we haven't spoken in days. Maybe because you haven't returned any of my messages.* "You didn't tell me you were coming," she answered, the safest option.

"You didn't tell me you were leaving," he countered.

"What?" *Why was he bringing this up now?* "I called your office," she reminded him.

"And left a message with my assistant. Told her you had to go back home because of a family emergency."

"Which was true."

"It was also something of an understatement, wouldn't you say?"

"Yes, okay. But at the time I didn't really know what was going on and I didn't want to worry you . . ."

"So you were thinking about me?"

"Well, no, I probably wasn't thinking at all." *What's happening here? Why are we having this discussion? Why do I feel as if I have to defend myself?* "Okay. Look. Maybe I should have insisted on speaking to you before I left. I'm sorry if I hurt your feelings, but we've spoken a number of times since then and . . ."

"You think this is about hurt feelings?" he interrupted.

"To be honest, I don't know what this is." She stopped when she realized that Blake was no longer beside her. She turned around to see him standing several paces back, not moving. "What's wrong?" she asked, returning to his side.

"You tell me."

Really? "Well, Tara is dead and my father is barely hanging on. My brother's car was photographed in Red Bluff on the night of the shootings, and he seems to have disappeared off the face of the earth. The sheriff obviously considers him a suspect, along with my nephew. Then there's some guy named Donny Warren who may or may not have been having an affair with Tara and . . ."

"All very interesting, but that's not what I meant and you know it."

"I don't understand."

"Neither do I."

"Tell me what you don't understand," Robin said, adopting a more conciliatory tone and picturing herself leaning back in her office chair, pen poised over her notebook, encouraging a shy client with a friendly smile.

Blake shook his head, clearly picturing the same thing. "You're doing it again."

"What am I doing?"

"Whenever I try to have any kind of a serious discussion with you these days, you turn into a therapist."

"I *am* a therapist."

"You're also my fiancée. We're supposed to be on the same page. We're supposed to tell each other things, to be there for each other. Why are you cutting me off?"

"I'm not cutting you off."

"The hell you aren't."

"You've been very busy at work, with meetings . . ." *With your new assistant.*

"You're saying this is my fault?"

"I'm not saying this is anybody's fault. I'm not even sure what you're talking about."

"I'm talking about *us*. I'm talking about the fact that something's changed with us, and I don't know what it is and I don't understand why."

"My father's been shot. My best friend is dead." *You're screwing your assistant.*

"You don't have any friends," he said. "You haven't talked to your 'best friend' in almost six years. The minute anybody gets too close, you pull away."

"Whoa. Hold on. *You're* the one who hasn't been returning *my* phone calls."

"Because we never say anything," Blake said. " *'Hello. How are you? I'm fine. How are you?'* What the hell, Robin? Your life gets turned upside down and you shut me out completely. What did I do to deserve that? When did I become the enemy?"

"You're not the enemy. I'm not shutting you out."

"You want to know why I didn't tell you I was coming? Because I knew you'd tell me not to bother. That you were *fine*. And maybe you *are* fine. But *we're* not."

Oh, God. Were they really having this discussion? Now?

"You're saying you want to call off our engagement?"

Blake looked stunned. "No. Of course I don't want to call off our engagement. Is that what *you* want?"

"No, that's not what I want."

"What *do* you want?"

"I want *you*."

"Well, I'm here. And I drove all night to get here. Damn it, Robin. I'm standing right in front of you."

The first few notes of Beethoven's Fifth Symphony began emanating from Blake's pocket. "Shit. Sorry," he said, pulling out his cell phone and glancing at the caller ID. "It's the office."

"Then you'd better answer it."

Blake turned away, lowering his voice. "Kelly, what's up?"

Robin resumed walking up the road, the sun beating down on the top of her head like hot liquid gold. She was perspiring heavily. *I bet Kelly doesn't perspire,* she thought. *I bet the humidity never causes her perfectly straight blond hair to spiral out of control. I bet that when Blake runs his hands through it, it feels soft and silky, not like a ball of steel wool.*

"Sorry about that," Blake said, returning his cell phone to his pocket as he hurried to catch up to her.

"How long have you been sleeping with your assistant?" Robin asked, the words out of her mouth before she could stop them.

"What!"

"Please answer the question, counselor."

"You think Kelly and I are sleeping together?"

"Aren't you?"

"No. *No,*" he repeated. "Why would you even think that?"

"Kelly's a beautiful girl."

"So what? L.A. is filled with beautiful girls."

"And you could have any one of them."

"There's only one girl I want. *You*."

"We haven't made love in weeks. You're always working late."

"It's been a crazy busy time, that's all, and you're always asleep when I get home."

"Because you don't get home till after midnight."

"I know that I've been working a lot of late nights. I'm trying to make partner." Blake's hands fluttered aimlessly in the air. "Maybe I haven't been as attentive as I should. I've been preoccupied, and I'm sorry about that. But I'm *not* having an affair with my assistant. I'm not having an affair with anyone." He hesitated. "I'm not your father, Robin."

Shit.

"You have to stop projecting his face onto mine."

"Now who's playing therapist?"

"I'm just saying . . ."

"I know what you're saying, and you're way off the mark."

"Am I?"

"I'm not some little girl with daddy issues."

"Nobody said you were a little girl."

"Really? What *are* you saying?"

"I'm saying that I would never cheat on you."

"All men cheat," she heard Tara say.

"You have to trust me."

"Okay."

"Okay?" Blake repeated. "What does that mean?"

Robin looked toward the ground, his words swirling around in her head like a swarm of angry bees. "I don't know."

She heard a rumble in the distance, and for a second she thought it might be thunder. *Which would be good.* Thunder meant rain. And a little rain would cool things off, give them a chance to catch their breath. It was only as the rumble drew closer that she recognized it as the sound of an approaching motorcycle.

The large bike slowed down as it passed. *The same one that had picked Landon up last night?* The rider wasn't wearing a helmet, affording Robin a fleeting glance of his deeply tanned face and the sandy-colored hair that stopped just short of dark, deep-set eyes. His arms, stretched out before him on the handlebars, were muscular and bare beneath his sleeveless black leather vest. In the next second, he picked up speed and the motorcycle disappeared down the road.

"You know that guy?" Blake asked.

Robin shook her head. "We should go back." She turned and hurried down the road, Blake on her heels.

The man and his Harley were nowhere in sight when they reached her sister's driveway.

They stood for several seconds in silence, Robin aware that Landon was staring down at them from his bedroom window.

"Do you want me to leave?" Blake asked.

"I want you to do whatever you feel is right."

"Damn it, Robin. I'm asking what *you* want."

Robin stared into Blake's face, catching her father's reflection in the shadow falling across his eyes. It took all her resolve to push that image aside, although she felt it lingering just outside her line of vision. "I want you to stay."

—EIGHTEEN—

They left for the hospital before ten the next morning.

"Somebody looks happy," Melanie commented, climbing into the backseat of Blake's car. "I take it you two slept well."

"We did," Robin said from the front seat, smiling as she snapped her seat belt into place.

"The bed big enough for the two of you?"

"We managed," Blake said.

"Hopefully you managed quietly. Teenage boys are quite impressionable, as I'm sure you remember."

"I think we were pretty quiet," Blake said easily. "Don't you, Robin?"

Robin smiled. The fact was they'd gone right to sleep. They were both completely spent—Blake from his long drive, Robin from the events of the day, and both of them from tiptoeing around the eggshells that Melanie had been constantly scattering at their feet. They'd managed a few tender kisses and tentative caresses before being overwhelmed by a combination of fatigue and the relentless rocking from the next room. Robin had lain beside him, wrapped in the comforting cocoon of his embrace, feeling the steady beat of his heart against her back.

"I'm not your father," he'd told her. *"You have to stop projecting his face onto mine. You have to trust me."*

He was right, of course.

But it would be hard. To do it, she'd have to let go of the only thing that connected her to her father, to loosen her viselike grip on the past. Could she do it?

Did she want to?

However destructive, there was something inherently comforting about familiar patterns. As a therapist, she knew that efforts to change, to break free of ingrained habits, were usually accompanied by counter-instincts to "change back," to take refuge in the way things had always been.

The past is always with us.

Did it have to be?

She woke to the touch of Blake's lips grazing the top of her shoulder as his hands reached around to cup her breasts. *Was she dreaming?* Seconds later, he was lifting her nightgown and pushing gently into her, his face buried in the nape of her neck. They rocked together, their bodies unconsciously mimicking the rocking coming from the next room. *If this is a dream,* Robin thought, *it's the best dream I've had in a long while.*

Except there was no question now that they were awake. Instead of Blake's warm breath on the nape of her neck, she felt the heat of Melanie's impatient sighs from the backseat.

"Everything all right back there?" Blake asked, checking his rearview mirror.

"Hunky-dory," Melanie replied.

"I take it that Landon won't be joining us."

"Landon's not very keen on hospitals."

"Don't know many people who are," Blake said, backing down the driveway. "You'll tell me where to go?" he asked as they reached the road.

"With pleasure," Melanie said.

Robin released a sigh of her own. "Can we please give the sarcasm a rest for a few hours?"

Melanie laughed. "Oh, lighten up." She sat forward in her seat, stretching toward Blake. "Tell me, Blake. Is my sister always this humorless?"

"Are you always this angry?" he asked in return.

"You think I'm angry?"

"Aren't you?"

"Maybe," Melanie surprised Robin by answering. "Wouldn't you be, if your sister suspected your son was a murderer?"

"What?" Robin said. "I never said that."

"Not in so many words. But you'd rather think Landon is a killer than your precious Alec."

"If I really thought Landon is a killer," Robin protested, sidestepping the real issue, "wouldn't I be afraid to sleep under the same roof?"

"Not necessarily," Melanie said, as calmly as if she were discussing the weather. "I mean, even if he did shoot everybody else, he'd have no reason for killing you. Other than that you're a bit of a wet blanket," she added. "See what I mean, Blake? Not even a chuckle."

Blake squeezed Robin's hand, the gesture telling her not to snap at Melanie's bait.

"Any idea how long you'll be staying in Red Bluff, Blake?" Melanie asked.

"Guess it will depend on what happens."

"You mean on how long it takes my father to die," Melanie replied. "Your office doesn't mind?" she continued, not waiting for Blake's response.

"I have my computer, my phone," he said. "I can pretty much work from anywhere."

"We can move to a hotel, if you'd prefer," Robin offered.

"Yeah, that might not be such a bad idea." Melanie leaned back into her seat. "The press seems to have lost interest. Turn left here. In two more blocks, make a right."

They drove the rest of the way in silence, Robin feeling lighter than she had in days at the thought of leaving her sister's house. Fifteen minutes later, they arrived at the hospital parking lot. Five minutes after that, they were pushing open the door to their father's room.

A woman—dark-haired, well dressed, mid-fifties—was sitting in the chair beside Greg Davis's bed, her right arm extended, resting on the sheet covering his torso. She jumped up when she heard the door open.

"Who are you?" Melanie asked before Robin could form the words.

The woman was about five feet six inches tall and slender. Her hair was pulled into a bun at the back of her neck, and the buttons of her suit jacket strained around the ample swell of her bosom. It was obvious she'd been crying. "My name is Jackie Ingram. You must be Greg's daughters." She looked from Melanie to Robin, her lips quivering in her attempt to smile.

"And what is *your* relationship to my father?" Melanie pressed.

"I'm his office manager."

"Oh. So you were sleeping together," Melanie said.

"What? No . . ."

"Oh, please. He sleeps with all his office managers. It's a matter of principle."

Jackie Ingram looked as if she didn't know whether to laugh or cry.

My sister has that effect on people, Robin thought, feeling genuinely sorry for the woman.

"I should go."

"Yes, you probably should," Melanie agreed.

Jackie Ingram fled the room.

"Was that really necessary?" Robin asked as the door closed behind her.

"Probably not," Melanie said. "But it *was* fun. Come on, you have to admit, it was fun to see the look on her face."

"You really think she was . . ."

"Fucking dear old Dad? I don't think there's any doubt. Rumor has it that her husband found out about the affair a few weeks back and threatened all sorts of nasty things. You can ask Sheriff Prescott if you don't believe me."

"So her husband's a suspect?"

"I believe there are several husbands on that list. Isn't that right, Dad?" Melanie approached his bed. "Lots of people had it in for you, didn't they? Not just members of your immediate family." She glanced over her shoulder at Blake. "And in case you're wondering who this person is, he's Robin's fiancé."

Blake stepped closer to the bed.

"Handsome guy, isn't he?" Melanie said, referring to her father. "Quite the stud in his day."

A groan emanated from deep within Greg Davis's chest, followed by another.

"Dad?" Robin asked, approaching cautiously. "Dad, can you hear us?"

"Maybe we should get the nurse," Blake said.

The nurse confirmed that there had been several indications during the night that their father might be on the verge of regaining consciousness, although she cautioned them not to get their hopes up. He was still in an exceptionally precarious position. Even in the unlikely event that he woke up, his brain had suffered a tremendous trauma and it would be a miracle if he survived, let alone ever returned to being the man he once was.

"Which, depending on how you look at it, could be a good thing," Melanie said, her voice radiating fake cheer.

"He might be able to tell us who did this to him," Blake said.

"We should tell Cassidy," Robin said.

"Think I'll stay here," Melanie said.

"You'll come get us if anything . . ."

"My shouts of hallelujah will echo down the halls."

—

The door to Cassidy's room was closed, and Robin heard voices coming from inside as she drew closer. She knocked.

"Come in," Cassidy called, her voice sounding stronger than it had in days. She was sitting up in bed, her hair brushed away from her face and secured with a pink ribbon. Standing at the foot of her bed were two teenage girls, both in tight denim cutoffs and Day-Glo halter tops. Kenny Stapleton was leaning against the far wall, watching them. "Robin! Come in. Meet my friends. I think you've already met Kenny."

Robin smiled as she approached the bed. "Yes. Hello, Kenny."

He nodded, glancing from her to the floor.

"This is Kara and Skylar. They go to my school."

"Are you classmates?" Robin thought the girls looked a few years older than Cassidy.

"We're juniors," Kara said. "But we wanted to come by and say hello, make sure our girl Cassidy was okay."

You mean you wanted to find out what happened, get the dirt straight from the horse's mouth, Robin thought. *Impress the senior boys.*

"This is Robin," Cassidy said. "She and my mother were best friends."

"It's so awful about Cassidy's mother," Skylar said, her voice low.

"Yes, it is."

"Cassidy was telling us about what happened." Kara shuddered. "I don't think I would have been so brave."

"Who are you?" Cassidy asked Blake.

"This is my fiancé, Blake."

"Nice to meet you, Cassidy," he said. "You're looking amazingly well."

"Isn't she?" Kara enthused.

"They took out my IV this morning," Cassidy said.

"I'm Kara," the girl said to Blake.

Am I imagining things or did she just stick out her chest?

"And I'm Skylar."

Skylar with the round little bottom sticking out from under her very short shorts.

"Nice to meet you, girls."

"He's really good-looking," Cassidy whispered to Robin.

Robin saw Kenny Stapleton's back stiffen as he looked over at Blake.

"The doctor says I might be able to leave the hospital in a few days."

"That's great, sweetheart."

"Well, I guess we should be going," Kara said, staring at Blake as she wrapped a strand of long brown hair around her finger and twirled it.

Way to go, Lolita.

"It was nice meeting you, girls," Robin said.

"You, too," Kara said to Blake, glancing only briefly at Robin.

"Hope we see you again," Skylar echoed. "You—get better," she said to Cassidy on her way out, an obvious afterthought.

"That was nice of them to stop by," Robin said when they were gone.

"Yeah," Cassidy agreed. "I was so surprised. I didn't

even think they knew who I was. When did you get here, Blake?"

"Drove in yesterday," he said.

"Are you staying at the house?"

"I have been."

"Then we'll all be together," Cassidy said.

So much for moving to a motel, Robin thought. *Who's going to be the lucky one to tell Melanie?* "We have some news," she said.

The girl looked warily from Robin to Blake and back. "Is it about Daddy?"

"The doctors think he might be regaining consciousness."

"He's awake?" Kenny asked.

Robin spun in his direction. She'd forgotten he was there. "No, he isn't awake," she said to Cassidy, whose eyes were bright and big as saucers. "But he's making sounds, and the nurse said there were some indications . . ."

"That he's coming around?" Cassidy said, completing the sentence.

"That he *might*."

"So, he's going to be all right?"

"You can't get your hopes up."

"But you just said . . ."

"I said that he *might* regain consciousness. 'Might' is a really big word."

"But it's a really *good* word," Cassidy protested. "Can I see him?"

"We should check with the doctor."

"The doctor said I could see him once my IV was out."

"Well, then, I guess it's all right. If you think you're strong enough . . ."

Cassidy pushed her covers aside and swung her legs off the bed. Kenny was immediately at her side. "No, it's okay," Cassidy told him. "I can manage. You've been here all morning. You should go home. Blake can help me. Can't you, Blake?"

"Absolutely." Blake came forward to offer his arm.

Kenny stepped back as Cassidy took Blake's hand, leaning against his side as his arm reached around her waist to support her.

"Maybe I should get a wheelchair," Robin suggested.

"No," Cassidy said. "The doctor said that I should try to get as much exercise as I can. You really think there's a chance that Daddy's going to be all right?"

"Please don't get too excited," Robin told her, putting her arm around Cassidy, her hand folding inside Blake's as they led her from the room.

"See you later, Cassidy," Kenny called after them.

Only Robin acknowledged him with a goodbye wave.

—NINETEEN—

"Wow. Look at you!" Melanie exclaimed as Robin and Blake escorted Cassidy into Greg Davis's hospital room. "Should you be out of bed?"

"Is he awake?" Cassidy asked, ignoring the question as she moved closer to her stepfather.

"No. Nothing's changed."

"He's so . . . still," Cassidy said, her voice trembling as her eyes filled with tears. "I've never seen him so still."

Robin felt her own eyes well up. "Still" was the last word she would ever have expected to hear to describe the man who, for as long as she could remember, always seemed to be moving. A local journalist had once described him as "someone who never walks when he can march, who never whispers when he can shout, whose effortless authority vibrates through even the simplest of gestures." It occurred to Robin that up until the shooting, she'd never seen her father asleep, never so much as caught him napping.

"Can he hear us?" Cassidy asked.

"We don't know," Robin said.

"Is he in pain? Are you in pain, Daddy?"

"He's not in pain," Melanie told her. "How are *you* doing?"

"I'm okay," Cassidy said. "Everything's still pretty sore, and sometimes it hurts to take a deep breath. But the doctor says I should be able to go home in a couple of days."

"So soon?" Melanie asked. "Is that wise?"

"The doctor says that the faster I get back to my normal routine, the better."

"Of course, she'll have to take it easy for a little while," Robin elaborated.

"Of course," Melanie said. Her lips curled into a stiff smile. "You can have your old room back. Robin and Blake are moving to a hotel."

"Oh, no. Please," Cassidy said, her eyes widening in panic. "You can't do that."

"It's getting a little crowded," Melanie said. "And they'd have to move into my old room across the hall, which is much smaller—"

"*I'll* take the smaller room," Cassidy offered quickly. "Please. You have to stay," she begged Robin.

Robin glanced at Blake, and both of them simultaneously nodded their assent.

"Then it's settled." Cassidy turned from Robin to her stepfather. "And when you get better, Daddy, you can come home, too. You can have *your* old room back."

Robin watched Melanie's jaw tense. She wasn't sure whether this was due to Cassidy's continued use of the word "daddy" or the thought of having to relinquish the master bedroom.

"I think we're getting a little ahead of ourselves," Melanie said. "Even if Dad regains consciousness, the doctors aren't optimistic . . ."

"I don't understand," Cassidy interrupted. "If he regains consciousness, doesn't that mean he's getting better?" Cassidy's gaze bounced frantically around the room. "Doesn't it?"

"Hopefully, yes," Blake told her.

"He's suffered grievous injuries," Melanie said.

" 'Grievous' . . . What does that mean?" Cassidy asked.

"It means that whether or not he regains consciousness, we shouldn't get our hopes up."

"He has to get better." Cassidy spun back toward her stepfather. "You have to get better, Daddy. Please. You're all I have left."

"Oh, sweetheart," Robin said, taking Cassidy in her arms.

Cassidy collapsed against Robin, her legs weakening, so that Robin was virtually holding her up. "They killed my mommy," she cried, her voice disappearing into Robin's curls. "Daddy can't die. He can't leave me."

"I'm sure he's doing everything in his power to get better," Robin said.

"He's made it this far," Blake added. "And from what little I know about him, if anyone can survive this, he can."

"That's true," Melanie conceded. "I just think it's a mistake to cling to false hope."

"Sometimes hope is all we've got," Robin said, kissing Cassidy's forehead. "Maybe we should get you back in bed."

"No. I want to stay here." Cassidy backed slowly out of Robin's arms, fresh resolve straightening her shoulders. "Daddy?" She reached over the bed's handrail to take his hand in hers. "It's me, Cassidy. I'm here. And the doctors say I'm going to be fine. But I need you, Daddy. I need you to wake up." She looked back at Robin. "He's cold. He needs more covers."

Robin looked around the room, locating a lightweight cotton blanket in the closet. She tucked it around her father's legs, watching as Cassidy drew it up toward his chin.

"That's better," the child said. "Isn't it, Daddy? You're warmer now." She looked back at Melanie. "Where's Landon?"

"He's at home."

"He should be here. Daddy should be surrounded by the people he loves."

"I'm not sure that would be such a good idea," Melanie protested. "You know Landon's behavior can be a bit . . . unpredictable."

"I know that Landon loves Daddy and Daddy loves him."

Melanie's skepticism registered on her face. "Maybe so, but . . ."

"He said he thought Landon had come a really long way, that you'd done an awesome job with him."

"He told you that?" Tears sprang to Melanie's eyes. Quickly, she turned aside, swiping at them with the back of her hand. "What else did he say?"

"Just that he loved you."

Wow, Robin thought.

"Wow," Melanie echoed out loud. Then, her voice a whisper: "If only he'd said that to *me*."

"He will," Cassidy said. "When he wakes up." She squeezed her stepfather's hand. "I love you, Daddy. We all do."

Robin held her breath, half-expecting her father to summon up all his inner strength and shout out in his booming voice, "I love you, too." But he didn't.

He never had.

She pictured her brother, saw the lingering hurt in his eyes at their father's betrayal, and felt the rage behind it. Had he been angry enough to kill?

Where are you, Alec? What were you doing in Red Bluff the night of the shootings?

"Maybe you should sit down," she said to Cassidy, in an effort to quiet those thoughts.

"No, I'm okay." Cassidy smiled shyly at Blake. "You didn't tell me you were engaged," she said to Robin.

"Well, we really haven't talked that much," Robin said.

"I'm sure there were more important things on her mind," Blake said.

Robin wondered if he was merely being generous, masking his hurt feelings, or if he really meant what he said. It occurred to her that she didn't know the man she was engaged to marry very well at all.

"So when are you getting married? Can I be a bridesmaid?" Cassidy asked, one question tumbling on top of the other.

"Most certainly," Blake said graciously.

"That's so cool. And I guess you'll be maid of honor," she said to Melanie.

Melanie looked over at Robin. Robin glanced toward the floor.

"First things first," Blake interjected. "And first, we have to set a date."

"How about as soon as Daddy gets out of the hospital?"

"That's certainly something to consider," Robin said, deciding to let the child cling to her optimism, however unrealistic.

Plenty of time for reality later.

Cassidy clapped her hands with excitement. "Did you hear that, Daddy? There's going to be a wedding. So you have to get better, so you can give the bride away." She glanced at Robin for confirmation.

Robin nodded. *What the hell? What harm could it do?*

"Have you met Robin's fiancé, Blake? Oh—I don't know your last name."

"It's Upton," Blake said.

"Blake Upton," Cassidy repeated. "That's a really cool name."

"Thank you." Blake smiled. "I had absolutely nothing to do with it."

"Are you related to Kate?" Cassidy asked.

"Who?"

"Kate Upton. She's a famous model."

"Pretty sure we're not related."

"That's too bad. I'd really like to meet her. I want to be a model one day."

"I don't think that *Daddy* would be too happy about that," Melanie said.

Robin recalled Melanie's early dreams of being a model, how their father had dismissed those dreams with a few terse words. *"Fat chance of that,"* he'd said.

"I think you'd be a great model," Blake told Cassidy.

"Really? That's what Kenny says."

"Kenny Stapleton?" Melanie's eyes narrowed, her head tilting to one side.

"He was here earlier," Robin said.

"Really." The word was no longer a question.

"And Kara Richardson and Skylar Marshall, from my school," Cassidy said. "They're juniors. I didn't think they even knew who I was. It was so cool they came to see me. Don't you think?"

"So cool," Robin repeated with a smile. One minute Cassidy seemed mature far beyond her years, and the next she reverted to the child she was. It was hard to keep up without getting dizzy.

"My mother could have been a famous model," Cassidy told Blake. "She was really beautiful."

"Yes, she was," Robin agreed, trying not to imagine that beautiful face torn apart by bullets.

"But she didn't care about that stuff. She just wanted to be a good wife and mother. That's what she always said. That Daddy and I were plenty for her. Didn't she, Daddy?" Cassidy leaned in toward her father. "She loved you so much. You know that, don't you, Daddy?"

"I'm sure he knows," Blake said, and Cassidy fell back against his chest, sobbing quietly.

"Maybe we should go," Melanie said after several minutes had passed. "There's no point just standing around waiting for something to happen. What is it they say—'a watched pot never boils'?"

"What does that mean?" Cassidy asked.

"It means that it could be days, weeks . . ."

Their father groaned.

"Oh, my God," Cassidy cried. "Is he . . . ?"

"He's just making noises . . ."

The groan became louder, more insistent.

"I'll get the nurse," Blake said, hurrying out of the room.

"Daddy?" Cassidy said.

"Dad? Can you hear me?" Melanie said, approaching.

Robin hung back, holding her breath.

"Dad?" Melanie said again. "It's me, Melanie."

A low wail emanated from deep inside their father's throat, gurgling toward the surface of his lips. After a few seconds, the gurgle became a name.

"Cassidy."

Melanie fell back, as if she'd been physically struck.

"Daddy!" Cassidy cried, grabbing his hand. "I'm here, Daddy. I'm right here."

"Cassidy," he said again.

Cassidy tried to throw herself over the handrail of the bed, crying out as the rail dug into her side. "Daddy! Daddy!"

"Cassidy," he repeated, his eyes opening even as his voice grew fainter.

"Daddy! He's awake! He's awake!"

Robin inched toward the bed. "Dad?"

Slowly, almost imperceptibly, her father's eyes gravitated toward her. "Robin?"

Melanie pushed herself in front of Robin. "Dad, it's me—Melanie." She leaned in close, her lips brushing the side of his cheek. "Dad?"

"Melanie? No . . ." His eyes rolled back in his head and he began to shake.

"What's happening?" Cassidy shouted as a series of loud beeps sounded and the room filled with medical personnel.

"Okay, everybody who doesn't need to be here, leave now," a male voice directed. "Mr. Davis . . . Mr. Davis . . . It's Dr. Barber. Can you hear me?" He turned toward the others. "He's seizing."

"What did you say to him?" Cassidy asked Melanie, panic lacing her voice.

"Get everybody out now," the doctor said.

"I'm not leaving," Cassidy said.

"It's just for a little while," Blake said, gently taking hold of Cassidy's shoulders. Immediately Robin was at her other side.

Together they led the sobbing child out of the room.

—TWENTY—

"Well, that was fun," Melanie exclaimed as they left the hospital two hours later.

"You have a strange definition of fun," Blake said, walking ahead of Robin and her sister through the parking lot, using his fob to unlock the car doors and open the windows.

Melanie shrugged. "Come on. You have to admit it was rather exciting there for a few minutes. Even though the outcome was something of a letdown."

"Our father didn't die," Robin reminded her sister.

"Precisely my point. All that drama, then nothing. Back to where we started."

"I can't believe he's still alive," Robin said.

"Are you kidding?" Melanie said. "He's not going anywhere. Not till you and I are dead. Then he can die happy."

"That's a terrible thing to say," Robin said.

"Oh, please. You hated the man. And now, just because he suddenly remembers your existence and whispers your name, you're going to go all biblical and forgive him his transgressions?"

"It's *trespasses,* not transgressions, and I'm not forgiving anything." Threads of anxiety began weaving through Robin's insides. *Now? I'm going to have a panic attack now?* After *everything that just went down?*

Robin reached Blake's car, the disparate threads of anxiety now uniting to wind their way around her throat, digging deep into her flesh like barbed wire and cutting off her air supply. She grabbed the door handle, clinging to it despite the heat of the steel that seared the palm of her hand, certain that if she let go, she would crumple to the ground. "What *did* you say to him?" she managed to spit out.

"What do you mean—what did I say to him?" Melanie asked. "When?"

"You whispered something."

"No, I didn't."

Robin pictured Melanie leaning over their father, her lips moving toward his ear.

"I didn't get the chance to say anything," Melanie insisted.

Robin pulled open the car door and climbed into the front seat as Blake got behind the wheel and started the engine. A noisy blast of air shot toward her head, scattering the threads of panic still clinging to her neck, although it did little to break through the oppressive heat surrounding her.

Melanie climbed into the backseat, slamming the car door after her. "What—you think I threatened him? Or better yet, confessed the whole thing was my idea? Is that what you think? Damn it, can we get some of that cold air back here? I'm suffocating."

"It'll take a minute," Blake said.

"You have a hell of a nerve, you know that?" Melanie said to Robin.

"I just asked you what you said to him."

"You implied I caused his seizure."

"I did no such thing," Robin said.

"Ladies . . . ladies," Blake interrupted, pulling out of the parking lot. "Can we not do this now?"

There was a welcome moment of silence.

"Just so we're clear . . . ," Melanie started up again.

"I think we're pretty clear," Blake said.

"I think you should stay out of this," said Melanie.

"Please don't talk to him that way," Robin said.

"What way?"

"The way you talk to everyone."

"I would think you'd be pleased. I'm treating him like family."

"Which is exactly the problem."

"In which case, he might want to reconsider marrying into this family."

"Oh, shut up," said Robin.

"*You* shut up," said Melanie.

"Okay, then," said Blake, clearly at a loss.

"I had nothing to do with the shootings," Melanie said. "And neither did Landon."

"Fine," said Robin.

"You are so full of shit."

"*I'm* full of shit?"

"Look," Blake said. "This bickering isn't doing anybody any good. Cassidy is going to need all the love and support we can give her, which at the very least means we have to get along."

Robin nodded. The doctors had had to give Cassidy a sedative to calm her down after their father's seizure. She was still asleep when they'd left the hospital.

"Speaking of Cassidy," Melanie said, "what the hell was Kenny Stapleton doing in her room this morning?"

"I assume he was checking in to see how she's doing."

"You don't find his concern a little . . . troubling?"

"Should I?"

"You're the therapist. You tell me."

"I'm not sure what you're getting at."

"Then let me ask *you*, Blake," Melanie said. "As a man, what do you think of a boy Kenny's age being this concerned about a twelve-year-old girl? I know the sheriff finds it odd."

"Under the circumstances, it doesn't seem that unreasonable."

"Well, Tara wasn't too happy about his always hanging around," Melanie said. "I can tell you that."

"I thought he came to see Landon," Robin said.

"So did I," Melanie agreed. "Now I wonder."

"Is he a suspect?" Blake asked.

"The sheriff doesn't think so. It's not like he had anything to gain. And he doesn't match the description Cassidy gave of the men she saw in the house that night." Melanie shrugged, as if she was already bored with the topic. "I'm hungry. Anybody feel like Chinese food?"

"Seriously?" Blake asked.

"Actually, yes," Robin said, surprising herself. "Chinese food is exactly what I feel like."

"Turn right at the next corner," Melanie directed Blake. "We'll go to the Golden Dragon over at Main and Union." She checked her watch. "It's after two. The lunch crowd should be gone. I don't think we'll be bothered."

"Should we call Landon?" Blake asked. "See if he wants to join us?"

"Landon hates Chinese food. Turn here."

"What exactly does he do all day?" Blake asked.

"He keeps busy."

"Doing what?"

"What difference does it make?"

"He likes to draw," Robin offered.

"How would you know that?" Melanie asked.

"I came across some of his pictures in a box in the mudroom."

"Why would you be going through the boxes in the mudroom?"

Robin's eyes appealed silently to Blake for help.

"Where to now?" he obliged by asking as they crossed Highway 647A.

"Go straight till we hit Union," Melanie said. "You shouldn't have any trouble finding a parking space."

They didn't. Blake found a spot about half a block from the restaurant and they exited the car, walking briskly down the tree-lined street.

Melanie was right—the lunch crowd had pretty much cleared out, although a few stragglers remained. They glanced up when the front door opened. Robin saw a woman at one table immediately reach for her cell phone.

Don't be paranoid. Just because she's reaching for her phone doesn't mean it has anything to do with you.

A smiling hostess with shiny black hair and a handful of menus approached and directed them to a booth at the back. They passed the table with the woman whispering into her phone. She turned away and covered her mouth as they walked by. Her male companion was studiously rearranging his cutlery and didn't look up.

Robin slid into the seat beside Blake. Everything about the restaurant was exactly as she remembered—the deep red walls, the red leather booths, the middle of the room crowded with small square tables for two, a mirrored bar opposite the front door, colorful Chinese lanterns and green plastic vines laden with white plastic flowers scattered among unframed pictures of frolicking panda bears.

"The decor may be a cliché, but the food's great," Melanie said, taking a seat opposite them. "Not *fancy*, mind you." She waved away the hostess's offer of a menu. "I'll have the wonton soup and the beef chow mein." Melanie nodded at Robin. "She'll have the lemon chicken with extra sauce. Right?"

"I'm surprised you remember."

"Hard to forget. It's all you ever ordered."

"Lemon chicken sounds good," Blake said. "Anybody for an egg roll?"

Both sisters raised their hands.

Blake's cell phone rang. He pulled it from his pocket. "Sorry about this. I'll be right back." He stood up and headed for the door.

"Good-looking man," Melanie said, watching him leave. "Kind of reminds me of Dad."

"He's nothing like Dad," said Robin, fresh stirrings of anxiety circling her heart.

"You sure about that?"

Robin leaned back in her seat and closed her eyes, keeping them closed until she felt Blake returning to his seat.

"Are you okay?" he asked.

"I'm fine," Robin said. "What about you? Problems?"

"Good news for a change. Looks like the deal I've been working on is finally wrapping up."

"What kind of law do you practice?" Melanie asked.

"Corporate and commercial."

"Sounds complicated. And by 'complicated,' I mean boring."

He laughed. "I guess it can be both."

Why can't I do that? Robin wondered. *Just shrug and laugh off Melanie's more caustic remarks. Why do I always react?*

"Do you understand any of it?" Melanie was asking her.

"Not really," Robin admitted, determined to try harder, to not let her sister get to her.

"I try not to bring my work home with me," Blake said.

"Probably wise. Our dad had much the same philosophy. Didn't he, Robin?"

"Fuck off," Robin said. *So much for shrugging and laughing it off.*

"What'd I do now?" Melanie asked. "Honestly, Blake, is this how she is with you?"

Blake smiled. "Fuck off," he said.

Robin burst into tears of gratitude as the waitress appeared with their egg rolls.

"It's okay. She's just really hungry," Melanie told the startled young woman. The waitress deposited the food on the table, then backed quickly away. "Well," Melanie said, smiling as she dipped her egg roll into the accompanying plum sauce and lifted it into the air. "Cheers, everyone."

A phone rang.

"Again?" Melanie asked.

"Not mine," Blake said as it rang a second time.

"Oh, what do you know? It's mine." Melanie laughed as she extricated her cell phone from her purse and raised it to her ear. "Hello?" A brief pause and a roll of her eyes. "Yes. What can I do for you?"

A longer pause. Melanie pressed the button to disconnect the call.

"Well?" Robin asked.

Melanie took a big bite of her egg roll. "That was our illustrious sheriff. Apparently the San Francisco police have located Alec and they're escorting him to Red Bluff as we speak. They should be here in about an hour. Looks like we're going to have to eat fast."

—TWENTY-ONE—

The Tehama County Sheriff's Office is located on Antelope Boulevard near the intersection of Highways 99 and 36, far from the center of town. According to its website, it exists to protect the lives and property of the more than 63,000 permanent residents of Tehama County, which includes the city of Red Bluff, as well as the thousands of visitors who enjoy hunting, fishing, and vacationing in the area's vast wilderness. It is staffed by the sheriff, the assistant sheriff, one captain, three lieutenants, nine sergeants, seven detectives, and twenty-nine deputy sheriffs, all of whom proudly sport the seven-pointed badge on the front of their uniforms. The department's motto, prominently displayed throughout the uninteresting brown-brick low-rise building, is Serving Our Community with P.R.I.D.E., the initials standing for Professionalism, Respect, Integrity, Dedication, and Equality.

"As if," Melanie said, pushing open the heavy glass front door.

Sheriff Prescott was waiting for them in the lobby, in front of a high reception counter, behind which a series of glassed-in offices ran down a wide corridor in both directions.

"Where is he?" Robin said instead of "Hello."

"Why don't we sit down for a minute?" The sheriff motioned toward a group of brown leather chairs. "Relax, catch your breath . . ."

"Why don't you just skip the bullshit and let us see our brother?" Melanie said.

The deputy behind the counter looked up at the word "bullshit," his hand moving instinctively toward the gun in his holster. The sheriff smiled and turned toward Blake. "I'm Sheriff Alan Prescott. And you are?"

"Blake Upton." Blake shook the sheriff's hand, his own hand disappearing inside the larger man's palm.

"My fiancé," Robin explained. "He drove up yesterday from L.A."

"Nice to meet you, although I wish it were under . . ."

"Yeah, yeah," Melanie said dismissively. "Better circumstances and all that. Isn't that what people tell each other at funerals?"

"And always a pleasure seeing you, Melanie." Again Sheriff Prescott motioned toward the nearby chairs. "Please, everyone, have a seat. You'll be able to see your brother shortly."

Robin looked nervously down the hallway, its off-white walls lined with diplomas, citations, and photographs of men and women in and out of uniform, along with the department's ubiquitous P.R.I.D.E. motto. She saw doors, all of them closed, with labels such as *Civil Division*, *Operation Division*, and *Jail Division*, even though the jail itself was housed in a separate building at the corner of Oak and Madison, in the center of town. *At least they haven't taken Alec there,* she was thinking as she and Blake sat down. "Is my brother under arrest?"

"Not yet. At the moment he's merely a person of interest." The sheriff lowered himself into a chair across from them.

"I've always loved that expression," Melanie said, remaining stubbornly on her feet and hovering beside the sheriff's chair. "As if the rest of us are of no interest whatsoever."

"If he's not under arrest, then why is he here?" Blake asked. "Why the police escort?"

"He didn't leave us much choice," Prescott answered. "It appears that he was on his way to Canada, judging by the fact that he had his passport with him and a considerable amount of cash."

"Since when is it a crime to carry money and a passport?" Robin said.

"What has he told you?" Melanie asked.

"He hasn't told us anything," the sheriff replied. "Your brother is being most uncooperative, I'm afraid."

"Which is his right," Blake reminded the sheriff.

"Yes, but if he's innocent, why be difficult?"

"Maybe your so-called person of interest isn't interested in doing your job for you," Melanie said.

"Look—" the sheriff began.

Robin could hear the constriction in his voice when he said the word, as if he was struggling to keep his cool, as if the very act of keeping his voice down was an effort of almost superhuman proportions. *You're not alone,* she wanted to tell him. *Melanie has that effect on many people.*

"I understand he's your brother and your instinct is to protect him," Prescott continued. "But he's not doing himself any favors by refusing to talk to us. I was hoping you'd be able to convince him that it's in his best interests—"

"A person of interest's best interests," Melanie interrupted. "Interesting."

The sheriff looked toward Blake, as if to say, "We're both men here. Help me out."

"Have you advised him of his rights?" Blake asked.

Sheriff Prescott ran his hand over the top of his head. "We have."

"And has he asked for an attorney?"

"He has not."

"Well, it appears he's got one, anyway," Blake said, rising to his feet. "I'd like to see my client now, if you don't mind."

Sheriff Prescott pushed himself out of his chair, sighing in defeat. "You didn't mention you were a lawyer."

"I was hoping it wouldn't be necessary."

The sheriff turned toward the reception counter. "Mike, could you have Mr. Davis brought out, please?"

The deputy relayed the request into his phone.

"What happens now?" Robin asked.

"That's up to you," Prescott said. "And your brother."

"But he's free to go?"

"Provided he doesn't leave town, yes."

"So you're not going to arrest him?"

"Not at this time. No."

"They don't have enough evidence to arrest him," Melanie said, her tone stopping just short of a sneer. "All they have is his car on tape."

"We have motive," Sheriff Prescott reminded them. "As well as opportunity."

"Pretty weak as far as motives go," Robin said. "It's been almost six years since he saw Tara or my father. The rest is strictly circumstantial."

"Juries have convicted on less."

"There are at least a dozen people in this city, myself included, with both motive and opportunity to shoot them," Melanie said. "I'd say that's more than enough to create reasonable doubt in a juror's mind."

"And I haven't eliminated anyone as a suspect. Including you," the sheriff said pointedly.

And then there Alec stood, appearing before them as if by magic, to the left of a uniformed deputy in front of the reception counter, trying to look defiant and unflappable, but instead looking shell-shocked and exhausted. His narrow face was in need of a shave, and his soft gray eyes were swollen and red-rimmed, as if he'd been crying. He was wearing faded, loose-fitting jeans and a wrinkled white T-shirt, the front of which was spattered with a sweeping arc of coin-size coffee stains.

"Alec!" Robin cried, rushing into his arms.

"Hey, you," he replied, his fingernails digging into her sides as his chin sank heavily onto her shoulder.

"Are you okay?"

"I've been better."

"Hi, there, little brother," Melanie said, joining them,

although she made no move to hug him even after Robin took a few steps back. "Long time no see."

"Melanie," he said, glancing at her only briefly before shifting his attention to Blake. "And Blake. Wow—the man himself. Didn't expect to see you here in Red Bluff."

"I could say the same about you," Blake said, patting Alec's arm.

"Let's get out of here," Melanie said.

Sheriff Prescott stopped them before they could take a step. "A word, if I may."

"Sure thing, Sheriff," Alec said, although the straight line of his lips made it clear he wasn't about to say anything.

"You understand that you're not to leave town . . ."

"Understood."

". . . and that should you try, you will immediately be placed under arrest."

Alec began rubbing his jaw. "Also understood."

"I'm hoping that after talking to your lawyer here, you'll decide to be more cooperative."

"My lawyer." Alec's lips curled into a half-smile.

"Are we done here?" Blake asked.

"For now."

They walked toward the parking lot, Robin holding tight to her brother's hand, Melanie and Blake flanking them on both sides, Sheriff Prescott following.

"Nice car," Prescott said as they approached Blake's Lexus, a standout among the half dozen police cruisers.

"You can get in front with Blake," Melanie directed her brother as she climbed into the backseat. "Robin will sit back here with me." She patted the seat beside her.

"I'll be in touch," the sheriff called as Blake pulled out of his parking spot.

"Looking forward to it," Alec said with a wave.

"What is it with you two?" Blake snapped, looking from Alec to Melanie and then back at Alec. "May I remind you that you're a suspect in a murder investigation? That man you just blew off so cavalierly is a sheriff. Don't deliberately antagonize the people with the power to throw your ass in jail."

"They don't have enough evidence to arrest him," Melanie said, as she'd said earlier.

"Since when has that ever stopped anyone?"

"Since when did you start doing criminal law?" Alec asked, sounding genuinely interested.

"I didn't. But I'll do for now. If and when the time comes . . ." Blake looked around the mostly barren landscape, the mountains shimmering in the distance. "Where the hell am I?"

"Turn left at the next intersection," Melanie said.

There was a moment's silence and then everyone spoke at once.

"Thanks for doing this." Alec.

"You must be exhausted." Robin.

"What happened to your car?" Blake.

"So, did you do it?" Melanie.

"Wow," said Alec, answering their questions one at a time. "Yes, I'm exhausted. The San Francisco police seized my car. And no, I didn't do it. Thanks for asking."

"But you *were* here in Red Bluff on the night of the shooting," Melanie said.

"I don't think I have to respond to that, do I, counselor?"

"What were you doing here?" Melanie persisted.

"How's Landon?" Alec asked in return, ignoring the question.

Beside her, Robin felt Melanie's body tense.

"Don't do this, Alec," Robin said, as exasperated as her sister. "Our father is in a coma, Tara is dead, and a twelve-year-old girl is without her mother. The police have proof you were in Red Bluff on the night of the shootings. This is not the time for evasions and obfuscations."

"Wow—'evasions and obfuscations.' Impressive words."

"How about 'glib'? You like that word better?" Melanie asked.

Alec twisted in his seat and peered over his shoulder into the back of the car. "Look. I understand your concern and I'm grateful for it."

"We don't need your understanding or your gratitude," Melanie said.

"And I don't need to be cross-examined." Alec turned back to face the windshield.

"For God's sake, Alec," Robin said. *Why was he being so damn difficult? Was it possible he* was *guilty?* "We're family. We just want to help."

"You can't. Trust me, the less you know, the better off we'll be."

"What does that mean?" Robin and Melanie asked together, their voices overlapping.

"I think we've all seen enough *Law & Order* to know that anything I tell you *can* and *will* be used against me in a court of law. If I'm arrested and this thing actually goes to trial, you could be subpoenaed and compelled to testify against me. Am I right?" he asked Blake.

"That's right. On the other hand," Blake said, "I'm your attorney. At least for the moment. And anything you tell *me* is strictly confidential."

Alec let out an audible sigh, nervously massaging his jaw as he lay back against his headrest and closed his eyes. "Then we'll talk later," he said.

—TWENTY-TWO—

"Okay, who needs a drink?" Melanie asked as soon as they stepped inside the house.

"Beer for me." Alec made a beeline for the kitchen, as if it hadn't been almost six years since his last visit and this were still his home.

"Me, too," echoed Blake, tossing his key fob onto the side table by the front door.

"I'm okay," Robin said.

Except she wasn't okay. She was in the midst of a full-blown panic attack, knives of anxiety stabbing her chest with each step, flailing at her carotid artery. If she wasn't careful, she'd bleed out in front of everyone. "If you'll excuse me, I need to use the bathroom."

"You all right?" Blake asked.

"I'm fine. The Chinese food . . ." Robin hurried up the stairs, hearing Landon rocking behind his closed door as she raced for the bathroom. "Damn it," she muttered, locking the door behind her. *Damn it, damn it, damn it.* "Okay. Settle down. Take deep breaths. You'll be fine."

But every time she tried to breathe, newly sharpened daggers pierced deeper into her flesh.

"Calm down. Calm down."

Except how could she calm down when Alec refused to answer any questions about what he'd been doing in Red Bluff on the night Tara was murdered and their father and Cassidy shot, which meant that at the very least he had something to hide? How could she calm down when the only Tom Richards from Red Bluff who'd moved to San Francisco had been dead for two years, which meant that her brother and Tom Richards were likely one and the same? How could she calm down when there was a good chance Alec had been one of the shooters?

Was it possible?

No, it couldn't be possible.

Shit. Shit. Shit.

She splashed cold water on her face, staring at her reflection in the mirror over the sink. "Damn scrunched-up face," she muttered, pushing at her skin, trying to smooth away the telltale signs of her anxiety. "Alec did not do this," she told her reflection. *He did not do this.*

There had to be a rational explanation for his refusal to explain his actions. "What? What possible explanation can there be?"

Shit. Shit. Shit.

"Shit! Goddamn it! Fuck!"

There was a knock on the bathroom door.

Robin froze.

Another knock, stronger than the first. "Aunt Robin?"

"Landon?" *Landon?* She unlocked the door and pulled

it open, the shock of seeing her nephew standing on the other side temporarily interrupting her panic attack.

He was wearing a bright orange T-shirt with a Harley-Davidson logo, his shoulder-length hair uncombed and falling into his eyes, eyes that shot to the floor the instant she opened the door. "I heard yelling," he mumbled, staring at his bare toes protruding from under the frayed hem of his too-long jeans.

"Oh, sorry," Robin said, following his gaze. "I didn't mean to alarm you. I . . . I stubbed my toe."

"Ouch," Landon said without looking up. "That hurts."

"Yes."

He turned to leave.

"I like your T-shirt," she said quickly.

Landon smiled and patted the shirt's logo.

"You like motorcycles, huh?"

No response.

"Can I ask you something?"

He shrugged, looked toward the stairs.

"I saw that you went for a motorcycle ride the other night."

Landon's head bolted up, his eyes boring into hers for half a second before returning to the floor. He began swaying from one foot to the other.

"Who do you know who drives a motorcycle?"

Silence.

"Is it anyone I know?"

"His name's Donny."

"Donny Warren?"

"He's my friend," Landon said, speaking into his chest.

"Your friend," Robin repeated.

"He takes me for rides on his bike."

After midnight?

"My mom says it's okay."

"It sounds like fun. Where do you go?"

"To his ranch. He has horses. I like horses."

Robin nodded. It was the longest conversation she'd ever had with her nephew. "Can I ask you something else?"

Landon glanced back at the stairs.

"I notice you spend a lot of time looking out your bedroom window."

He began rocking back and forth on his heels.

"And I was wondering . . . if maybe you happened to be looking out your window . . . on the night . . . of the shootings . . ."

"Landon?" Melanie called from the foot of the stairs. "Is that you up there? What are you doing? Come on down. Your uncle Alec is here."

"Landon, did you see anything that night?" Robin asked.

But his back was already to her, and in the next second, he was halfway down the stairs.

Robin remained in the bathroom doorway for several seconds before proceeding to her bedroom and closing the door. She lay down on the bed and stared up at the overhead ceiling fan, questions circling her head like flies. *Had Alec killed Tara? Had he tried to kill their father and Cassidy? Had Landon? Maybe it had been*

Alec and Landon together. Or Landon and Donny Warren. Maybe Melanie had *planned the whole thing.*

"Shit."

What a family.

What a mess.

Why wasn't she better equipped to deal with messes like this? Wasn't family dysfunction something she encountered on an almost daily basis? Wasn't her own family history at least part of the reason she became a therapist?

She tried to think of how she would advise a client.

"*Take it one step at a time,*" she would say. "*One issue at a time.*"

There was certainly no shortage of issues: her anger, her disappointment, her defensiveness in the face of Melanie's nearly constant attacks. But perhaps all these issues were the result of an even bigger issue—guilt.

For not telling her mother about her father's infidelities.

For abandoning her mother during her illness.

For abandoning her best friend.

For believing Melanie could be capable of murder.

For believing Landon could be capable of murder.

For believing Alec could be capable of murder.

"That's a shitload of guilt," she said out loud.

She shook her head. She was always telling clients that guilt was a useless emotion whose only purpose was to keep you stuck in the past and prevent you from moving forward. That it was easier—less scary—to feel guilty than it was to make positive changes in your life. That guilt was the coward's way out. "Am I really such a fucking coward?" she asked out loud.

There was a gentle tapping on the door. "Robin?" Blake called softly.

And what about Blake? she wondered, sitting up in bed. Was he the man he claimed to be or just a younger, more polished version of her father? Could she really trust him?

"Robin," Blake called again, opening the door a crack, then stepping inside. "Sorry. Were you asleep?"

"No."

He walked to the bed and sat down beside her, the mattress dipping slightly with his weight. "How's your stomach?"

"Better. What's happening downstairs?"

"Not much. Your brother has decided he's going to sleep in the mudroom."

"The mudroom? It's a mess."

"Says he likes it that way."

Robin looked toward the window opposite the bed, catching their reflection in the glass and thinking that they complemented each other well. "Do you believe that guilt is the coward's way out?" she asked.

He seemed puzzled by the question. "I'm not sure I even understand what that means."

She smiled. Her father would never have admitted to not understanding anything. "There's nothing the matter with my stomach," she told him. "It was a panic attack."

"I thought it might be." He squeezed her hand.

"Sorry."

"For what?"

"For not telling you the truth in the first place."

"I'm the one who owes *you* an apology."

"My turn to ask for what?"

"For thinking you were exaggerating when you talked about your sister."

She laughed. "Thank you for telling her to fuck off earlier."

"It was my pleasure."

"In her defense, it's been difficult—"

"She doesn't need you to defend her." He shrugged. "I guess everybody has a story."

"I guess." She paused. "What's yours?"

Robin waited for him to smile and say that she already knew his story, that all things considered, he'd enjoyed a life of relative ease and rare privilege. He was smart and good-looking. His family was both wealthy and well connected. True, his parents were divorced, but the divorce had been amicable and both were now remarried and settled comfortably on the East Coast, his mother in New York, his father in Connecticut. She knew he had an older brother who was off teaching English in China and a younger brother who'd died as the result of an asthma attack in his early twenties. They'd discussed all that when they first started dating. She'd assumed that because he rarely spoke of his family, there wasn't much else to say.

She should have known better.

"My brother didn't die because he was asthmatic," Blake said now.

"What?"

"He died because he overdosed on a combination of cocaine and heroin. Actually the coroner said he had so many drugs in his system that it was a wonder he'd survived as long as he had."

"Oh, my God. I'm so sorry. Why didn't you tell me this before?"

He ran his hand through his hair. "I don't know. Maybe I thought you had enough on your plate. Maybe I thought another fucked-up family would scare you away. Maybe I just didn't want to deal with it."

"You didn't trust me," Robin acknowledged quietly.

"No. I . . ."

"It's okay. I didn't trust you either."

He smiled sadly. "So what do we do now?"

Robin exhaled a long deep breath. "We make the decision to trust each other. Or else what's the point?"

"You think it's that simple?"

"I think it has to be."

He nodded.

"Tell me about your brother," she said.

"It was such a stupid waste." The words tumbled effortlessly from his lips, as if they'd been sitting on the tip of his tongue for years, just waiting for a push. "He was this charming, charismatic guy. Which I guess was part of the problem. Everything always came so easily for him. He never had to try, never had to put himself out there. School, job offers, women. All he had to do was smile. A movie producer actually spotted him on the street one afternoon and offered him a small part in a film. The lead actress was supposed to walk into a party and grab some random guy and start making out with him. Naturally she picked my brother. He told me that they spent all day making out on set and all night fucking in her mansion overlooking the ocean." Blake shook his head at the memory. "You can still see that dumb movie on TV sometimes. Don't ask me what it's called. *House Party*? *Pool Party*? *Frat Party*? Something like that."

"Did you ever watch it?"

"I did—once. But it was too painful. You can see he was stoned out of his mind. Goddamn drugs."

That's why you never take so much as an aspirin, why you were so concerned about my taking Valium.

"He was only twenty-four when he died. He'd had asthma when he was a kid, so my parents decided to tell everyone he'd suffered a fatal attack. Pretty soon I adopted that story as well. It was easier that way." Blake brought his hands together, as if to signal the story was coming to an end. "Anyway, my parents divorced soon after that, my older brother took off for China, and I buried myself in my career." He looked directly into Robin's eyes. "Then one night I reluctantly agreed to accompany a colleague to a party, and who should walk in . . . but the love of my life."

Robin covered his hand with her own.

There was a knock on the door. Robin spun around to see Melanie in the doorway.

"Sorry to interrupt, but . . ." Melanie took a deep breath.

Robin rose slowly to her feet. "What's the matter?"

"Alec is gone."

"What do you mean, he's gone?"

"I mean he stole your fiancé's car and took off."

"Please tell me this is your sick idea of a joke."

"Sorry, little sister," Melanie said solemnly. "Looks like the joke is on us."

—TWENTY-THREE—

They waited until almost midnight before giving up on Alec and going to bed.

"Why would he do such a stupid thing?" Robin had lost track of how many times she'd asked that question. "What the hell was he thinking?"

"Obviously he wasn't." Melanie stood up from the kitchen table, where the three of them had been lingering since dinner. No one had had much of an appetite except Landon, who'd wolfed down two hot dogs and three helpings of beans before retreating to his room and resuming his rocking. "But at least the sheriff hasn't called to say they picked him up, which means they probably don't know he's gone. So maybe he'll get smart and come back before it's too late."

Sheriff Prescott would no doubt be checking in with them in the morning. It wouldn't take long for him to realize that Alec had gone AWOL. It would take even less time for a warrant to be issued for their brother's arrest.

"Unless, of course, he's guilty," Melanie said.

"He isn't," Robin insisted.

"There's also the little matter of your fiancé's car."

"Looks like your brother's going to need a good criminal attorney sooner than we thought," Blake said.

"Do you know anyone?" Robin asked him.

"Not from around here."

"I hear Jeff McAllister's pretty good," Melanie said. "I'll phone him in the morning. Anyway, I'm calling it a night, and I suggest you do the same. Tomorrow is shaping up to be a very eventful day."

Robin listened to her sister's footsteps as they retreated up the stairs. "Do you think she could be right?" she asked Blake, reluctant to accept the possibility that Melanie could be right about anything.

"I don't know," Blake said honestly. "But if he doesn't come back by morning, then I'm going to have to report my car stolen or risk being charged as an accomplice after the fact."

"I know."

"I'm really sorry."

"You have nothing to be sorry about. This is Alec's fault. Not yours."

They went upstairs and lay down on top of the bed, not bothering to change out of their street clothes or climb under the covers. Robin felt the weight of Blake's arm as it wrapped around her waist, his breath steady and reassuring on the back of her neck. *Thank God you're here,* she thought. Then, *Where the hell is my brother? Why isn't he answering his phone? Is he, at this very minute, barreling down a distant, dark highway, headed for the Canadian border?*

Did you do it, Alec? Did you shoot our father and Cassidy? Did you murder Tara?

She tried picturing her brother with a gun in his hand, a ski mask covering his thin face and full mouth, hiding everything but his beautiful gray eyes.

Did you do it, Alec? Were you so consumed with bitterness, even after all this time, that you murdered one person and tried to kill two more, including your own father? Did you hate them that much?

Her father and Alec had always had a contentious relationship, even before Greg's marriage to Tara. Alec had never lived up to their father's stereotypical expectations of what a man should be, what *a son of his* should be.

"Do you have to be so hard on him?" she remembered her mother asking repeatedly throughout Alec's childhood.

"Do you have to be so soft?" had been her father's automatic response. "You have to stop babying him. He needs to toughen up. You want the kids at school to walk all over him?"

But who needs outsiders when your own father's footprints are already imprinted on your back?

It was even worse the few times Alec had tried standing up to him.

Robin recalled her father's indignation when Alec refused his advice regarding a school project. The first-grade class had been told to design a park, and Alec had come home full of enthusiasm. He'd been . . . how old . . . six, maybe seven? His park would consist of a swing set and a sandbox made out of construction paper, he'd announced, as well as a Lego boy hanging from a set of monkey bars constructed from straws. There would be two cardboard trees.

"Two trees?" their father had bellowed. "What kind of park has only two trees? You need more goddamn trees."

Alec had stared at his father. "Whose project is this?" he'd asked. "Yours or mine?"

Their mother had glowed with quiet pride, but Greg Davis had stormed angrily out of the room, viewing his son's legitimate question as a threat to his authority and vowing never to help him again. His anger had resurfaced when Alec came home a week later, beaming with delight at the B-plus he'd received. "I bet all the other kids got an A," his father said dismissively. "It was the damn trees. I told you. What kind of stupid park has only two goddamn trees?"

The next time Robin saw Alec's project, it was stuffed in the garbage bin under the kitchen sink, its monkey bars dismantled, its cardboard trees upended and shredded beyond recognition.

Alec's teen years were no better. If he answered nine out of ten questions correctly on a test, his father would harp on the one question he'd missed. If he came in second in a track-and-field meet, he would be berated for not coming in first. His accomplishments were consistently viewed through the lens of failure, and no matter how hard he tried, he came up short. He was always a disappointment.

Eventually he stopped trying. What was the point when you were never going to be good enough? His grades slipped. He had to repeat his final year. He didn't even bother applying to college. "What are you going to do now?" his father had demanded. "Start your own business?" Then, without waiting for a response, "I'll tell you what you need to start a business—you need capital and you need balls. I didn't have a dime when I started up, but I had enormous balls. You don't have either. Looks like you'll be working for me full-time. And don't expect any favors because you're my son."

In truth, it was unlikely that Alec had expected anything from his father, other than abuse. And if he harbored any hopes that Greg Davis would miraculously turn into some sort of mentor, he'd been quickly relieved of those illusions. The man in charge showed no inclination to share anything of what he'd learned over the years. Alec was quickly relegated to the role of glorified errand boy, there to do his father's bidding and bear the brunt of his daily rants.

Robin recalled stopping by the office one day to get her father's signature on a scholarship application form, when she heard him berating Alec long and loud from behind his office door, unmindful or unconcerned about the fact that two clients sat waiting in his outer office. "Some men should never have sons," the female client whispered to her male colleague.

The man nodded. "I hear he eats his young."

My father the cannibal, Robin thought now, feeling Blake's arm slip from around her waist as he turned onto his back, giving in to sleep.

The one bright spot in Alec's life had been Tara.

They'd known each other for years, as a result of Tara's friendship with Robin. Even though Tara was a few years older than Alec, she never looked down on him. She seemed to value his opinion, regularly seeking his advice on everything from the boys she was dating to the clothes she should wear.

"What are you asking him for?" their father had scoffed once in passing. "He doesn't know anything."

"Sure he does," Tara had responded easily. "He knows lots. You're being a bully, Mr. D."

Robin had held her breath, waiting for her father to erupt and order Tara out of the house. But instead, he'd laughed out loud.

"That girl's a little firecracker," he'd pronounced at dinner that night.

Robin knew her brother was in love with Tara even before he did. The few girls he dated all looked vaguely like her—the blue eyes, the long, straight brown hair, the willowy, athletic bodies. But these romances never lasted long. "What was the matter with that one?" Tara had asked him after one breakup.

Alec had shrugged. "I don't know. She just wasn't . . . I don't know."

She wasn't you, Robin had answered silently, staring at her friend. If Tara knew about the crush Alec had on her, she never mentioned it to Robin. Still, how could she not know?

"So, Alec, what do you think about Dylan Campbell?" Tara had asked when she and Dylan first started dating.

"Don't like him much," came Alec's quick response. "He's kind of rough."

"I know," said Tara, with a laugh. "That's what I like about him."

Tara married Dylan and Alec never said another word against him until Tara showed up at their house one day covered in bruises, her infant daughter in her arms. "You have to leave him," he'd said simply. "He's going to kill you."

And now Tara was dead.

But it wasn't Dylan Campbell who'd killed her.

Was it Alec?

"Can I talk to you a minute?" Alec had asked Robin one night. She was home from Berkeley for the week of spring break. They were sitting in the backyard, staring up at the thousands of stars surrounding the full moon, like freckles. "It's about Tara."

"What about her?"

"Do you think she'd . . . ?"

"Do I think she'd what?" Robin pressed, although she didn't have to hear the rest of the question to know what it was.

"Do you think . . . I mean, now that Dylan's out of the picture for good . . . if I were to . . ."

". . . ask her out?"

"Do you think she'd go?"

Robin smiled. "I think she'd be a fool not to."

Tara was no fool.

"I don't get it," Greg Davis had sneered. "A girl like that. What the hell does she see in a lightweight like Alec?"

"Alec isn't a lightweight," Robin's mother had protested. "He's sweet and he's sensitive—"

"He's a goddamn wimp. What that girl needs is a man."

Robin wondered now if her father had set his sights on Tara even then, if he'd deliberately set out to sabotage his own son.

Some men should never have sons.

I hear he eats his young.

She sat up in bed, careful not to disturb Blake. She stared down at his handsome face, his mouth partly open in sleep, nighttime stubble grazing his cheeks and jaw. He'd been so good about everything, so patient and understanding. If he was upset about Alec running off with his car—and how could he not be?—he hadn't taken it out on her. Unlike her father, who'd always found a way to blame everyone else whenever anything didn't go exactly according to his plan, Blake had been quick to shoulder part of the responsibility for what Alec had done. "I should never have left my fob out where he could just pick it up," he'd offered generously.

"You couldn't have known he'd do something like this."

"I should have at least considered the possibility. It was careless."

She reached over and gently flicked several stray hairs away from his eyes. He was right—he was not her father. They weren't anything alike.

Still, she couldn't blame her father for everything, despite the temptation to do exactly that. She wasn't a child. At some point, you had to grow up, accept responsibility for your own actions. You could blame your parents for only so long.

Wasn't that what she regularly advised clients?

Maybe she wasn't such a bad therapist after all.

Try to remember this resolve in the morning, she told herself, about to lie back down when she heard the rumble of tires on gravel. She got out of bed and opened the bedroom window, straining to hear more.

Had she heard anything at all?

It was several more seconds before she heard a car door close. In the next instant, she was downstairs and at the front door. The second after that, she was outside, her eyes straining through the darkness.

Slowly a figure emerged.

Her brother.

Thank God.

She was assaulted by a multitude of conflicting emotions—anger, gratitude, apprehension. Above all, relief. She burst into tears. "Alec, what the hell . . . ?"

He stopped several feet from where she stood, his sigh sending ripples through the heavy air. "Follow me," he said.

–TWENTY-FOUR–

"Where are we going?" Robin demanded. "And where in God's name have you been?"

Alec had already started up the path to the road. Robin raced to catch up to him.

"Where have you been?" she asked again as she reached his side. "We've been worried sick. Why didn't you answer your phone?"

"Don't have one." He stuffed his hands into the pockets of his jeans and refused to look at her.

"What do you mean, you don't have one?"

"Tossed it in the trash before I left San Francisco."

"You tossed it in the trash?"

"Yes. Are you going to keep repeating everything I say?"

"Why would you throw your phone in the garbage?" Robin asked, making a conscious effort to rephrase the question.

"Didn't want the police searching through its history," he said, as if this fact should be self-evident.

"You didn't want the police . . ." Robin left the sentence hanging. "Why not? What were you afraid they'd find?"

He shrugged, brought his fingers to his lips, his eyes searching the darkness. "*Ssh,*" he said.

"What do you mean, *ssh*? Don't shush me."

"There are ears everywhere."

"It's almost one o'clock in the morning. Who do you think is out here?"

"Oh, you'd be surprised who might be listening."

"Where the hell have you been? And where the hell are we going?" Robin asked as he turned left at the road.

"Nowhere in particular."

"We just happen to be walking toward our father's new house?"

"Not quite so imposing in the dark, is it?" Alec said.

It was her turn to stop. "You called it the biggest fucking house in Red Bluff."

"So I did."

"How did you know that unless you'd seen it?"

"Lucky guess?"

"Alec . . ."

"Come on," he urged. "Enough questions. Can't we just go for a pleasant evening stroll?"

"Evening was six hours ago. Are you going to tell me where you've been since then? How could you just take off in Blake's car like that?" She continued without pause. "Do you know how . . . ?"

". . . stupid that was?" Alec said, finishing her question.

Robin felt a pang of guilt. "Stupid" had been their father's favorite insult for his son. "It was *reckless,* Alec," she said. "What if Sheriff Prescott had seen you . . ."

"Oh, he saw me."

"He saw you?"

"You're doing it again."

"What the *fuck,* Alec? What do you mean, he saw you?"

"Okay, okay. Take it down a notch. Look over there." He pointed down the road.

"What am I looking at? I don't see anything."

"Down there. Under that big tree."

Robin strained to see through the darkness. "I still don't see . . . Is that a car?"

"A patrol car, if I'm not mistaken."

"Sheriff Prescott?"

"Or one of his deputies. He's been on my tail since I left the house this afternoon."

"You knew he was watching you when you took Blake's car?"

"Not right away, no. But we're kind of in the middle of nowhere. Not hard to figure out when you're being followed."

Robin sank down onto the grass at the side of the road. "I'm not taking another step until you tell me what's going on."

Alec lowered himself to the ground beside her, crossing his legs and tearing at the surrounding grass with his fingers. "I'm sorry. I honestly didn't plan to take your fiancé's car."

"Then why did you?"

"I don't know. I was tired, confused. Being back in that house, seeing the old mudroom, being around Melanie, hearing Landon rocking away. I guess I panicked."

Robin nodded. Panic was a feeling she understood all too well.

"I saw Blake's fob on the table by the front door, and next thing I knew, I was behind the wheel—car drives real nice, by the way—and heading for the highway. Until I spotted the patrol car in the rearview mirror and decided that maybe it wasn't such a good idea."

"But you didn't come home."

"This isn't my home," he said.

Robin sighed in frustration. "You know what I mean."

"Yeah, I do. And I'm sorry about taking Blake's car and sorry about not contacting you. It was inconsiderate, to say the least."

"Yes, you're very good at saying the least. So, that's it? You just went for a drive?"

He sighed. "I went to Walmart."

"You went to Walmart?" she repeated, the question out of her mouth before she could stop it.

"I needed some clothes, some fresh underwear, a toothbrush. Stuff like that. Figured I might as well buy them in case I'm here for a while. And if I'm being honest, I was probably hoping to lose that damn deputy, or at least bore the guy to death. I spent hours in that fucking store. I bet I can tell you the price of every damn item on their shelves."

"Walmart doesn't stay open all night. Where'd you go after the store closed? To see Dad?"

"Are you kidding?" Alec looked genuinely shocked. He began rubbing his jaw. "That's the last fucking place I'd go."

"So where *did* you go?"

"Well, I was pretty hungry by that point and I gave some thought to coming home. But then I remembered Melanie saying something about hot dogs and beans, and that didn't appeal to me a whole lot, so I went to this new sushi restaurant over on Aloha Street. You been there yet?"

You went to a sushi restaurant? Robin repeated silently, biting her lower lip to keep from saying it out loud.

"It's good. I was surprised." He threw a fistful of grass into the air. It disappeared in the darkness. "Anyway, the patrol car was parked down the street when I got out, and even though I'd pretty much abandoned my plans for the great escape, I still wasn't ready to come home. So I went to the movies. Saw the new one with Melissa McCarthy. She's great. Sat through it twice. I actually went out and bought another ticket. Didn't want the sheriff arresting me for trying to sneak in without paying."

"I take it they were still waiting for you when you left the theater."

"They were probably hoping for some kind of high-speed chase up Highway 5. Something to tell their grandkids about. But my heart wasn't in it, so I just drove around until I figured everyone had gone to bed, then came back. Okay? Satisfied?" He pushed himself to his feet, brushed the grass off the seat of his pants. "Remind me to take my purchases out of the car when we get back to the house."

Robin clambered to her feet. "Were you really on your way to Canada when the police picked you up?" she asked as they started back toward the house.

"British Columbia's one of my favorite places," Alec answered. "Tara and I talked about moving there one day."

Robin held her breath at the mention of Tara's name, waiting for him to say more.

"How are you and Melanie getting along these days?" he asked instead.

"Okay, I guess," she answered. "She hasn't changed much."

"People don't change, Robin. You're the therapist. You should know that."

"To be fair . . ."

"Oh, no, please. Don't be fair. Our sister's a cunt and you know it."

Robin swallowed a gasp at the word "cunt." It had been Tara's favorite word for Melanie.

"Tara used to say that Melanie was Dad in a dress," Alec said. "You know what she needs, don't you?"

"Please don't tell me she needs to get laid."

Alec laughed, inadvertently kicking a pebble at his feet and bending down to scoop it up before throwing it back into the night. "How long do you think it's been, anyway?"

"I can't say I've ever given the matter any thought."

"You don't suppose it could be since she got pregnant with Landon, do you? I mean, you'd get pretty cranky, too, if you hadn't had sex in almost two decades."

"I can't imagine . . ."

"What? That she has? Or that she hasn't?"

"Either," Robin said, turning down their driveway. "Besides, she was like that before she got pregnant."

"Like what?"

"You know like what."

"I want to hear you say it."

"No."

"Why not?"

"Because it's not nice to call your sister a . . ."

". . . cunt? Go on, you can do it."

"I won't."

"I dare you. I double dare you."

Robin was laughing now. "You're crazy."

The front door opened. Melanie appeared in the doorway, framed by the light of the hall behind her. She was wearing a pair of blue cotton pajamas and an expression of weary exasperation. "What the hell is going on out here?"

"Alec is back," Robin said, trying to keep the laughter gurgling inside her throat from escaping.

"So I see. Nice of you to come home, Alec. Are you intent on broadcasting your presence to the whole neighborhood?"

"Sorry about that," Alec said. Then under his breath, "Told you she's a cunt."

"Stop it."

The two of them collapsed in a fresh fit of giggles.

"What's the matter with you?" Melanie said. "Are you ten years old?"

"Sorry," Robin managed to spit out as Melanie turned on her heel and disappeared inside the house.

"Way to go, Robin," Alec said. "Now you've made her mad."

Robin motioned toward Blake's car. "Don't forget your stuff."

Alec used the fob to unlock the rear passenger door of the Lexus. It made a loud squeaking noise, as if in protest. He removed half a dozen large shopping bags from the backseat, handing half of them to Robin as he looked toward Landon's bedroom. "Looks like we woke him up."

Robin shook her head. "No. He's always standing there."

Alec waved at his nephew. Landon immediately disappeared from view. "Do you think he was there the night of the shootings? That he might have seen something?"

Was Alec curious, or was he afraid? Robin couldn't help wondering. "I don't know. I tried to talk to him once about it, but no luck."

"Maybe I'll give it a try."

"Alec . . ." She wanted to ask if he and Tara had crossed paths in San Francisco, if seeing her again had reopened old wounds. *Did you do it?* she asked with her eyes. *Are you guilty?*

"What?"

She shook her head. "Nothing." It was late. She was exhausted. And if she was completely honest with herself, she was afraid of what Alec's answer might be.

—TWENTY-FIVE—

The law office of McAllister and Associates was located on the second floor of a red-brick building at the corner of Main and Crittenden, half a block from the bright blue, two-story concrete building that housed Davis Developers. Melanie pulled into a parking space midway between the two, and the three siblings emerged from the front and back seats of the car almost simultaneously.

Robin looked toward her father's office. "What do you think will happen to Dad's business if . . . ?" She let the sentence dangle, unfinished.

". . . he croaks?" Alec finished for her. "I think you mean *when*, not *if*."

"Guess we'll worry about that *if and when* the time comes," Melanie said, pulling open the outer door of the brick building.

"I think I remember Jeff McAllister," Alec said as they headed up the steep flight of stairs to the office. "Short guy, right?"

"Tiny. Dad used to say his balls were bigger than he was."

"The man's a poet," Alec said.

Melanie pushed the door open without knocking. "We're here to see Jeff McAllister," she announced to the young woman behind an old-fashioned wooden desk. "I'm Melanie Davis. This is my brother, Alec, and my sister, Robin."

The young woman smiled, revealing two large dimples and a prominent upper gum. "I'll tell Mr. McAllister you're here. If you'd care to have a seat . . ." She indicated the four white plastic chairs, two sitting at right angles to the other two, against ecru-colored walls covered with framed mottoes: It's Always Darkest Before the Dawn, read one. Everyone's Entitled to at Least One Good Day, began another. This Is Not One of Yours.

Not exactly designed to give one confidence, Robin thought.

"We'll stand," Melanie said, perhaps thinking the same thing.

"You're sure he's a real lawyer?"

"This isn't L.A.," Melanie reminded her.

Robin's body ached to sit down. She'd spent the balance of last night tossing and turning, worrying about Alec, about their father, about Cassidy, about everything that had happened and everything that might happen, unable to fall back to sleep. As anxious as she was to leave Red Bluff, how could she go anywhere until they knew what had happened? At the very least, she had to know the extent of her brother's involvement.

Melanie had called Jeff McAllister first thing in the

morning, and he'd agreed to see them at one o'clock that afternoon. Blake had a conference call scheduled for two o'clock and hadn't been able to join them.

"You'll be fine," Blake told Robin as they were leaving. "Just remember to breathe."

Not so easy, she thought now, her eyes traveling to six black-and-white photographs of rodeo scenes hanging on the opposite wall. She took four deep breaths, one immediately following the other.

"Are you going to faint again?" Melanie asked.

"No. Sorry." *Sorry for breathing.*

"They're here," she heard the receptionist whisper into her phone, not bothering with names.

Seconds later, Jeff McAllister was standing in front of them, his right arm outstretched to shake their hands. He had a grip of steel, as if to make up for his lack of height, but Robin thought he had a nice face. It was round and reassuring. She estimated his age as mid-sixties. He still had all his hair.

"Very nice to meet you," he said. "We were all so shocked to hear about the shootings. How is your father doing?"

"Not great," Melanie said. "It appears my brother is in need of legal counsel."

The receptionist smiled shyly at Alec.

Melanie shot the young woman a look that said, *You've got to be kidding.*

The receptionist immediately began moving papers around on her desk, as if she'd just remembered something important.

"This way, please." McAllister led them toward the inner offices. His was the last of three and occupied the corner.

"This is as far as you go," Alec told his sisters when they reached McAllister's door.

"You've got to be kidding," Melanie said, this time out loud. She was still bristling minutes later, as she and Robin sat fidgeting on the uncomfortable plastic chairs in the reception area.

"We could go for a coffee," Robin suggested.

"Not thirsty."

"This may take a while."

"You go, if you want."

"No. I . . ."

Melanie's cell phone rang. She reached inside her purse and brought it to her ear. "Hello?" Her face immediately softened, and she turned away, lowering her chin. "Hi. Yeah, I'm okay. It's been a little rough." She stood up, took several steps away from Robin. "Uh-huh. Yeah. That would be great. Okay. Sure. I really appreciate it. Okay. See you later." She returned to her seat, dropping her phone into her purse and leaning her head back against the wall.

"Who was that?" Robin asked.

"No one."

"Obviously it was someone."

"It was just a friend."

"What friend?" To Robin's knowledge, her sister didn't have any friends. It was one of the few things they had in common.

"Just someone I know. What's the big deal?"

"It's not a big deal. I'm just curious."

"There's nothing to be curious about."

"Was it a man?" Robin pressed, mindful of the conversation she'd had with Alec the previous night. "Are you seeing someone?"

"Seriously?" Melanie asked. "That's what you're concerned about? With everything else that's going on, you're asking me if I'm seeing anyone?"

"Are you?" Robin said.

Melanie rolled her eyes toward the recessed ceiling. "No, of course not. Don't be ridiculous."

"Why is it ridiculous? You're still young and attractive."

"And my son's still autistic."

"Which doesn't mean you can't have a social life. Come on. There must have been *some* men over the years."

"What are you asking me? If I've had lovers?"

"Have you?"

Melanie slumped down in her seat, stretching her long legs out in front of her, her denim skirt riding up on her thighs.

"*Dad in a dress,*" Robin heard her brother say.

"There've been a few," Melanie surprised her by admitting.

"Really? Who?"

"Seriously?" Melanie said again.

"Anybody I know?"

There was such a long pause that Robin assumed Melanie either hadn't heard her or was deliberately ignoring the question. "You remember Steve Clark?" she asked just as Robin had given up hope of a response and was reconsidering going out for that cup of coffee.

"Steve Clark?" Robin flipped the name over on her tongue. "You mean that fat kid with the bad complexion who used to follow you around in high school?"

"He lost weight and his skin cleared up. He actually looks pretty good now."

"You're sleeping with him?"

"Not anymore, no. This was years ago. He married Pamela Haggar. You remember her?"

Robin shook her head.

"She was fat, too. Still is, actually. They have three kids, a boy and twin girls, all under the age of five."

"Who else?" Robin asked. "You said that was years ago."

"Oh, God. Let's see." Melanie sighed, although she was clearly warming to her subject. "Mark Best . . . Surely you remember him."

Robin narrowed her eyes, a picture taking shape in her mind. "Tall, dark hair, green eyes? Played basketball?"

"That's the one."

"Was he? The best, I mean?"

Melanie chuckled. "Sadly he was not." She shook her head. "No. That honor would have to go to Ronnie Simon." She nodded, agreeing with her own assessment. "Yep. He was something else."

"I don't think I know him."

"No, you wouldn't. You were long gone when they moved here."

"They?"

"He and his wife and kids."

"He was married?"

"Still is."

"Did you know?"

"Of course."

"Was that him just now, on the phone?"

"No. That was months ago."

"What happened?"

"What usually happens. It ended. And don't you dare get all judgmental. Like you've never had an affair with a married man?"

Robin shook her head. She remembered the damage her father's multiple affairs had done to her family, and she had made a solemn vow that she would never knowingly sleep with a married man.

"Can I get you ladies anything? Something to drink, perhaps?" the receptionist asked.

"No, thank you," the women said together.

"Were you in love with him?" Robin ventured after several seconds.

"With who? Ronnie Simon? Don't be insane."

Another moment of silence.

"Have you ever been in love?" Robin asked.

"As if I have time for that nonsense."

"Love isn't nonsense."

"It isn't?"

"What about Landon's father?"

"That jerk? Biggest mistake of my life."

"Do you ever hear from him?"

"Never. Are we done with the interrogation yet?"

"I didn't think it was an interrogation."

"What would you call it?" Melanie asked.

"A conversation?" Robin asked in return. She'd actually been enjoying the last few minutes.

"Conversations usually work both ways," Melanie said. "How would you feel if I were to pepper you with questions about *your* sex life?"

"Go ahead," Robin said, her back stiffening, as if she were physically bracing herself for what was to follow. "Ask me anything."

Melanie shrugged. "I have nothing to ask."

"You're not curious about my life at all?"

"Not particularly. I think I know pretty much all I need to know."

"And what's that?"

Melanie swiveled around in her chair, crossing one knee over the other and staring directly at Robin. "I don't think you really want to get into this now."

"Might as well," Robin said, tingles of anxiety starting to ferret through her veins. "Not much else to do."

"*Breathe,*" she heard Blake say.

"Fine. I think you're a spoiled brat who assumes the world revolves around her."

The breath caught in Robin's lungs. "But I *don't* think—"

"Sorry. I thought you were interested in what *I* thought," Melanie said.

"I am, but . . ." Invisible hands reached for her throat.

"I think you feel entitled and superior. You and Alec both. The two of you always uniting against me, laughing behind my back. Or right to my face, judging by last night."

"We weren't . . ." Unseen fingers pressed down on her throat.

"You think you're better than me. You think you have

all the answers because you have a college diploma, and you think that gives you the right to sit in judgment of my life, my parenting, my relationships . . ."

"I was just trying to get to know you."

Breathe. Just breathe.

"Why? What's the point? Are you planning to stick around when this is over?"

Robin said nothing.

Melanie sneered. "Yeah, that's what I thought."

"It doesn't mean that we . . ."

"What? Can't be friends? News flash—we've *never* been friends."

"Because you've never given me a chance," Robin said, the words shooting directly from her lungs. "You've hated me since the day I was born."

Melanie looked toward the ceiling, as if she were seriously considering what Robin had said. "You know, you might finally be right about something." She shrugged. "Anyway, you were Mom's favorite, so what does it matter? What's that stupid saying—'It is what it is'? When this is all over, when our father dies and Alec is either in jail or back in San Francisco, you're going to return to L.A. and marry the Ken doll of your dreams. And maybe it'll work out, and maybe it won't, but one thing is certain: I'm going to be stuck here in Red Bluff."

"You don't have to be stuck," Robin said.

Melanie raised both eyebrows.

"You'll have money," Robin said. "You'll be able to afford professional help for Landon. You can put him in a special school . . ."

"You mean an institution."

"No," Robin said. "I was thinking maybe an art school." Then, "I don't know."

"Really? There's something you don't know?"

Robin sank back in her chair, anxiety swirling through her head, her energy spent. "Okay. You win. I give up."

"And Cassidy? You gonna give her up, too?"

"I won't abandon Cassidy."

"No? How noble. What does that mean in practical terms?"

The receptionist was suddenly standing in front of them. "Are you sure I can't get you anything?"

Robin pushed herself to her feet. "Actually I think I'll take a walk." She crossed to the door and opened it. "I could use some air."

"No need to hurry back," she heard Melanie say as the door closed behind her.

–TWENTY-SIX–

Breathe. Just breathe.

Robin stood on the sidewalk in front of Jeff McAllister's office building and gulped at the surrounding air as if it were water. "Damn it," she whispered. Just when she thought she and her sister were making progress, that they were on the verge of a real breakthrough, that they might actually be able to forge a relationship, reality had to rear its ugly head, like a rattlesnake disturbed at the side of the road by an unwary hiker.

How many times did she have to bang her head against this same brick wall?

"That's it," she said out loud. "I'm done."

"I'm sorry," someone said. "Are you talking to me?"

Robin looked up to see a woman perhaps a decade her senior standing in front of her, an inquisitive look on her wide face. "Oh, no. I'm sorry. Just talking to myself, I'm afraid."

The woman laughed. "I do it all the time. No worries."

Unfortunately, I have nothing but worries, Robin thought, as the woman continued on her way.

Robin looked up and down the long main street, stopping at the bright blue building that housed Davis Developers. It had been years since she'd been inside the attractive two-story structure; her father had frowned on unscheduled drop-ins. She remembered the place as a beehive of activity—employees rushing back and forth between offices, phones constantly ringing, designers toiling away to create something new and innovative, draftsmen making last-minute changes to blueprints, marketers struggling to develop fresh campaigns, the sales staff trying to persuade new clients to come on board. In addition to the creative staff, a substantial support staff served the business side of the company—the chief financial officer, two accountants, an office manager, and at least a dozen secretaries and assistants.

Still, only one person really counted, the one man they were all there to serve.

Her father.

Davis Developers was his business, his baby, his mistress. Robin thought it was probably the only thing, other than himself, that he'd ever truly loved. Nothing else came close. Not his wife. Not his other women. Certainly not his children.

"Cassidy," she'd heard him whisper, his eyes searching the hospital room for the child who was not his own, but who had somehow managed to scale the wall of his self-absorption, a feat that none of his natural-born children had been able to achieve. *I won't abandon you,* she thought now, recalling the look of skepticism on Melanie's face, and wondering how Blake would react to the idea of Cassidy returning with Robin and him

to L.A. She desperately hoped she wouldn't be forced to choose between them.

So don't tell me I have no worries, she called silently after the woman as she disappeared down the street. Taking another deep breath, Robin opened the elaborately carved wooden door of her father's building and stepped inside the small lobby. She was greeted by a one-two punch of silence and frigid air.

"It's freezing in here," she said, more to herself than to the attractive, rosy-cheeked blonde behind the marble-and-glass reception desk. The nameplate on the desk's black marble surface identified her as Shannon Leacock. She was wearing a heavy white sweater over her yellow sundress.

"I know. They keep it so cold," Shannon commiserated. "Can I help you?"

"It's so quiet," Robin said, not really sure what she was doing here. "I wasn't expecting it to be so quiet."

"Well, we're operating with a skeleton staff at the moment. Until we know . . . I'm sorry. Do you have an appointment?"

"No," Robin said quickly. "I'm . . . I'm Robin Davis."

"Robin Davis? Robin *Davis*?" Shannon repeated. "Are you related to Mr. Davis?"

"I'm his daughter."

Shannon jumped to her feet, almost upending her black leather chair. "I'm so sorry. Your father . . . has something happened? Is he . . . ?"

"Still hanging in there."

"Oh, thank God. Just a minute, I'll get Jackie. She's our office manager." Shannon grabbed her phone, pressing the numbers for Jackie Ingram's extension before Robin could stop her.

Jackie Ingram was probably the last person Robin wanted to talk to right now. "It's not necess—"

"Oh, no worries," Shannon said.

Dear God.

"She'll be right with you," Shannon said, hanging up the phone. "How's the little girl? Cassidy, right?"

"Yes, Cassidy," Robin agreed. "It looks like she'll be okay."

"Well, thank God for that. Oh, here comes Jackie now."

Robin turned as Jackie Ingram rounded the corner. A look of relief instantly flooded the woman's face. Clearly she'd been expecting Melanie. *No worries,* Robin thought with a smile. *She has that effect on all of us.*

"Is . . . has something . . . your father . . . ?" Jackie began, but was unable to complete a sentence.

"There's been no change."

Jackie nodded, tapping her hand lightly on her heart. She was wearing a dark blue suit, and her hair was pulled into the same soft bun that she'd had the first time they'd met, in Greg Davis's hospital room. She wasn't quite as attractive as Robin remembered—her features a little too doughy, her nose a tad too prominent. She had dark circles under her eyes and looked every bit of her fifty-plus years. It was hard to imagine her father choosing her as a lover. Especially with Tara waiting for him at home.

Unless, of course, Tara wasn't waiting, at home or anywhere else.

What's good for the goose . . .

Jackie Ingram stared at her expectantly. "Is there something I can do for you?"

"I don't know," Robin began. *Why was she here?* "I don't know." Tears filled her eyes and began streaming down her cheeks.

"Why don't we go into my office?" Jackie wrapped her arms around Robin and led her down the hall without waiting for an answer.

"I'm sorry. I'm really embarrassed," Robin said as they entered the first office on the left and Jackie directed her to one of the two beige velvet tub chairs opposite her desk. A tissue appeared in her hand, as if she'd pulled it magically from her sleeve, and she handed it to Robin, then sat down in the chair beside her.

"There's no need to be embarrassed."

Robin blew her nose, then dabbed at her eyes, although it did no good. The tears kept coming. "I'm sorry," she said again. "I can't seem to stop."

"It's okay," Jackie said. "This can't be an easy time for you."

"You're very kind." Behind Jackie's desk a large window revealed a view of mountains in the distance, peeking out beyond the tops of the surrounding buildings. Inside the crowded office, stacks of *Architectural Digest* and assorted other architecture and design magazines stretched across the beige-carpeted floor, climbing up the pale blue walls like vines.

"Are these your grandchildren?" Robin asked, referring to three framed photographs on the wall to her right, one of two little boys bearing proud, toothless grins, another of three little girls in lacy dresses, the last of a smiling baby asleep in its mother's arms.

Was my father really sleeping with a grandmother?

"Aren't they beautiful? Three girls, three boys. But you didn't come here to talk about my grandchildren."

"To be honest, I have no idea why I'm here."

"You want to know about your father and me," Jackie Ingram stated without rancor.

"My sister was out of line the other day," Robin said. "I'm sorry."

"Your sister *was* out of line," Jackie agreed. "But she was also right."

"You were sleeping with my father?"

"We were having an affair, yes," Jackie said, making the subtle correction.

"When? For how long? If you don't mind my asking."

"I don't mind," Jackie said. "Let's see. I came to work here two years ago, after Lisa Holt left, and it probably started about six months after that. Did you know Lisa?"

Robin shook her head. "Was my father having an affair with her, too?"

"I can't say for sure. But it wouldn't surprise me. I'm sorry. I don't mean to upset you."

"You're not. I've known about my father's extracurricular activities for years. I just thought maybe he'd changed after he married Tara."

"You mean because she was so much younger than he was?"

"Yes," Robin admitted. "I guess I figured she'd be more than enough for him."

"I actually think that was part of the problem."

"I don't understand."

"Can I be blunt?"

Robin almost laughed. Tara was dead, her father was gravely injured, and she was sitting in an office being comforted by her father's last known mistress. A grandmother, no less. "By all means," she said, lifting her hands in resignation. "Be blunt."

"I think your father didn't quite know what he was getting into when he married Tara. Not only was she much younger, but she also had a very young child. He'd forgotten what it was like to have a youngster underfoot all day, every day. Not that he didn't love Cassidy. He did. But as she got older . . . well, you know what girls Cassidy's age are like. They're not the easiest. She and her mother fought a lot. Your father hated that. And Tara hated having to share a house with your sister and that poor boy of hers. She was always after him to move into a place of their own. And then there were problems . . . in the bedroom."

"Problems?"

"Unfortunately, instead of making your father feel young again, Tara made him feel pretty old pretty damn fast. Not her fault, really. But she had a lot of energy. Your father had a hard time keeping up, if you get my drift."

Robin nodded, trying to erase the image of her father and Tara in bed together that was already forming in her mind.

"He once told me that he'd forgotten what you thirty-year-olds were like in bed." Jackie chuckled, remembering. "He was worried about his heart, said he was afraid she was going to kill him. Not intentionally, of course." She took a deep breath. "Do you want anything to drink? Some water, perhaps? You're looking a little . . ."

Robin made a deliberate effort to relax the muscles in her face. "No, nothing. Thank you. I'm fine. You were saying . . ."

"You're sure you want to hear this?"

"Quite sure." *Actually, not sure at all.*

"It was just that your father had this image of himself as a great lover. Don't get me wrong—he *was*. For a man his age, and for a woman *my* age. Girls your age expect more . . . stamina. And these days they want—no, they *demand*—orgasms. Women my age—well, we're just happy the man shows up. We don't expect—hell, we don't want—all-nighters. They're painful, and truthfully, they're a little boring. We've had the years of foreplay. We know what works; we know what doesn't. We just want to get to the point. Am I shocking you?"

"No." *Yes.*

"At any rate, what I'm getting at here is that I think your father liked the fact that with me he didn't have to work so hard. He *needed* to be admired. I admired him. It's as simple as that."

"And your husband?" Robin asked. "What about his needs?"

"Oh, my husband lost interest in sex years ago. At least with me."

"He was seeing other women?"

"Other men, as it turns out," Jackie said with a shrug. "Amazing how you can live with someone for years and have no idea who they really are."

"What about how angry he was when he learned of your affair, the threats he made?"

"Purely for show. A way of keeping up the pretense. Not many people know about his other . . . interests."

"So you don't think . . ."

"That he shot your father? Not a chance. Why would he? I actually think he was relieved when he found out about Greg and me. It meant he didn't have to feel so guilty anymore. And don't forget, your father was not only my lover but also a very generous employer. Now, God only knows what's going to happen, if I'll still have a job—" She broke off. "Anyway, not your concern."

"Can you think of anyone else who might have done this?" Robin asked, relieved that they were no longer talking about her father's sex life. "A disgruntled employee, an unhappy client . . . ?"

Jackie Ingram shook her head with such vehemence that the bun at the nape of her neck came loose, sending strands of dark hair cascading onto her shoulders. "Your father could be stubborn and imperious, even ruthless at times, and it's true that not everybody was a big fan, but to do something like this, to kill people, *to shoot a child,* no, I can't imagine any of our employees or clients ever being that angry." She paused. "Your father's not going to make it, is he?"

"It doesn't look good." Robin stood up. "I should go."

Jackie Ingram was immediately on her feet. "Will you tell him that we're all praying for him, that we . . . that *I* miss him."

"I will."

"Thank you."

"Thank *you*." Robin allowed the other woman to take her in her arms and hug her close. "I can find my way out."

"Take care," Jackie called after her.

Her sister and brother were waiting by the car when Robin emerged into the bright sunshine. "Told you that's where she was," Melanie said to Alec.

"I'm sorry," Robin said, a blanket of heat falling on her head. "Were you waiting long?"

"Long enough." Melanie unlocked the car doors and climbed behind the wheel. "Get in."

"Where are we going?" Robin asked, getting in beside her.

Melanie was pulling away from the curb even before Robin had her seat belt fastened. "To see a friend of mine."

—TWENTY-SEVEN—

"Are you going to tell me who this friend is?" Robin asked when Melanie failed to elaborate.

"Don't think so," her sister said.

"Is this the same friend you were talking to earlier?"

"Could be."

"Are we playing Twenty Questions?"

"Only if you insist on asking them."

Robin swiveled around in her seat to face her brother. "What happened with McAllister?"

"Confidential," he said.

"Seriously?" she asked. "Nobody's telling me anything?" Robin returned to her previous position, staring at the scenery beyond the side window as it quickly changed from urban to rural, barren fields taking the place of sidewalks and offices. The only constant was the heat, which rose like waves from the pavement. "And no one's curious about my visit to Dad's office?" she asked after several seconds had passed.

"Not particularly," said Alec.

"Not at all," said Melanie.

Clearly, her siblings weren't in the mood for conversation or speculation, so there was little point in trying to pursue either. They drove for a good five minutes without a word, the only sounds coming from the country music on the radio. Something about loss and heartache. *Welcome to the club.*

Her phone rang.

Thank God. At least someone wants to talk to me. Robin pulled the phone from her purse, saw it was Blake, and lifted it to her ear. "How's it going?"

"Slowly. Taking a fifteen-minute break," he told her. "Looks like I'm going to be tied up for the rest of the afternoon."

"That's okay. We won't be home for a while."

"Alec still with the lawyer?"

"No. He's done."

"Anything to report?"

"Apparently not."

"Okay, listen. Something you should know."

"What's that?"

"Landon—he went out shortly after you guys left. Hasn't come home."

Robin's eyes shot to her sister.

"What?" Melanie asked without looking at her.

"Okay, thanks," Robin said to Blake. "See you later." She returned the phone to her purse, debating whether or not to tell Melanie about Landon, imagining how the conversation might go.

"Blake says Landon's not home."

"So? He's allowed out. He's not a prisoner."

"I'm just saying . . ."

"Don't say."

She felt the car speed up, then slow down, then speed up again. "What's happening?"

"I think someone's following us," Melanie said.

Both Robin and her brother immediately spun around in their seats to look.

"Is it the sheriff?" Robin asked.

"It doesn't look like a patrol car," said Alec.

"Can you see who's driving?"

"No."

"Maybe they're not following us," Robin said.

"They've been behind us since we left Main Street. I'm pulling over."

"Maybe that's not such a good idea," Robin said.

"You have a better one?"

"Mom always said you shouldn't go looking for trouble," Robin reminded her sister as Melanie pulled the car to the side of the road and stopped.

"Yeah, and look where that philosophy got her. Maybe if she'd looked for trouble a little earlier, she'd still be alive." The car behind them continued past. "Okay. Good. Looks like I was wrong."

"No," Alec said. "Look. They're pulling over."

"Shit," said Robin when the dark blue Buick stopped about fifty yards down the road.

"Who the hell is that?" Melanie asked, as the driver exited the car and began walking toward them.

Despite the sun in her eyes, Robin had no trouble recognizing Dylan Campbell. There was no way to disguise either his swagger or the unspoken dare in the tilt of his head. "Shit," she said again.

"Is that who I think it is?" said Melanie.

"You gotta be kidding me," said Alec, pushing open his car door.

"Alec, don't . . . ," Robin began, but Alec was already out of the car. "Goddamn it." She opened her car door at the same time Melanie opened hers. A fistful of hot air hit her like a punch to the jaw, almost knocking her to the dry ground.

"Well, hail, hail," Dylan said. "Looks like the gang's all here."

"Why are you following us?" Robin said.

Dylan's face relaxed into a big grin. Despite the heat, he was dressed all in black, and seemed none the worse for wear. "That's my girl. No time wasted on foreplay. Hi, Melanie. You're looking well. And Alec. How you doin', buddy? Haven't seen you in forever."

"Forever isn't long enough, you piece of shit."

"At least this piece of shit wasn't in Red Bluff the night someone shot the face off his beloved ex-wife. Which I understand is more than can be said for you."

"Okay," Robin said, "you've said enough."

"Did you shoot her, Alec?" Dylan asked, ignoring her, and asking the question she was afraid to. "Did you kill Tara? Did you leave my little girl without a mother?"

"I wouldn't get too cocky if I were you," Robin said, her voice carrying more bravado than she actually felt. "That alibi of yours isn't all that airtight. You could easily have hired someone."

"You should know me better than that, Robin. I'm strictly a hands-on kind of guy. I'd never hire anyone to hurt Tara. If I wanted the bitch dead, I'd have taken care of it myself. I wouldn't let someone else have all the fun." He shook his head. "And I sure as hell wouldn't have left any witnesses." He pushed his hair away from his forehead, smiled as it fell right back. "Besides, I'm a changed man. Prison will do that to a guy. And I would have thought that you, of all people, would believe that everyone deserves a second chance. Gotta say, I'm kind of disappointed."

"Gotta say, I couldn't give a shit."

"What do you want, Dylan?" Melanie said.

"What do I want?" he repeated. "Well, let's see. For starters, access to my daughter would be nice."

"She doesn't want to see you," Robin said.

"I'm sure she could be persuaded, if *you* were to talk to her, get her to see reason."

"The reason being?"

"That I'm her daddy. Her *real* daddy. And I want to take care of her, make up for all the time we lost."

"Not happening."

"We'll talk to her," Melanie said. "See what we can do."

"What?" Robin gasped. "We'll do no such thing."

"The man has a right to see his daughter," Melanie said.

"Finally. The voice of reason." Dylan tipped an invisible hat toward Melanie.

"There is no way I am letting you anywhere near that little girl," Robin insisted.

"We'll talk to Cassidy," Melanie said as another car pulled to a stop behind them.

Robin watched the car door open and a pair of scuffed brown leather cowboy boots hit the gravel shoulder of the road.

"Is there a problem here?" Sheriff Prescott asked, the rest of him emerging from behind the wheel.

"Well, hello there, Sheriff," Dylan said. "Now isn't this a coincidence? Us all being out here together."

"Problems?" the sheriff asked again.

"Nothing we can't handle," said Melanie.

"Dylan was just leaving," Robin said.

Dylan nodded toward Alec. "When are you gonna arrest this man, Sheriff?"

"When I damn well feel like it, Dylan."

Dylan chuckled. "Okay. Seems like we're all a bit sensitive today. Must be the heat. Guess I'll get going, leave you guys to it. I'm staying at the Red Rooster Motel, if you need to get ahold of me. You'll talk to Cassidy?" he asked Melanie.

"I'll see what I can do."

"You'll do no such thing," Robin said as Dylan sauntered back to his car.

"Please don't tell me what I can and can't do."

"Well, you won't get any help from me," Robin said.

"When have I *ever* gotten any help from you?"

Robin bit down on her tongue to keep from snapping back as she watched Dylan get into his car and drive off.

"The man is Cassidy's biological father," Melanie said. "As far as I'm concerned, if he's willing to take Cassidy off my hands, then I'm more than willing to let him."

"There's no way I'll ever let him get his hooks into Cassidy," Robin said.

"You may not be able to stop him. He has rights, whether you like it or not. Whether Cassidy likes it or not. She's a minor. He's her father. What do you say, Sheriff?"

"I say that you'll probably have to talk to a lawyer about that," Prescott said. "Jeff McAllister, for instance. I hear you've already paid him a visit. Care to share, Alec?"

Alec laughed. "Not much in a sharing mood, I'm afraid."

"What are you doing here, Sheriff?" Robin asked. "Surely you have better things to do than trail after us all day."

"Just doing my job. Keeping tabs on the good citizens of Red Bluff. Hoping they stay out of trouble. You *do* know that the city limit is just a few miles up the road. Wouldn't want to see your brother get hauled off to jail because he was unfamiliar with the town's boundaries. Or you, for inadvertently aiding and abetting."

"My brother has no intention of leaving Red Bluff."

"Glad to hear it."

"So why don't you stop harassing us and concentrate on finding out who shot my family?" Robin said as the sheriff turned to leave.

"That's exactly what I'm trying to do, Robin. I'll be in touch." He climbed back in his car and drove off.

"Wow," Alec said to Robin. "When did you get so feisty?"

Robin spun toward her brother. "Shut the fuck up."

"Whoa. What?"

"Did you do it, Alec?"

"What?" he repeated, looking helplessly toward Melanie.

Melanie shrugged. The shrug said, *Don't look at me.*

"Because I gotta tell you," Robin continued, a line of perspiration wriggling down her neck, "I'm getting really sick and tired of all this bullshit."

"What bullshit?"

"I want you to stop with the excuses and the evasions and the smart mouth and tell me the truth."

"I *have* told you the truth."

"You didn't shoot anybody," Robin stated.

"I didn't shoot anybody," Alec confirmed.

"Then what the hell were you doing in Red Bluff that night? I need to know, and I need to know now. Do you hear me?"

"I can't tell you. If they call on you to testify in court . . ."

"Then I'll plead the fifth, or I'll lie, or God forbid, I'll tell the truth. God knows somebody around here has to start."

"Shit," Alec said.

"Now, Alec. Or I swear I'm going back to L.A. and you can deal with this crap on your own. Is that what you really want?"

There was a long pause. Alec swept his hair off his forehead, unconsciously mimicking Dylan Campbell. He looked up and down the dried-out, deserted stretch of country road, as if hoping for someone to come to his rescue. "I came to see Tara," he said finally, his voice so low that Robin had to strain to hear him.

It took another beat for his words to register. "You came to see Tara?"

"What do you mean, you came to see Tara?" Melanie demanded. "You were in their house that night?"

"No," Alec said quickly. "I never went inside. Tara and I were supposed to meet at the Riverbank Inn. She called around nine, said there were problems and she couldn't get away."

"Wait—go back," Melanie said. "What do you mean, you were supposed to meet?"

Robin fell back against the side of her sister's car, the heat of its exterior burning through her clothes. *So her suspicions about Alec and Tara had been correct.* "They were having an affair."

"It was more than an affair," Alec said sharply. "We were in love. We always have been. She knew marrying Dad had been a huge mistake. She was planning to leave him."

"Holy shit," said Melanie.

Robin stared at her brother, her eyes filling with tears. "I think you better start at the beginning."

—TWENTY-EIGHT—

"Can we at least get in the car, so I can put on the air conditioner?" Melanie pleaded.

The three siblings climbed back into the old Impala, Melanie in front, Robin and Alec in the back, Robin holding tight to her brother's hand. Melanie started the engine, and a weak blast of tepid air shot toward the backseat.

"It started about a year ago," Alec began without prompting. "Tara emailed me, said she was unhappy, that Dad was up to his old tricks, that she had no one to talk to, that she missed me, that sort of thing. I wasn't going to respond, but I never did have a whole lot of willpower where Tara was concerned, and soon we were emailing each other pretty much every day.

"I guess Dad figured that something was up, that Tara was unhappy and maybe getting restless," Alec continued, "because he suddenly agreed they should move into their own place. Tara had been after him to do that ever since they got married, but you know how stubborn Dad could be, and he wouldn't budge. Suddenly, out of the blue, he up and decides she's right—they need their own space. He's going to build her the home of her dreams, yada, yada, yada. Of course, since this is Dad, what he's going to build her is really the home of *his* dreams. He's making all the decisions—where they're going to build, how they're going to decorate. He knows everything, after all.

"Except what he *doesn't* know is that the prestigious decorating firm he hires, McMillan and Loftus, is a mere ten blocks from my apartment in San Francisco, which makes it very easy for Tara and me to get together.

"At first, nothing happened. We'd meet for coffee. We'd talk. The first time, she actually brought Cassidy with her. We pretended to be just a couple of old friends who'd happened to bump into each other on the street. Tara introduced me to Cassidy as Tom Richards, this guy she went to school with. Luckily, Cassidy didn't remember me, and I probably wouldn't have recognized her, she'd grown up so much. We went back to my apartment, I made the kid some hot chocolate, Tara and I pretended to catch up on old times. Anyway, after that, Tara usually came alone. It didn't take long for things to heat up. Soon I was driving three hours to Red Bluff on a semi-regular basis. We'd meet at various motels on the outskirts of town."

"And Dad never suspected?" Melanie asked.

"If he suspected Tara was having an affair, which frankly I doubt his ego would permit, he certainly never suspected it was with me."

"Okay," Robin said, perspiring profusely despite the now cooler air. "So you and Tara were having an affair—"

"We were in love," Alec corrected a second time.

"You were in love," Robin repeated. "Was she planning to tell Dad?"

"She was going to, but then there was the move to the new house and the house-warming party. She didn't want to embarrass Dad, and she didn't want to upset Cassidy, who for some inexplicable reason seems to really love our father. It just never felt like the right time. Plus Tara was worried about how Dad would react when she told him she was planning to leave him. I offered to be there with her, but she didn't think that was a good idea. We were going to figure it out that night, make concrete plans, but then she called, said there were problems and she wouldn't be able to make it, said she'd phone me later."

Alec looked toward the window, as if watching the scene play out in the reflection of the glass.

"When it was after midnight and she still hadn't phoned, I got worried and called her, but she didn't pick up. So I drove over to the house. As soon as I got to the street, I saw the police cars and the ambulance. I thought maybe Dad had had a heart attack when she told him she was leaving, or that he'd done something crazy, maybe threatened her and she'd called the cops. To be honest, I don't know *what* I thought. So I drove around for a while, trying to figure out what I should do, and I ended up driving back to San Francisco. Next thing I knew, the two of you were leaving frantic messages on my voice mail."

"But why not just tell us the truth?"

"Honestly, at first I was too stunned. When you told me that Dad had been shot, my first thought was that

Tara had shot him. Then you told me that Tara had been shot, too, and my next thought was that Dad had shot her and then turned the gun on himself. But then you said that someone had shot Cassidy, which was just inconceivable, and that it looked like some sort of home invasion."

He slumped forward in his seat, lowering his head into his hands.

"I couldn't believe it. I didn't know what to do. There didn't seem to be anything to be gained by telling anyone about Tara and me. I thought it would only complicate things, and things were already complicated enough. And then a few days later, you started asking about my car, and I realized that the sheriff had found out I was in Red Bluff, and I knew how it would look and that nobody would believe me. It was only my word that Tara was going to leave Dad. The sheriff was probably going to assume I killed Tara and shot Dad and Cassidy because Tara had decided *not* to leave him. He'd say that I was furious at being made a fool of a second time and I wasn't going to let Tara get away with it again."

"Would he be right?" Melanie asked from the front seat.

"Shit," said Alec, looking imploringly at Robin. "You see."

"Just asking," Melanie said.

Alec turned back to Robin. "Look. As motives go, it's a bit of a stretch to think I would still be carrying a grudge after more than five years, especially if I hadn't seen Tara in all that time. But once I admit to an ongoing affair, it's a whole different ball game. Put it together with my being here in Red Bluff that night, and they have a pretty solid case."

"What did McAllister say?"

"He agrees. Says there'll be plenty of time for the truth if and when they make an arrest. In the meantime, it's not necessary for me to do their job for them."

Robin sank back in her seat. "Shit," she said. *What else was there to say?*

"I'm sorry," Alec said. "I screwed up."

"That's putting it mildly." Melanie threw the car into gear and pulled away from the shoulder.

"I didn't shoot them. I swear it."

"I believe you," Robin said, watching Melanie's eyes narrow in the rearview mirror.

"Thank you."

"Where are we going?" Robin asked her sister.

"Same place we were headed before this little episode of *True Confessions*. Fasten your seat belts, everyone," she said, channeling Bette Davis in *All About Eve*. "Looks like we're in for a bumpy ride."

They arrived at an isolated stretch of land on the outskirts of Red Bluff less than ten minutes later. Melanie got out of the car to open a wooden gate, then turned the car onto the wide dirt path inside the wire fence that ran along the treeless perimeter of the property. It was the polar opposite of the lush farmland along the Sacramento River. *We might as well be on the moon,* Robin thought, although she understood why tourists might find it fascinating. *This place gives new meaning to the phrase "wide-open spaces."*

A bright orange barn stood to the right of the path, a small log cabin to the left, surrounded by dry yellowing grass everywhere she looked. A rusty old Chevy was parked to one side of the cabin, a shiny Harley-Davidson on the other, leaving no doubt in her mind whose property this was.

"Everybody out." Melanie turned off the car's engine and opened the door.

The smell of horses instantly invaded Robin's nostrils, causing her to sneeze three times in quick succession.

"This way." Melanie strode purposefully toward the barn.

"You going to tell us why we're here?" Alec asked as he and Robin trailed after her.

In reply, Melanie pointed past the barn to the field beyond.

Robin brought her hands to her forehead to shield her eyes. Even with her sunglasses on, the light was almost blinding, there being no shade to provide even minimal protection from the blistering sun. In the distance she saw two men on horseback, their gaits measured and in complete sync. "Is that Landon?" Robin asked, straining to find something familiar in the black-filled outlines of the men's faces.

"It is," Melanie said, a surprising but unmistakable trace of pride in her voice.

"And the man with him is Donny Warren?"

"It is," Melanie said again, the pride lingering.

"What's going on?" Alec asked. "Who's Donny Warren?"

The riders turned in their direction, one of them waving. "A friend of Landon's," Melanie said. "He's been teaching him how to ride."

Robin had read reports that animals—dogs and especially horses—could be an effective tool in the treatment of autism.

"He called while you were with McAllister, said Landon was with him and that I shouldn't worry."

"Very interesting," Alec said.

Robin sensed something in her brother's tone that made her uneasy.

"Correct me if I'm wrong," he continued, confirming her worst fears, "but didn't Cassidy tell the sheriff that there were two men in Dad's house the night of the shootings, and that both men were tall and muscular?"

"Alec . . . ," Robin warned, although the question wasn't entirely unreasonable.

"Just asking," Alec said with a sly smile.

The men on horseback drew closer, their faces emerging from the shadows. Beneath the wide-brimmed hat he wore, Landon was grinning from ear to ear.

Robin thought it was the first time she'd ever seen her nephew smile.

Melanie was also smiling, albeit faintly, a sight almost as rare.

"Hold on," Alec said, his eyes narrowing. "Are you fucking this guy?"

Melanie's head snapped toward her brother.

"You *are,*" Alec said. "You're fucking him."

"Shut up," Melanie said.

"Melanie's got a boyfriend; Melanie's got a boyfriend," he taunted.

"I'm warning you . . ."

"Don't get me wrong. I think it's terrific," Alec said as Donny Warren jumped off his dark brown horse, removing his hat and walking toward them. "Hypothetically, of course, if someone hated her father and Tara enough, she might enlist the help of her lover and son . . ."

"Shut the fuck up."

Robin sneezed.

"God bless you," Donny Warren said as he approached, pulling a tissue from the pocket of his jeans and offering it to Robin.

"Thank you."

"I'm Donny. You must be Robin. I think I saw you the other day on the side of the road."

Robin nodded. "Nice to meet you."

"And I'm Melanie's brother, Alec," Alec interjected, extending his hand and wincing as Donny shook it. "Whoa there, cowboy. That's some grip you've got."

"Sorry." Donny took a step back, and Robin saw that in profile his face was less intimidating than it appeared full on. There was a softness, even a twinkle, in his coal-black eyes. And despite the intense heat, he looked entirely comfortable in his deeply tanned skin, his checkered shirt unstained by sweat. *A man at peace with himself and his surroundings,* she thought. Robin couldn't imagine him killing anyone.

Then she remembered he'd served two tours in Afghanistan.

"I was explaining that you've been teaching Landon how to ride," Melanie said, watching as Landon dismounted from his dappled gray horse.

"Yeah. He's a quick learner. He did great today. Didn't you, Landon?"

Landon looked toward the ground at his feet, still holding tight to the horse's reins.

"It's very generous of you," Alec said, "to spend so much time with Landon."

"Well, I like the kid. And we both like horses and motorcycles," Donny said. "Plus I grew up with a brother with learning disabilities, so it's really no big deal for me. You want to come inside for a drink?"

"I think we better be heading back," Melanie said.

"Sure," Donny said. "Anytime." He glanced at Landon. "I'll take those, partner," he said, lifting the reins from Landon's hands.

"Come on, Landon," Melanie said.

"Nice meeting you," Donny said to Robin and Alec as they turned to leave. "Same time tomorrow, Landon? You, too," he said to Alec, "if you feel like going for a ride."

"Just might take you up on that," Alec said, smiling at Melanie.

"If somebody doesn't shoot you first," came Melanie's quick reply.

—TWENTY-NINE—

The call came the next morning.

"Robin?" The small voice vibrated with enthusiasm.

"Cassidy?" Robin responded.

"Guess what? The doctor says I'm ready to be discharged."

Robin looked toward Blake, who was sitting at the kitchen table, answering his email on his laptop.

"*What?*" he asked with his eyes.

"The doctor says Cassidy's ready to come home," she whispered. "That's fantastic, sweetheart. Did he say when exactly?"

"He said you can come and get me anytime. *Now,* even. I mean, if it isn't too much trouble."

What do I do? Robin wondered. This wasn't her home anymore, and Melanie wouldn't take kindly to Robin making a decision like this on her own. But Melanie wasn't here, and she couldn't very well tell the child she'd have to think about it and call her back. "Of course it's no trouble," she said. "We'll be there as soon as we can."

"Robin . . ."

"Yes?"

"Can you bring me something to wear? I was wearing pajamas when . . . you know. And they got kind of ruined . . ."

Robin pictured a child's pajama top shredded by bullets and soaked through with blood. "Sure. We'll go to the house and get something." The police tape had been removed from around her father's mansion, but the thought of returning there, of seeing the blood that covered Cassidy's bed like a blanket, made her stomach lurch. "You know what? This is the first good news we've had in a while and you deserve something special. We'll stop at a store and get you something new to wear."

"Really? There's this awesome shop on Main Street called Trendsetters. I love their stuff."

"Anything in particular?"

"No. You pick."

"Okay. I'll do my best. We'll see you soon." Robin hung up the phone as Blake closed his laptop. "Melanie's not going to be happy."

"Is she ever?"

"She hates surprises."

"She hates everything. You going to call her?"

"No," Robin said. "The day is young. Why spoil it so early?"

"You're learning," said Blake, with a smile.

Melanie had been in a bad mood when she woke up, and it had only worsened as the morning progressed. It reached its peak when Alec decided to tag along with her and Landon to Donny Warren's ranch. "What?"

he'd said. "I like horses. And your lover invited me." Melanie's only response had been steely silence. They'd left about an hour ago, and Robin wasn't sure what time they would be back.

Melanie had refused to comment further about her relationship with Donny, saying only that he'd told Landon he could call him whenever he was agitated and felt like going for a ride, either on horseback or on the back of his motorcycle. Apparently Donny suffered from insomnia as a result of his time in Afghanistan, so he had said that Landon was free to call him anytime, day or night. "How do you know he suffers from insomnia unless you've been spending the night?" Alec had asked. The daggers that shot from Melanie's eyes gave new meaning to the phrase "if looks could kill."

"You don't have to come to the hospital with me," Robin told Blake now.

"You don't want me to come?"

"That's not what I'm saying."

"What *are* you saying?"

Robin took a deep breath. "I want you to come."

Trendsetters was a small, upscale boutique located on Main Street between an old-fashioned hardware store and a modern hairdressing salon, directly across the street from the gold-domed clock tower. The shop was relatively new, having opened sometime in the last five years. "I don't know," Robin said, surveying the off-the-shoulder tops and short skirts on the mannequins in the window. "All these clothes seem a little too old for Cassidy."

"Let's have a look." Blake held the door open for her.

A young woman approached even before the door was fully closed. She was in her early twenties, tall and slender, with waist-length brown hair and makeup that was several shades too orange for her complexion. Her eyelashes were so laden with mascara that Robin wondered how she managed to keep her eyes open. "Hi. I'm Miranda," she said in greeting. "Can I help you?"

Robin took a quick glance around the brightly lit store. It was nicely laid out, with clothes hanging along both sides of the wide room, and three tables containing a variety of folded items running up the center. At the rear of the shop, a salesgirl was sharing a joke with a customer whose headband-secured bouffant blond hairdo was reminiscent of *Alice in Wonderland.* "I'm not sure," Robin said. "We're looking for something for a young girl. Your stuff seems a little, I don't know, maybe too mature." She noted that Miranda was wearing a loose-fitting lime-green top and a pair of yellow-and-green-patterned shorts that were for sale on the first table.

"Oh, no," Miranda said quickly. "We get lots of teenagers in here."

"She's twelve."

Miranda looked unconcerned. "What size is she?"

"I'm not sure."

"Is she tall, thin, heavyset . . . ?"

"She's shorter than me, around five feet three or four, I guess. Kind of delicate-looking, weighs maybe ninety-five pounds soaking wet. She's twelve," Robin repeated, as if this said it all.

"Sounds like a size zero. What sort of style does she like?"

"I have no idea. She just said that she likes your stuff."

"Really? Who is she? If she shops here, I probably know her."

Robin hesitated. "Her name is Cassidy."

Miranda's eyes widened, despite their many coats of mascara. "Are you talking about Cassidy Davis?"

For a second, Robin considered lying. But how many Cassidys could there be in a city the size of Red Bluff? "Yes."

"Of course I know Cassidy. She's in here all the time. Loves our clothes. How's she doing?"

"Much better. She's actually being released . . ."

"That's so great," Miranda said without waiting for Robin to finish the sentence. She pivoted toward the back of the store. "Tiffany, did you hear that? Cassidy Davis is getting out of the hospital."

"Are you kidding?" Tiffany squealed in response.

"The little girl who was shot?" her customer asked, turning around so that Robin could see her face.

Not Alice in Wonderland.

Shit.

"Terri Glover," she said, her heart sinking as the woman approached. Terri Glover was the most notorious busybody in Red Bluff. "Nice to see you again. It's been a while."

"Yes, it has. And I traded in a Glover for a Norris two years ago, so it's Terri Norris now. How *are* you?"

"I'm okay."

"Well, considering the circumstances," Terri said. "I can't believe what happened. The whole town's in shock." Terri reached in her purse and removed her cell phone, punching in a series of numbers while she spoke. "But it's fabulous news about Cassidy. You must be so relieved."

"I am. Wait—what are you doing?"

"I'm just going to tell Grant, my husband. He's a reporter for the Tehama Today section of the *Redding Record Searchlight.* It's included in the Sunday edition of the paper. You must read it. Yes, hello," she said into her phone. "Can I speak to Grant Norris? It's important."

"No. Please don't do that."

"Put your phone away," Blake said.

"Who are you?" Terri took several steps back, holding her phone close to her chest.

"This is Blake Upton, my fiancé."

"Well, nice to meet you, Blake. But it's a free country."

"Please, Terri," Robin began, "I'm sure you understand what a difficult time this is—"

"And I'm sure that *you* understand that this is the biggest thing to happen in Red Bluff in years. People have a right to know."

"Look, Terri," Robin said, fighting to maintain control when what she really wanted to do was punch the woman in her stupid *Alice in Wonderland* face. "I would consider it a great favor if you would keep this quiet, at least for a couple of hours, until we can get Cassidy home. The last thing she needs right now is to be hounded by a bunch of reporters."

Terri looked from Robin to Blake, then back to Robin.

She returned the phone to her ear. "Grant," she said, "I'll have to call you back."

"Thank you. I really appreciate it."

"Guess a few hours won't make much difference. Tehama Today doesn't come out till Sunday anyway."

"Thank you," Robin said again, eager now to get out of the store. She turned back to Miranda, whose eyes were open so wide that her lashes appeared stuck to her eyebrows. "Do you think Cassidy would like what you're wearing?"

"Are you kidding? Cassidy would love this. And I'm pretty sure we have it in her size. Yep," she said, locating both the shirt and the shorts on the display table. "Here they are."

"Great."

Blake insisted on paying for the items, and they hurriedly left the store. Robin turned back briefly and saw Terri already talking on her phone.

They arrived at the hospital half an hour later, having stopped at Walmart to pick up underwear and a pair of Crocs.

"This is so cool," Cassidy exclaimed from her bed, clutching the lime-green top and the patterned shorts to her chest. Her hair was brushed away from her pale face and secured behind both ears with matching butterfly barrettes, making her look even younger than her twelve years. "I love everything."

"We're glad," Robin said. "I was afraid they might be a little too . . . I don't know . . ."

"Oh, no. They're perfect. Did you pick them out, Blake?"

"No, they were Robin's choice."

"The salesgirl was wearing them," Robin explained. "Miranda."

"Oh, Miranda. I love her. Didn't you love her?"

"She was very helpful." Robin handed Cassidy the bag from Walmart. "Some underwear and a pair of green Crocs. I hope they fit."

Cassidy withdrew the panties from the bag, laughing as she turned them over in her hands. "They're kind of gross."

"Gross?"

"Mommy always used to buy me thongs."

Of course she did, Robin thought. "Oh. Well, I guess we can stop and get you some of those."

"It's all right. I have lots at home. I can get them later."

Robin and Blake exchanged worried looks.

"No, it's okay," Cassidy said. "Sheriff Prescott was here before. He said that he'd go with me whenever I felt ready."

"There's plenty of time for that," Robin said. "I wouldn't rush it."

"No, it's important," Cassidy insisted. "Sheriff Prescott said the sooner, the better. He said that maybe if I'm back in the house, I might remember something. Something important." She smiled, as if trying to reassure them. "And I can pick up my clothes when I'm there."

"Well, we can talk about that later," Blake said. "What do you say we get you home first?"

"Okay." Cassidy pushed back her covers, swiveling gently around and swinging her bare legs over the side of the bed. She paused for a second to take a deep breath before looking up at Blake. "Could you help me?"

"Sure thing." He was instantly at her side, holding on to her waist as her feet touched the floor.

"Do you need help putting these things on?" Robin asked.

"Maybe."

"I'll wait in the hall," Blake said.

Robin undid the ties at the back of Cassidy's hospital gown, noting the large bandage wrapped around the child's upper torso. *Dear God.* "There's a bra in the bag. Nothing fancy," she said, hearing Melanie's voice twist through her words. "I wasn't sure what size you are."

"I don't usually wear a bra," Cassidy said. "I never even had boobs till I got my period. And it might kind of dig in."

"Of course. How stupid of me."

"You're not stupid," Cassidy said. "You're the best." She turned and buried her head in Robin's chest as her arms wrapped tightly around her waist.

Tears sprang to Robin's eyes. "Let's get you home."

—THIRTY—

Three reporters and a photographer were waiting in the parking lot when Robin and Blake, pushing Cassidy in a wheelchair and flanked by two deputies, reached the front door of the hospital.

"Damn that Terri Glover," Robin said.

"Norris," Blake corrected. "She traded in the Glover, remember?"

"What do we do?"

"I'll get the car," Blake said. "Bring it up to the door."

"What do they want?" Cassidy asked.

"Some sort of statement, I guess. Some pictures."

"Of me?"

"You don't have to talk to anyone," Blake told her. "Just hang tight. I'll be right back."

"Who are *you*?" one reporter called out as Blake pushed the door open.

"Cassidy!" cried another. "Cassidy, look this way."

"How are you feeling, Cassidy?" the third one shouted. "Can you tell us what happened?"

"Who shot you?"

"Oh, God," said Cassidy as the door swung shut.

"It's okay, sweetheart." Robin looked from one deputy to the other. "Can't you do something?"

"They've been warned to keep their distance," one of the deputies replied. "The sheriff's on his way."

"I'm scared," said Cassidy.

"Don't be," Robin said. Then, "Hell. I'm scared, too."

"Really? You get scared?"

Pretty much every day of my life, Robin thought. "We'll be okay," she said.

"What about Daddy?" Cassidy asked. "Will *he* be okay?"

"I don't know, sweetheart."

Cassidy had insisted on seeing their father before they left the hospital. Robin had wheeled her into his room, and the child had sat beside his bed for ten long minutes, holding his hand and crying quietly. "Please wake up, Daddy," she kept repeating. "Please wake up."

But Greg Davis didn't wake up, and every hour brought less hope that he ever would. He'd suffered another seizure the previous night. The next one would likely kill him, his doctor had confided. Still, if anyone could prove them wrong, Robin thought, it was her father.

"Cassidy?" a woman said, approaching from behind.

Robin's first thought was that a reporter had somehow managed to get past the guard, but when she turned around she saw that it was one of the nurses assigned to Cassidy's care. The young woman was holding a bouquet of white tulips. "We wanted you to have these," she said, nodding toward two older nurses standing behind her as she transferred the floral bouquet to Cassidy.

"Thank you so much," said Cassidy. "They're so beautiful."

"You're our little miracle child," the nurse said.

"Take care of yourself," said another.

"Come back and see us whenever you want."

"That was really nice of them," Cassidy said after they were gone.

"Yes, it was."

"Can I tell you something awful?"

"Something awful?"

Cassidy motioned for Robin to lean closer. "I don't like tulips," she whispered.

"You don't?" Robin smiled. "I thought everybody liked tulips."

"Mommy always said that they don't smell, they droop, and then they die."

Robin decided that was a pretty fair assessment.

"I like roses better."

"I'll keep that in mind," Robin said as Blake pulled his car up to the front door.

"Ready?" asked one of the deputies.

Robin nodded as the deputy opened the door. Immediately a flood of voices washed over them.

"Do you know who shot you, Cassidy?"

"Did you recognize the person who killed your mother?"

"Was it someone you know?"

"Cassidy, look this way."

"Can you give us a smile?"

And still more voices, disembodied, relentless, pummeling them like angry fists as Robin raised her arms in front of her face, trying to block the prying gaze of the camera. "Robin, is it true you haven't talked to your father in over five years?"

"Is your brother a suspect?"

"Who do you think is responsible?"

The sheriff pulled into the parking lot as Blake was helping Cassidy out of her wheelchair and into the backseat of his car. "Okay, guys, back off. Now," he commanded. "You've got your pictures. Nobody's answering any questions today. The child's terrified. Get the hell out of here."

Miraculously, the reporters obeyed, dispersing as quickly as if the sheriff had tossed a smoke bomb into their midst, although the cameraman stayed behind, clicking away. Robin took her seat beside Cassidy as Blake got behind the wheel, about to drive off when the sheriff knocked on his side window.

"I'll give you a police escort home," Prescott said.

"Appreciate that."

"Can't promise the vultures won't follow us." The sheriff peered into the backseat. "How you doin', kiddo?"

"I'm okay. I got flowers," Cassidy said, holding up her bouquet.

Robin put her arms around the child and hugged her close, careful not to apply too much pressure. "I want to be just like you when I grow up," she said.

They arrived home fifteen minutes later. The sheriff parked at the top of the driveway to allow Blake entry, and Blake pulled his car as close to the front door as possible.

Melanie's car was nowhere in sight. Which was good, Robin decided. Melanie was going to be far from thrilled to see Cassidy, and even less thrilled to see the sheriff.

"Doesn't look as if anybody's home," Prescott said, helping Blake and Robin with Cassidy. "Must still be at Donny's ranch."

"I take it that means you're still following us," Robin said, bristling.

"Just making sure nobody gets any bad ideas."

"What do you mean?" Cassidy asked. "What bad ideas?"

"Nothing for you to worry about, sweetheart," he answered. "Now, you think you're strong enough to walk to the door on your own?"

"How about I carry you?" Blake offered before Cassidy could answer.

Relief flashed through Cassidy's doe-like brown eyes. "Thank you." She leaned her head against Blake's shoulder as he lifted her into his arms and carried her to the house.

Robin glanced toward the road, where three cars had already stopped to unload photographers with long-range lenses. As she watched, a small truck with a FOX News logo pulled up and a man jumped out, balancing a camera on one shoulder. "Shit," Robin said. *Melanie is going to have a fit when she sees the growing media circus.* Not even a town the size of Red Bluff was safe. "Isn't there anything you can do about this?" she asked the sheriff.

"As long as they stay on public property, my hands

are tied. I can have a deputy posted at the top of your driveway if you'd like, make sure nobody trespasses. But you should probably consult with your sister about that."

Won't that be fun? Robin thought, leaving his side to unlock the front door, then standing back as Blake carried Cassidy through the hallway and into the living room. He deposited her gently on the sofa, then sat down beside her, the child still clinging to his side.

"Well, thank you, Sheriff," Robin said, surprised to find him still hovering, "for making sure we got home safely. We can manage things from here."

"You wouldn't happen to have a drink of something cold, would you?" he asked.

"I'll get it," Blake offered. "I could use a drink myself."

"No," said Cassidy, her hand clutching tight to his arm. "Don't leave me."

"How about I put those flowers in a vase," Robin said, taking the bouquet from Cassidy's hands, "and bring a pitcher of water in here. Sheriff, would you mind giving me a hand?"

Prescott looked skeptical. "It would be my pleasure." He followed her down the hall. "I take it you have something you want to say to me," he said when they reached the kitchen.

"What the hell are you trying to do to that child?" Robin demanded angrily, setting the flowers on the counter.

"I'm not sure I under—"

"The hell you don't! What are you doing suggesting to Cassidy that she go back to my father's house?"

"It's not an unreasonable idea."

"She's twelve years old! Her mother was murdered. She's been through a terrible trauma. And you're asking her to relive it?"

Sheriff Prescott lowered his voice, perhaps hoping Robin would do the same. "I'm conducting a murder investigation, Robin. Cassidy is our only witness."

"She's also a victim. And she's already told you that she can't identify the men who were in the house that night."

"She *thinks* she can't identify them, but being back in the house might—"

"No. I won't allow it."

"I don't think that's your decision to make. Cassidy seems ready . . ."

"Cassidy's a minor," Robin reminded him. "And if I have to hire a lawyer and get a court order to stop you, that's exactly what I'll do."

"Anything else?"

"As a matter of fact, yes, there is."

The sheriff cocked his head to one side, like a curious bulldog.

"Stop harassing my brother. You can't make him stay in Red Bluff indefinitely, hoping to come up with enough evidence to arrest him. He has a life in San Francisco, and you have no right to keep him here. The way I see it is that you have two choices: either you arrest him or you leave him alone. Shit or get off the pot, as my father used to say." Robin was stunned by her outburst. She was even more stunned to hear herself quoting her father.

"Everything all right in there?" Blake called from the other room.

"Everything's fine," Robin called back. She found a glass vase in the cupboard over the sink, filled it with water, then arranged the tulips inside it, watching as they almost instantly drooped. "Here," she said to the sheriff, removing a pitcher from the same cupboard and all but pushing it against his hard stomach. "You can fill this with ice." She reached into the cupboard for glasses.

She heard the front door open, then slam shut, as Melanie sprayed the air with questions. "Robin, what's going on? What's with all the reporters? What's the sheriff's car doing here?"

Robin put the glasses on the counter and stepped into the hallway, the sheriff behind her. Melanie, Alec, and Landon were standing just inside the front door. The smell of horses galloped toward Robin, almost knocking her down. She sneezed twice.

"Bless you," said the sheriff.

"Thank you," Robin acknowledged. Then, seeing the confusion in Melanie's eyes, "Why don't you go into the living room—"

"Why don't you just tell me what's going on?"

"Melanie," Robin said, "go into the living room."

"Fine." Melanie marched into the living room, Alec and Landon behind her, Robin and the sheriff bringing up the rear.

"Hi, Melanie," Cassidy said in greeting, her eyes shifting toward the two men behind her. "Hi, Landon." A slight pause. Then, "Tom? Is that you? What are you doing here?"

Alec turned pale, his mouth falling open in shock.

Robin felt a jolt of anxiety so strong that it reverberated throughout her entire body. "Oh, God," she muttered, understanding that it wouldn't take long for the sheriff to put two and two together. Motive and opportunity. All that was needed for the sheriff to make an arrest.

"Who's Tom?" the sheriff asked.

"Tom," Cassidy repeated. "My mother's friend from San Francisco."

"You're confused," Melanie said. "This man is Alec, my brother."

"Alec? No. It's Tom. Tom Richards. We used to visit him."

The sheriff stepped forward, his hand on his holster, the full meaning of what he'd just heard clicking into place behind his eyes. "Okay, everybody, stay nice and calm. Alec, suppose we step outside."

"Sheriff—" Robin began.

"Let's not make this any more unpleasant for everyone than we have to," Prescott said, cutting her off. He put a hand on Alec's arm and led him from the room.

"I don't understand. What's happening?" Cassidy asked.

Robin ran outside after them. "What are you doing?" she asked as the sheriff cuffed her brother's hands behind his back.

"I believe you advised me earlier to shit or get off the pot," Prescott said. "Alec Davis," he began, guiding him up the gravel driveway toward his patrol car as the waiting reporters and photographers descended en masse, "I remind you that you have the right to remain silent . . ."

—THIRTY-ONE—

The Tehama Superior Court is located at 445 Pine Street, a few blocks from Main Street and a block from the Tehama County Jail. Unlike the unassuming low-rise brown-brick jailhouse, the courthouse is an imposing two-story white concrete-and-marble building, whose front entrance is flanked by tall decorative columns and towering evergreens.

The interior is equally impressive—a large, open lobby in white-and-beige marble, more decorative columns, skylights, and a sweeping staircase leading to a balcony that surrounds and overlooks the lobby below. The court's mission statement is "to ensure the prompt and fair adjudication of all cases and to improve public confidence in the Courts through accessibility, communication and education." There are a total of five courtrooms, presided over by Tehama County magistrates.

Robin and Blake stood in the hall outside Courtroom One, waiting for the bailiff to unlock the doors. It was almost nine-thirty. Alec's hearing was scheduled for ten o'clock. "What do you think is going to happen?" she asked.

"I don't know."

"Do you think they'll grant Alec bail?"

"I don't know."

"Do you think he's all right? Please don't say you don't know."

"I think he's all right," Blake responded dutifully, although his eyes said, "I don't know."

"Poor Alec," Robin checked that her white blouse was tucked securely in the waistband of her blue skirt. "Do you think he got any sleep at all last night?"

"Probably more than you did."

"I'm sorry. Did I keep you up?"

"Don't worry about me."

"I'm sorry," Robin apologized again. "I just feel so helpless. What do you think is going to happen?"

"McAllister will be here soon. He should be able to tell us something."

Robin looked down the wide corridor for some sign of her brother's lawyer, but while the building was filling up with people, Jeff McAllister wasn't one of them.

She'd called him as soon as Alec had been arrested and told him what had happened. The lawyer had listened and said he'd be in touch. When Robin hadn't heard from him an hour later, she and Blake drove to the sheriff's office themselves, only to be told that Alec had been transferred to the Tehama County Jail.

"He's in jail," Robin had reported to Melanie, who'd stayed back at the house with Cassidy and Landon. The jail was more than forty years old and had a capacity for two hundred and twenty-seven inmates, both those who had been sentenced and those who were awaiting sentencing. Alec was now one of the latter. "They won't let us see him. And his bail hearing isn't till tomorrow morning. Which means he has to spend the night in that awful place."

"Which is probably a good thing," Melanie said. "He certainly can't come back here. Cassidy's upset enough as it is. She keeps asking me if I think Alec killed her mother."

"I hope you told her that he didn't."

"What makes you so sure?"

Robin promptly disconnected the call.

Cassidy had been sleeping when Robin and Blake left the house this morning. Which was probably a good thing, Robin decided, borrowing Melanie's phrase. It had been difficult enough trying to explain Alec's relationship with Tara. "You mean they were having an affair?" Cassidy asked, eyes wide with disbelief. "She was cheating on Daddy?"

"She wasn't happy, sweetheart."

"No, you're wrong," Cassidy had insisted. "She loved Daddy. They were really happy together."

Now Robin stared at the beige marble tiles at her feet, wondering if Alec had been entirely truthful with her. She didn't doubt that Tara and her brother had been having an affair, but what if Tara had merely been playing with him? What if she'd had no intention of leaving her husband and told Alec so that night and he snapped?

No, it wasn't possible. She knew her brother. He was no more capable of shooting anyone than she was. *But if he didn't shoot them, who did?*

A young woman with a pronounced pout and long blond hair falling in waves down her back approached. She was dressed in tight white jeans and an even tighter cherry-red tank top. *Obviously not the district attorney,* Robin thought.

The woman came to a stop directly in front of Blake. "Hi," she said to him, as if Robin didn't exist.

"Can we help you?" Robin asked.

The young woman didn't so much as glance in Robin's direction. "I was just wondering where to go to pay my traffic ticket?" Her voice curled up flirtatiously at the end of the sentence.

"Sorry," Blake said, "I have no idea."

"I think the office is that way." Robin pointed down the hall to her right.

"Guess I must have walked right by it." The woman lingered, smiling expectantly at Blake, as if it was his turn to say something. "Okay. Well, thanks," she said, wiggling away when he didn't speak.

"You get that often?" Robin asked Blake, almost grateful for the diversion the blonde had provided.

"Get what?"

I love you, thought Robin.

Two men came bounding down the corridor, one with a camera.

"Keep your head down and don't look up," Blake advised, guiding Robin to a nearby bench and sitting down beside her. "Pretend they're not there."

They sat in silence, Blake scrolling his phone for messages, Robin staring at her feet. She looked up several minutes later to see Jeff McAllister approaching. "That's him." She jumped to her feet as the lawyer drew nearer, the reporter and his photographer nipping at his heels.

"Excuse me, Mr. McAllister," the reporter shouted as the photographer began snapping pictures.

"I must ask you to back away," McAllister said. "I'll have a statement for you later."

"Do you think there's any chance your client will get bail?" the reporter asked, ignoring the lawyer's directive.

"As I said, I'll have a statement for you later. Now, if you don't mind . . ."

The reporter and his cameraman reluctantly withdrew. Outside Courtroom One, a small crowd was gathering.

"My brother will get bail, won't he?" Robin asked, reworking the reporter's question.

"Highly doubtful," McAllister replied. "But I'll do my best." He looked at Blake. "You are?"

Robin introduced the two attorneys, Blake towering over the shorter man. Despite the outside heat, McAllister was wearing a dark blue three-piece suit, a white shirt complete with cuff links, and a paisley tie.

"How is Alec?" Robin asked. "Have you seen him?"

"Not this morning, no. But they'll be bringing him over shortly from the jail."

Robin felt tiny bubbles of panic bursting like champagne inside her chest. "What kind of jail has two hundred and twenty-seven inmates?" she asked, hoping that the sound of her voice would keep her panic in check.

"I mean, who came up with that number? Why not two hundred and twenty-five or two hundred and thirty? What genius decided on two hundred and twenty-seven?"

"Robin," Blake said, "are you all right?"

"It just seems stupid to me, that's all."

"Maybe you should wait out here," McAllister said, as the bailiff unlocked the courtroom doors.

"No," Robin insisted. "It's important for Alec to know we're here, that we believe in his innocence. My brother is innocent," she announced to the reporters now crowding the doorway.

"Did you know about your brother and Tara?" one asked as they made their way into the courtroom.

"Is it true they were having an affair?" asked another.

"Did Cassidy identify your brother as the man who shot her?"

"My brother is innocent," Robin repeated, her voice a full octave higher and multi-decibels louder than it had been just seconds ago.

"Okay, that's enough," McAllister cautioned, although Robin wasn't sure if he was talking to her or to the reporters.

Blake led Robin to a bench at the front of the visitors section. Her eyes scanned the judge's podium, the witness stand, the court recorder's desk, the jury box, the long tables used by the prosecution and defense teams, and the five rows of benches reserved for spectators. *Just like on TV,* she thought. Maybe a little brighter, since the wall opposite the jury box was mostly windows. There was a lot of impressive-looking wood, but little color save for the large American flag on prominent display at the front of the room. The walls were beige, as was the floor. There was no carpet. The rest of the room was a blur, like a photograph that was slightly out of focus.

"You sure you're okay?" Blake asked.

"I'm not sure of anything."

Blake took her hand and held it as the bailiff announced that court was in session and directed everyone to stand for the arrival of the presiding magistrate. The judge's name was Robert West and he was appropriately white-haired and distinguished-looking. A pair of wire-rimmed reading glasses were balanced low on the bridge of his nose, completing the picture of a folksy, fair-minded grandfather.

"He's looks nice," Robin said, her voice hopeful.

The judge directed the bailiff to bring in the first of the accused, a man charged with robbing a local 7-Eleven. He pleaded not guilty and was released on bail to await trial.

"That's good," said Robin, watching as the second prisoner was brought before the magistrate. The charge was simple assault, and he, too, was granted bail while awaiting trial. "Good," Robin said again. *Two out of two.*

Her brother was escorted in next. He was wearing the same orange jumpsuit as the two previously accused prisoners. *And after he spent all that money in Walmart,* Robin thought, noting the defeated slump of his shoulders, so similar to Melanie's. She rose slightly in her seat, lifting her right hand into the air, fingers fluttering, trying to get his attention. Only the pressure of Blake's hand on her arm brought her back into her seat.

If Alec saw her, he gave no sign. His back was to her, and he stared straight ahead as Jeff McAllister joined him in front of the judge. The charges were read, and Alec was asked for his plea.

"Not guilty, Your Honor," he replied.

Just like on TV, Robin thought again, wondering suddenly if this could be another of the strange dreams she'd been having since her arrival in Red Bluff. *Please let me wake up. Please let this awful nightmare be over.*

But, of course, she wasn't dreaming and she knew it. This nightmare was real and wouldn't end until Alec was exonerated and the men who'd murdered Tara and shot her father and Cassidy had been apprehended and brought to justice.

"The prosecution is seeking remand," the prosecutor argued. She was a woman of about forty, with short brown hair that emphasized the heavy bags beneath her eyes. She was wearing a black A-line skirt and a pale yellow blouse that Robin remembered seeing on the cover of a Brooks Brothers catalog. She wore little makeup beyond her coral lipstick, and her voice all but shook with righteous indignation. "The defendant is charged with murder and attempted murder, as well as breaking and entering, robbery, and vandalism. He killed his former lover in cold blood, and severely wounded her husband, a pillar of this community, who remains in the hospital in critical condition, not expected to survive. He also shot a helpless child. If he were to be granted bail, we have no doubt that he would attempt to flee the country, given that he has already tried once to do so."

"Your Honor," Jeff McAllister began, "the defendant is not a flight risk. He has long-standing ties to this community, having lived here most of his life. He is currently staying with his sister, and his car and passport have already been seized."

"His car and passport were seized during a failed attempt to flee to Canada," the prosecutor interrupted, "and he left Red Bluff more than five years ago after his father, whom he stands accused of shooting, married his then-fiancée, whom he stands accused of murdering. He's refusing to cooperate in any way . . ."

"Application for bail is denied," the judge pronounced before the prosecutor could finish. "Defendant is remanded for trial." He banged his gavel, and Alec was escorted from the room.

"Oh, no," Robin cried. "Poor Alec."

"Getting bail was always a long shot," Jeff McAllister reminded her. In the background, reporters hovered, waiting for the statement McAllister had promised them earlier.

"What happens now?" Blake asked McAllister.

"We meet next week, set a trial date, get a look at their evidence. From what I can gather, the case against your brother isn't very strong, and it's entirely circumstantial. There's nothing physical linking him to the crime scene, no DNA, no eyewitnesses, except for a traumatized twelve-year-old girl who isn't even sure how many men were in the house. Your father had no shortage of enemies. I think a good case can be made for reasonable doubt."

He repeated essentially the same account to the press, downplaying both motive and opportunity while emphasizing the prosecution's lack of hard evidence. He said that since Alec had been denied bail, he would insist on his client's right to a speedy trial.

"Which means what, exactly?" Robin asked Blake. "Are we talking weeks? Months?"

"My guess would be nothing happens until the fall."

"The fall?"

"At least."

"Oh, God. We can't let that happen. He'll die in there. We have to find out who did this."

Blake took her arm, led her toward the front door of the courthouse.

The sheriff was waiting beside it. "Robin . . . Blake," he said, tipping his hat. "I was hoping I might be able to stop by this afternoon—"

Robin neither slowed down nor looked in his direction. "Go to hell," she said.

—THIRTY-TWO—

The sheriff showed up at their door at just after two o'clock that afternoon.

"We don't want any," Melanie told him, about to shut the door in his face.

"I'm here to see Cassidy."

"She doesn't want to see you," Robin said, coming up behind her sister, their bodies forming a human barricade.

"I have a right to question the girl."

"She has nothing to say to you."

"Is that Sheriff Prescott?" Cassidy called from inside the house.

"It's all right, sweetheart," Robin called back. "You don't have to talk to him."

"No, that's okay. I want to see him."

"I think that's my cue." The sheriff waited for Robin and her sister to step aside before taking off his hat and entering the house.

"I'm in here," Cassidy said.

Robin and Melanie followed the sheriff into the living room where Cassidy was sitting on the sofa, Blake beside her, watching an afternoon soap opera on TV. She was wearing the outfit that Robin and Blake had purchased at Trendsetters the day before. Her feet were bare.

"Sorry to bother you," the sheriff said. "Hope I'm not interrupting anything too important." He motioned toward the big-haired, big-bosomed actress on the screen who was almost drowning in tears, lines of black mascara trailing down her cheeks.

"It's my favorite show. *Bleeding Hearts,*" Cassidy informed him. "That's Penny. She just told her twin sister, Emily, that their father's been molesting her for years, and now poor Emily doesn't know what to believe."

I know exactly how she feels, Robin thought, sitting down beside Cassidy and taking the child's hand in hers.

"How are you feeling today?" the sheriff asked, shifting awkwardly from one foot to the other.

"Pretty good." Cassidy clicked the remote on her lap, and the television screen went blank.

"I brought you your phone." The sheriff removed it from his pocket and handed it to her.

Cassidy hugged it to her chest as if it were a stuffed toy. "Thank you so much. I wondered what happened to it."

"You had it in your hand when the paramedics found you. We cleaned it up . . ." He didn't bother finishing the sentence. "They treating you well here?"

"No," Melanie said from the doorway. "We're torturing her. In fact, until seconds before you got here, we had her hanging by her thumbs from the ceiling."

"Perhaps Cassidy and I should talk in private," the sheriff said.

"That's out of the question." Robin looked to Blake for support.

"Afraid you're stuck with us, Sheriff," he said. "The girl's a minor."

"Yes, she is," Prescott concurred. "And I could call Child Welfare Services, I suppose. I was hoping not to get them involved, but . . ."

"What do you mean, Child Welfare Services?" Cassidy asked, glancing around the room with a look of panic on her face. "Why would you call Child Welfare Services?"

"If I'm being prevented from doing my job, if you're being coerced or pressured in any way not to talk to me . . ."

"I'm not being pressured," Cassidy said. "I'll tell you anything you want to know. Please don't call them. I don't want them to take me away."

"You feel safe here?"

"Why wouldn't I?"

"Well, Alec has been arrested."

"He didn't do it."

"Did someone ask you to say that?" The sheriff looked from Robin to Melanie, then back to Cassidy.

"No. *No*."

"What *did* they say to you about Alec's arrest?"

Cassidy paused to consider the question. "They said you think Mommy and Alec were having an affair, and that Alec killed her and shot Daddy and me. But it's not true."

"How can you be sure? He fits the description of the men you gave us—tall, muscular—"

"Yes, but—"

"But?"

"I just know it wasn't him. He's Robin's brother," she said, as if this was all the evidence she needed.

He's also Melanie's *brother,* Robin thought, knowing that the sheriff was thinking the same thing.

"And besides, even if it *was* him," Cassidy added as Robin felt her heart drop into the pit of her stomach, "then I'm safe here because he's in jail. But it wasn't him," she added quickly, seeing the look on Robin's face. She glanced toward the ceiling, where a faint rocking could be heard. "Landon fits the description, too. He's tall and muscular. But it wasn't him either," she added quickly.

"Why are we talking about Landon?" Melanie asked, her voice stretched as tight as an elastic band.

"I was just saying he fits the description," Cassidy said. "The same as Alec."

"The same as a lot of people," Robin said, sensing that in spite of Cassidy's best efforts, by linking Alec and Landon she'd only made things worse. There'd been at least two men in the house that night, two men matching the general description of her brother and her nephew. "Any other questions, Sheriff?"

He smiled at Cassidy. "I was wondering if you felt strong enough to accompany me to the house—"

"We've already discussed this," Robin interrupted. "She's not going anywhere near that house."

"No, I want to go," Cassidy said. "All my stuff, my clothes . . ."

"We'll get you new clothes."

"But I might remember something," Cassidy insisted. "Something that could help Alec."

Or hurt him, Robin thought. "I just don't think it's a good idea."

Cassidy took a deep breath, exhaling audibly. "What about Mommy?"

"What about her?" Melanie asked.

"Where is she?" Cassidy asked the sheriff. "Can I see her?"

"We'll be releasing her body for burial in another day or two," Prescott said.

"Then I'll need something to wear." Cassidy nodded several times to emphasize that her mind was made up. "We should go soon."

"How's tomorrow morning?" the sheriff asked.

"Tomorrow morning is good."

"You're sure you want to do this?" Robin asked.

"I'm sure."

The sheriff arrived at precisely nine o'clock the next morning. Cassidy was waiting in the front hall, Robin and Blake on either side of her. "How are you doing today, Cassidy?" Prescott asked. "You ready to do this?"

Cassidy nodded, grabbing both Robin's and Blake's hands for support.

"I take it you'll be joining us." Prescott's tone indicated that he was resigned to their presence.

"We will," Robin said.

"Then I must instruct you not to interfere in any way."

"Wouldn't dream of it."

"And Melanie?"

"Staying right here," she called from the kitchen.

"My lucky day," Prescott muttered, not quite under his breath. "Shall we?" He opened the door, and they stepped into the warm morning air. "We can walk or take my car." He motioned toward the end of the driveway where his patrol car was parked.

"The doctors said I should get as much exercise as I can," Cassidy said.

"Fine. If you think you're strong enough."

"I'm strong enough."

Robin smiled proudly. Cassidy was one of the strongest people she'd ever met. She wondered where that kind of fortitude came from. Tara probably. *God knows I've never had it,* she thought, squeezing Cassidy's hand as they proceeded slowly up the driveway and along the side of the road to the house next door.

"Ready?" the sheriff asked when they reached the front door, where a deputy was waiting.

Cassidy nodded, the deputy unlocked the door, and they stepped inside the large circular foyer. Robin followed Blake's gaze from the high ceiling and huge crystal chandelier to the two staircases off the center hall. She saw his lips form an unspoken "Wow."

"How you doin' so far?" the sheriff asked Cassidy.

"Okay," Cassidy said, although the slight wobble in her voice said otherwise. Her fingernails dug into the back of Robin's hand.

"I thought we could start by going over the events of

that night again." Prescott paused to let his words sink in. "You woke up to loud voices and came down the stairs to see what was happening . . ."

Cassidy's eyes glazed over, as if she were watching the scene play out before her. She let go of Robin's and Blake's hands and, as if she were sleepwalking, moved toward the staircase on the left side of the hall, the others following close behind her. "It sounded like arguing," she said, stopping at the base of the staircase, "so I got out of bed and tiptoed down the stairs to see what was going on. The voices got louder." She began inching toward the living room. "This one guy was yelling. He was really mad."

"Can you hear him now?" the sheriff asked. "Do you recognize his voice?"

Cassidy tilted her head, as if she were listening. "No." She stopped, gasping when she saw the blood covering the living room rug and much of the furniture. "Oh, God."

"Don't go in there," Robin said, catching the warning not to interfere in the sheriff's eyes.

"I saw two men," Cassidy continued. "One of them was waving a gun and shouting, '*Stop fucking with me, you piece of shit, or I swear I'll shoot the bitch. I'll shoot the bitch right now.*'"

Robin closed her eyes. The words coming out of the child's mouth were as jarring as the first time she'd heard them.

"And the other man? What did he say?" the sheriff asked.

"He never said anything."

Robin tried to gauge what the sheriff was thinking. Two men, both muscular and tall, one barking orders in a voice that Cassidy couldn't identify, the other silent.

Alec and Landon?

Cassidy's eyes widened in alarm at the vision taking shape in her mind's eye. "Daddy lunged and the man whacked him with the gun on the side of his head. Daddy went down, and Mommy started screaming."

"Which of the men struck your father?" Prescott asked. "The one who was yelling or the silent one?"

"The one who was yelling."

"And where were you standing exactly?"

Cassidy spoke from her position at the entrance to the living room. "Here."

"And no one saw you?"

"No. Not yet."

"And then what happened?"

"The guy shot Mommy."

"Which guy?" the sheriff prodded. "The one who was yelling or the other one?"

"The other one."

"The silent one?"

"Yes."

Robin did a quick mental calculation, trying to put herself in the sheriff's head, to figure out how his brain was processing this information. If Alec and Landon were indeed the two men in the house that night, then Alec was undoubtedly the man yelling. Surely Cassidy would have recognized Landon's voice.

Still, while it made perverse sense that Alec might hate his father enough to shoot him, it made no sense at all for Landon to kill Tara. If revenge was the true motive, wouldn't Alec have shot Tara himself? She recalled Dylan Campbell's chilling words: *"If I wanted the bitch dead, I'd have taken care of it myself. I wouldn't let someone else have all the fun."*

Unless, of course, Landon had panicked and just started firing.

Except that the gunman had shot Tara in the face. That was personal. Not panic.

Another nagging question: if Alec had come to Red Bluff expecting to rendezvous with Tara, as he claimed, and Tara told him she'd changed her mind, enraging him enough to kill, as the sheriff speculated, when had he had time to contact Landon?

Unless Tara had already broken up with him, giving her brother sufficient time to nurse his grudge and plot his revenge, to contact Landon, to enlist his help . . .

Unless. Unless. Unless.

"You're sure it was the silent one who shot your mother?" Robin asked, her head spinning with *unless.*

"Robin, please," the sheriff warned.

"Yes, I'm sure," Cassidy said, eyes darting between Robin and Blake. Then, "No. Wait. I don't know. Maybe it was the other guy. It could have been the other guy." Her eyes filled with tears. "I don't know."

Prescott checked his notes. "You told us in the hospital that it was the second man, the silent one, who shot your mother. You were very clear about that, very sure."

"Yes," Cassidy said. "But now I'm not. It could have been the other guy. It all happened so fast, and I was so scared."

"It's okay, sweetheart," Robin said.

"It's not really important who shot who," Prescott said, the sudden gruffness in his voice betraying his impatience. "Both men were there. Both men are equally guilty under the law."

Robin understood that while both men might be equally guilty, regardless of who pulled the trigger, in a case like this one, every detail was important. If Cassidy couldn't be certain who shot her mother, if she wasn't even sure if there'd been two men or three in the house that night, what else could she be mistaken about?

"What happened next?" the sheriff asked.

"I screamed," Cassidy said, "and that's when the men saw me and came after me."

"They both came after you?"

"No. Just one."

"Which one?"

"I don't know. They were wearing ski masks. They looked the same." Cassidy was crying now, her words escaping her mouth in gulps. "I ran up the stairs to my room and grabbed my phone to call nine-one-one. That's when the man burst through the door. He pointed the gun at my chest. Oh, God."

"That's enough," Robin said. "She's told you everything. We're out of here."

"Okay," the sheriff reluctantly agreed. "We'll call it a day."

"I still need my clothes," Cassidy whispered.

"I'll get them," Robin said.

"There's a suitcase in my closet," Cassidy told her.

"You can dump my stuff in it. And there's a bag for my shoes . . . somewhere . . ."

"I'll find it."

"I'll give you a hand," Blake said.

"No," Cassidy cried, grabbing his arm. "Stay with me."

"It's okay," Robin said. "I can manage."

Sheriff Prescott motioned for the deputy to accompany Robin upstairs. He remained in the doorway as Robin walked straight to the closet in Cassidy's room, trying not to see the blood staining the bed. She located the blue canvas suitcase on the floor and unzipped it, dragging Cassidy's clothes from their hangers and stuffing them inside the bag, then moving to the nearby chest of drawers and emptying each one. Luckily, Cassidy's wardrobe consisted mostly of jeans and T-shirts. And thongs, Robin realized, counting one for every day of the week. There were a few items with Trendsetters labels, including a pretty white dress that she could wear to her mother's funeral.

Dear God. Tara's funeral. Did this nightmare never end?

She zipped the suitcase back up, then tossed half a dozen pairs of sandals and sneakers into a brown leather bag she found at the back of the closet, allowing the deputy to take both bags from her hands and carry them down the stairs. "Okay," she said when she reached the bottom. "Let's get the hell out of here."

—THIRTY-THREE—

Oak Hill Cemetery is located at 735 Cemetery Lane, off West Walnut Street, not far from Larie Lane. More than a century and a half old, it was established in 1859 and completed in 1861. An elaborate wrought-iron archway at the cemetery's entrance was added several decades ago, the words "Oak Hill Cemetery" written across its surface. Tall, shady trees are everywhere along the gentle curves and subtle undulations of the landscape.

"I'd forgotten how beautiful it is here," Robin said as Blake's car followed the hearse containing Tara's body along the winding, picturesque road to the gravesite. Cassidy was in the backseat beside Robin, holding tight to her hand. Melanie was in the front seat beside Blake, having made the decision that it would be better for everyone concerned if Landon stayed home. Now that news of Alec's arrest was public knowledge, speculation was rampant that Landon had been his accomplice.

"It's beautiful, all right," Melanie agreed. She shot Robin a knowing look over her shoulder, and Robin remembered the joke from their childhood that Melanie used to love: *"It's so beautiful that people are dying to get in."* Mercifully, Melanie refrained from saying this out loud.

Robin twisted around in her seat to glance out the back window. The sheriff and several of his deputies were among the small procession of cars behind them. Despite the family's best efforts to stay under the radar and their appeal to the press for privacy, word had leaked out about Tara's funeral. There was no telling how many curious spectators would show up. Robin wondered if the men who'd killed Tara would be among them.

It had been two days since their visit to the house, two more days that Alec had languished behind bars. The police seemed confident that they had their man. Their only concern now was identifying his accomplice.

"Is your mom buried here?" Cassidy asked.

"Yes," Robin said.

Cassidy stared out the side window at the rows of gravesites, each one marked by a small rectangular block of white stone in the ground. Bouquets of plastic flowers were scattered across the dry earth. "Where is she?"

"Not really sure." While Robin had a general sense of the part of the cemetery where her mother had been laid to rest, she couldn't pinpoint the grave's precise location. She hadn't been back to Oak Hill since her mother's funeral.

"Over that way," Melanie said, pointing in the direction opposite to the one in which they were headed. *"It wouldn't do to have our father's wives lying too close to each other for all eternity,"* Melanie had opined when choosing a plot. And while Robin might not have put it exactly that way, she'd agreed with the sentiment.

The hearse came to a stop underneath an impressive cluster of weeping willow trees, and Blake pulled up directly behind it, the patrol cars forming a line behind him.

Robin gave Cassidy's hand a gentle squeeze. "Ready?"

Cassidy nodded, tucking her freshly washed hair behind her ears and smoothing out the creases of her sleeveless white dress as she exited the car. Immediately, a man with a camera came rushing toward her.

"Back off," the sheriff shouted, punching the air with his fist. "Back off right now."

"Public property, Sheriff," the cameraman shouted back.

"And this is a private funeral. Come within fifty feet of us and I'll have your ass hauled off to jail."

"You can't do that."

"Yeah, I can. You can sue me later."

The cameraman backed away, grumbling, although he kept his camera raised and ready. "He threatened me," he said to the reporter beside him. "Did you hear him?"

"Sorry about that," Prescott said to no one in particular as he positioned his substantial girth between the spectators and Cassidy. Robin and Blake, both wearing black, quickly formed a protective semicircle around her. Melanie stood off to the side, looking uncomfortable in her denim skirt and blue cotton blouse, as she waited for Tara's casket to be removed from the hearse.

"Oh, poor Mommy," Cassidy whispered, glancing at the elegantly simple light walnut casket that Robin had selected.

The small group gathered around the gravesite as Tara's casket was lowered into the freshly dug grave. Robin's eyes filled with tears at the thought of the most vibrant person she'd ever known lying lifeless inside it. In spite of her conflicted feelings for her former friend, she couldn't deny that Tara had been a force of nature.

"Shouldn't we say something?" Cassidy asked. They'd decided against a formal service or a religious officiant, Tara having been decidedly anti-religion ever since her mother had run off to join a cult.

"Like what?" Melanie asked.

"I don't know. Something." Cassidy turned to Robin. "Maybe you could . . . ?"

Robin took a few seconds to gather her thoughts. "I loved your mother," she said finally, her eyes daring Melanie to contradict her. "She came to my rescue when we were in grade school and I didn't know a soul, didn't have a friend, had no clue how to make one. She grabbed my hand and said she'd be my best friend forever." She paused. "It didn't quite work out that way, but despite everything that happened, deep down I still loved her. And missed her. I missed her spunk and her spirit. She was a real little firecracker." Robin choked back a laugh full of tears. "That's what my father used to call her. And while he was so wrong about so many things, he was certainly right about that. Tara was fearless; some might even say reckless. She would rush in where not only angels but the devil himself feared to tread. And while I know that she came to regret some of her rasher decisions, the one thing she never regretted was being a mother." She turned to face Cassidy. "I can still picture her rocking you in her arms after you were born. I can see the love in her eyes, and feel the pride in her heart when you took your first steps and spoke your first words. I remember how she worried when you went off to school for the first time. 'Please let her find a forever friend like Robin,' she said." An involuntary cry escaped Robin's throat, and Cassidy grabbed her hand. "I loved your mother. I miss her. And I will miss my 'forever friend' forever."

There was a moment of absolute silence. Robin waited for Melanie to offer a customary barb, but she didn't, and Robin breathed a small sigh of relief.

"Thank you," Cassidy said.

"Your mother loved you more than anything on earth," Robin told her. "I hope that no matter what happens, you'll always remember that."

"I will."

They fell into each other's arms.

"Oh, shit," said Melanie. She grabbed Robin's arm and spun her around.

"Shit," Robin repeated, shaking her head in dismay as Dylan Campbell separated himself from the small gathering of spectators still hovering. He was wearing a white T-shirt, black jeans, and a blue baseball cap with a Yankees logo.

"I'll get rid of him," the sheriff offered before Robin could ask.

"Who is it?" Cassidy asked, eyes widening with each step Dylan took toward them.

"It's your father," Melanie said.

"My father's in the hospital," Cassidy corrected Melanie, her voice a rebuke. "I don't know this person."

Robin strained to hear the words exchanged between Dylan and the sheriff, but was able to make out only a few snatches.

"What do you think you're . . . ?"

"I have as much right as . . ."

"I'll tell you the same thing I told that reporter . . ."

". . . just want to see my kid."

"Blake," Robin said, "can you take Cassidy back to the car? I'll handle this."

"No," said Cassidy firmly. "I want to talk to him."

"Sweetheart, I don't think . . ."

"It's all right, Robin." Cassidy's eyes were on Dylan as he maneuvered around the sheriff and took half a dozen steps toward her. "I'm okay."

"That's my girl." Dylan removed his baseball cap and extended his arms, as if preparing to embrace her.

"I'm not your girl," Cassidy said, stopping him in his tracks.

He smiled, deep dimples creasing his cheeks. "You're my flesh and blood."

"Don't take another step," Robin warned as he was about to.

"What do you want?" Cassidy asked.

"I want to see you."

"You saw me twelve years ago. Seemed like more than enough for you at the time."

"Times change."

"People don't."

Dylan cocked his thumb toward Robin. "She tell you that?"

"She didn't have to. One look at you tells me everything I need to know."

He laughed. "You sound so grown up."

"What is it you want, Dylan?" Robin asked.

"Look," he said, ignoring her. "I can only imagine the things your mother said about me, but . . ."

"She said you were no good."

"Uh . . ."

"She said you used to beat her."

"Yeah, well, truth is she could throw a pretty mean punch herself."

"She said you were scum," Cassidy continued, clearly warming to her subject.

"'Scum's' a little strong . . ."

"She said you were a lowlife and a liar and a thief."

Dylan grinned. "Your mother always did have a way with words."

"She said that you never sent her the support money the court ordered you to pay."

"Because she wouldn't let me see you."

"Did you ever try?"

"I knew there'd be no point."

"There's no point now."

"Ah, come on, Cassie. I'm your daddy. The only real family you got left."

Cassidy grabbed Robin's hand. "That's not true. I have Daddy, and Robin, and Melanie, and Blake."

"And I have rights." Dylan shifted his weight from one foot to the other. "Come on, Cassie. Don't be like this." He looked toward Sheriff Prescott. "Can't you talk some sense into the girl, Sheriff?"

"She's making a lot of sense to me," Prescott replied.

"Look, I tell you what," Dylan said, returning his attention to Cassidy and his baseball cap to his head. "It looks like I made a mistake coming here today. I wanted to pay my respects—to you, to your mother, to these kind people here who've been looking after you. But I can see now that this wasn't the best time or place to get reacquainted or make amends. You're grieving and not thinking straight. So I'm gonna back off, give you a few days to mull things over, then try again. How's that?"

"How much do you want, Dylan?" Cassidy asked.

"What do you mean?"

"How much money will it take to make you go away for good?"

"Ah, honey. You got me all wrong. This isn't about money."

"It isn't? Well, then, I guess there's nothing left to talk about."

"Well, I mean, sure," Dylan said quickly. "It's not the reason I came, but if my daughter would like to help me out a bit financially, well, I wouldn't turn it down."

"How much?" Cassidy asked.

"A hundred thousand?" He glanced quickly at the sheriff. "That's not blackmail or anything. You heard her. She offered."

"A hundred thousand," Cassidy repeated. "What would you do with all that money?"

"I was thinking about maybe starting up a business."

"Cool. What kind of business?"

"Well, I haven't thought that far ahead yet." Dylan tried for his most endearing smile, but managed only a twitch instead.

There was a long pause.

"I don't think so," Cassidy said. She turned to Robin. "We can go now."

"Okay. Wait," Dylan said. "Maybe that was a little steep. Fifty thousand would probably do me."

"No," Cassidy said, grabbing both Robin's and Blake's hands. "Mommy was right. You're scum."

"You little bitch," Dylan said, his voice a combination of anger and admiration. "You were just playing with me, weren't you?"

"Sheriff," Cassidy said, "please make this man stop bothering us."

"Time to move on, Dylan," the sheriff said.

"I'll get a lawyer," Dylan said.

Cassidy smiled. "Give it your best shot."

—THIRTY-FOUR—

"I've got to hand it to you, kiddo," Melanie was saying as Blake's car was pulling away from the gravesite. "For a twelve-year-old, that was impressive as hell. Don't think I could have handled it any better myself."

"Can I tell you something?" Cassidy asked, looking sheepish.

"Of course," Robin said.

"Those things I said . . . I kind of borrowed them from *Bleeding Hearts*."

"*Bleeding Hearts*?"

"That TV show we were watching the other day?" Blake asked.

Cassidy nodded. "It was a few months ago. Penny was being blackmailed by Jason. He's her third—no, her fourth—husband. He showed up just as she was about to marry Reed and told her that he was a changed man and begged her to give him another chance. And she said that one look at him told her everything she needed to know, and asked how much was it going to take to make him go away for good. And then she told him to give it his best shot."

"Wow," said Melanie. "You remembered all that?"

"Do you think he'll really hire a lawyer?" Cassidy asked.

"With Dylan Campbell, anything is possible," Robin said.

Panic filled Cassidy's eyes. "But he wouldn't get custody, would he? I mean, if he went to court, there's no chance that he . . ."

"No," said Robin. "We would never let that happen."

"How could you stop him?"

"We'll stop him," Blake said from the front seat.

"You promise?"

"I promise," Blake said.

Cassidy breathed a deep sigh of relief and settled back into Robin's arms as Blake turned the car toward the exit.

"Wait," Robin said, lurching forward in her seat.

"Something wrong?"

"No. I just thought . . ."

"Oh, dear," said Melanie. "She's thinking again."

"Could we stop at Mom's grave?" Robin swiveled toward Cassidy. "I haven't seen the headstone and . . . I won't be long, I promise. I just thought . . . since we're already here . . ."

"Sure," Cassidy said. "It's down that way, right?" She pointed in the direction that Melanie had indicated earlier.

"Why not?" Melanie said. "Stop here," she said a minute later. "It's the second-to-last row. Third from the end." She pointed to her left as Blake pulled the car to a stop.

"Do you want me to come with you?" Blake asked as Robin opened the rear door.

"No. I'll find it."

"Wait. *I'm* coming," Melanie said, exiting the front seat and catching up to her sister.

"It's all right. You don't have to . . ."

"I know I don't have to. Maybe I want to. Is that a problem?"

"No, of course not."

"Good. That's it—over there." She pointed to a rose-colored granite headstone several yards away.

Robin walked cautiously toward it, silently reading the simple inscription etched across its surface as she approached: *Sarah Davis. Wife. Mother. Grandmother. In Our Hearts You Live Forever.*

"A cliché, I know, but what can you do?" Melanie said.

"It's lovely."

"Yeah? Well, I'm sure you would have come up with something more profound, but then . . ."

". . . I wasn't here," Robin acknowledged. She took a deep breath. "Look. I'm sorry that I let you down, that I wasn't here more. I know it wasn't easy for you, looking after Mom . . ."

Melanie shook off Robin's sympathy with a shrug of her shoulders. "It wasn't. But, hey, what's done is done. I wasn't exactly laying out the welcome mat."

"You never liked me very much," Robin said.

"Yeah, well, it's hard to like your sister when she's your mother's clear favorite."

"I wasn't her—" Robin started to protest.

"Sure you were. I knew it from the minute she brought you home from the hospital, and that was years before I heard her tell you so."

"You heard her . . . ?"

"Tell you that you were her favorite? Oh, yes. The memory is seared into my brain. There you were, all nice and cozy, curled up on her lap on the sofa, and there I was, watching from the shadows." She shrugged again, as if to say it didn't matter. Her eyes said something else.

"I'm sorry," Robin said again.

"You certainly didn't look sorry at the time. You looked about as pleased as a little girl could be."

Robin acknowledged the truth with a nod of her head and a long exhalation. It was several seconds before she spoke. "I knew you were there."

Melanie made a face halfway between a smile and a scowl. "I thought you did. I bet it made the moment that much sweeter."

"It did," Robin admitted. She looked across the rows of gravestones. "I was, what, ten? I'd spent my whole life trying to get my big sister's approval. All I ever got was a cold shoulder and a broken nose."

Melanie chuckled. "And even that worked in your favor. Gave your face some much-needed character."

Both sisters stared absently at the horizon.

"Did you ever confront Mom?" Robin asked.

"I thought about it once," Melanie said, "when she was making the usual round of excuses for you not coming home. But she was pretty sick by then, and what was I supposed to tell her without sounding like the jealous brat I was?"

Robin stared down at her mother's grave. "You could tell her now."

Melanie's eyes narrowed, a sneer tugging at her lips. "What are you—my therapist now?"

"I'm your sister," Robin said. "Go on. Tell her."

Melanie scoffed. "You think she's listening?"

"I don't think it matters."

There was a long pause. "Sure. Why not? I'll play along. Here goes nothing." She took a deep breath. "Not sure what I'm supposed to say, but . . ." Another pause, this one so long that Robin thought she'd decided not to continue. "Okay. Here's the thing, Mom. You shouldn't have played favorites. It wasn't fair. I know I wasn't an easy child to mother. But I *was* your child. And I loved you. And you hurt my feelings. Yes, surprise! I actually have them." She turned back to Robin, her cheeks flushing pink with embarrassment. "Okay, that's it. Happy now?"

Robin inched forward, her shoes sinking into the soft ground around her mother's grave, rooting her in place. "Do you think she knew about Dad's affairs?" she surprised herself by asking.

"Are you kidding me? Of course she did," Melanie said. "You think the whole town knew and she didn't?"

"All those years I thought I was protecting her," Robin said. "All those years I felt so guilty for keeping his secret. And she knew all along."

"What did she know?" a small voice asked from behind them.

The sisters turned to see Cassidy and Blake watching from a few feet away.

"Sorry," Blake said. "Didn't mean to sneak up on you. We were starting to get worried."

"That's okay," Melanie said, walking toward them. "We're done here."

A few minutes later, they turned onto Larie Lane. Robin spotted a black Honda Civic parked behind Melanie's car in the driveway. "Whose car is that?"

Cassidy stretched forward in her seat. "Looks like Kenny's."

"Who's Kenny?" Blake asked.

"The boy who visited Cassidy in the hospital," Robin reminded him.

"Landon's friend," Cassidy clarified.

Blake parked his car, leaving enough room for Kenny to get his car out, then ran around to help Cassidy out of the backseat. She collapsed against his side. "Whoa," Blake said. "You okay?"

"A little dizzy," Cassidy said.

Blake scooped her into his arms. "Let me carry you inside."

"No. I can walk."

"No arguments," said Robin, walking beside them as Melanie hurried ahead to unlock the front door.

"Landon," she called out as they entered the house, "we're home."

There was no answer.

"I'll see what we have for lunch." Melanie headed for the kitchen as Blake carried Cassidy into the living room and deposited her on the sofa.

His cell phone rang and he reached into his pocket, glancing at the caller ID. "Sorry. It's the office. I've got to take this." He walked into the hallway.

Cassidy's eyes brimmed over with sudden tears. "What's going to happen to me if Daddy doesn't get better?" she asked Robin.

"Please stop worrying about that. We'll figure something out."

"What?"

"I don't know. You heard Blake. He won't let anything bad happen."

"Do you believe that everything happens for a reason?" Cassidy asked.

Robin gave the question a moment's thought. "No," she answered, deciding that the child deserved honesty, not platitudes. "I know that lots of people find it comforting to think that, but I just don't buy it. Things happen because they happen. I actually find it more comforting to believe things happen randomly than to believe there's some sort of divine plan that justifies a child dying of cancer or people starving to death." *Or forever friends being gunned down in cold blood.* "But even if things *don't* happen for a reason," she added, trying to soften her words, "I think they still have a way of working out."

"Isn't it the same thing?"

"I think there's a subtle difference."

"A subtle difference between what and what?" Blake asked, re-entering the room.

"Do you think everything happens for a reason?" Cassidy asked him.

"I think there are reasons things happen," Blake said. "But do I believe in some sort of greater plan? No. I guess I subscribe to Albert Camus's theory of 'the benign indifference of the universe.' "

"What does *that* mean?" Cassidy asked.

"It means I'm hungry," Blake said with a laugh. "I always quote Camus when I get hungry."

Robin wanted to jump up and hug him. "What did the office want?"

Blake sank down beside Cassidy. "Unfortunately, the deal we thought was in the bag appears to be unraveling at the seams. There's a meeting scheduled for Monday to address the issues, so it looks as if I'll be heading back to L.A. on Sunday."

"No!" Cassidy cried. "That's only a few more days."

"It's okay, sweetheart," Robin said. "I'll be here." *How could she leave with things still so up in the air? She couldn't very well just dump everything in Melanie's lap again.*

"For how long?" Cassidy asked. "You're not gonna hang around forever once Blake goes home. What's gonna happen to me when you leave? What's gonna happen to me if Daddy dies?"

Robin looked to Blake.

"We'll work something out," he said.

"What?" Cassidy pressed. "Can I go with you to L.A.?"

They heard a shuffling noise and turned to see Kenny standing in the doorway, Landon behind him. "Somebody going to L.A.?" Kenny asked. He pushed his hair off his forehead, then buried his hands in the pockets of his skinny jeans.

"We were just talking," Cassidy said.

"About you going to L.A.?"

"Nothing's been decided," Cassidy told him.

"I don't think you should go."

"Well, we'll see. You know I've always wanted to live there."

"Your dad could get better."

"Then, of course, I'll stay."

"But if he doesn't, you'll go?"

There was an edge to Kenny's voice that made Robin uncomfortable.

"Nobody's going anywhere today," Robin said, trying to ease the sudden tension in the room. "Melanie," she called out, "can I give you a hand in there?"

"A little late for that," Melanie said, appearing behind Landon with a large tray of sandwiches.

"What kind of sandwiches did you make?" Cassidy asked.

"Just tuna. Nothing fancy." Melanie put the tray on the coffee table, then took a step back. "Knock yourselves out."

Kenny promptly grabbed a sandwich from the top of the pile and took a large bite. "They're good," he said to no one in particular.

Blake pointedly picked up the tray and offered it to Cassidy.

"Thanks." She smiled up at him as she lifted a sandwich to her mouth.

Robin took a sandwich, noticing the scowl in Kenny's eyes as Blake held the tray toward Landon.

Landon shook his head.

"You gotta eat, big guy," Kenny said, grabbing another sandwich from the tray and pushing it against Landon's chest.

"When did you get here, Kenny?" Melanie asked.

"About an hour ago. Landon said I just missed you. I would have come to the funeral if somebody had told me about it."

"We wanted to keep things as private as possible," Robin explained.

Kenny finished the last of his sandwich and helped himself to another. "Because of your brother being arrested?"

"That's part of it."

"Do you think he did it?" Kenny asked.

"No, I don't think he did it."

"Who did, then?"

"Not Robin's brother." Cassidy fidgeted with agitation. "What's your problem, Kenny? You're acting weird."

"No, I'm not."

"Yes, you are."

Kenny turned toward Melanie. "Did you know that Cassidy's thinking of moving to L.A.?"

"She is?" Melanie looked surprised, but not displeased. "That's news to me."

"Yeah. To me, too," Kenny said. "What about you, Landon? She ever mention anything about wanting to live in L.A. to you?"

Landon's response was to turn and run from the room.

"Now look what you've done," Cassidy said as Landon's feet banged up the stairs. "He's all upset."

"He's fine."

"He isn't fine. You know how sensitive he is."

"He doesn't want you to go to L.A."

"I don't think it's such a bad idea." Melanie lifted a sandwich off the tray. "After everything that's happened, a fresh start might be just what the doctor ordered. And if Robin and Blake are willing . . ."

"I think we're getting ahead of ourselves here," Blake said. "At the moment, I'm the only one who's going anywhere."

"You're leaving us?" Melanie asked.

"On Sunday."

The door to Landon's room slammed shut.

"I think you should go up there," Cassidy said to Kenny. "Make sure he's all right."

"Only if you come, too," Kenny said. "It's because of you he's upset."

Cassidy sighed. She tried to stand up from the sofa but collapsed back onto it from the strain.

"Here," Blake said, "let me help you."

"I'll do it," Kenny said, rushing forward to grab Cassidy's arm.

"Get away," Cassidy said to Kenny. "You're being weird." She allowed Blake to help her to her feet, then walk her out of the room and slowly up the stairs, Kenny on their heels.

Robin stood up. "Well, that was . . ."

"Weird?" Melanie made her I-told-you-so face. "You know you're crazy if you're seriously considering taking that girl back to L.A. with you, don't you?"

"Didn't you just say you thought it was a good idea?"

"Oh, don't get me wrong. I'd be thrilled. I just thought you were smarter than that."

"What are you talking about?"

"I'm talking about the obvious crush Cassidy has on your boyfriend, which might not seem like much of a threat to you now, but she won't be twelve forever. And if she's anything like her mother was at eighteen . . ."

"Now you're just being mean."

"And you're being obtuse."

Blake returned to the living room to find the two women standing at opposite ends of the couch, glaring at each other. "What just happened?"

The phone rang. Melanie turned on her heel and marched into the kitchen without a word. Seconds later, she was back. "That was the sheriff. Apparently the San Francisco police obtained a warrant to search Alec's apartment and guess what they found?"

Robin's mind raced through the incriminating possibilities: the murder weapon, the contents of their father's safe . . . "Our mother's jewelry?" she said out loud.

"Close, but no cigar."

"Are you going to tell us or do I have to keep guessing?"

"A ski mask. Just like the ones Cassidy described."

"Shit."

"Still convinced he's innocent?"

Robin sank down onto the sofa, cradling her head in her hands. "There has to be some sort of explanation."

"There is," Melanie said. "He's guilty."

—THIRTY-FIVE—

The Tehama County Jail is a coed, medium-security facility whose primary function is to confine inmates for relatively short periods of time while they await processing or trial. Both unimaginative and unattractive in design, it was built in 1974, with additions completed twenty years later, including a reinforced perimeter fence and electronic detection system to ensure that inmates remain inside its ugly brown-brick walls until their release.

"Oh, God," Robin said, as Blake pulled his car into the parking lot and turned off the engine. It was the morning after the funeral, the fourth day of Alec's incarceration and the first time she'd been permitted to visit.

"You don't have to do this," Blake said, swiveling toward her.

"Yes, I do. Guilty or not, he's still my brother." She closed her eyes and took a long, deep breath.

"Are you having a panic attack?"

Robin searched her body for familiar signs of anxiety. Surprisingly, there were none—no trapped birds fluttering wildly against her chest, no razor-sharp knives stabbing at her flesh, no overwhelming urge to flee the scene. "No," she said, opening her eyes. "I'm okay."

"I wish I could go with you."

"I wish you could, too."

Jeff McAllister had already informed them of the prison rules: inmates were allowed a thirty-minute visit twice a week; all visits had to be non-contact and were limited to one person at a time; visitors had to be over eighteen and produce photo IDs; all visitors were subject to search.

"Just remember that you have no expectation of privacy and that your conversation is likely being recorded."

Robin nodded and took another deep breath, smoothing her hair and playing with the top button of her sleeveless mauve sundress. "Do I look all right?"

"You look terrific."

"My face isn't all scrunched up?"

"Your face is beautiful."

Robin smiled and opened her car door.

"Wait," Blake said.

She turned back.

"I love you," he told her.

Robin stretched across the front seat to kiss him gently on the lips. "I love you, too."

She walked up the concrete path to the prison's front door, then stopped for one last deep breath before stepping inside. She was greeted by an unsmiling male officer in a glass booth who asked for her ID, after which she was patted down by a female deputy and her purse was passed through a metal detector. She was then escorted into a waiting area filled with gray plastic chairs and instructed to wait until her name was called.

There were three people already waiting, a middle-aged man and two women. They looked up briefly when she walked in, the younger of the two women offering an almost imperceptible nod in her direction. Robin took a seat in one corner of the room, noting the long tubes of too-bright fluorescent lights lining the recessed ceiling and shining down on the dull white walls. Abundant signs warned visitors against bringing items such as guns, explosive devices, and chewing gum into the jail.

"First time here?" a voice asked from beside her, and Robin jumped. "Sorry. Didn't mean to scare you. Mind if I sit down?"

Robin turned to see the woman who'd acknowledged her arrival. She was in her mid-twenties and auburn-haired, wearing blue jeans and a red V-neck T-shirt that exaggerated the multiple folds of flesh beneath it. She smiled and sat down before Robin could object. "First time, huh," she said, turning her earlier question into a statement.

"Is it that obvious?"

"The dress is a dead giveaway. I wore a dress the first time I came, too. But then you realize there's no point. Do I know you? You look sort of familiar."

"No, I don't think so."

"My name's Brenda. I'm visiting my boyfriend. He got laid off from his job and didn't take it too good, went back the next day and shot up the place. Didn't hurt anybody, but that's more a case of dumb luck than anything else. Turns out it's not as easy to hit your target as it looks on TV. The jackass. Got six years." She shrugged. "What's your guy in for?"

Robin hesitated, wondering if the woman was a plant, if their conversation was being recorded. "It's a mistake . . ."

Brenda laughed. "That what he told you?"

"He didn't have to."

"Yeah, well, good luck with that. What'd you say your name was?"

Robin briefly considered giving Brenda a fake name, but decided against it. "It's Robin."

"You're sure? You kind of hesitated."

"I'm sure."

"Robin," the woman repeated. "Like the bird." She squinted, small hazel eyes all but disappearing inside fleshy cheeks. "You sure do look familiar."

The door at the far end of the room opened and a deputy appeared. "Robin Davis," he announced.

"Davis?" Brenda repeated as Robin was standing up. "Robin *Davis*? No shit. You're related to those people who got shot? I saw your picture in the paper. Damn it, I knew you looked familiar."

"This way," the deputy directed, and Robin eagerly followed him into a small adjoining room. "Empty your purse, please." He pointed toward a scuffed metal table that was the room's only furniture.

"It's already been through the scanner."

"Empty your purse, please," the deputy repeated.

Robin dumped the contents of her beige canvas bag onto the table, revealing a mint-green leather wallet, a bright orange change purse, her cell phone, a checkbook with a torn black plastic cover, three ballpoint pens, a small notebook, a pair of sunglasses in a red faux-ostrich case, and a bunch of crumpled tissues. "No chewing gum," she said, hoping to elicit a smile from the officer, but receiving only the hint of a scowl instead. Robin decided that the poor man had probably heard that line at least a hundred times. "Sorry."

The scowl became fixed. "For what?"

"Bad joke," she muttered, deciding to volunteer nothing further unless asked a direct question. If she wasn't careful, they would throw her in jail, too.

"Okay," the deputy said after rechecking the inside of the bag to make sure it was empty. He handed it back to her, indicating that she could refill it, then directed her to the door opposite the one from which she'd entered. "Your brother will be in shortly. You have thirty minutes."

"Thank you." Robin stepped inside a long, narrow room divided down the middle by a wall of individual glass partitions. Ten round wooden stools were secured to the dividing wall by metal bars, and the concrete floor had been painted an unpleasant shade of butterscotch. An elderly woman sat on a stool at the far end of the room, crying into the telephone on the wall beside her as she spoke to the prisoner on the other side of the partition. Robin slid onto the closest stool, staring at the empty space in front of her, her solemn expression reflected in the glass. *What must it feel like to be on the other side?*

A minute later, her brother was led into his half of the room and directed to the stool across from her. He was wearing the same orange jumpsuit he'd worn to court. His hair was combed away from his face, but he looked gaunt and a decade older than when she'd last seen him. He sat down, lifting the phone to his ear at the same moment that Robin lifted hers.

"Hi," she said.

"Hi."

"How are you doing?"

"Not bad."

"Not good," Robin corrected.

"I've been better."

"Are you eating?"

"A bit. Food's not exactly gourmet. How about you?"

"I'm fine."

"The others?"

"Fine."

"Cassidy?"

"She's doing well, all things considered."

"Must have been quite a shock for her, seeing me," Alec said. "Realizing I wasn't who she thought I was."

"Yes, that was quite a shock for all of us."

Alec looked sheepish. "Sorry about that."

Robin wondered how he'd been planning to handle seeing Cassidy again, but decided not to ask in case their conversation was being monitored.

"I guess I figured I'd be long gone by the time she got out of the hospital, and I wouldn't have to see her at all," he said, as if reading Robin's mind.

She sighed, trying to decide what topics would be safe to broach.

"I didn't do it, Robin," he told her.

So much for that. "I know you didn't."

"Everything I told you that day was the truth."

"I know. I believe you," Robin said, knowing in her bones that no matter how bad it looked or how strong the evidence was against him, Alec was incapable of hurting anyone. She also understood that it was up to her, that she would have to work as hard to prove her brother's innocence as the sheriff's department was working to prove his guilt.

"I loved Tara," Alec said. "She loved me. We were gonna build a life together."

"I'm so sorry."

"Please tell Cassidy that I'm innocent, that I could never hurt her mother."

"I will. I *did*."

"Did she believe you?"

"I don't know."

The door opened and Brenda walked into the room, glancing pointedly at Alec as she walked past Robin and sat down on the stool next to hers. "Your brother's hot," she said out of the corner of her mouth as her boyfriend took a seat next to Alec and picked up his phone.

"Don't look," Robin heard Brenda tell her boyfriend, "but you're sitting next to a real celebrity. The guy who shot his father and murdered his ex-girlfriend. Oh, and shot her kid, too. No, I'm *not* shitting you."

"Robin?" Alec asked. "What's the matter?"

"Nothing. I just hate seeing you in this awful place."

"You and me both." He rubbed his jaw. "Did you speak to Prescott?"

"Yes."

"Then you know about the ski mask the cops found in my apartment."

"Maybe we shouldn't talk about this," Robin said.

"Why not? It's a black ski mask, for fuck's sake. Not some rare artifact. There must be a million like it around."

"Why would *you* have one?"

"Why would *I* have one?" he repeated, looking at the ceiling in obvious frustration. "I ski, for God's sake. The police found ski boots, too. Did the sheriff tell you that?"

Robin felt a rush of hope. "Since when do you ski?"

"Since after I left Red Bluff. I was depressed. Hell, I was almost suicidal. Thought skiing would be as good a way to kill myself as any. Discovered to my shock that I was actually good at it. And I loved it. It's very therapeutic. You should try it."

She smiled. "Maybe you'll give me lessons when you get out."

"Might not be for another thirty years."

The smile froze on Robin's lips. "Please don't talk like that."

"Sorry. A little jailhouse humor."

"Not very funny."

"There's something else you should know."

Robin held her breath. Had the search of Alec's apartment turned up any other potentially incriminating evidence? "What else?"

"McAllister thinks they might be willing to offer me a deal."

"What kind of deal?"

"He thinks the State might be willing to agree to a charge of murder two, providing I agree to name my accomplice."

"But you didn't do it. You don't have an accomplice."

Alec smiled. "Aye, there's the rub."

They sat for several seconds in silence. "So what are we going to do?" Robin said finally.

"There is no 'we' here, Robin. Just me. You need to pack your bags, grab your fiancé, and get your ass out of town."

"No way. I'm not leaving until you're out of here."

"Yeah," Alec said, "you are." He stood up, the phone cord stretching into a straight line as he motioned for the deputy standing guard at the door.

"What are you doing? We still have lots of time."

"Don't come back, Robin. Get out of here while you can still breathe."

"Alec . . . ," Robin called as the deputy led him from the room. But he didn't stop, didn't so much as turn around. She returned the phone to its receiver, then lowered her chin to her chest and cried.

"It gets easier," Brenda said, leaning toward her. "You'll see. A few more weeks and this place'll feel just like home."

—THIRTY-SIX—

The doorbell rang at just after six o'clock that evening.

"Pizza's here," Melanie called from the kitchen. "Can somebody please answer the door?"

"I'll get it." Robin finished setting the last place at the dining room table and walked into the hallway. Cassidy and Blake were watching TV in the living room, and Robin gave a little wave when she passed by. She heard Landon's bedroom door open and his footsteps on the stairs as she opened the front door, unprepared for what she would see. "Oh, my God."

"Robin," said the woman on the other side of the threshold. "It's been a long time. You're looking well. May I come in?"

Robin stepped back to allow the woman to enter. She glanced over her shoulder at Landon, who stood watching from the foot of the stairs.

"What's happening with that pizza?" Melanie called, coming out of the kitchen, then stopping dead in her tracks. "Holy shit."

The woman's shoulders stiffened at the profanity.

"Melanie," she said. "My goodness. You girls haven't changed a bit."

"You sure have," Melanie said. "What's with the hair?"

Robin shot her sister a look of disapproval, although she'd been thinking the same thing. The woman's hair, once black and luxurious, was now stringy and gray. It hung in uncombed strands halfway down her back. Her dress was a shapeless beige sack, her feet bare in her worn Birkenstocks. She looked like the stereotype of an aging hippie, a throwback to a time that was never as simple or loving as it had once seemed.

"What are you doing here?" Melanie asked.

"Where else would I be?"

"Wherever you've been for the last decade, I guess."

"Is the pizza here?" Blake asked, joining them in the hall. "Oh, sorry." He looked toward the gray-haired woman. "Who's this?"

"Blake," Robin said, "this is Holly Bishop." She took a long, deep breath. "Tara's mother."

"Oh, dear Lord." The woman burst into tears. "My poor baby." She flung herself into Robin's arms, sobbing on her shoulder. "How could this happen?"

Robin's arms inched reluctantly around the woman's thickening waist. "I'm so sorry, Mrs. Bishop."

"Took you long enough to get here," Melanie said, her voice cold. "It's been almost two weeks since Tara died."

"I just found out." Holly Bishop pulled out of Robin's embrace. "I left Oregon as soon as I heard."

Robin couldn't help noticing that the woman's eyes were dry despite the sobs that had racked her body only seconds earlier.

"I live in a pretty isolated area. We don't have TVs or personal computers."

"So how did you find out?"

"Reverend Sampson, our leader. He told me."

"Your leader has a computer?" Robin asked.

"Yes, of course. An old one. Someone has to be aware of what's happening in the world. He relays all pertinent information."

"To his flock," Melanie said.

"To his followers, yes," Holly corrected. "He heard about the shootings and came to me. He remembered that I used to live in Red Bluff, that I still had family here."

"And figured out that your granddaughter would be coming into a lot of money that might allow him to upgrade his equipment," Melanie said. "A godsend, you might say."

"That's not why I'm here."

"Why *are* you here?" Robin asked.

"I came to see Cassidy. That poor child." Holly's voice quivered, but once again there were no actual tears.

"What's going on?"

Robin turned to see Cassidy standing in the living room doorway.

"Hello," Cassidy said to the woman.

"Oh, my," Holly said. "Is this my precious baby?"

"Who are you?"

Holly crossed both hands over her heart. "I'm your grandmother, darling."

"My grandmother?"

"Your mother's mother," Holly explained, inching toward her.

"The one who disowned her after she married Dylan," Melanie clarified.

Holly came to an abrupt halt. Her mouth opened, but it was several seconds before any sounds emerged. "Well, I didn't approve of her marriage, that's true," she sputtered, "but I never actually disowned her."

"You didn't talk to her. You didn't help her," Robin said.

"She didn't want my help."

"You ran off with a cult—"

"It's not a cult, dear. It's a religious order."

"Really? What church?"

"Well, it's not an actual church, but—"

"But you joined it anyway. And you ran off, left Tara to fend for herself."

"It was what she wanted."

"It was what *you* wanted," Melanie said.

"It was what the Lord wanted," Holly said, as if that was the final word.

"Did the Lord want Tara to be murdered?" Robin asked. "Is that the kind of God you ran off to serve?"

"The Lord works in mysterious ways," Holly began. "We can't hope to understand—"

"You think things happen for a reason?" Cassidy interrupted, glancing at Robin.

Robin smiled, marveling at the child's composure.

"I do."

"So you think there's a good reason that some moron blew Mommy's face off? That Daddy Greg is in a coma? That *I* almost died? You think God planned for that to happen?"

"I have to think there's a reason that we mortals can't comprehend, yes."

"Why?"

"Why?" Holly repeated. "Because—"

"Because you're too stupid to think for yourself?" Cassidy challenged. "That's what Mommy always said about you, you know, that you were too stupid to think for yourself, and that you joined a cult so someone else could do it for you."

Holly visibly stiffened.

"She told me about how mean you were to her," Cassidy continued. "How you were always putting her down, telling her she'd never amount to anything. She said that my grandfather was so starved for affection that he ran off with the first woman who was nice to him."

"Oh, yes. She always took his side. Even after he left us for that whore, she blamed me and made excuses for him. And where is that poor love-deprived man now?" Holly asked. "Has he shown up to comfort you? Is he here?"

"Not yet," Melanie said. "But I'm sure he'll be arriving any day now."

"Cassidy's suddenly very popular," Robin chimed in. "Why is that, I wonder?"

"I don't know about anyone else," Holly began, ignoring the two sisters and speaking directly to Cassidy. "But I'm here because, in spite of everything, and no matter what you might think, I loved your mother. And I love you. You're all I have left of her. My baby is dead . . ."

"And you haven't seen me since *I* was a baby. I wouldn't have known you if I tripped over you on the street. And now you suddenly show up and want to be my nana? Give me a break. You're here for the same reason that Dylan Campbell is here."

"Dylan's here?"

"Staying at the Red Rooster," Melanie said.

"You might want to get in touch," Robin added.

"Dylan Campbell may be here because he smells a payoff, but I'm not." Holly Bishop looked down at her plain beige dress. "Material goods have never been important to me. I'm here because—"

"Because you loved Mommy, you love me, I'm all you have left, your baby's dead, it's the Lord's plan. Did I miss anything?" Cassidy said. "I'm tired. I don't want to talk to you anymore." She moved toward Landon. "Come on, Landon. Let's go upstairs." She took Landon's hand and together they started to climb the steps.

"Cassidy, wait," Holly called after them.

"Call me when the pizza gets here," Cassidy said, without looking back.

Robin watched them disappear up the stairs.

"Wow," Melanie said. "I don't know about you, but I'm liking that girl more every day."

"She's her mother's daughter, all right," Holly said. "God help us."

"What exactly did you think was going to happen?" Robin demanded. "Did you really expect that after all this time, after everything that's happened, Cassidy was just going to welcome you into her life with open arms?"

"I don't know what I thought," Holly admitted. "Maybe that she'd want to come back to Oregon with me." A lone tear tracked down her cheek and disappeared inside the corner of her mouth. "Wishful thinking, I guess. And now I should go." She reached inside the pocket of her dress and pulled out a small white card. "It's Reverend Sampson's private line," she said, handing the card to Robin. "In case Cassidy changes her mind."

"Drive carefully," Robin told Holly, opening the front door, then watching her climb behind the wheel of her rented Ford and drive away. "Don't think we'll be needing this," she said, crumpling the card in her fist.

"Wait," Melanie said, taking the card from Robin's hand and smoothing it out.

"What are you doing?"

"You never know."

"I know that Cassidy made her feelings about her grandmother very clear."

"Cassidy's a child. Children's feelings change every hour."

"Wow," Robin said. "I thought we were on the same page."

"Look. I'm no fan of Holly's, but she *is* Cassidy's grandmother. And decisions eventually have to be made about who's going to look after her long-term. Because it sure as hell ain't gonna be me. Not when she has a father and a grandmother both eager to take her."

"You know as well as I do that they're only interested in her inheritance," Robin argued.

"Which isn't my problem. *Cassidy's* not my problem. And if you're smart you won't let guilt and a misguided sense of loyalty make her yours either."

"So what are you suggesting? That we just abandon her?"

"I'm not suggesting anything. I'm coming right out and saying that I have no intention of being a mother to that child. I've done my time as far as motherhood is concerned. Trust me, it's not all it's cracked up to be. So it looks like (a) she goes to live with either her father or her grandmother, (b) she becomes a ward of the court, or (c) you take her back with you to L.A. Those are the options." Melanie looked to Blake, her eyes challenging his. "What say you, Blake? Are you ready to be a father to a teenage girl you barely know?"

"It's a lot to think about," he admitted after a silence of several seconds.

"Yes, and unfortunately, we don't have a lot of time. Even if our father survives the weekend, the odds are he'll be a vegetable for whatever time he has left, and much as I've enjoyed our time together, I can't play hostess forever. I have to get back to work. Tillie's won't hold my job forever. And nothing is going to be accomplished by your hanging around indefinitely."

"Our brother . . ."

". . . is in jail. There's nothing you can do about that, except maybe visit him for half an hour twice a week until he goes to trial, which might not be for another six months. And that's assuming he'll agree to see you. Are you really going to put your life on hold that long? I don't think so. No. The party's over. Your fiancé is heading back to L.A. on Sunday, and I strongly suggest you go with him. What you do with Cassidy is up to you. But face it, Robin. You really don't want her any more than I do."

Robin lowered her head, the weight of her sister's words falling squarely on her shoulders. As much as she hated hearing them, she couldn't dismiss them out of hand. Did she really want the responsibility of taking Cassidy back to L.A. to live with her and Blake? Was she ready to be the mother of a teenage girl, to raise Tara's child as her own?

"We'll figure things out," Blake said, putting his arm around her and turning her toward the living room.

Which was when they saw her.

Cassidy was standing at the foot of the stairs, her mouth open, her eyes brimming with tears.

"Cassidy . . . ," Robin said, reaching for her. *How long had she been standing there? How much had she overheard?*

In response, Cassidy turned on her heel and ran back up the stairs. Seconds later, the door to her room slammed shut.

"I honestly didn't know she was there," Melanie said.

"I'll talk to her," Robin said.

"And say what?"

Robin shook her head. "I have no idea."

—THIRTY-SEVEN—

"So what are we going to do?" Robin asked, lying beside Blake in bed, flutters of anxiety weaving between her heartbeats.

"What do you *want* to do? Ultimately it's your decision."

"No. It affects you as much as it affects me. It has to be something we decide together."

"And if I say I'm not ready?"

"Is that what you're saying?"

"I don't know."

It was almost midnight. They'd been going back and forth like this ever since dinner, reviewing their options, listing the pros and cons. Nobody except Melanie had been hungry, so most of the extra-large pizza they'd ordered had remained in the box. Landon had come downstairs eventually and helped himself to a couple of slices, but Cassidy had remained locked in her room, despite repeated attempts by both Robin and Blake to get her to talk.

"Okay," Blake said. "What if we suggest a compromise? Offer to have Cassidy with us for part of the time."

Robin sat up beside him, considering his suggestion. "It wouldn't work, even if Melanie agreed to it, which she won't. Cassidy needs stability. She needs love." She closed her eyes and took a deep breath. "She needs *us*."

There was a long pause. "Then I guess that settles that," Blake said. "Decision made."

"Is it the right one?"

"Time will tell."

"What about us?" she asked.

"What *about* us?"

"I don't want to lose you."

Another long pause. "You won't lose me," Blake said. "Don't you know that by now?"

Robin swiveled around to face him. "I love you so much."

"I love you, too."

They fell back against the pillows, wrapped in each other's arms.

"Should I go wake up Cassidy and tell her?" she asked.

"Sure. Why not?"

Robin got out of bed, threw a housecoat over her nightgown, and left the room. She tiptoed across the hall, listening at Cassidy's door, about to knock.

She heard the sound of a door opening and turned around, expecting to see Blake. Instead she saw Landon, wearing pajama bottoms and naked from the waist up. He was even more massive than she'd imagined, his neck thick, his chest chiseled and muscular.

"Landon," she acknowledged. "Sorry. Did I wake you?"

"Leave Cassidy alone."

"I was just—"

"Leave her alone." His hands formed fists at his sides.

"It's good news, Landon. I think she'd want to hear—"

"Leave her alone." Even though his voice was barely above a whisper, it had the intensity of a shout.

Blake appeared in the doorway of their bedroom, looking from Robin to Landon and back again. "Is there a problem?"

"Landon doesn't think I should wake Cassidy up."

Landon took a menacing step forward.

"Okay," Blake said. "Maybe Landon's right. It's late. Cassidy needs her rest. We can talk to her in the morning."

"Why don't we all try to get some sleep?" Robin agreed, crossing back to her room. "You, too, Landon," she said when he didn't move. "I promise I won't try to talk to Cassidy again tonight."

Landon hesitated, but then returned to his room and closed the door.

"That was creepy," Robin said, climbing back into her bed.

Blake crawled in beside her. "Your sister's right," he said, folding her in his arms. "It's time we got out of here."

"You're out of your minds," Melanie pronounced at breakfast when Robin informed her of their decision.

"I would have thought you'd be ecstatic." Robin finished the last of her coffee and smiled across the table at Blake. "Assuming Dad's condition remains unchanged and Cassidy agrees, we'll all be out of your hair first thing Sunday morning."

"What'll you tell the sheriff?"

"The truth. That we're taking Cassidy back to L.A. and that if he needs to talk to her, he knows where to find us."

"And Alec?"

"I'll come back as often as possible, do whatever I can to help him."

"Like what?"

I wish I knew, Robin thought. "It's kind of late," she said, checking her watch. "Do you think Cassidy's all right?"

"The kid survived a bullet," Melanie said. "A few harsh words won't kill her."

Robin pushed herself away from the table. "I should check."

"Suit yourself."

Robin headed up the stairs, stopping at the top of the landing to listen for the sound of Landon rocking. But there was nothing. Which meant he was probably standing at the window, she decided, tiptoeing toward Cassidy's room. She didn't want a repeat of last night's confrontation.

"Cassidy," she said, knocking gently on the door. "Cassidy, it's Robin. I have some news. Cassidy?" She knocked louder. "Wake up, honey. I have something to tell you."

She twisted the handle. The door opened.

Even before Robin stepped into the room, she knew it was empty. She crossed to the window and pulled open the drapes, flooding the room with sunshine. The sun shone a spotlight on Cassidy's empty, unmade bed. "Oh, God. Where are you?"

Robin hurried down the stairs and into the kitchen. "She's gone."

"What do you mean, she's gone?" Melanie asked.

"I mean, she's gone."

"So she went out. I'm sure there's nothing to worry about."

"Cassidy was very upset last night. She thinks that nobody wants her."

"Maybe Landon knows where she is," Melanie suggested.

Robin turned and ran back up the steps, Blake right behind her. "Landon!" She banged loudly on his door. "Landon, I need to speak to you." She pushed his door open.

He wasn't there.

"Shit."

"Take it easy," Melanie said when they returned to the kitchen. "They're obviously together, and if Landon's with her, she'll be fine."

Robin thought of last night's confrontation. "Maybe we should call the sheriff."

"A little early to be calling in the troops, don't you think?"

The doorbell rang, followed by loud knocking.

"There. See," Melanie said. "The prodigal daughter returns."

Robin marched to the front door and opened it.

The sheriff was standing on the other side.

"Oh, God. Cassidy . . ."

Sheriff Prescott looked confused, his eyebrows knitting together above the bridge of his nose. "Is there a problem?"

"What are you doing here?"

"Is your sister home?"

"My sister?" Robin looked over her shoulder toward the kitchen. "Melanie," she called. "Sheriff Prescott's here." She turned back to the sheriff, noticing for the first time that he hadn't come alone, that there were two other patrol cars parked behind his in the driveway.

"Has something happened?" Blake asked, joining her at the door.

"I have a search warrant," the sheriff said, holding it in his right hand.

"A search warrant?" Robin repeated. "What do you mean?"

"It's a warrant giving us permission to search the house." He signaled to the waiting deputies.

"Can I see that?" Blake extended his open palm.

Melanie approached, hands on her hips, a frown on her face. "What's going on?"

"They have a warrant to search the house," Robin said.

"Let me see that." Melanie grabbed the warrant from Blake's hands.

"It looks to be in order," Blake said.

"I don't care what kind of order it's in," Melanie said. "You're not setting foot inside this house."

"Come on, Melanie," Prescott said. "Let's not make this any more unpleasant than it has to be. I don't want to have to arrest you."

"I don't understand," Robin said. "Why do you want to search the house? What are you looking for?"

"They're looking for evidence, obviously," Melanie said. "They think Landon was Alec's accomplice."

"But Alec didn't do anything."

"And neither did Landon."

"Is Landon home?" Prescott asked.

"No," Robin said.

"And Cassidy?"

"Not here," Robin said, deciding this probably wasn't the best time to elaborate.

"Good. Then let us inside to do our job," Prescott said. "Hopefully we'll be out of here before they get back. We'll try not to make too much of a mess." He waved the deputies inside the house.

"You piece of shit," Melanie muttered as they entered the hallway. "You won't find anything."

"We'll start with the upstairs," the sheriff said, stopping at the foot of the steps. "If you'd be kind enough to direct me to Landon's room."

"You're the one with the search warrant," Melanie told him. "Find it yourself."

—THIRTY-EIGHT—

One deputy remained downstairs while the sheriff and the other three officers headed for the upstairs bedrooms. Prescott directed one deputy to Melanie's room, another to the room Robin and Blake were sharing, and the third to Cassidy's room, leaving Landon's bedroom for himself. "We'll be as quick and as careful as we can," Prescott told Robin and Blake as he donned a pair of latex gloves to pull back the curtains in Landon's room and flip on the overhead light.

"You break anything, you pay for it," Melanie warned.

"I'm going to need you to stand back," Prescott said. "You can watch if you want, but you're not to interfere in any way."

"You are one miserable son of a bitch," Melanie told him.

"Melanie . . . ," Robin cautioned.

"What? Are you going to tell me he's just doing his job? That this isn't personal?"

"Why would it be personal?" Robin's eyes shot

between her sister and the sheriff, the reason for their enmity suddenly clear. "Whoa," she gasped. "Seriously? You and the sheriff?"

"Guess I forgot to mention it," Melanie acknowledged. "Guess he wasn't all that memorable."

"Can we not do this now?" the sheriff said.

"Yeah, I think that's what you said when you told me you'd decided to patch things up with your wife."

"And I'm deeply sorry that I hurt you. It was never my—"

"You didn't hurt me," Melanie interrupted. "Shit. Don't flatter yourself. Just don't try to tell me this isn't personal."

"I'm sorry," he apologized again, looking sheepishly at Robin. "But none of this has anything to do with my investigation or why I'm here. Believe me, I'd rather be anywhere else."

I believe you, thought Robin.

"Now, we've wasted enough time."

"You can say that again," Melanie said.

The sheriff sighed in defeat and pulled open the top drawer of the dresser, sweeping his gloved hand through Landon's underwear, then moving on to the drawer below, which contained his T-shirts and socks.

The third drawer was filled to overflowing with sweatpants and sweatshirts, all of which Prescott shook out before tossing them across the bed.

"So much for not making a mess," Melanie said.

"Come on, Melanie," Robin said, still reeling from the realization of her sister's affair with Prescott. "You're only making things worse."

The bottom drawer contained sweaters and a crumpled black rain jacket. The sheriff checked the jacket's pockets, then returned it to the drawer before getting down on his hands and knees in front of the bed.

"Careful, Sheriff," Melanie warned. "If I remember correctly, you don't have a lot of stamina."

Prescott's jaw visibly clenched as he flattened himself on the floor to shine a flashlight underneath the bed.

"Take your time getting back up," Melanie said. "You don't want to give yourself a hernia."

"Okay," Prescott said, noticeably out of breath as he sank down onto the bed, although whether it was with exertion or impatience was impossible to tell. "I think I've had just about enough of your sarcasm, so you can either stop with the smart-ass remarks or you can wait in my patrol car. The choice is yours."

Melanie raised her hands in mock surrender, then drew a line across her mouth with her fingers, as if she were zipping it closed.

"Thank you." Prescott reached over to pull open the top drawer of the nightstand.

You won't find much in there but pencils and paper clips, Robin thought, recalling her own search of Landon's belongings.

The sheriff withdrew the large ball of elastic bands, turning it over in his hands several times before tossing it back into the drawer. He moved on to the drawer below and leafed through a stack of comic books. "That's quite a collection he's got here," Prescott remarked as he walked around the bed to the nightstand on the other side. More paper clips, more pens, more pencils, along with several loose scraps of paper, including the sketches of Cassidy.

Except that Cassidy was no longer recognizable; her face had been completely scribbled over with angry black lines.

"Somebody wasn't very happy with his work," the sheriff said, returning the papers to the drawer as Robin suppressed a gasp.

What did it mean? Why would Landon have defaced his sketches of Cassidy?

"Hold on," Prescott said, stopping suddenly. "What's this?"

Robin leaned forward, expecting to see a dome-shaped snow globe with a tiny plastic ballerina twirling in its center. Instead she saw something black and bulky, made of wool.

The sheriff unfolded it with deliberate care and held it out.

It was a ski mask.

Robin bit her lip as Melanie stiffened beside her, her face draining of color. *How could I have missed that?*

"Brian!" the sheriff called. "Peter! Get in here."

Two deputies instantly came running, pushing past Robin, Blake, and Melanie.

"Bag this," Prescott said.

"You planted that," Melanie said, her voice quivering.

"Bullshit and you know it." The sheriff dropped the ski mask into the plastic bag the deputy held out. "You guys find anything?"

"Not so far."

"Take this to the car, then keep checking."

The deputies left the room.

"You going to tell me that Landon's been taking skiing lessons?" Prescott asked Melanie.

For once, Melanie was silent.

In the closet, the sheriff removed each item from its hanger, checking the pockets of every pair of jeans and every shirt before tossing each item to the bed.

I've been through those pockets, Robin thought. *There was nothing.* She had to admit, though, that her examination had been perfunctory at best. She breathed a sigh of relief when Prescott's search of Landon's clothes turned up nothing.

He crouched on the floor, his knees cracking loudly with the effort.

This time there were no smart remarks from Melanie. Robin reached out to stroke her sister's arm, but Melanie jerked away as if she'd been burned.

Robin held her breath as the sheriff shone his flashlight into every corner of the long, narrow closet, then pushed his fingers into the toes of each sneaker and shoe. *Please don't let him find anything else,* she prayed, suddenly realizing that Prescott had stopped moving. "What is it?"

The sheriff sighed and struggled to his feet, the effort showing on his face, which had turned a frightening shade of pink. He held out his hand, slowly opening his right fist to reveal a crumpled piece of tissue, the tissue unfolding to reveal a small emerald-and-ruby pin in the shape of a butterfly. Beside it lay a diamond engagement ring and a matching eternity band.

"Oh, God." Robin collapsed against Blake's side.

"I believe these were Tara's," Prescott said, once again calling for his deputies to bag the evidence.

Melanie slid down the wall to the floor, her body as limp as a rag doll.

Robin knelt beside her sister. "Can somebody please get us some water?"

Seconds later, a deputy appeared with a plastic glass, and Robin raised it to her sister's lips. Melanie pushed the glass aside with an angry flick of her hand. It flew across the room, bouncing toward the sheriff's feet and leaving a snaking trail of water in its wake.

"Where is Landon now?" Prescott asked.

Melanie said nothing.

The sheriff looked at Robin. "Where is he?"

Robin shook her head. "I don't know."

"You realize that you're not doing the boy any favors by not cooperating. We're going to find him, and I'm sure we'd all prefer if no one else got hurt."

"We don't know where he is," Robin said. "He's been out all morning."

"With Cassidy?"

"They were gone when we woke up. We assume they're together."

Prescott took a deep breath. "Which means that Cassidy could be in danger."

"Oh, God," Robin said again, thinking of the sketches, Cassidy's sweet face all but obliterated. *Just like her mother's.* "Oh, God," she said a third time.

"I don't care what you found," Melanie said, her voice as flat as if it had been run over by a steamroller.

"Landon would never hurt Cassidy. He's always been very protective of her."

"I think it's time you started telling us the truth, don't you?" the sheriff said.

"What are you talking about?" Robin asked.

"Melanie," Prescott said, a rare note of tenderness creeping into his voice, "you can't account for Landon's whereabouts on the night of the shooting, can you?"

Melanie said nothing. She didn't have to. Her face said it all.

"One person is dead," he continued, "and your father and a twelve-year-old girl were grievously injured. Now, I understand your desire to protect your son, but continuing to lie to us is not only *not* protecting him—it could get him killed."

Melanie stared blankly ahead. It was several seconds before she spoke. "He wasn't having a very good day," she began in a voice not her own. "He was rocking and pacing. He wouldn't talk to me. He wouldn't draw or look at his comic books. I couldn't get him to calm down. I phoned Donny . . ."

"Donny Warren?" the sheriff asked, looking perplexed.

"Donny's always been very good with him. They go for rides on his motorbike; they go horseback riding. He knows how to reach him when I can't. So I called him, told him I was worried. He came right over, took Landon back to his ranch."

"You're saying that Landon was with Donny Warren that night?"

"Yes."

"All night?"

"I don't know. I was exhausted, so I took a sleeping pill and went to bed."

"So you have no idea what time Landon came home."

Melanie shook her head no.

Robin struggled to make sense of what was happening. Tara's jewelry had been found in Landon's room, implicating him in Tara's murder. Her sister had just admitted that Landon had been with Donny Warren for at least part of that night, implicating Donny as well. What did it mean? "What about Alec?" she asked. *If Landon was with Donny that night, wouldn't that exonerate her brother?*

"They could have all been working together," the sheriff said, squashing that hope like a bug underfoot. "Cassidy couldn't say for sure how many men were in the house that night. And don't forget about the ski mask the San Francisco police found in your brother's apartment."

"Which could be a coincidence."

"Never cared much for coincidences in murder investigations," the sheriff said, moving to the bedroom door.

"But Donny didn't even know Alec," Melanie protested. "It doesn't make sense. What motive would he possibly have? What motive would Landon have?"

The sheriff didn't answer, but Robin guessed that he was thinking it was probably personal for Alec and financial for Donny. Maybe some sort of combination of the two as far as Landon was concerned. Or maybe Landon had been nothing more than a convenient pawn, someone they used so they could get into the house without arousing suspicion.

"What happens now?" Blake asked.

"We pay Donny a visit. He has no idea what's happened here or that we found anything. Hopefully we'll find Landon and Cassidy. Fingers crossed that nobody's done anything stupid and that the girl's all right."

Oh, God. Cassidy . . .

"I'm coming with you," Melanie said, scrambling to her feet.

"No, you're not."

"You'll scare Landon. He's liable to panic . . . I don't want him hurt. Please. I might be able to help."

Robin thought it was the first time she'd ever heard her sister plead for anything. "We're coming, too," she said, and Blake nodded his agreement.

Prescott sighed. "All right. But you'll all stay back and do exactly what I say. Do I have your word?"

Robin and Blake nodded their assent, and Melanie agreed half a beat later.

The sheriff assigned one of the deputies to stay at the house in case Landon and Cassidy returned. He dispatched another to the courthouse to get a search warrant for Donny's house and property, and then he and the remaining deputies got into their cars. Blake climbed behind the wheel of his Lexus, and Robin got into the backseat beside her sister.

Tears streamed down Melanie's cheeks, and Robin instinctively reached over to take her hand.

To her shock, Melanie didn't pull away.

—THIRTY-NINE—

Donny Warren's Harley was parked in its usual spot at the side of the cabin when the small procession of cars turned onto his property. His old Chevy was parked down the road, closer to the barn.

"Looks like he's home," Melanie said as Blake pulled his car to a stop behind the sheriff.

The smell of horses hit Robin as soon as she opened her car door and she sneezed four times, one sneeze immediately following the other.

"Bless you," Melanie said as they got out of the car.

"I'm going to need you to stay back here," the sheriff told them.

"What about Landon?"

"If I need you, I'll call you."

"Please don't hurt him," Melanie begged.

Robin watched Prescott pivot toward the small log cabin, his deputies behind him, hands on their holsters as they neared the front door. Her eyes scanned the horizon, but she saw nothing besides acres of dried and yellowing grass. There were no riders in the distance, happily galloping across the barren expanse. If Landon and Cassidy were here, they were inside either the house or the barn, she thought, staring in that direction.

The sheriff knocked on Donny's door and it opened almost immediately to reveal Donny, wearing jeans and a white T-shirt that emphasized the size of his biceps. His hair was uncombed and fell lazily across his forehead. "Sheriff," he said, waving in their direction, his hand stopping in midair. "What can I do for you?"

"Is Landon here?"

"Landon? No. Why? Has something happened?"

"We're just trying to find the boy. We thought he might be here."

"He's not."

"You're sure?"

"Of course I'm sure."

"Any chance he's in the barn?"

"Not that I'm aware of. You can check it yourself if you want."

The sheriff motioned for one of his deputies to do just that.

"What's going on?" Donny asked, his eyes circling back to Melanie.

"When was the last time you saw Landon?"

"A few days ago. Why?"

"What about Cassidy?"

"Cassidy? What about her?"

"Have you seen her?"

"No. I haven't seen Cassidy since before . . ."

". . . she got shot?"

"Right," Donny said.

"You wouldn't have had anything to do with that, would you?" Prescott asked almost casually, as if it were an afterthought.

Donny's face froze before breaking into a wide grin. "Is this a joke? Some kind of hidden-camera thing?"

"No joke, Donny."

"Hold on. You think I had something to do with the shootings?" He stared at Melanie. "You think I shot your father?"

Melanie stepped forward. "No, I don't. I honestly don't."

"Stay back," the sheriff warned.

Robin reached for Melanie's arm to restrain her, but Melanie shook off her sister's hand and continued walking.

"I don't think for a minute that you had anything to do with what happened," Melanie told Donny. "No more than I think Landon had anything to do with it."

The second deputy moved to block Melanie's path.

"Landon?" Donny's focus returned to the sheriff. "You think Landon was involved?"

"They think you were in it together," Melanie said. "Along with Alec."

"Your brother? That's absurd. I just met the man."

"I tried to tell them—"

"You've said more than enough," the sheriff cautioned Melanie. "Get back in the car before I arrest you for interfering with a police investigation."

"They're getting a warrant to search your house and property," Melanie continued as she sidestepped the deputy.

"They don't need a warrant," Donny said. He motioned toward the cabin with a sweep of his hands. "Have at it."

"Maybe you should consult a lawyer," Blake advised.

"I don't need a lawyer. I've got nothing to hide."

"We're going to do this by the book," Prescott said as the deputy returned from the barn, shaking his head to indicate he'd found nothing, "and wait for a warrant. In the meantime, we're going to put out an APB on Landon, and you guys are going to get the hell out of here and go home until I send for you. Am I making myself very clear?"

Robin nodded. "Come on, Melanie."

Melanie shifted her weight from one foot to the other, almost as if she were considering making an end run around the deputy. Then she stopped and turned back to Robin, allowing her to take her arm and guide her toward the car. "What now?" she asked as she crawled into the backseat beside Robin. "We go home and wait for the good sheriff to shoot my son?"

"Not quite," Robin said. "I have another idea."

"What makes you think they're here?" Melanie asked as they were approaching the run-down Loma Vista Trailer Park on Vista Way.

"I can't think of anywhere else," Robin admitted. "Were you ever going to tell me about you and the sheriff?"

"Probably not. Why?"

"Would have been nice to know, that's all."

"Why?" Melanie repeated. "So you'd have another reason to look down your nose at me?"

"I don't look down my nose at you."

"Really? Tell that to your face. It gets all . . ."

". . . scrunched up?"

"Is that a technical term?"

"It's just what happens to my face when I get worried."

Melanie did her own variation of a scrunched-up face. "Yeah, well, you don't have to worry about me. Turn left here. You can park in the lot. His trailer's down that way."

"Did you love him?" Robin asked as Blake pulled his car into the narrow space between a relatively new Toyota and a rusted-over Dodge.

"Are we still talking about the sheriff?" Melanie asked.

"How long were the two of you . . . involved?"

"Four months, give or take a couple of weeks. He stopped me for speeding one afternoon. We started talking. He asked how Dad's house was coming along, how Landon was doing. He told me that he and his wife had separated. One thing led to another. Four months later he was back with his wife. End of affair. End of story."

"And Donny?"

"Probably the end of that story as well, thanks to what just happened." Melanie opened her car door and stepped onto the sand and gravel of the small parking lot. In front of them stood half a dozen rows of dilapidated trailers. "If memory serves, his trailer's down this way."

Robin took Blake's hand and they followed Melanie, turning right at the end of the first row, then right again.

"Shit." Melanie came to a sudden stop. "I don't know. Maybe it's that way. Wait. That's it. Magnolia Lane. This way. Number 24. Over here." She marched toward the second of four squat trailers in obvious need of repair and knocked on its door.

No one answered.

"Kenny?" Melanie knocked again. "Kenny? Anyone home?" She took a step back, waited half a beat, then stood on her tiptoes to peer in the high window. "It's dark. Looks empty."

"Damn it," Robin said. "I really thought there was a chance Cassidy might have come here."

"It was a good thought," Melanie conceded. "Oh, God." She sank to the step in front of the door. "What if Prescott is right? What if Landon *was* involved? What if he was one of the shooters? What if Cassidy *is* in danger?" A low moan escaped her lips. "What if it's too late?"

The door to the trailer suddenly opened, striking Melanie's back. She jumped up and out of the way. Kenny stood in the doorway, shirtless and holding a half-full bottle of beer, the smell of marijuana circling his head like a halo.

"Mrs. Davis?" he said. "What are you doing here?"

"Is Landon with you?" Melanie asked.

"No." He glanced around, as if checking to make sure.

"What about Cassidy?"

"No."

"Damn. Okay. Sorry to bother you."

"They left a while ago," he said as they were turning to go back to their car.

Melanie spun around. "They were here?"

"How long ago?" Robin asked.

"A few hours, maybe."

"How did they get here?" Blake asked. "They can't have walked."

"Cassidy called first thing this morning. She was pretty upset, said to come pick her up."

"And Landon?"

"He's like her shadow, man. Doesn't let her go anywhere without him. You know how he gets . . ."

"What were they doing here?"

Kenny shrugged, his ribs clearly outlined beneath the thin layer of flesh covering them. "You know."

"We *don't* know," Melanie said. "That's why we're asking."

"Just chilling, smoking a little weed."

"You gave my son marijuana?"

Not to mention giving it to a twelve-year-old girl, Robin thought.

"It's not like it's the first time," Kenny said defensively.

"I don't believe this," Melanie said. "This is the last thing the sheriff needs to find out."

Kenny's body tensed. "Who said anything about the sheriff?"

"Do you know where Cassidy and Landon are now?" Robin asked.

Kenny shrugged. "Home, I guess. They caught a ride with one of my neighbors."

"When did they leave?"

Kenny looked confused. "What time is it?"

Robin checked her watch. "Almost twelve."

"Noon?"

"No, midnight," Melanie said. "Of course, noon, you idiot."

"Hey," Kenny said, managing to look both offended and on the verge of unconsciousness at the same time.

"Let's go," Blake said.

"Wait," Kenny said. "I'll come with you."

"No," Robin told him. "You'll stay here. If Landon and Cassidy come back or contact you, call us immediately. Okay? Do you understand me?"

Kenny raised his hand in a mock salute that missed his forehead by several inches. "Aye, aye, Captain."

Melanie was already halfway down the lane. "Let's go, people," she shouted. "We haven't got all day."

—FORTY—

Melanie was out of the car before Blake could pull to a complete stop in her driveway. The deputy Prescott had assigned to stay at the house was nowhere in sight, and neither was his car.

"Landon?" Melanie called, pushing open the front door; Robin was right behind her. "Cassidy?"

There was no answer.

"Landon?" she called again, running up the stairs.

Robin did a quick check of the downstairs rooms. "Cassidy?" she shouted. But there was no sign of her.

"Up here," Melanie yelled, her voice stopping just short of a scream.

"Oh, God," said Robin, grabbing Blake's hand as he reached her side.

Melanie was waiting for them at the top of the stairs, her hands shaking, her face gray with the strain. The door to Landon's room was open. The room was empty.

"What?" Robin asked.

Melanie pointed across the hall at the open door to Cassidy's room.

"What is it?" Robin asked. "Is she there? Is she . . . ?"

"She's on the bed. She's not moving."

Robin bolted from Blake's side, rushing into Cassidy's room and approaching the small figure sprawled face-down across the bed. "Cassidy," she said, her shaking hand reaching out to touch the girl's shoulder, her eyes scanning the comforter for blood. "Oh, God." *Had Landon strangled the child to death with his bare hands?*

"Robin?"

Robin gasped as Cassidy twisted around on the bed to face her.

"What's the matter? Are you all right?"

"Oh, God. Oh, God," Robin cried, hugging the child and motioning the others into the room. "She's okay. She's okay!"

"Shit," Melanie said. "You scared the hell out of us!"

"I don't understand," Cassidy said.

Robin detected the faint but stubborn scent of marijuana laced through the girl's hair.

"Where's Landon?" Melanie said.

"I don't know. He went with that deputy."

"What are you talking about?"

Cassidy rubbed the sleep from her eyes. "When we got home, there was this deputy waiting. He told Landon to get in the patrol car, and they drove off. I wasn't feeling so hot, so I came upstairs to lie down. I guess I fell asleep."

"How long ago was this?"

She glanced at Robin's watch. "About an hour ago, maybe."

"I've got to go," Melanie said.

"Wait," Robin said. "Where are you going?"

"To the sheriff's department. Hopefully they haven't placed Landon under arrest yet."

"Why would they arrest Landon?" Cassidy asked.

"Call McAllister," Melanie said. "Tell him to meet me there."

"I'll take you," Blake offered. "You're in no condition to drive."

For once Melanie didn't argue.

"I'll stay with Cassidy. Phone me as soon as you know anything," Robin called after them. She reached into the pocket of her jeans for her cell phone and called the lawyer's office, relaying Melanie's instructions to his assistant.

"I don't understand. Why would they arrest Landon?" Cassidy asked again.

Robin told her about the warrant to search the house and what they had uncovered.

"They found Mommy's jewelry in Landon's room?"

"Yes."

"And a ski mask?"

"Yes."

Cassidy shook her head. "No. I don't believe it."

"I know. It's inconceivable."

"So they think that Landon and your brother . . ."

"And maybe Donny Warren," Robin said, shocked at the words coming out of her mouth.

"They killed Mommy? They shot me and Daddy?"

Robin said nothing. Inconceivable as it may have been, the evidence against the three men was mounting every day: Alec had had both motive and opportunity to carry out the attack; Landon had obvious behavior problems, and some of Tara's stolen jewelry had been found hidden in his room; Landon had been with Donny on the night of the shootings; identical ski masks had been found in both Landon's room and Alec's apartment. There was no telling what the search of Donny's cabin might uncover. "I'm so sorry," she said, not knowing what else to say.

"I think I'm going to be sick." Cassidy bolted off the bed and ran out of the room.

Robin remained where she was, unable to move, the enormity of the day's events weighing her down like an anchor. She stared blankly ahead, her mind reeling, her head spinning.

Gradually the room returned to focus around her: the small window overlooking the backyard, the bare ecru walls, the ceiling fan whirring gently overhead, the double bed with its billowy beige comforter, the mirrored nightstand beside the bed, the small stack of fashion magazines on top of it, the familiar snow globe beside the magazines.

Robin reached out and picked up the snow globe, turning it over in her hands and watching the flakes of pretend snow cascade around the tiny ballerina at its center.

A sliver of anxiety burrowed into Robin's side.

"That was awful," Cassidy said, returning to the room.

"Are you okay?"

Cassidy plopped down on the bed. "Yeah. I hate throwing up. Don't you?"

"I don't think anybody likes it."

"I remember when I was really little," Cassidy said, "and I ate all this junk—candies and jellies and a whole bag of red licorice—and Mommy warned me I'd be sick to my stomach, but I ate it all anyway, and then I spent most of the night throwing it all up. It was the worst. I haven't been able to look at red licorice since."

Robin marveled at the child's ability to compartmentalize—one minute she was discussing her mother's murder, the next she was going on about red licorice—and wished she could do the same.

"And after that, every night when I went to bed," Cassidy continued, "I used to grit my teeth, 'cause I thought that would keep me from throwing up again. I did that for a long time, till the dentist told Mommy I was ruining my teeth and I had to stop." She motioned toward the stack of fashion magazines. "Some of these models, they have eating disorders. They actually make themselves throw up. On purpose." She looked horrified by the thought. "That's really gross. Don't you think?"

"Gross," Robin agreed, turning the snow globe over again, watching the snowflakes dance around the ballerina's head. "Maybe it was the marijuana that made you sick."

Cassidy stiffened. "What marijuana?"

Robin lowered the snow globe to her lap. "I can smell it in your hair."

There was a long pause before Cassidy spoke. "It's because I was so upset about you leaving, and Kenny said it would make me feel better," she admitted sheepishly. "I just had a couple of puffs. I swear. I didn't like it and I promise I won't do it again."

"Okay. That's good. You're too young for that sort of thing." Robin held up the snow globe. "Where did you get this?"

"I have a whole bunch. I used to collect them. This one was always my favorite."

"I've seen it before," Robin said.

"There's probably hundreds like it."

"I saw it in Landon's room."

"Really?" Cassidy asked. "It was there on the nightstand when I got home from the hospital. Guess he must have put it there. So I'd have it."

"Guess so," Robin agreed.

"Which means he would never shoot me," Cassidy insisted. "Don't you see? Deep down, Landon's kind and he's sensitive, and he loves me. He would never do anything to hurt me. I don't care what they found in his room."

"I hope you're right."

"I *am* right. At least I think I am." Cassidy jumped to her feet. "Oh, God. I don't know what to think anymore. I'm so confused."

"Me, too, sweetheart," Robin said, taking the girl in her arms. "I wish there was something I could say to reassure you." *To reassure both of us.*

"I don't know who to trust."

"You can trust me."

"You're leaving," Cassidy said.

"Not till we know what's going on," Robin told her. "And not without you."

"What do you mean?"

"Blake and I talked about it. We decided that if my dad doesn't pull through, you'll come back to L.A. and live with us. I wanted to tell you last night, but . . ."

"Oh, my God. Oh, my God!" Cassidy danced around

the room with excitement. "I can't believe it! This is so wonderful! Do you promise?"

"I promise."

"Can we go right now? Please? We can transfer Daddy to a hospital in L.A."

"I don't think that's possible."

"I don't want to stay here anymore. I want to get out of here now."

"We'll go soon, I promise, but—"

The doorbell rang.

Robin and Cassidy froze. "Who's that?" Cassidy asked.

Robin left Cassidy's side and headed for the master bedroom at the front of the house. She stared out the window at the driveway below, feeling Cassidy right behind her, the girl's chin resting on her shoulder.

"It's Kenny," Cassidy said. "That's his car." She was out of Melanie's room before Robin had even turned around.

"Cassidy, wait!" Robin called as the child's footsteps receded down the stairs.

A multitude of thoughts began swarming around in Robin's head, like a horde of locusts, their insistent buzzing getting louder, stronger. According to Melanie, Tara had been concerned about Kenny's interest in her daughter. Had Tara told the young man to stop coming around? Had he gotten angry? Angry enough to kill?

It would have been so easy for him to blame everything on Landon once suspicions arose. Kenny had been in the house multiple times since the shootings. He'd had ample opportunity to hide both the jewelry and the balaclava among Landon's things.

I searched that room, Robin thought, mentally retracing her steps that night. *I checked each pocket and the inside of every shoe. I went through everything and found nothing. No ski mask stuck to the back of a drawer, no jewelry secreted in the toe of a sneaker. And while it's possible I might have missed one or the other, there's no way I missed both. I'm sure of it.*

"Cassidy," she called, "wait. Don't answer that."

But it was too late. Cassidy was already opening the front door. Kenny was inside the house.

—FORTY-ONE—

Robin heard them moving around in the kitchen as she approached the top of the stairs. She took her cell phone from her pocket and pressed Blake's number. The call went straight to voice mail. "Get home as fast as you can," she whispered. "Bring the sheriff with you."

She could hear Cassidy and Kenny arguing as she crept slowly down the stairs and tiptoed cautiously across the hall.

"What the hell, Cassidy?"

"Why are you being such a jerk? It's not like you can't come and visit."

"Yeah, sure. With *him* there?"

"*Him?* You mean Blake?"

"Yeah, I mean Blake. Everything was going great until he got here."

"Going great? Are you kidding me? I just got out of the hospital. I almost died!"

"This morning you told me there was nothing to worry about, that you definitely *weren't* going to L.A."

"That's what I thought, but then Robin said—"

"I don't give a shit what Robin said. You're not going."

"I *am* going. I've always wanted to live in L.A. You know that. This is my big chance. I'm gonna be a famous model, like Kate Upton."

"Yeah, right."

"I am, and you can't stop me."

Next she heard the sound of a chair crashing to the floor. "Wanna bet?"

"Sit down. You're drunk."

"What's going on in here?" Robin asked, taking a deep breath as she straightened her shoulders and pushed herself into the room.

"Nothing," Cassidy said, her voice heavy with disgust. "Kenny's just being weird."

Kenny was standing beside the kitchen table, an upturned chair at his feet, a freshly opened bottle of beer in his hand. He quickly righted the chair and plopped down across from where Cassidy was sitting. Robin thought he looked even worse than when she'd seen him earlier, the cocktail of drugs and alcohol in his system wreaking havoc with his focus, his eyes seeming to dart in all directions at once. Cassidy, on the other hand, looked cool and unfazed.

What's wrong with this picture? Robin found herself thinking.

"Cassidy tells me it's a done deal," Kenny said. "That she's going to L.A. with you." He sniffed and scratched the side of his nose. "When exactly are you planning to take off?"

"That will depend," Robin said, wondering what other drugs he'd taken in the last hour.

"On what?"

"On what happens with Daddy and Landon," Cassidy told him, filling Kenny in on the search of Landon's room and his arrest.

Kenny made a sound halfway between a scoff and a laugh. "No kidding. Landon was one of the shooters?" He took a long sip of his beer. "To be honest, I have to say I'm not all that surprised."

Robin waited for him to elaborate. "What do you mean, you're not surprised?" she asked when he didn't. "I thought you two were friends."

"We are. But, well, he's got a temper. And you gotta admit, he's not exactly operating with a full deck."

"Just because he's autistic doesn't mean he's stupid," Robin said, hearing echoes of her sister in her voice.

Kenny shrugged and took another swig of his beer.

What am I missing?

"A little early to be drinking, isn't it?"

Kenny laughed. "Not where I come from. My daddy used to start drinking before he even got out of bed in the morning. My mama wasn't far behind." He took another long swallow, as if to underline his point.

"Where are they now?"

"My parents?" Kenny looked toward the mudroom, as if they might be standing just outside the back door. "Around somewhere, I guess. They got divorced when I was nine. Both been married a bunch of times since. My father has an apartment somewhere in town. Lost track of my mom and stepdad after they kicked me out of the house. Been on my own since I was sixteen."

"That can't have been easy for you," Robin said, stealing a look at her watch.

"I manage."

"How?"

"What?" Kenny asked.

"How do you manage? It doesn't seem that you have a job . . ."

He smiled. "Let's just say I'm in supply and demand."

"What does that mean?"

"Simple. If there's a demand, I supply."

"You're a drug dealer," Robin stated.

The smile widened. "We do what we gotta do." He raised his beer bottle in a mock toast.

"Don't say stuff like that," Cassidy admonished. "He's drunk and he's just being silly," she said to Robin. "He doesn't mean it."

"Yeah," Kenny said, "I don't mean it." He took another swig from the bottle. "Anything else you want to know? Like, do I have any brothers or sisters or anything?"

"Do you?" Robin wasn't sure if she was genuinely interested or just stalling until Blake and the sheriff could get there.

"Had a sister. She died when I was seven. Menin . . . menin . . . something."

"Meningitis?"

"Yeah, that's it. Why're you so interested all of a sudden?"

"Robin's a therapist," Cassidy told him.

"That like a shrink?"

"Sort of," Robin said.

"You trying to get inside my head? Find out my deep, dark secrets?"

"Do you have any?"

"Oh, we all got some of those," Kenny said, a note of pride in his voice.

"Maybe I'm just trying to get to know you."

"What's the point? You're leaving soon."

Robin said nothing. *Where are you, Blake? Please pick up my message.*

"What about you?" Kenny asked.

"Me?"

"What are your deep, dark secrets?"

Robin shrugged. "I'm pretty much an open book."

Kenny sneered. "What you are is full of shit."

"Kenny!" Cassidy gasped. "You can't talk to Robin that way."

"Why can't I? You think that just because she's a therapist, she's the only one who gets to ask questions?"

"You want to ask me something?" Robin stole another glance at her watch. "Go ahead."

Kenny paused for a moment, as if considering his options. "Why do you want to take Cassidy back to L.A. with you? What's in it for you?"

"There's nothing in it for me. I just think it's for the best."

"How do you know what's best for Cassidy? You hardly know her."

"I knew her mother. I think it's what she would want."

"Her mother was a fucking bitch. Who cares what she wanted?"

"Kenny!" Cassidy cried.

"Okay," Robin said, feeling the situation beginning to slip from her control. "I think that's quite enough."

"Oh, you think it's *quite* enough?"

"Stop it, Kenny," Cassidy said. "Why are you being so mean?"

"*I'm* being mean?"

"You shouldn't talk about my mother like that."

"Like what? You hated the bitch!"

"Did not."

"How many times did you tell me she was ruining your life?"

"Maybe, when I was mad at her. I didn't mean it!"

"The hell you didn't."

"Okay. Let's drop this, shall we?" Robin said.

"*Shall* we?" Kenny repeated.

"You're obviously very angry." She had to calm things down before they went totally sideways.

"Fuckin' right I'm angry," Kenny said. "Cassidy belongs here. This is her home."

"It *was* my home," Cassidy said.

"It still is."

"Melanie doesn't want me here."

"So, you'll come live with me. I'll take care of you."

"That's impossible," Robin said.

"Why? Because you think I'm a drug dealer?"

"No. Well, yes, that's certainly part of it, but . . ." The conversation was becoming surreal.

"What's the rest?"

"You're what, Kenny . . . eighteen?"

"Nineteen," he said, correcting her.

"Cassidy's *twelve*." Robin glanced at her watch again, praying that Blake and the sheriff were on their way.

"So? She'll be thirteen in July," Kenny said. "Six years isn't such a big difference."

"It is when you're thirteen."

"My dad used to talk about this country singer who married his cousin when she was thirteen."

Robin felt her knees wobble and she leaned back against the wall for support. "Are you saying that you want to marry Cassidy?"

"Well, not now, of course," Kenny said. "But in a few years, maybe, when the State says she's legal."

"That's not going to happen, Kenny."

"Not if you take her to L.A. with you, it isn't." He looked at Cassidy, the agitation returning to his voice. "It's because of *him*, isn't it? That's why you want to go to L.A. so bad all of a sudden."

"You're talking crazy again, Kenny," Cassidy said.

"You're not going anywhere without me, Cassidy. We had plans."

"Plans?" Robin asked. *What kind of plans?*

"Plans change."

"This is so fucked up," Kenny said, shaking his head. "You said you loved me. You said you wanted us to be together. '*Oh, Kenny, that feels so good. I love it when you touch me like that,*'" he said, mimicking Cassidy's girlish voice. "'*I want us to be together for always and forever.*'"

"He's lying. I never said that."

"You told me there was only one way that was ever gonna happen."

Cassidy pushed herself slowly out of her chair, her eyes wide with horror. "What are you saying? That you shot Daddy Greg? That you murdered Mommy?"

Kenny's eyes darted around the room, like splinters of plastic in a child's kaleidoscope. He shook his head, as if desperately trying to get the pieces to fall into place, to form a cohesive pattern. "Wait," he said. "What's happening? What are you doing?"

"How could you?"

"You throwing me under the bus?" He looked from Cassidy to Robin, then back to Cassidy. "No. No way. If I go down, *you* go down."

"You're crazy," Cassidy said. "He's crazy," she said to Robin.

"*I'm* crazy?" Kenny shouted, jumping up and slamming his beer bottle against the table with such force that it broke in his hand. Beer and blood dripped from his open palm. "I'm not the one who shot her mother's face off!"

"Oh, God!" Robin cried.

"He's lying," Cassidy cried. "You're a damn liar, Kenny Stapleton!"

"The whole thing was her idea."

"No!"

"You want to know how it went down?" Kenny asked Robin. "I'll tell you exactly how it went down."

"Don't listen to him, Robin. He's drunk and high on coke."

"Her mother didn't like me always hanging around," Kenny said, ignoring her. "She was getting suspicious that something was going on. And she was right. We were going at it like rabbits. Have been for months."

"He's making all this up," Cassidy said, crying now. "I swear—"

"Her mother told Cassidy she couldn't see me anymore, and Cassidy got real pissed off, said her mother had no right to tell her anything, that she was ruining her life. Said her mother was cheating on her dad and planning to run off with some old boyfriend, which would've meant no more big house, no more money for nice clothes, no more nothin'. She said her mother was gonna spoil everything and that we had to stop her."

"I told him that Mommy was cheating on Daddy and I was afraid he'd find out and divorce her and that would ruin everything, yes, that's true," Cassidy explained, choking back tears. "I was upset and I needed someone to talk to. I thought Kenny was my friend. I thought I could confide in him."

"Cassidy heard her mother talking on the phone that night, making plans to meet up with your brother," Kenny continued, ignoring Cassidy. "She and her mom had this big fight and she called me, said we couldn't wait any longer, that they were coming to install the security cameras that week, so we had to take care of things right away, and to bring my gun. I went to the house. Cassidy let me in. Her mother saw me and right away started yelling. Her dad ordered me to leave. I pulled out my gun, and told them both to shut up. Cassidy already had the gun your dad kept in his bedroom. Shit, you should have seen her. The damn thing was bigger than she is. She held it on her mom while I made your dad open the safe. Cassidy knew your dad kept a lot of cash in there and we were gonna need it to start our life together once things calmed down. Her mom was crying and begging her to think about what she was doing, telling her that she loved her and stuff. And that's when Cassidy shot her." He laughed. "Shot her right in the fucking face. And then just kept on shooting her. I didn't have a whole lot of choice but to finish off Mr. Davis. Then we messed up the place to make it look like a home invasion."

Cassidy was sobbing. "That's not what happened. Please, Robin. Can I tell you what really happened?"

Robin nodded, unable to find her voice.

"It's true I was angry with Mommy. I knew about her and Alec. I recognized him the minute I saw him in San Francisco, even though he said his name was Tom Richards. I knew they didn't just run into each other by accident. I figured out that they were having an affair, and that she was planning to leave Daddy. And make me go with her. Make me leave the only father I've ever known. And I love him, Robin. I love him so much. He's been so good to me.

"I heard Mommy talking to Alec on the phone that night, making plans to meet him, and I was so upset, we had a big fight, and I called Kenny to come over. I just wanted somebody to talk to. But then when Mommy saw him, she went ballistic. Daddy told Kenny to get out, and that's when Kenny pulled out his gun. I didn't even know he *had* a gun. Guns scare me. I begged him to put it away, to leave before anything really bad happened. But Kenny wouldn't listen. He made Daddy open the safe and Mommy started screaming, and . . . and . . . that's when he shot her. And then he shot Daddy. And I tried to get away, to call nine-one-one, but he came after me. I screamed at him to stop, but he just smiled and pulled the trigger. I almost died, Robin. Did I plan that, too?"

Robin's head was spinning, her whole body tingling. "But why didn't you tell anyone?"

"I couldn't. At first I was in shock. I didn't remember anything. It was like what you see on TV. What do they call it? Am— am—"

"Amnesia?"

"Yes. That's it. From the trauma and everything. And then when things *did* start coming back to me, Kenny was always there. And he said if I told anyone what had happened, he'd tell the police it was all my idea. Just like he's doing now. So I didn't say anything, and I pleaded with you to take me back to L.A. Please, Robin. That's the honest-to-God truth. You have to believe me. I would never shoot Mommy. I would never hurt Daddy Greg. Please, please believe me."

Robin closed her eyes. What Kenny was suggesting was impossible. Cassidy was twelve years old. She was a child, for God's sake.

"Well, you can believe whatever the hell you want," Kenny said, brandishing the piece of broken glass in his hand, "but I'm getting out of here and Cassidy's coming with me."

"No," Cassidy said. "I'm not going anywhere with you."

"The hell you aren't." He grabbed for her hand.

Instinctively Robin threw herself in front of Cassidy. The child screamed as the jagged piece of brown glass in Kenny's hand swooped through the air. A sudden sharp pain sliced across Robin's abdomen, a thin line of blood slowly seeping through the white cotton of her blouse and expanding like a sponge.

There was a loud banging on the front door. Kenny disappeared through the mudroom seconds before Blake and Sheriff Prescott came rushing into the kitchen.

"Robin, my God!"

Robin collapsed in Blake's arms. The last thing she heard before she gave in to unconsciousness was Cassidy screaming her name.

—FORTY-TWO—

In her dream, Robin was lying in a narrow bed in an all-white room when a doctor with red hair and an upturned nose covered in bright orange freckles approached, her stethoscope pointed toward Robin's chest, like a gun. "How are we doing?"

What's wrong with this picture?

"You're looking pretty good for a woman who almost got herself killed," the doctor continued, morphing into Brenda, the woman she'd met in the waiting room at the Tehama jail. "Good thing that boy's aim wasn't better. Turns out it's not as easy to hit your target as it looks on TV."

What am I missing?

In the next second, she was in the lobby of the Tremont Hotel, crouching next to Tara behind a large potted plant.

"Here comes your father," Tara said. "That shit's been cheating on me with his office manager."

Robin rose to confront him. "Cassidy," he said as Robin approached.

"No, Dad. It's me, Robin."

"Cassidy," her father insisted as Kenny Stapleton burst onto the scene, a broken beer bottle in his hand, blood dripping from his closed fist.

Robin groaned.

"I think she's waking up," Blake said from somewhere above her head.

"Robin?" Cassidy said. "Robin, can you hear us?"

Robin opened her eyes to find her sister, the sheriff, Blake, and Cassidy gathered around her bed, staring down at her expectantly.

"You're in Emergency," Blake told her before she could say anything.

"What happened?"

"You've been stabbed. But you're going to be fine. Luckily, the wound was more horizontal than vertical. No vital organs were pierced. The doctors stitched you up. Twenty-six stitches. They've given you some pretty powerful painkillers, so you might be a bit woozy for a while."

"You've been drifting in and out for the past hour," Melanie said.

The afternoon's events flashed through Robin's consciousness like a strobe light, creating a series of frozen, hyper-bright images. She gasped as Kenny broke free from one such image and lunged toward her.

"What is it?" Blake asked.

"Kenny Stapleton," Robin said. "Did he get away?"

"We have every available officer out looking for him," Sheriff Prescott said. "And we'll have deputies guarding the house until he's caught."

"This is all my fault," Cassidy cried. "I should have told you about Kenny."

"Yes, you should have," Melanie said. "Landon and Alec are in jail because of you. Donny Warren was almost in there with them. You caused a lot of people a lot of grief."

"I'm sorry. I was just so scared."

"The important thing is that we know everything now," the sheriff said.

"Everything?" Robin asked, Kenny's more outlandish accusations echoing in her ears.

"I told the sheriff all the horrible things Kenny said," Cassidy explained.

"Just when you think you've heard it all." Prescott shook his head. "I'll stop by the house later to take formal statements from both of you."

"What about my brother and my nephew?" Robin asked.

"Once we have your statements, we can work on getting them released."

"Thank God."

"Thank Cassidy," Prescott said.

Except it had been Cassidy's statements that had implicated Alec and Landon in the first place, Robin thought. *Her words were what had linked the two men together. She'd deliberately steered suspicion away from Kenny, describing the shooters as big and muscular. Did she do so out of fear, as she claimed, or was there something more sinister at play?*

What am I missing?

Robin pushed the troubling questions aside. Cassidy was twelve years old, for God's sake. A child.

A child who could discuss her mother's murder in one breath and her revulsion for red licorice in the next. A child who'd more than held her own against an accomplished criminal like Dylan Campbell, a child who'd delighted in cruelly dismissing her hapless grandmother, a child who'd had even more opportunity than Kenny Stapleton to plant incriminating evidence in Landon's room.

Was that why Landon had defaced his sketches of her? Had he figured out what had happened that night?

Robin pictured the snow globe with its twirling little ballerina. *Cassidy could have come across the snow globe when she was planting the balaclava. She could have transferred it to her room. And she'd been inside Alec's San Francisco apartment. She could have spotted the ski mask in his closet and used it when formulating her plan to murder her mother and stepfather.*

Except she'd been shot as well, Robin reminded herself. *It was a miracle she hadn't died.*

What kind of monster shoots a twelve-year-old girl?

Then, an even more troubling question: *what if the monster* is *a twelve-year-old girl?*

"When can I go home?" Robin asked, once again shutting down such conjecture. The painkillers in her system were affecting her judgment, making her delusional.

"As soon as the doctor gives you the okay."

"Think you're strong enough to leave the hospital?" Blake asked.

"I think so."

As if on cue, Dr. Arla Simpson walked into the room, a stethoscope around her neck. "Well, well. Look who's conscious."

"Hello, Arlene." Robin dug her nails into the palms of her hands, no longer sure if she was awake or back in one of her strange dreams.

"It's Arla now," the doctor said with a smile "You gave us quite a scare. Luckily, the injury looked much worse than it was. The wound is actually pretty superficial, even though I'm sure it hurts like hell. And will probably hurt for quite some time. At least you'll have an interesting scar to tell your grandchildren about."

"It's pretty sexy, actually," Blake said.

Arla looked from Robin to Blake and back again. "He's a keeper," she whispered, unwrapping the stethoscope from her neck and holding it against Robin's chest. "Nice strong heartbeat." She reached for the blood pressure unit on the wall beside Robin's head and wrapped its sleeve around Robin's upper arm.

Robin felt the pressure building as the sleeve tightened its grip, as if a hungry boa constrictor had latched onto her arm and was coiling toward her throat, preparing to swallow her whole.

"Blood pressure's a little elevated, but that's to be expected under the circumstances." Arla removed the apparatus from Robin's arm. "I'll write you a prescription for some antibiotics and a few painkillers for when this one wears off. You'll come back tomorrow, we'll change the bandages, and have another look. For now, if you feel up to it, you're good to go." Arla patted Robin's knee, then left the room.

"Thank you. My blouse . . . ?"

"Evidence," the sheriff said.

"I brought some clothes from home," Melanie said.

"Thank you."

"Can we see Daddy before we leave?" Cassidy asked.

Robin nodded.

Cassidy smiled, and Robin saw Tara in her face.

Someone shot Tara in the face, she thought. *Someone had slashed the nude painting of her in half, which suggested the attack had been personal and fueled with rage. Cassidy had admitted to being angry with her mother.*

Angry enough to shoot her?

"Robin?" Cassidy was asking. "Is something wrong?"

"What?"

"You kind of froze up."

"You want me to get the doctor back in here?" Blake asked.

"No, I'm okay."

"I'll give you some privacy," the sheriff said, walking to the door. "I'll come by to get those statements in a few hours, if that's all right."

"The sooner, the better," Melanie said. "Never thought I'd hear myself say that," she said after he was gone.

Robin allowed Blake to help her off the bed, out of her hospital gown, and into the loose-fitting sundress Melanie had brought from home.

"I'll get a wheelchair," Cassidy offered, running into the hall.

"Sweet kid," Blake said.

Was she? Robin found herself thinking. *Or was it possible that everything Kenny had said was true?*

"Are you sure you're up for this?" Blake asked as Cassidy returned with the wheelchair. "Your face is a little . . ."

"Scrunched up?" Robin said, resigned.

Blake laughed. "Still cute, though."

Robin sank into the wheelchair's black leather seat, and Blake pushed the chair through the door, wheeling her out of the emergency room and down the corridor to the next wing, Melanie and Cassidy beside them.

"Well, if it isn't our little miracle girl," a nurse said, approaching Cassidy with open arms. "How are you, angel?"

"Fine," Cassidy said, returning the embrace.

Our little miracle girl, Robin repeated silently. *What am I missing?*

Cassidy had been shot and almost killed. It had been a miracle that she'd survived, a miracle that the bullet had missed both her heart and her lungs.

There was no way anyone could have planned that. No one was that good a shot.

Unless Kenny wasn't a good shot at all.

"Turns out it's not as easy to hit your target as it looks on TV."

"Good thing that boy's aim wasn't better."

"Oh, God."

"What is it?" Melanie asked.

"Robin," Blake said. "Are you okay?"

"I assume you're here to see your father," the nurse said, cutting short her conjecture.

"How is he?"

"He's very low," the nurse replied. "It won't be much longer."

Cassidy grabbed Robin's hand.

"You don't have to go in there," Robin told her.

"Yes, I do. I need to see him. To say goodbye."

"Then let's get this show on the road." Melanie marched into their father's room.

Blake pushed Robin's wheelchair through the door. Robin saw immediately that her father's once hardy complexion was the color of ash. His lips were partly open and his cheeks caved in, as if he were sucking on a lemon.

"Looks like this is really it," Melanie said.

Cassidy approached the bed. The side rails were down, allowing her to lay her head against his chest. "Oh, poor Daddy."

What's wrong with this picture?

Robin watched her father's face, half-expecting him to open his eyes and call out Cassidy's name, as he had the last time they'd been here together.

"Cassidy," he'd cried.

So glad to see her. So relieved she was alive and well.

Unless he hadn't been glad at all, Robin thought as Cassidy stretched to kiss his cheek. *Unless relief had been the last thing he was feeling.*

Instead of being relieved and happy to see his stepdaughter, had he been trying to identify her as the person who shot him?

"We should go," Melanie said.

They filed out of the room.

"Do you think he's going to a better place?" Cassidy asked.

"Better than Red Bluff?" Melanie asked. "Hard to imagine."

They drove home in silence, Robin lost in a swirling labyrinth of conflicting thoughts. By the time Blake pulled his car into Melanie's driveway, Robin had almost managed to convince herself that her suspicions were both ridiculous and unfounded. Once the drugs were out of her system, she'd start thinking clearly again.

Blake turned off the car's engine and came around to open the passenger door for Robin as Melanie and Cassidy exited the backseat.

Cassidy immediately got between Robin and Blake, throwing her arms around their waists. "Can we have pizza tonight for dinner?" she asked.

—FORTY-THREE—

The sheriff and a deputy arrived as they were finishing their pizza. "This is Deputy Reinhardt," Prescott announced, introducing the younger man, the two officers joining Robin, Blake, Melanie, and Cassidy at the dining room table. The sheriff removed his hat and put it on the chair beside him, pulling a small recording device from his pocket while Deputy Reinhardt produced a pad of paper and a ballpoint pen. "Before we start, I have some good news," the sheriff said. "We arrested Kenny Stapleton an hour ago."

"That's a relief." Blake reached over to squeeze Robin's hand.

"Where did you find him?" Cassidy asked.

"At his father's. It was actually his dad who turned him in. Wanted to know if there was any reward money."

"Families," Melanie muttered, clearing the dinner dishes off the table and carrying them into the kitchen.

"How are you feeling?" Prescott asked Robin.

"Tired, sore."

"We'll try to make this as painless as possible."

"Did Kenny say anything about . . . you know?" Cassidy asked.

"Let's not worry about Kenny right now. At the moment, I'm much more interested in what *you* have to tell me. And this time, young lady, I need the truth."

"The whole truth and nothing but," Cassidy said with a shy smile.

The smile sent an unpleasant shiver up Robin's spine. Cassidy had told so many stories about that night. Would they ever know the whole truth about what had happened? Or would it die with her father?

"Good," Prescott pronounced. "You might as well get the ball rolling, Cassidy." He glanced across the table at Robin. "I'll need you to wait in another room, if you don't mind. To ensure that her statement doesn't influence yours."

"I understand." Robin pushed herself away from the table, and Blake helped her to her feet.

"Can't Blake stay?" Cassidy asked. "Please? For support. I'd feel so much better."

Blake looked toward Robin.

"As long as it's okay with the sheriff." The shiver in Robin's spine twisted its way through her rib cage, like a snake trapped in a maze.

"As long as you don't interrupt or interfere in any way," Prescott told Blake, "then I don't have a problem with you being here."

"So you'll stay?"

"You'll be all right?" Blake asked Robin.

"I'll be fine." She moved slowly toward the kitchen, looking back briefly to see Cassidy reach for Blake's hand.

"What's going on in there?" her sister asked as Robin entered the kitchen.

"The sheriff is taking Cassidy's statement."

"Wonder what it'll be this time." Melanie put the last of the dishes in the dishwasher and turned it on.

"Do you think—" Robin began, then stopped. "No, it's too crazy."

" 'Crazy' is a relative term around here. Do I think what?"

Robin glanced guiltily toward the dining room. "Do you think there's any possibility that Kenny could be telling the truth about Cassidy?"

The two sisters stared at each other for several long seconds, their eyes measuring the chasm of distrust between them.

"Do you?" Melanie asked.

The sound of water from the dishwasher filled the room. "I need you to do something for me," Robin told her sister. "And I need you to not ask questions." She held her breath, waiting for Melanie to object.

"What is it you need?" Melanie said.

"There you are," Blake said, entering the living room approximately forty minutes later, Cassidy on his heels. "How are you feeling?"

Robin was sitting on the living room sofa, the TV turned to some inane reality show, her heart pounding so hard she was afraid it might burst the fresh stitches in her abdomen. *Could they see how nervous she was?*

"I'm okay," she said.

"You look really tired," Cassidy said.

"It's been a long day. How'd it go in there?"

"Good."

"She did great," Blake said, and Cassidy beamed. "Where's Melanie?"

"Upstairs. Said she'd had enough of all the drama and was going to bed."

"That's our girl." Blake sat down beside Robin, taking her hand in his.

"The sheriff said you should go in now," Cassidy said, squeezing in beside Blake.

A phone rang in the other room. Robin heard the sheriff talking softly. Seconds later, he stood in the doorway to the living room, a vaguely stunned look on his face.

"What's wrong?" Robin asked.

"That was the hospital," Prescott said. "Your father . . ."

"Daddy's dead?" Cassidy cried.

"No." The sheriff lifted his hands into the air, the gesture mirroring the disbelief in his eyes. "That's just it. He's awake."

Robin swung her feet off the sofa. She was so light-headed, she feared she might faint. "I don't understand. How can he be awake? We just saw him. The doctors were certain he wouldn't make it through the night."

"The doctors can't explain it. One minute the man was at death's door, the next minute he was awake and talking."

"He's talking?" Cassidy asked.

"Apparently they can't get him to shut up. Obviously I have to get over there right away."

"We'll go with you." Robin reached for Blake's hand to steady her as she stood. "Melanie," she yelled as they approached the stairway. "Melanie, get down here. It's Dad! He's awake!"

They followed the sheriff to the front door.

Only Cassidy held back. "Wait!" she cried as Prescott was reaching for the doorknob. "You can't go."

Everyone stopped.

"You can't go," she repeated, looking from the sheriff to Blake to Robin, to the top of the stairs where Melanie stood, then back finally to Robin.

"I don't understand," Robin said.

"Please," Cassidy said. "You can't go."

"Why not?"

"Because I have to tell you something."

The sheriff closed the front door.

"We're listening," Robin said.

"I lied." Cassidy looked toward the floor.

"You lied," Prescott repeated.

Dear God.

"Yes. Before. And in my statement. I lied."

"About what?" Prescott asked.

"About what happened that night."

"Okay, Cassidy," the sheriff said. "Before you say another word, I have to advise you of your rights."

"I know my rights. I waive them. I don't need an attorney. I need to tell you the truth before you talk to Daddy."

"All right," the sheriff said.

"It's true what Kenny said," Cassidy began.

Robin collapsed against Blake's side as Melanie joined them at the bottom of the stairs.

"You're telling us that you killed your mother?"

"It's not like you think."

"You didn't shoot her?"

"Yes, I did. I shot her." She looked directly at Robin. "But there was a reason."

"The reason being that she was about to ruin your cushy little lifestyle by running off with my brother?" Melanie interjected.

"No. That's not why I did it."

"Why, then?" Robin asked.

"Because . . ."

"Because what?"

Cassidy's gaze shifted toward Blake, her voice a whisper. "Because . . . because she knew about Daddy."

"You mean she knew about his affairs?" Robin said.

"No. I mean . . . I mean she knew about Daddy and me . . . what he was doing to me, what he'd been doing to me since I was six years old."

What?

"Are you saying that your father molested you?" the sheriff asked.

"You lying little bitch," Melanie said.

"I'm not lying. It's the truth. He's been molesting me ever since he married Mommy. And she knew all about it and didn't do anything to stop him."

Why does this sound so familiar? Robin wondered.

"He was molesting me," Cassidy insisted. "And Mommy knew about it and she let it happen. She didn't care."

"*It's my favorite show,* Bleeding Hearts," Robin heard Cassidy say. "*That's Penny. She just told her twin sister,*

Emily, that their father has been molesting her for years, and now poor Emily doesn't know what to believe."

She recalled that Cassidy had overheard her conversation with Melanie at their mother's gravesite, regarding their father's multiple affairs. *"She knew all along,"* Robin had told her sister. Cassidy had been standing just feet away.

The child was indiscriminate in her borrowing, Robin realized. A little bit of this, a little bit of that. She would use whatever her instincts told her would work. *She's been playing me all along.*

"She was gonna run off with Alec and leave me with him. So I called Kenny and told him everything. And that's when we decided what had to be done."

"You decided to kill your mother and stepfather," the sheriff said.

"I had to do it. Don't you understand?"

"Tell us what happened."

Cassidy shrugged. "It went down pretty much the way Kenny said. My mom and I had been fighting all night. I called Kenny. He came over. We did what had to be done," she said again.

"Just like you *had* to set up Alec and Landon?" Melanie asked.

"No. We didn't plan that. At least not right away. It was supposed to look like a home invasion. But the sheriff kept asking questions. And I remembered seeing a ski mask in Alec's apartment, and I thought it was kind of a neat detail, so I said the men who shot us were wearing ski masks. And I said that they were big and muscular so no one would suspect Kenny. And then the sheriff found out Alec was in town that night and, I don't know, everything just kind of fell into place."

It was kind of a neat detail? Everything just kind of fell into place?

"And Landon?" Melanie asked.

"I like Landon," Cassidy said. "But, well, it was kind of his own fault."

"His own fault," Robin repeated.

"He was getting suspicious, sticking to me like glue. Kenny said not to worry, that even if he figured it out and said something, nobody was gonna believe a retard. But just in case, we hid some jewelry in his room." She shrugged. "It wasn't personal. It just . . ."

"Had to be done," Robin and Melanie said together.

"Was almost killing you part of the plan as well?" the sheriff asked.

"No. Kenny was just supposed to shoot me in the shoulder, but the idiot missed. And now he's trying to make it look like I'm some sort of psycho when all I was doing was trying to stop Daddy from molesting me." She brought her hands to her lips, almost as if she were praying. Tears filled her eyes. "Please, Robin. You have to believe me. I loved Daddy Greg. In spite of everything, I loved him. I still do. I didn't tell you the truth because I didn't want you to ever have to find out about him."

"You did this for me?"

"I lied to protect you."

"You shot my father."

"Because of what he was doing to me."

"You killed your mother."

"Because she knew and didn't stop him."

"Tara would never have let anyone hurt you. She loved you more than anything on earth."

"She didn't know anything about love. Neither of them did. They were always fighting. She was cheating on him. He was cheating on her."

Cheating on Tara with a grandmother, for God's sake. Does that sound like a man who would sexually abuse a child?

"There are many words to describe my father," Robin said—*bastard, prick, cad, asshole, jerk, scoundrel, son of a bitch*—"but 'pedophile' isn't one of them."

Tears began streaming down Cassidy's cheeks. "You don't believe me?"

"Here's what I believe," Robin said. "I believe you shot your mother and my father because they were in your way. And because you thought you could get away with it. Maybe it was because they tried to stop you from seeing Kenny. Maybe because Tara was planning to leave my father and put a dent in your cozy lifestyle. Maybe you wanted the money so you could take off to L.A. and be a famous model. Or maybe it was a combination of all those things. I don't know and I don't really care. Just like you didn't care about Kenny once you thought you saw a better opportunity. Just like you don't care about Landon or Melanie or me or anyone but yourself."

Cassidy's tears came to an abrupt halt, freezing like tiny icicles on her cheeks. "Well, then, I guess it's your father's word against mine."

"Oh, I think your words are going to be all we need," Robin said.

"What's that supposed to mean?"

"It means that my father is still in a coma. He isn't talking to anyone."

"I don't understand." Cassidy's eyes shot toward the sheriff. "You said the hospital called . . ."

Melanie raised her hand. "Yes, that would have been me. The sheriff was kind enough to play along."

"Cassidy Campbell," the sheriff said as Deputy Reinhardt approached, "I'm placing you under arrest for the murder of Tara Davis and—"

"Wait! Robin, please . . ."

"What are you talking to her for?" Melanie asked. "This whole charade was her idea."

Deputy Reinhardt pulled Cassidy's hands behind her back and snapped the handcuffs around her tiny wrists.

"I want my father," Cassidy said. "My *real* father."

"Of course you do," Robin said. "You two deserve each other."

The sheriff took Cassidy's elbow, pushed her toward the front door.

"You think you're so smart, don't you?" Cassidy said, spinning back around. "Tell me, big shot L.A. therapist, do you really think any jury in the country is going to believe a twelve-year-old girl shot her own mother for no good reason? When I get through testifying, there won't be a dry eye in the place."

A slow smile played around the corners of Robin's lips as she recalled Cassidy's parting words to Dylan Campbell. "Give it your best shot," she said.

—FORTY-FOUR—

Greg Davis succumbed to his wounds just after midnight.

Robin stood beside her father's hospital bed the following morning, staring down at his once handsome face, but the man she'd both loved and loathed was no longer present. In his place was a waxen shell, slack-jawed and devoid of humanity.

"Well, well," Alec said from somewhere beside her. As if that said it all. And maybe it did.

Robin glanced at her brother, trying not to wince at how thin he'd become during his brief stint behind bars. He and Landon had been released first thing in the morning, and the sheriff had personally driven them from the jail to the hospital. Landon had nodded silently, tears filling his eyes, when told of Cassidy's involvement. Now he stood beside Blake in a corner of the room, staring at the floor and rocking gently back and forth.

"You know," Alec said, "I must have wished the man dead a hundred times over the years."

"And now?" Robin asked.

"And now?" Alec repeated. "I expected to stare down at his dead body and tell him I hoped he'd rot in hell. But I can't. I thought I'd say that he got what he deserved. But I can't do that either. Nobody deserves this. Not even him. I get no satisfaction seeing him like this. There's no relief, no closure. The sad truth is, I feel nothing. Nothing at all."

Robin touched her brother's arm while looking at her father's face. "I'm afraid you weren't a very nice man, Daddy," she said. "You were selfish and self-absorbed. It was always your way or no way. You did a lot of damage. You hurt a lot of people. Especially the people you were supposed to love, the people who tried desperately to love you. I'm sorry you weren't a better father. I'm sorry you weren't a better man. Not just for our sake. But for yours."

"I'll second that," said Melanie.

"So what happens now?" Alec asked.

"Apparently there has to be an autopsy," Robin said, "even though we know what killed him."

"It's the law," Blake explained. "They need an official cause of death for when the case goes to trial."

"A twelve-year-old girl on trial for murder." Alec shook his head in disbelief.

"Sheriff Prescott said they're going to do their best to have Cassidy tried as an adult," Robin said.

"To think I actually liked the kid," Alec said.

"Is there any chance she could get off?" Melanie asked.

"It's possible," Blake acknowledged. "All Cassidy needs is one sympathetic juror who buys her story."

God help us.

"So I guess the answer to 'What happens now?'" Melanie said, referring to Alec's earlier question, "is 'Who the hell knows?' We'll have to talk to Dad's lawyer, I suppose, sort out the will, figure out what to do with the business. Stuff like that." She looked at Robin. "I guess you'll be taking off after you get those bandages changed."

"You're leaving?" Alec asked.

"Well, Blake has to get back to L.A.," Robin said, her eyes on Melanie. "But I thought I'd stick around for another week, if that's all right."

In response, Landon shot forward, throwing his arms around Robin and hugging her so tightly she could barely breathe.

It's okay, she thought, returning his embrace. *I'll breathe later.*

"I guess I can hang around for a few more days, too," Alec said. "Maybe Landon and I could go horseback riding later this afternoon. I think we could use some of those wide-open spaces. What do you think, big guy?"

Landon pulled slowly out of Robin's arms. But even though his gaze was steadfastly on the floor, Robin could tell he was smiling.

"We should probably get out of here," Melanie said. "Let the nurses do their thing." She looked at Robin. "Unless you have anything else you want to say to our father."

Robin shook her head. She'd said it all.

—

It was late afternoon and she was alone in the house.

Dr. Arla Simpson had changed her bandages and pronounced the wound healing nicely. Blake had taken off for L.A., promising to call as soon as he arrived. Melanie had left thirty minutes ago to pick up Landon and Alec at Donny Warren's ranch. Now Robin found herself wandering restlessly from room to room, emptying the dishwasher, setting the dining room table for dinner, lying down on the living room sofa, getting up, going upstairs, lying down on her bed, sitting up, going to the window, looking toward her father's house, a thousand disparate thoughts swirling through her head.

What am I missing? she recalled wondering. *What's wrong with this picture?*

The answer to both those questions had been there all along: Cassidy.

All those years of study, the classes she'd taken in aberrant behavior, the many articles she'd read on the subject, only to be fooled by an adolescent girl. A child without a conscience. *A twelve-year-old sociopath.*

Was Cassidy a bad seed or a product of her environment? Perhaps a combination of the two. Nature versus nurture, the eternal debate.

"Don't be too hard on yourself," Robin said out loud. After all, fooling people was what sociopaths did best.

She pulled her cell phone from her pocket and called her L.A. office, recording a new message for her voice mail, informing callers that she would be away for another week, and wondering if anyone would care. Then she checked for messages. There was only one, from four days ago.

"Hi," the message began. "This is Adeline Sullivan, the client who ran out on you in the middle of our session. I believe I said at the time that I didn't think we were a good fit, and that might still be true. But the fact is that I took your advice. After a particularly unpleasant evening, I told my husband that I would no longer be inviting his mother over for dinner and that if he wanted to see her, then *he* could take her grocery shopping and out to lunch. He wasn't very happy about it, but I have to say—I am! Of course my daughter is still treating me like shit, but I thought maybe we could work on that. If you'd agree to see me again, that is. Anyway, you can let me know. I completely understand if you'd rather not, but I really hope you'll give me a second chance. I look forward to hearing from you. Goodbye."

Robin replayed the message to make sure she'd heard it correctly. Then she tucked the phone back into her pocket and left the room, not sure where she was going until she found herself in Cassidy's bedroom. The snow globe was still on the night table, and Robin reached for it, turning it over in her hands and watching the flakes of fake snow dance gracefully through the clear liquid surrounding the delicate ballerina.

She stood absolutely still for several long seconds before returning the snow globe to the nightstand. Then slowly, deliberately, she lifted her hands into the air, feeling the painful pull on her stitches as her hands came together above her head in a graceful arc, her fingers touching. She closed her eyes and pushed her weight into her toes, lifting her heels off the floor and swaying from side to side, then dancing in slow circles around the room, as invisible flakes of snow cascaded gently around her head. She twirled around the room, her head back, her chin raised, breathing in through her nose and out through her mouth. Inhaling the good energy, exhaling the bad.

Her phone rang.

Robin came to a halt, then waited for the room to stop spinning before reaching into her pocket for her cell. "Hello?"

"It's me," said her sister. "I need you to set an extra place for dinner."

"For Donny?"

"No, for Brad Pitt."

Robin smiled. "I'll set another place."

"Good. Are you all right? You sound out of breath. You're not having one of your panic attacks, are you?"

"No. I'm good."

"You're sure?"

"Yes," Robin said. "I'm sure."

ACKNOWLEDGMENTS

My thanks to my husband, Warren, who after all these years has finally learned how to critique my manuscripts without my wanting to (literally) throw the book at him. Thanks also to my daughter Shannon (please check out her website at shannonmicol.com), for her insightful editorial comments and overall assistance. And, of course, my thanks and gratitude to Larry Mirkin, whose suggestions and support were as invaluable as always.

Normally I would also thank Bev Slopen for her help in the writing of my novel, but this year our schedules didn't quite mesh. Having said that, I'll thank her anyway—for being a generous sounding board and a good friend.

Thanks and a hearty "Welcome aboard" to my new editor, Anne Speyer. I've had quite a few editors during my career, and it's sometimes hard learning to trust a new voice. But Anne has been nothing short of amazing. She "gets" me and what I'm trying to do, and I feel very grateful that she's on my team.

Speaking of teams, I want to thank everyone at WME

Entertainment, especially my longtime agent, Tracy Fisher, who, like a fine wine, gets better every year, and her assistants past and present—most recently Alli Dwyer, Drew Factor, and Fiona Smith. I also want to thank everyone in every department—the list gets longer with each book, so please forgive me for not naming you individually as I dread leaving anybody out—at Ballantine in New York and at Doubleday Canada (both of which are divisions of Penguin Random House) for all their hard work and efforts on my behalf, as well as my publishers and translators all over the world. In these days of shrinking audiences and fewer publishing houses, I feel very fortunate indeed. (I'll miss you, Helga! Take care of yourself.)

Special thanks to Corinne Assayag, who has done and continues to do such an incredible job with my website.

Hugs and kisses to my daughter Annie, her husband, Courtney, and their gorgeous, fabulous children, Hayden and Skylar. Another hug to my sister, Renee (who, I promise, is nothing at all like Melanie), and to Aurora, for continuing to take such good care of me and for making the best cranberry muffins and strawberry-banana-mango smoothies in town.

Thank you also to Peter Araian, who came to my rescue when my computer crashed as I was trying to review the copyediting of this manuscript, and I was in my usual panic and railing away furiously at modern technology.

And, as always, thanks to you, my readers. I look forward to meeting each and every one of you—either in person or through email. Don't be shy. Drop me a line.

ABOUT THE AUTHOR

JOY FIELDING is the *New York Times* bestselling author of *She's Not There, Someone Is Watching, Now You See Her, Still Life, Mad River Road, See Jane Run,* and other acclaimed novels. She divides her time between Toronto and Palm Beach, Florida.

Joyfielding.com
Twitter: @JoyFielding
Instagram: @fieldingjoy
Find Joy Fielding on Facebook